THE SHATTERED CROWN

THE SHATTERED CROWN

BOOK TWO OF THE STEELHAVEN TRILOGY

R S FORD

WORDHOG

THIS ONE IS FOR ALL THE READERS WHO
HAVE BOUGHT MY WORK AND SUPPORTED
ME OVER THE YEARS. I APPRECIATE IT
MORE THAN YOU KNOW.

PROLOGUE

Saviour's Bridge spanned the River Storway where it ran between Steelhaven and the Old City. It was no doubt named to venerate the Teutonian saviour Arlor – that deified hero of old, raised to godhood by the teeming, ignorant masses.

From the centre of the bridge, facing north, the river could be seen slithering its way for miles, wending through the fields and woodland. As it flowed towards the city it brought with it all manner of offerings from the land, the flotsam and jetsam of the Free States, bloated carcasses of a nation condemned.

It was also bringing Forest's mark.

Rain hammered down, soaking his cloak, bouncing off the bridge and running in a fast flood into the river. Watching from the centre of the bridge, Forest could see the wide river barge sitting low in the water, cruising towards him. Its four oars either side dipped in rhythm, pulled smoothly by powerful rowers. At its prow stood a tall man, his hood thrown back despite the inclement weather. His proud bearing was obvious even from a distance. But that was to be expected – he was a general of one of the famed Free Companies, a mercenary lord, tempered on the battlefield, and not just skilled in the sword but equally cunning of mind – he had to be to have lived for so long. No one survived at the head of one of the Free Companies without a certain shrewd ruthlessness. No one could command men who fought for coin without being able to outwit those who would try to usurp his position.

The general was flanked by his men, grizzled veterans all, ready to give their lives for him, though here at least he need anticipate no danger. This was Steelhaven, seat of power within the Free States, and its enemies, the savage Khurtas, were still hundreds of leagues to the north. Besides, its enemies were not *his* enemies – the general had not yet pledged the service of his company and his men to the defence of Steelhaven.

And Forest had been sent to ensure he never would.

The barge was within range now, and Forest reached beneath his cloak for his yew bow. In a pouch at his belt was the hempen bowstring, treated with beeswax to resist the wet. Though the rain would eventually slacken the string, he would not linger long enough for it to hamper his shot.

In one swift and graceful movement Forest strung his bow and pulled an arrow from his quiver. Alone on the bridge in the pouring rain, he was unobserved. Though the gate at the eastern side of the bridge was guarded by Greencoats, they were hunkered beneath their shelter and wouldn't see him. Down on the barge, the general and his men, blinded by the downpour, would not spot him until it was too late.

Forest nocked and drew, aiming through the rain, as the general's barge came closer with every breath. The slight breeze at his back, blowing in from the Midral Sea, would only make the flight of his arrow swifter.

As he drew in one last breath, the rain seemed to slow. His target was all at once perfectly clear as Forest saw the path of the arrow in his mind's eye; saw it streaking through the air. In that moment of stillness, in which time seemed to wait in anticipation, he loosed.

The arrow was true; the mercenary general could not even see it through the deluge as it flew towards his head, twisting through the air, the head spinning towards its target. Forest held his breath, watching in anticipation of the kill.

At the very last moment a shield came up. One of the mercenaries had leapt to defend his general; the arrow pierced the wood but stopped short of its target. Aboard the barge the hells broke loose as the other mercenaries rushed to defend their leader with a wall of shields, and orders were barked for the rowers to change direction and make for the nearest bank.

There was no time to lament the miss, or wonder how the bodyguard had intercepted the arrow so deftly. Forest leapt onto the bridge's parapet, throwing his cloak back so he could more easily reach his quiver. The barge had slowed now, the rowers frantically adjusting themselves in their seats to try and make their way upriver. Oars splashed in the water, men grunted, steam rising from their sweat soaked bodies.

Arrows hummed from Forest's bow, one after the other, in quick succession. As the first rower cried out in pain from a shaft buried in his back, two more arrows were already in flight, whipping towards their targets. It was as though a rank of archers was firing down. Eight shots, eight dead men. The last rower managing to stand and turn in a vain attempt to avoid his fate, but he was not quick enough. His lifeless body pitched into the water as Forest nocked a final arrow.

The general's bodyguard stood in front him, covering him with their shields. Even the best-placed shot would not pierce that defence, and so Forest waited. Lacking rowers to power it through the water, the barge drifted, borne ever closer to Saviour's Bridge by the Storway's current. Forest watched the approaching boat, saw the general's men eyeing him warily, swords drawn, shields raised. But he did nothing, allowing the boat to drift below him and under the bridge.

As soon as the boat was out of sight Forest discarded his bow and quiver, stepped off the parapet and grasped the keystone to enable him to swing under the bridge. He landed at the barge's stern, drawing rapier and poniard, rapidly assessing the four men who guarded the general, searching for their weaknesses. This was not what he had planned, but the Father had been adamant: the general must die. Forest would adapt to the situation, *sweeping them aside like a swift wind through the branches.* He knew his duty. His mark could not be allowed to escape.

Three of the men moved forward unsteadily as the barge rocked, while the fourth, the one who had intercepted the arrow, hung back as the last line of defence. The trio of warriors advanced, shields held up, swords low. Forest was impressed with their discipline – though facing a single assailant they remained wary. These men were seasoned and he would need to exact care in taking them down, but that did not mean waiting for them to take the initiative.

Without pause Forest sidestepped, skipped off the barge's gunwale and leapt at the first warrior. The mercenary raised his shield to block the rapier coming towards him, but Forest had already altered his attack, kicking out with one foot before he landed and knocking the shield upwards. His rapier thrust in as the warrior, realising his defence was open, desperately stabbed out with his own weapon. Forest twisted away, the incoming blade slicing open his tunic but no more. His poniard punched into the warrior's chest between his ribs. As the first mercenary fell back with a gurgle, a second hacked in. Forest was already spinning, his rapier coming up to deflect the blow. His poniard stabbed forward, taking the second warrior in the neck. The man stared, gritting his teeth against the pain. Forest could see in his eyes that the man knew he was doomed and there wasn't a damned thing he could do about it. When, with a jerk, Forest pulled out the blade, the warrior fell back, vainly clamping his hand to staunch the flow of blood.

The third mercenary charged, screaming in fury, his voice almost lost in the torrential downpour, his shield held forward with the intention of smashing his foe into the flowing waters. Forest waited, presenting himself as an easy target – until the last moment. Then he crouched, his rapier thrusting beneath the shield, allowing the mercenary to impale himself with the impetus of his own attack. The man stopped dead, his sword and shield clattering to the deck before he toppled after them.

Forest saw a flash of fear cross the general's eyes, but he knew that the last bodyguard would be the most formidable.

The barge had drifted out from underneath the bridge now, heading down the Storway towards the sea, the rudder was free, sending it spinning as though caught in a whirlpool.

The last bodyguard had already saved his general's life once, blocking a shot that should have been impossible to see, let alone intercept. But Forest was undaunted – there was no way this man's training could have been as punishing as that given by the Father of Killers. There was no way he could ever be his match.

As the barge lurched violently, Forest charged, his approach intending to seem rash, attempting to draw the mercenary forward. But the man stood his ground, crouching lower behind his shield. With a flourish, Forest feinted to the left, then right, then left again, and cut in with his rapier, but the warrior anticipated his move, blocking it easily with his shield. Forest drew back, ready for the counter, ready with his short blade to slice the mercenary's sword hand, but no counter came.

'Kill him,' shouted the general. 'What are you waiting for?'

But the mercenary paid no heed. Forest almost felt sympathy for the man – he was clearly a far superior warrior to his commander, and unquestionably loyal. Nevertheless, because he stood in the way of Forest's mark, he had to die.

Forest leapt to the side, dodging the mercenary, sword raised high, aiming at the general. Seeing his commander was about to die the last defender rushed to intercept. Forest had counted on the man's loyalty – on his determination to guard his leader with his life. A loyalty that would cost him dearly.

Twisting in midair, Forest thrust his rapier, aiming past the shield at the mercenary's heart. In a last effort to save himself the man brought his sword up, deflecting Forest's lunge so it only pierced his shoulder. He growled in defiance at the biting pain as Forest quickly tore the blade free, preparing for the killing blow. The mercenary staggered back as Forest lashed in again, but before he could strike the barge smashed against the vast stone curtain wall that ran along the Storway. The barge listed violently. The mercenary lost his footing and was pitched over the side, plunging into the water as the sound of snapping timbers cracked the air.

The deck was fast filling with water now, and Forest turned to the general. The man's sword was drawn, his face twisted in anger, but there was fear in his eyes.

Forest advanced through the ankle deep water as the barge smashed against the wall once more. He could hear the decking crack and splinter, the noise ringing out over the sound of the heavy rain hitting the river. The general was crouched at the bow, grasping his sword in a defensive posture. His form was perfect, but it was still not enough to deter Forest.

The general growled in defiance, pressing to attack, but he was old and sluggish, his best days long behind him. Forest easily parried and countered the clumsy blow. There was a clang of metal on metal as he swept the general's sword aside, before thrusting his rapier into the mark's chest. As Forest pulled his bloody rapier free, for a brief moment the general looked bewildered, as though he could barely believe he was dead. Then the light in his eyes slowly dimmed and his body slumped to the bottom of the barge.

Forest saw the vessel was headed straight at the stone stanchion of Steelhaven's derelict Carrion Bridge. He waited in the deepening water as the barge span towards its final doom. In the last moment before it hit, he leapt from the boat's prow, grasping the crumbling stanchion and pulling himself up. The barge smashed against what remained of the bridge, broke in two, and was quickly consumed by the river. The bodies of the general and his men were swept into the treacherous arms of the Midral Sea.

It was nothing for Forest to scale the wall into Steelhaven. Nothing for him to avoid the attention of the Greencoats, their duty ineffectual as they sheltered from the rain.

The streets were deserted, swept clear of the drudges who usually filled them by the torrential rain. Forest was glad of it; he would rather have suffered the cold and rain any day, than endure the multitude of city folk who walked this place as though in a stupor. He hated them, hated this place, but he was bound here by his devotion to the Father of Killers. Nothing would ever see that devotion questioned.

It took little time to return to the sanctum where the cloying dark of the subterranean tunnels offered shelter from the driving rain. In places the tunnels were flooded, the rainwater flowing in rivers through the underground passages, but Forest knew the secret ways, and in no time was at the central cavern.

He knelt in silence waiting for the Father. It could be a long vigil; the Father of Killers came at his own behest and Forest had sometimes waited for days. Mercifully, the Father was eager to learn that his son had succeeded.

'The general?' came a deep voice from the darkness.

'Is dead.' Forest kept to himself that achieving this had been neither quick nor easy.

The Father moved closer. 'I am pleased,' he said, stepping into the winking torchlight, his face drawn, troubled. For days he had mourned the loss of Mountain, and even more the loss of River – his favoured son. Forest hated River for that. Hated him more than ever for his betrayal and what he had done to their Father.

'I live to serve, Father. I live to destroy the enemies—'

'I know, my son,' the Father interrupted. His voice held an edge of annoyance and for a second Forest wondered if he would indeed feel the sting of the whip, but instead the Father of Killers laid a hand on his head. 'You are the most loyal of all, my one remaining son. And I have a further task for you.'

'Name it, Father,' Forest replied looking up eagerly, yearning for another chance to make his Father proud. As he did so he noticed the Father held two iron nails in his hands, rubbing them between his thumb and finger as though they gave him comfort.

'You might be less willing when you learn of the task I would have you perform.'

'I will do anything you ask.'

The Father smiled. 'I know you will, my son.'

He took a step back and gestured for his son to rise. Forest obeyed, eager to know what would be asked of him.

'River is at Keidro Bay. The Lords of the Serpent Road are being brought to heel as we speak and his task almost done. You will travel to Aluk Vadir. When River has completed his mission, he will travel there to receive his next instruction.' The Father fixed Forest with his stare. 'And there you will kill him.'

Forest understood the Father's words, but could barely believe what he was hearing. Any other time he would have obeyed immediately, would already be on his way to carry out the Father's bidding. Instead, he shook his head.

'But we entered into a pact with him. He has upheld his part of the bargain. Why are we—?'

'Do you question me, Forest?'

The Father's words stung more than any whip and Forest quickly bowed his head in shame.

'No, Father. I will do as you command.'

The Father of Killers laid a hand on his shoulder, saying again, 'I know you will, my son.' His words were calm once more, his ire forgotten. 'I understand your concern; we have entered into an accord and it should be honoured, for without honour we are nothing. But there are greater things to consider, Forest. Things you are not yet able to understand.'

Forest trusted his Father, trusted his words, and he could only think those 'things' were something to do with the message and the battered leather wallet that had been delivered all those days ago by the foreign herald. Since then, his Father, usually so composed, had behaved strangely, his mood erratic, at times almost anxious and Forest had become concerned. On occasion he had spied the Father staring inside that wallet, his lips moving silently, though Forest had never had the courage to ask what lay inside.

Some things he simply could not question.

'I do not need to understand, Father. I will do your bidding.' Yet Forest wondered if it was the bidding of his Father or of the warlord Amon Tugha, to whom his Father seemed beholden.

'That pleases me, my son. I know I ask much of you. River was your brother, and it is only natural you would retain some feeling for him.'

'I bear no loyalty to that traitor.'

The Father of Killers smiled. 'His betrayal burns inside you as it does in me. But fear not. You will have your vengeance. And I will have mine.' With that he pressed the iron nails to his lips, as though they brought him some kind of comfort.

Forest's brow furrowed. 'You will, Father?'

'Yes. River's beloved queen still lives. But before your brother dies you will tell him that the pact we made was a traitor's bargain, and worthless. And by the time you reach him, I will have torn out his lover's heart and laid it at Amon Tugha's feet.'

'Then I will leave immediately,' Forest said.

As he walked from the cavern he could sense the Father's eyes on him, and felt the weight of this mission on his heart.

River had betrayed them, had murdered Mountain and turned his back on their Father. But was it right to break a pact – even a so-called traitor's bargain?

Whatever the rights or wrongs of it, Forest knew he had no choice.

River would soon be dead. And so would his queen.

ONE

Waylian had never known cold like it. It crept through his cloak and his jerkin, into his very bones. The chill giving way to shivers giving way to numbness.

Of course there had been tough winters in Ankavern. The little hamlet of Groffham had been cut off for almost a month one year, but a judicious use of their stores had meant they could weather the isolation with nothing worse than a few grumbling bellies. Waylian had been small then, barely seven summers old, and hadn't appreciated the danger. All he had wanted to do was play in the drifts and throw snowballs at trees to loosen the icicles hanging from their branches. He'd been wrapped up against the elements, and when his fingers had started to go numb there had been a hearth to warm himself in front off and hot broth to stoke a fire in his belly.

Well, there's no hot broth now, is there! There's not much of bloody anything up here other than the prospect of a cold and lonely death!

The wind howled, whipping the snow into his face; it blew his cloak about him, making it flap like an unkindness of angry ravens. Occasionally its fierceness threatened to sweep him off the mountain path and send him spinning to his death far below. He wanted to cry, to weep in sorrow at his lot, but the tears would have only frozen on his cheeks. If he could remember the way back down the Kriega Mountains to Silverwall he would have taken it, but he was hopelessly lost. Every path looked the same up here and it wasn't like he could even see with the thick snow flurries blinding him at every turn. Of course there was a map – there was always a bloody map – but right now it was about as much use as a paper axe.

Waylian tried to find shelter, huddling behind a rock, but the wind still screamed in his ears, still whipped through his clothes. He wrenched the pack from his shoulder and opened it. Before he looked he knew what would be in there – a damp and useless map, a single apple and half a hunk of bread. All his dried beef was gone, along with the cheese. As though to remind him he'd been an idiot for eating it all so quickly his stomach suddenly grumbled.

Waylian let out a sob. He stared hopefully into the pack again, as though he might somehow conjure more food from the ether, but there was still just that apple and the mouldy old bread. Oh, and the letter she'd given him – the little roll of paper with the wax wyvern seal. He still had that at least. Good old Magistra Gelredida.

The fucking bitch.

This was all her fault. Every bit of it. He was going to die up here, of starvation or from the cold, and it was all her bloody fault. Why had he said yes? He was no grand explorer, no kind of hero. But how could he have refused? It had been his one big chance to prove himself. His one opportunity to show her he was more than just an apprentice.

And you've well and truly fucked that up, haven't you.

All at once Waylian yearned for Groffham. For the quiet life he could have led – not the silent death that was slowly creeping up on him. He yearned for that winter so long ago, when the snows had seemed so harmless, and he cursed the day he had ever been sent to the Tower of Magisters. This was where his ambition had got him: an ignominious end on a lonely mountaintop.

Well, we all get what we deserve, don't we, Waylian Grimm.

He should have known it was never going to end well. It was written in the stars – the omens were there for him to see. The journey from Steelhaven to Silverwall had been uneventful enough, if you discounted saddle sores and a randy horse, but that had been nothing compared to what awaited him once he reached the city. Oh, it had looked impressive enough – high spires and vast walls under the shadow of the mighty Kriega Mountains – but what Silverwall possessed in splendour it certainly lacked in integrity. Or that's what Waylian decided when three robbers stripped his coinpurse from his belt then demanded his sandals for good measure. They'd been kind enough to leave him his robe, so at least he didn't have to suffer the shame of wandering around Silverwall's streets naked.

Could things have become any worse after that?

Of course they could.

When Waylian had finally tracked down Crozius Bowe, he was not a stuffy scholar as he'd been led to believe, but a mad old codger, crazy as a bat. Half a day it had taken Waylian to convince the venerable loon who he was and why he was in Silverwall in the first place. He had almost been tempted to stuff the sealed letter up the man's nose. Even after Bowe had decided to believe Waylian, he still made little sense, blithering on about ancient pacts and distant mountain keeps.

It was Bowe who'd given Waylian his altogether useless map and directions into the Kriega Mountains. He'd also given him travel advice, but Waylian had chosen to ignore that, making his way to a supply house for the requisite equipment and some sane guidance. Of course said 'sane guidance' had been not to travel at all. Venturing into the mountains alone was tantamount to suicide, but Waylian had been given his task and he was determined to see it through. And so, raising his chin like some fabled hero, he had set off to complete his task.

Looking back, such stubbornness had been foolish – suicidal even. Not much he could do about it now, though.

As he squatted down on the icy ledge he waited for the grumbling in his stomach to subside. It had got to the stage where he only ate if he was feeling sick or light headed. Who knew how much longer he would have to wander the mountain passes before he found what he was looking for. *If* he found what he was looking for. Waylian had been wandering for three days now, growing weaker, sicker and, it seemed, nowhere nearer to his goal.

When the grumbling had gone he staggered to his feet once more, clutching his cloak about him and pulling down the hood to try to shield his face from the blinding snow. It did little good, the snow seeming to fly every which way, even upwards to sting his eyes and assail his nostrils. He walked on blindly, keeping his eyes on the path in cased he slipped of the edge. It was sheer luck that made him look up. Simple good fortune that he spotted the beast crouched there on an overhanging ledge.

Waylian froze, staring through the snowstorm. The thing was barely visible, but he could see its eyes watching him, two dark holes peering through the whiteness.

What should he do? Back away slowly? Turn tail and flee? Run at the beast screaming his lungs out in the hope of scaring it into flight?

No. Definitely not that last one.

The longer he stared, the more he could make out. At first he had thought it feline, like the mountain leopards of the north, but the more he looked the more it seemed a cross between wolf and bear. Whatever it was, it crouched ready to pounce, shoulders hunched, every muscle tensed.

Waylian took a single step back, not taking his eyes from the creature. He put one hand out, touching the wall lest he move too far along the precarious ledge and drop to his death. Still the beast did not move. Maybe, just maybe, it wasn't interested in him.

Then it leapt.

Waylian didn't wait to see what it did next. He shot off, boots slapping along the mountain path, heavy cloak flapping behind him. The slope ran steeply downwards and Waylian almost toppled head over heels along it. He slipped on the rocky path, sent drifts of snow over the edge beside him, his breath blowing in wispy gasps. Behind him was only silence – no cry of rage, no animal panting, no sounds of huge paws padding after – but he wasn't about to stop and check. The thing must be coming, on the hunt, but there was no way Waylian was going to let it have him.

The path wound down the mountainside, and more than once he nearly fell, yet he always managed to right himself, running at a pace he'd have thought impossible. Was he less weak than he thought; or could being chased by a wild animal bring out the athlete in anyone?

Eventually the path levelled onto flat and he risked a glance over one shoulder to see if the thing was close.

That saved his life.

Waylian's scream was an icy breath shooting out of his mouth as he saw the creature was almost on him. In a panic he lost his footing, landing awkwardly on the icy path as the creature leapt at him, all fangs and claws and white bristling fur. The monster sailed over his head, to land in a flurry of snow. With a snarl of frustration it righted itself and Waylian watched from his numb arse, mesmerised with terror. If he didn't do something this death would be messy. Those claws looked unforgiving, the beast's fangs even more so.

Almost without thinking he grasped his pack; his only weapon. He was about to throw it when he recalled just why he was in this mess in the first place. It seemed insane, but as the creature stalked towards him he dipped a hand inside, fishing around for the sealed letter. Once he had it he began waving the pack in front of him.

'Come on then!' he screamed above the howling gale. 'Want some food, do you?'

Of course it wants some fucking food, Grimmy, you moron!

For its part, the beast tipped its head to one side in confusion, before letting out an angry roar. Waylian flung the bag with all his might and the beast snatched it out of the air, clamping the pack in its huge jaws and then viciously mauling it.

That was all the distraction Waylian needed – he was off back up the slope, hoping against hope the creature would be happy with what was in his sack, but knowing full well bread and fruit would in no way satisfy its hunger.

The wind blew hard but Waylian ignored it now, it was the least of his worries. As he ran he found himself whimpering, blurting profanities over and over again as he ran, cursing his luck and his parentage and Magistra bloody Gelredida.

A quick glance over his shoulder told him the beast wasn't close to him yet and he almost allowed himself a glimmer of hope, but he kept running despite the aching in his arms and legs and the hollow cold in his lungs. On and on he went until he was exhausted.

He reached a wide shelf where he was able to regain his breath, hands on his knees, sucking in the thin air and blowing out cloud upon cloud of freezing mist. He allowed himself the briefest glimmer of hope that perhaps the creature had given up the chase, but when finally he looked up those baleful eyes were once again staring at him through the snow.

It leered at him, this mountain wolf, or was it a bear? Whatever in the hells it was there was no escaping it now.

Waylian stumbled back feebly, slipping onto his backside, and the creature's howl of victory echoed up through the mountain. It was all Waylian could do not to piss himself with fright. He could only wish that some form of magick might well up within him, might blast this beast into oblivion, but he had not manifested any since that night at the Chapel of Ghouls, and it didn't feel like there would be a repeat performance any time soon.

He waited. Waited for that last leap. Waited for those rending claws. Waited for those fangs to sink deep into his throat and tear out lumps of flesh.

The beast just stood there and stared.

From behind Waylian came the sound of clinking metal, and then a snort. Reluctant as he was to take his eyes from the monster barely ten feet away, Waylian turned his head slowly. There, through the billowing snow he could just make out a horse and rider. For a moment his heart leapt as he allowed himself to think that maybe, just maybe, he was saved. Help had arrived, and if not help then perhaps someone else for this beast to eat.

He could see the rider was bedecked in bronze, his horse in barding to match. The armour was crafted in a design he'd never seen before; each piece forged to resemble a dragon's wing... or was it a wyvern's?

Waylian sat for what felt like an age, his backside getting colder as the beast and the rider just stood there. He began to wish they'd get on with fighting or running, one thing or the other, just so he knew which way to flee himself.

As last, the beast roared. It was a challenge, even Waylian could tell that. In response the rider spurred his mount and it walked forward, undaunted by the noise of the creature, or its talons and its teeth.

The rider dismounted holding his shield and spear confidently.

Then they were about it.

The warrior hefted his spear, bringing it to shoulder level, poised to throw, whilst the beast shifted its weight on its paws to take a defensive crouch, ready to attack. Waylian scrabbled out of their way, wading into the deep snow to huddle against the mountainside.

The warrior's throw was mighty, the spear cutting through air and snow, but the mountain beast was already leaping. The spear passed it by as it took to the air and Waylian felt any hope he had melt like snowflakes on a fire. It seemed obvious his saviour was about to be torn open and plucked from his armour like a whelk from its shell. But the knight had other ideas – moving impossibly fast, spinning beneath the beast as it leapt and pulling his sword from its sheath with a violent ring of metal.

The beast landed deftly, spinning around in the snow. The warrior faced off against it, crouched low, shield high. They both waited there in silence and all Waylian could hear above the wind was the chattering of his teeth. Then they both moved in unison, the beast scrabbling for purchase as it powered itself forward, the knight sprinting on through the snow. They leapt, leaving the ground together, but the knight jumped to the side, planting a foot against the hard rock of the mountainside and striking in as the beast shot past. It was a quick and nimble attack, the sword stabbing in and out in the briefest flash of steel. The knight landed on his feet, walking a couple of steps almost casually. Behind him, the bear or wolf or whatever in the hells it was, landed in a heap, the snow beneath it fast turning crimson.

Waylian almost laughed at the knight's victory. Almost. It was all he could do to struggle to his feet, using the wall of rock for purchase. Endless words of thanks would have come rolling off his tongue could he have moved it, but instead all he managed was a grateful groan.

The knight sheathed his sword, kneeling beside the creature as though examining its worth. Waylian stumbled forward, but the warrior paid him no attention.

'I say…' Waylian managed, his shoulders shivering more than ever. If the bronze-armoured knight heard he didn't acknowledge it. 'I say… you have my… eternal thanks.'

The knight turned, looked him up and down, then gave a nod.

Clearly a man of action rather than words.

'I… I am looking for the Keep,' said Waylian. 'I assume you are—'

'Not my problem,' said the knight, walking back towards his horse. He fished in one of the saddlebags as Waylian stumbled after him.

'Please… I have been sent from Steelhaven. I need…'

The knight ignored him, walking past with two lengths of twine in his hand. He knelt by the beast, securing its front and hind legs together. Then, with unbelievable strength, hefted the creature over his shoulders.

Waylian watched, feeling the cold creeping into his bones, gaining the dread impression he was going to be left alone up here to die.

'Please…' he said, letting out a sob. 'Please, you *have* to take me to the Keep. I have to deliver a message. If you don't help me… I'll die out here.'

'Not my problem,' the knight repeated.

Waylian felt anger burning in the pit of his stomach. It did little to warm him up but it made his words easier to speak through the cold.

'If you're just going to leave me here what was the point of saving me?'

The knight stopped and turned, looking on pitilessly from beneath his helm. 'Didn't do it for you,' he said. 'This thing's been making a nuisance of itself for days.'

Waylian suddenly felt guilty and a little foolish. 'I'm sorry. I suppose such a thing must have carried off more than its share of innocent mountain folk.'

That raised a smirk from the knight. 'Mountain folk? Who gives a shit about them? It took six of the Lord Marshal's goats. That's why it's dead.'

Waylian would find no compassion here, but he had to try one more time.

'Please. You have to take me to him. I have to speak with the Lord Marshal.'

'Not my problem?' replied the knight, turning to leave.

'But I have to deliver this,' Waylian snapped, lifting the sealed parchment between numbed fingers.

The knight regarded it for a moment, seeing the seal in the shape of a wyvern that matched the one on his breastplate. He shrugged.

'Why didn't you say that in the first place?'

He walked back to his warhorse, hefting the carcass over his saddle, then went to retrieve his spear. Waylian looked on, wondering if that was the end of the conversation.

The knight took his horse by the reins and made to lead it on through the mountains. After only three steps he looked back over his shoulder.

'Well? What are you waiting for?' Waylian needed no further encouragement, and stumbled after him through the snow. 'Here, make yourself useful.' The knight held out his spear expectantly.

Waylian grasped it in both hands, almost toppling backwards under the weight. Gratefully, he followed the knight and his charger, carrying his heavy burden. He only hoped the Keep wasn't far.

And that there was a fire.

A bloody big one.

TWO

E piak had died in the night. It had been a quiet death. Peaceful. Regulus Gor knew it was not how the young warrior would have wanted it.

No Zatani sought a peaceful end. They were a warrior people. Proud. Fierce. And the Gor'tana were among the fiercest. To run from enemies rather than face death was a supreme dishonour. That was why the shame of his flight now stung Regulus to the quick. Yet, he consoled himself, there would be time enough to regain his honour and his standing amongst the tribes of Equ'un. Time enough for vengeance For now, he would just have to bear the ignominy and survive long enough to plan his return.

Regulus watched in silent vigil as the sun rose over the mountains. He stood over seven feet, his powerfully muscled body silhouetted against the golden light of morning, a mane of thick locks crowning his head and flowing down his back. As he stood there he thumbed the pommel of his sword: five feet of black steel gifted to him by his father at his ascension ceremony. It was his only possession – but all he would ever need.

With no time to build a cairn for Epiak, they had laid him out on the ground. Leandran, the oldest and wisest of their number, had knelt over the young warrior, reciting the words that would speed him on his way, praising Kaga the Creator and Hama the Seeker. With luck, Epiak would make it to the stars before the Dark Walker could intercept him. Once there, Ancient Gorm would assess his worthiness and send him back to the earth either as warrior or slave. Regulus could not guess what the judgement would be. Epiak had fought bravely for days, but after being wounded he had died the quiet-death in his sleep. Only Gorm could decide whether he was worthy to return as a warrior.

The rest of the warparty, now only nine, watched along with Regulus. Just nine warriors left to represent the tribe of the Gor'tana. The legacy of his father had indeed been brought low. But Regulus would rise again; he would have warriors flocking to his banner. He was adamant. The glories he was determined to win in the north would re-establish his reputation.

Leandran finished saying his words and stood up. At a signal from Regulus they moved on. There would be no further ceremony – no mourning, no lamenting. Epiak was gone now, off to be judged by Ancient Gorm. None of them could change that. But if any of the warparty desired to avenge Epiak's death there would be chance aplenty.

They moved north at speed. The warriors had left the grassy plains of Equ'un behind them two days before, moving into the no man's land of the mountains that separated the southern continent of Equ'un from the Coldlands of the north. The lands of the Clawless Tribes.

Regulus had only been a boy when the Steel King had ridden down from those lands and defeated the Aeslanti. It had been his victory that led to freedom for all the tribes of Zatani, and this victory, this granting of freedom, was the reason Regulus and his warriors were now making their way north. Regulus hoped it would not prove a fool's journey.

As they moved onward, Leandran came up beside Regulus, his weathered features looking troubled. The old warrior's head was shaved bald, his limbs thin, his once powerful muscle little more than sinew, but his senses were keen and he could fight as well as any of the younger members of the tribe. His ebon skin had paled in places, which would have shamed another warrior, but not one who was as skilled as Leandran with spear and claw.

'They won't be far behind,' Leandran said. He had a habit of stating the obvious.

Regulus glanced back at his warriors. Their flight had taken days and most were carrying wounds. For now they were keeping pace but soon they would slow down. Their pursuers would not.

'Then we will have to fight them, Leandran,' Regulus replied, with barely concealed relish in his voice.

Leandran nodded, but Regulus could sense his apprehension. Never a coward, the old warrior was not eager to be killed in the mountains so far from home. For his part, neither was Regulus; but if that was what the gods decreed, then that was how he would meet his fate.

Regulus silently cursed Faro for leading them to this, and cursed the Kel'tana tribesmen who had aided him. Faro had been one of the Gor'tana's most honoured warriors, and the most trusted. By tribal custom Regulus was heir to the chieftaincy, but his father made no secret that if Faro proved himself worthy he would be the one to take on the mantle when the time was right. Faro, however, had been impatient and had made a secret pact with the warriors of the Kel'tana tribe. A pact made in blood.

The Gor and the Kel had been deadly rivals from before the Slave Uprisings, and Faro did not have to try hard to persuade the Kel that a coup was in their best interests.

They had come on a moonless night. By stealth, Faro and the Kel'tana slaughtered many Gor'tana and stole the clan from Regulus' father. Shamelessly they had pulled the old chief's teeth and his claws to bury them in the dirt and ensure he would never become a warrior in the next life.

Regulus had been on the hunt with his party of warriors when the ambush had taken place. When word reached him that his father had been murdered, Regulus knew what would follow. Faro would extend his hand to be bonded in blood and demand the fealty of Regulus and his warparty. Then, when he was off guard, Regulus would share his father's fate. Faro would never risk leaving Regulus alive to exact his vengeance. But neither could Regulus attack Faro while he had authority over the Gor'tana and the aid of the Kel'tana. There had been no choice but to flee. And – inevitably – Faro's hunters had come after him.

They had tracked his warparty quickly – so quickly that Regulus and his warriors were taken by surprise. Most of them had been killed in the battle that followed though all fought well and a few had managed to escape. Now, far from home and still hounded by a relentless enemy, they were becoming exhausted. Faro's allies would not stop until Regulus and any loyal to him were dead.

Regulus paused at the top of a promontory, surveying the few of his warriors that remained. Perhaps they should stop here and make a stand. But then they would all die, and he would never have a chance at vengeance. And it would almost certainly be an ignominious slaughter, not a glorious battle. Would his warriors want to stand and fight? Would they rather a slim chance at a heroic death here, or carry on running in ignominy? The Gor'tana were *his* tribe, *his* warriors to command. They would follow him unto death. Being scythed down here was not the glorious end he was determined to give them.

'The gate's not far,' said Leandran, breathing heavily. 'If we can make it that far, perhaps they'll stop following.'

Perhaps,' he replied. Regulus knew there was a slim chance the Kel'tana would give up their pursuit, but it was still better than no chance.

'Maybe we should find high ground, then. Make a stand?'

'If we make a stand there is every chance they will overwhelm us. A brave death, but death all the same. It might be a good fight, Leandran, and I want that more than you could know, but we deserve a heroic death. We deserve to have tales told of our final battle.'

'And they'll tell tales of us in the north?' Leandran looked sceptical.

'More likely in the north than in these mountains. Will tales be told of us if we perish here? In the Coldlands I hear their tellers travel far and wide spreading the word of their king and recounting their ancient fables. I would give them a tale to be told for a thousand years.'

'Was never one for tales, anyway,' muttered Leandran, as he loped off.

Regulus smiled wryly. The old warrior was irascible, but loyal to the end, and Regulus could forgive a man much for loyalty.

They ran on for most of the day, slowing as the sun drew its way across the sky. Cresting a high ridge, Regulus saw a sight that filled him with hope. Hope that they might yet salvage some glory from their flight.

Below was a deep valley, slicing its way through the mountains as though hewn by an axe-wielding god. Towering in the centre of that valley was a vast obsidian archway made up of two massive leaning towers, each half depicting gigantic warriors bound in an eternal struggle for supremacy, their weapons locked together at the summit. What race these stone warriors belonged to was impossible to tell, for both were armoured in heavy plate and full helms covered their faces.

The Clawless Tribes knew this place as Bakhaus Gate, probably named, as they named most things, after some ancient hero. It was where the Aeslanti had been defeated, where the seed of freedom had been sown for the Zatani. Regulus marvelled at the vast monolith and wondered what mighty hands could possibly have built it.

At seeing the huge arch he and his warriors moved down towards the valley with renewed vigour. This was the gateway to the north, marking the border with the Coldlands. Once through it, there was a chance their pursuers would give up the chase. There they had a chance of survival.

As they passed beneath the gate, Regulus stared up in awe. It was at least five hundred feet across, each of the carved warriors fifty feet wide at the base. The valley itself ran straight as an arrow as far as the eye could see. It was here the Aeslanti and the Clawless Tribes had done battle. It was here the beast-men who had kept the Zatani in bondage for so many centuries were finally defeated.

The Aeslanti had come north looking for slaves, seeking to pillage from the Coldlands everything of worth, but the Steel King had other ideas. Not only had he massed warriors from his own Clawless Tribes, but also those from Equ'un.

The Aeslanti had advanced along the valley, seeking to do battle beneath the gate so as to give themselves strength. It was said their war cries ripped through the mountains and echoed across the grasslands of Equ'un. Ten thousand warriors, armoured in steel, invincible, united.

It had not been enough.

As the Aeslanti assaulted the enemy lines they were beaten back again and again. Though the Coldlanders were small of stature compared to the Aeslanti they were their equals in ferocity, fighting with passion and honour. Nevertheless, their numbers dwindled and, as a river of blood flowed down the valley, it looked as if the Aeslanti would be victorious. But the Aeslanti had not bargained on the power of the northern warlocks, and when it seemed glory would be theirs, they were halted in their tracks, their armour closing about their bodies, their breath halting in their lungs, their blood freezing in their veins.

It was little effort for the northern king to lead his huge steeds through the Aeslanti ranks and crush any still standing.

As Regulus passed beneath the giant arch, part of him yearned to have been there, to have seen battle on such a huge scale, but the Zatani had not been able to fight alongside the other tribes of Equ'un. They had been a slave race, in bondage to the Aeslanti for centuries, bred to fight in the battlepits where their size and fierceness was highly prized. Though unmistakeably human, they bore fangs and claws said to be the result of Aeslanti sorceries and foul breeding practices. They had never known freedom, had only lived in chains, but with the Aeslanti defeat, that was all to change.

The uprising started the moment word of the Steel King's victory reached the slave pits of Equ'un. The Zatani saw their chance and took it, the ferocity they had learned over decades of fighting for the pleasure of their Aeslanti masters ensured their victory over the few weary lion-men that returned from Bakhaus Gate. It had been a glorious rebellion, and the Zatani won their freedom after crushing their former overlords.

Regulus was determined to show the people of the Clawless Tribes what a true Zatani warrior could do. He was determined to claim glory and honour for the Gor'tana and for his father. If he and his warparty made it north, if they survived the journey, he would kneel before the Steel King of the Clawless Tribes. He would offer his sword and show this Coldlander chieftain what true power and ferocity was. He would fight for him, destroy his enemies, make him the greatest king the Clawless Tribes had ever known. Then, when Regulus' reputation was such that word of his deeds had reached as far back as Equ'un, he would return to the grasslands and reclaim his place as chief of the Gor'tana. If Faro still lived Regulus could challenge him for leadership and they would fight, as was only right, with tooth and claw.

Had Faro offered any chance like that to Regulus' father perhaps things would have been different. Perhaps Regulus would have given fealty to Faro. But not now. Not ever.

All Faro would receive was a painful death.

They left Bakhaus Gate behind them and worked their way north up the valley. There was no time to hunt, no time to eat, and Regulus knew his men were becoming half starved, but they pressed on regardless. There would be time aplenty to hunt once they made it to the Coldlands.

The journey was not an easy one, and the sun had crested the sky by the time they came to the valley's end, where they were refreshed by a cool wind blowing down from the north. The valley led out onto flat grasslands, with

23

forest in the distance. They were nearing their goal and might well make it before the Kel'tana caught up with them. Regulus finally allowed himself a smile.

Seeing how fatigued his warriors were, Regulus at last ordered them to set up camp. Leandran barked instructions, sending off one scout to hunt down some game and another to search for firewood. Much as Regulus would have liked to help, it would not do for the tribe leader to engage in menial tasks. Crouching down he unfastened his greatsword, rested it across his knees and watched.

As his warriors busied themselves, Regulus felt a presence at his shoulder. Turning, he made out the powerful frame of Janto Sho standing in the shadows, his dark skin making him almost invisible in the waning light. His hair was shaven at the temples, and his remaining locks tied back in a knot. His eyes shone out of the darkness, sky blue in stark contrast to the bright green of the other Gor'tana. For a moment the two men stared at each other, then Janto moved forward to crouch beside Regulus.

'You think they will accept us, those weak, clawless fools?' said the warrior, fingering the handles of his twin axes.

'They were not weak when they defeated the Aeslanti at the gate. And a king who turns away willing warriors is a fool,' Regulus replied.

'But what do we really know of them and their ways? They could be our enemies.'

Regulus raised an eyebrow. 'As once you were mine, Janto of the Sho'tana.'

The dark warrior had no answer to that.

Hunting alone out in the grasslands Janto Sho had found that he himself was being hunted by three rogue Aeslanti. The beasts had stalked Janto for half a day, cornering him when he was too fatigued to flee further. Had Regulus not come to his aid he would surely have been torn to pieces. The pair of them had fought side by side, killing two of the Aeslanti before the last fled. That night they had eaten well of their slaughtered foes, and Janto had pledged his life-debt to Regulus, despite them being from differing tribes. Janto had remained in Regulus' warparty ever since, waiting for a chance to repay that debt. So far, no opportunity had arisen, and Regulus knew Janto was growing to resent his obligation. There was no guarantee of his loyalty once that debt was paid, and so Regulus was loath to turn his back on the warrior.

'The men of the Clawless Tribes are in need of warriors and their king most of all,' Regulus continued. 'A man does not sit on a throne for so long and not gather enemies. If we can prove to him our loyalty, then he will accept us.'

'You are so sure?'

Regulus shook his head. 'No. But what alternative do we have?'

Janto's blue eyes suddenly lit up. 'We make a stand here. We fight. We die with honour.'

'And who will tell of it, Janto? Who will present our defeat as glorious? Might we not just be forgotten? That is not the legacy I would leave.'

Regulus found himself fiercely gripping the sword that lay across his knees. Though he disagreed with Janto, a part of him that was eager to take his advice – to stand and fight. Yet it would only end with his passage to the stars and another life, whilst there was so much he had still to achieve in this one.

He had to exact vengeance before he stood before Ancient Gorm.

Their scout, Akkula, came running from his post up at the valley mouth and the two warriors rose as he approached.

'They're coming,' said Akkula breathlessly. 'The Kel'tana hunters are closing in on us. No more than two leagues across the valley.'

Regulus turned to his men who had already stopped making camp. He saw their exhaustion and felt their pain, their yearning for this constant flight to end. Yes, they could make a stand here, could even wait in ambush, but more than likely they would be defeated. It would not be a heroic end. If they continued to flee, eventually there might just be some opportunity for glory, a chance to salvage a spark of honour and pride.

'We travel through the night,' he said.

Some of his men showed their displeasure, but they all gathered their weapons obediently. Leandran led them off once more – the oldest amongst them seeming to hold the most vigour.

'We can't keep running forever,' said Janto, before Regulus started after his warriors. 'They'll catch us eventually.'

Regulus looked to him with steel in his green eyes. 'Then you will get your wish, Janto Sho. And we will all receive the deaths we deserve.'

Janto held his stare for some moments before lowering his eyes and running after the rest. After a last glance back to the mountains, towards his relentless pursuers, Regulus followed.

THREE

They had told Janessa that no seat of power was built for comfort. After so many days on Skyhelm's stone throne she could well believe it. She was Queen Janessa now, Sovereign of Steelhaven and the Free States, Protector of Teutonia and Keeper of the Faith of Arlor. But she didn't feel much different. How could she suddenly be more regal? Prouder of bearing? As wise as her father? People now expected so much of her. Janessa only hoped that she would find in herself some of her father's wisdom.

For weeks now she had struggled with the responsibilities of statehood and monarchy, and demands from men of importance who seemed reluctant to make their own decisions. Janessa found it ironic that such men, who had spent their lives striving to attain power, had seemingly buckled under the demands of that power, needing to defer tough decisions to a higher authority. She guessed most of them desired less the responsibilities of office and more its inevitable rewards.

Janessa herself had hardly wished for this great responsibility, but for her there had been no choice.

There had been entreaties from all across the Free States: from Lord Governor Argus of Coppergate and from the High Abbot in Ironhold, both terrified the Khurtas would besiege their cities; from Lord Cadran of Braega, or more likely his aunts who held the power there, for more troops to defend their lands as the Khurtas rampaged through. But no troops could be spared – the bannermen of Steelhaven had been forced into a rearguard action, only partially hampering the tide of savages as they laid waste to the land. Even Ankavern and Silverwall, places far from the onslaught, had badgered her for more men and supplies. Why could these places not organise their own defences? Had they not recognised that this massive wave of death and devastation had little interest in their cities? Its goal was to stab at the heart of the Free States – to destroy Steelhaven itself.

The weight of all this had almost crushed her, but Janessa had been determined to suffer it. She was lucky enough to be safe, for now, here in Skyhelm, while the people of the Free States, beyond the walls of the nation's capital, were being butchered by a merciless enemy. Her brave troops were laying down their lives to buy time for the city's defences to be bolstered before the inevitable attack.

And everything she did was subjected to the scrutiny of her court. For three hundred years the business of the Crown had been conducted in public – or at least as public as the great throne room got. It was always thronging with courtiers, nobles minor and major, an endless line of chancellors and chamberlains and stewards, most of whom Janessa did not recognise.

There was one face she *did* know, however. That of a woman who always seemed to be lurking, assessing her every decision, judging her and finding her wanting at every turn. Baroness Isabelle Magrida.

Oh, for the days of the Sword Kings, when they could execute their enemies, and sometimes their friends, with impunity.

Janessa sat patiently, trying to appear regal. She was relatively confident she looked the part, and did not expect to be told otherwise. Her short time as queen had shown her the sycophantic depths to which any man could sink and she had observed changes in the attitude of many who surrounded her. Only Odaka Du'ur remained the same; stern and stalwart, her constant rock. Without him she wasn't sure how she would have coped. But at this moment, in Odaka's absence, her only advisor was Rogan, the Seneschal of the Inquisition, who stood at her side, presiding over the throne room like a vulture over a rotting carcass.

Rogan usually kept himself to himself. His was a grim business, gathering information on the enemies of the Free States and acting upon it accordingly. Janessa was under no illusions how he gathered his information, and there were rumoured to be hidden chambers around the city, and elsewhere in the Free States, dedicated to the art of interrogation. Seneschal Rogan himself was said to have forgotten more about the history and techniques of torture than most men could ever learn in a lifetime. Janessa could barely stomach the man, but her father had felt the need to keep him and his Inquisition around for reasons that were increasingly obvious.

A grey haired figure came striding through the archway to the throne room. His jacket was green, emblazoned with the crown and swords of Steelhaven, and under the crook of one arm he carried a battered helm. Despite his advanced years his back was straight and his chin raised proudly.

Seneschal Rogan leaned in as the man approached and whispered, 'High Constable of the Greencoats, Majesty.'

Janessa made no acknowledgment. Though she found it annoying she had to rely on the inquisitor for such information, she was grateful for it. No sooner had the High Constable knelt before the throne than she beckoned him to stand.

'Majesty,' the High Constable began, his voice gruff from decades of barking orders, 'this is the third day we have had serious unrest in the Warehouse District. Our grain stores are still intact, but the rabble seems intent on smashing them open and helping themselves. Add to that the recent influx of Free Company mercenaries, and it's all we can do to stop the chaos consuming the city. Twelve of my men have been wounded stopping brawls in the street and damage to property is in the thousands of crowns. We need more men, Majesty.'

We need more men. Always the same words. *We need more men. We need more supplies. We are starving. We are dying.*

'As you know, High Constable, no men can be spared,' she replied. Words she had grown used to saying in recent days and weeks. 'I cannot request troops be brought back from the front.'

'Then we must establish martial law, Majesty. You must give my men the power to punish these rioters and quell the Free Companies with all Arlor's fury. If not, the grain stores will be overrun within the tenday and there may well not be an alehouse in the city safe to go in.'

Janessa had expected this – Odaka had warned her as much. To decree martial law, to allow the Greencoats the iron grip on her city that they wanted, was something she had hoped to avoid. There had been martial law in the city before, during the reign of Carcan the Usurper and, more recently, during the Long Drought. Neither time had it ended well for the kings involved, their heads having ended up on spikes above the city walls. But it was not her own head for which Janessa feared. Allowing the Greencoats to exact any means necessary might cost as many lives as it saved. If the grain silos were smashed open and the stores lost there might well be starving in the street, but would there be as many dead if the Greencoats were permitted to kill large numbers of rioters? What kind of ruler would she be if she presided over this? Would they call her Queen Janessa the Tyrant? Speak of her as the Crimson Queen who bathed in the blood of her own people. She had known wearing the Steel Crown would not be easy, that her first task was to fight back against a ruthless invader, but she had never imagined quelling the very people she hoped to protect.

'No,' she replied. 'You will have to find another way, High Constable.'

The man's grey brow creased into a frown as though he might have wanted to argue with his queen's decision, but his devotion to the Crown held him in check. She admired his loyalty, even had some sympathy for his position, but she would not be swayed in her decision.

'If I may, Majesty.' Seneschal Rogan leaned over her ominously. Janessa was aware how much she missed the imposing form of Odaka Du'ur, her one-time regent and her preferred advisor. 'There may be a way to allow the High Constable the men he needs. Were we to open the district gaols and house the mercenary companies within them, we could contain the violence, allowing the Greencoats to concentrate on guarding the Warehouse District silos.'

'You are suggesting we imprison the very men come to defend this city, Seneschal?'

Rogan flashed her a rare smile. It bore all the warmth of a snake about to consume a rat. 'Not imprison them, Majesty. Merely house them. They can be as raucous as they please within the confines of the gaol. A danger only to themselves, rather than the wider populace. And it frees up the High Constable's Greencoats, so they may carry out their allotted role within the city.'

Janessa regarded the inquisitor, trying her best to see a downside to Rogan's plan. She didn't trust the man at all, and felt he must have some ulterior motive for offering the gaols, which for the most part the Inquisition controlled. In the end though, she could think of no alternative.

'Very well,' said Janessa. 'Would such an arrangement satisfy your needs, High Constable?'

The grey-haired man looked at her open-mouthed – it was an expression Janessa had seen many times – but he knew this was as good a deal as he was going to get. Janessa had been in this position a score of times since taking the throne, and if she had gained a reputation for anything it was that once her mind was made it would not be swayed.

'It will have to, Majesty,' he said, quickly following his clear disappointment with a gracious bow. Then, without waiting to be dismissed, he turned on his heel and marched from the throne room.

'Most diplomatic, Majesty,' Rogan whispered. 'Your skills in statecraft blossom by the day.'

Janessa nodded, but somehow felt she had been manipulated. Rogan had a canny way of advising her, then making her think it was she alone who had made the right choice. It was obvious he was exerting his influence on her, but she couldn't yet see how he had steered her wrong. Perhaps that was part of his cunning. She knew she would have to keep a close eye on the Seneschal from now on, perhaps even have him followed, although whom she would choose to watch her watchman she had no idea.

No sooner had the High Constable left the throne room, than Janessa could hear marching feet approaching. It was with relief that she saw Odaka Du'ur entering at the head of an honour guard – four Knights of the Blood, bedecked in their crimson armour, each plate gilt-etched as though they were entwined within the branches of a brass thornbush. Since her coronation she had not seen Odaka out of his slate grey armour. His face had become more careworn with each passing day, and now more than ever he looked like a man weighed down by his responsibilities.

'Majesty,' he said, kneeling with bowed head, 'I would speak to you… in private.'

Janessa gestured or Odaka to rise and was about to dismiss those courtiers that still milled about the throne room when Rogan placed a claw-like hand on her arm. He quickly removed it when she glanced at where he had dared to touch her.

'Majesty, there is a protocol to observe. For matters of state the throne room cannot be—'

'Out!' barked Odaka, before the Seneschal could finish.

Every courtier immediately responded to Odaka's bellowed command, moving through the arch as quick as they could manage. Not one wished to provoke the towering figure.

Rogan raised an eyebrow in disapproval.

'You as well, Seneschal,' said Odaka, not bothering to hide his contempt for the man. 'Your presence is no longer required.'

If Rogan was offended, or indeed thought to argue, he covered it with a mask of apathy. After tipping his head to Janessa in a cursory bow he walked steadily across the chamber, seemingly in no hurry. For his part, Odaka stood waiting, not deigning even to glance in the Seneschal's direction. When Rogan was gone, Odaka moved closer, lowering his voice and sounding much like the Odaka of old.

'My apologies that you had to suffer the Seneschal while I was away, Majesty.'

'It was nothing. I am more than capable of handling Rogan.' Janessa hoped she sounded more confident about that than she felt. 'What is the news from the north?'

Odaka looked even more grave than usual. 'The armies of the Free States are sorely pressed. General Hawke leads what remains of the Steelhaven levies. Only Duke Logar has brought his bannermen from Valdor, the rest of the nobles have not joined the fight, choosing to bolster their own defences rather than come to the aid of the capital. We fight a brave rearguard action, but ultimately it will fail.'

'How long do we have?'

Odaka's expression grew even darker. 'A month. Perhaps less, depending on how valiantly our warriors fight. There is no doubt as to Amon Tugha's goal – he means to besiege the capital and take it for his own.'

Janessa had always known what the Elharim warlord wanted; after all he had tried to have her killed, though only succeeded in murdering her handmaid and Lord Raelan Logar. Though Janessa knew he would eventually fall upon her city, she hadn't wanted to believe it. Now Odaka forced her to confront the truth.

'We must make plans for the city's defence then,' she said, trying to instil some fire in her words.

'We will, Majesty. I will convene an emergency council meeting to discuss the matter. In the meantime, Marshal Farren has sent these men to ensure your safety.'

Janessa looked across at the four knights. They had been among her father's elite, warriors who would have gladly laid down their lives to save their king. She wondered if she too could inspire such loyalty, if they would do the same for her if called upon.

'No,' she replied. 'I have the Sentinels. These men should be north with their brothers, fighting the enemy at every step.'

'But Majesty, you *need* a personal lifeguard. And these men are the best we have.'

'I do not doubt it, Odaka. The more reason they should be north fighting our enemies, not here guarding me. Skyhelm is quite safe.'

Odaka shook his head. 'I think we both know it is not.' He looked at her, as though he might press his point, but then thought better of it. 'Very well. I will send these men back north.' Janessa was sure she could see relief in the faces of the knights. They wanted to be back in the thick of the fighting. 'However, I will have Garret select his best men to stay by your side at all times.' She opened her mouth to protest but Odaka leaned in, his eyes steely with determination. 'His best, Majesty. At all times.'

She knew this was one battle she could not win.

'Very well. Thank you, Odaka.'

'There is no need for thanks, Majesty. I only serve you as I served your father.'

Janessa rose. For the most fleeting of moments she wanted to reach out and embrace Odaka – to feel safe for just a short while. She was almost certain he would have placed his arms around her and returned the embrace. Instead she walked past him, down the stone stairs from the throne and across the chamber.

As she walked Skyhelm's torchlit corridors an ominous feeling began to rise in the pit of her stomach and not for the first time had she felt such a malady. Recently she had awoken with such a sickness she had retched into her chamber pot.

It must have been the pressure of her office, the strain of so much responsibility that was causing this sickness, but she had managed to keep it to herself. She had to stay strong, try to rule as her father had done and endure her burden in silence.

The palace seemed to be pressing in on her, and a sweat broke out on her forehead, her gown suddenly feeling as though it were constricting her. She just managed to reach her chamber without collapsing. Relief washed over her when she saw Governess Nordaine waiting patiently. Before Janessa could reach her bed, her knees gave way and she heaved once, twice, a thin line of vomit dribbling from her mouth. Nordaine was there in an instant, taking the heavy steel crown from her head and running a gentle hand through her hair.

Several weeks before, Janessa and Graye had been telling their cruel tales of Nordaine, but now she was the closest thing the young queen had to a confidante. Janessa still missed Graye, suddenly picturing her face, then her final scream as the giant Mountain closed his hands about her... Janessa retched again, ending it with a violent sob.

'Come on,' said Nordaine, helping her onto the bed. Janessa sat and looked up into Nordaine's eyes; eyes filled with kindness. To see such compassion made Janessa feel guiltier than ever that she had spoken in such a scurrilous way about this woman.

'What is wrong with me? I need to be strong.'

'You are,' Nordaine replied, the corners of her mouth curling into a smile. She reached around Janessa's back and unlaced the bodice of her gown, loosening it and immediately allowing Janessa to breath more easily. Over the past few days her gowns had seemed to grow tighter and tighter, despite the fact she was eating less and less.

'I'm not. I'm weak and sickly. Perhaps we should summon an apothecary.'

Nordaine's smile widened. 'No apothecary can help you, my dear.'

'What do you mean?' asked Janessa.

'I didn't want to think it, but it's obvious now.' Nordaine said, laying a gentle hand on Janessa's belly.

'What's obvious?'

Nordaine gave her a look of sympathy. 'Your Majesty is with child.'

Janessa stared at Nordaine for what seemed an eternity.

Then she doubled over and threw up on her skirts.

FOUR

The Skyhelm Sentinels were a martial order as old as the royal palace itself. Having studied their chequered history for long hours, Kaira knew well the tenets and traditions that made them such an honoured caste of knights. Established a mere forty years after the death of Arlor himself, they had been given stewardship of Skyhelm by King Burfain the Blue after his son attempted to usurp his crown. From that time, anyone wishing to depose a monarch of Steelhaven would have to take into account the unswerving loyalty of the Sentinels, and their capacity for retribution.

Of course history had shown the Sentinels could not always guarantee a long and untroubled reign, though almost a thousand years passed before the Steel Crown was usurped again and King Conrik the Second found his reign coming to an abrupt end. His brother Cedrik had raised an order of his own – the Knights of the Blood – and they had attacked Skyhelm in the night, murdering Conrik and driving out the Sentinels. Bloody civil war ensued as Conrik's son, Hadrik, led the Sentinels in a protracted siege. After much bloodshed, an accord was met, and both Cedrik and Hadrik ruled Steelhaven through an uneasy peace. When both kings were killed on the same day, it was Hadrik's heir Conhor who reinstated the Sentinels as stewards of Skyhelm once more, but also took the Knights of the Blood as his personal honour guard – an accord to which both orders had been bound ever since.

Kaira had found the Sentinels less pious in their worship of Arlor and Vorena, than the Shieldmaidens, but then for many days she had turned her back on piety and worship. She was a warrior-priestess no more. Now she was a servant to her queen and her city. Vorena would forever hold a place in her heart, would forever be her strength and her succour, but the Temple of Autumn was in her past. Though it pained her to have left her sisters behind, women she had grown up with, fought next to, she now had new warriors to stand by her side.

At first it had been odd, coming from the temple where she had been surrounded only by her sisters, but it had not taken long for her to gain as much respect from the men around her as she had from the Shieldmaidens. But then the Sentinels were a proud order, tempered long and hard in the training yard, each man picked for his prowess with sword and shield, each one devoted to his task. It was only natural that they should admire her skill and place the highest value on it. Kaira admired the dedication of these men to the Steel Crown and its city, and aspired to the same degree of commitment.

Despite being the only female in the barracks she was still housed with the men. Any doubts Captain Garret had harboured regarding the wisdom of this had soon been dispelled. Recognising her prowess, the other Sentinels quickly treated Kaira as one of their own.

If only the same could have seen said of Merrick.

Kaira glanced across the small chamber that passed for both refectory and lounge for the Sentinels. Merrick sat in his usual position, staring out of the small window, jaw clenching and unclenching, heel tapping out an incessant beat.

'We should head to the yard,' Kaira said, standing.

He glanced up at her, raising an eyebrow. 'Is that your answer to everything? More training?'

'Strength in body, strength in mind,' she replied.

'You'd just like to try me out again. I think you get some kind of sadistic thrill from it.'

She smiled at that. 'Can't say it hasn't crossed my mind. Though I am getting bored of beating you.' Kaira had found in recent days her attempts at levity were becoming more successful. Outside the cloistered environs of the temple she was gaining new talents all the time, but for Merrick the comparatively lenient regime of Skyhelm's barracks seemed like a prison.

Of course it had been difficult for him in those early days but, with a lot to prove to himself as much as anyone, he had actually thrown himself into his training as hard as she had. More recently though, she had seen him growing anxious, she suspected, for his old life, for the freedom it gave him, for the women… for the drink. Merrick *had* persevered, and she admired him for that. Every day he seemed to improve physically, his skills with a blade almost unparalleled, but his mind seemed elsewhere.

He returned her a smile, but Kaira could see through it. The easy confidence, the arrogance he had borne when they first met was gone now. She sensed the vulnerable, lonely child, abandoned by his father, who had watched his mother die from the plague, and eventually squandered his family's fortune.

Sometimes it seemed his only solace was in the training yard.

'Well, let's get to it then,' he said, apparently invigorated by the prospect.

She followed him out to the training yard where several others were already sparring under Captain Garret's watchful eye.

Garret's burden was taking its toll on him. Kaira did not envy his lot. He was tasked with protecting the palace of Skyhelm and their queen, and would be called on soon to defend the city against an invading army. The Sentinels would be at the forefront of the defence. All the more reason to spend as much time as they could practising their craft.

As they walked out into the yard, Kaira recognised the two Sentinels fighting in front of their fellows. Statton was young, handsome and probably the best sword in the order after Merrick and herself. When Merrick had first brought her here she had fought Statton and another warrior named Waldin. She had managed to best them both, but not easily.

Statton fought against Leofric, a promising recruit who had started soon after she and Merrick had joined. Though clearly a gifted swordsman, he was no match for the more experienced Statton.

As she and Merrick watched, Statton easily broke Leofric's defence again and again, choosing to toy with him rather than issuing a finishing blow. Kaira didn't consider it fair; Leofric would gain little unless instructed in how to remedy his weaknesses, but she never deigned to question Garret's way of teaching.

'Enough,' called Garret, after Statton easily parried Leofric's thrust for the umpteenth time. 'I see our sword masters have decided to join us.' He gestured to where she was standing.

The rest of the Sentinels turned to regard Merrick and Kaira. They had taken to calling the pair 'sword masters' some time ago and it made Kaira cringe every time it was uttered. Merrick, however, was unperturbed.

'It's clear our brother Sentinels are in need of further instruction,' he said to her with a grin, taking one of the wooden practice swords from its rack and deftly spinning it in his hand. 'We shouldn't disappoint them.'

Garret smiled and gestured him towards the practice square as though conceding to Merrick's suggestion. It never failed to surprise Kaira how much Merrick could get away with – Garret would never have tolerated such arrogance from any of the other Sentinels. Their captain was a stern taskmaster, but he seemed to hold Merrick in particular regard for some reason. She could only guess Garret felt somehow responsible for Merrick's fallow years after his father left.

Merrick strode to the centre of the square, glancing around as though goading someone, anyone, to challenge him. For Kaira this was becoming something of a tiresome charade. She looked at Leofric, who handed her his practice sword with the twitch of a smile. Having been humiliated by Merrick several times, the young novice was keen to see himself avenged.

Kaira walked forwards to face Merrick, whose face wore a confident grin. But Kaira had known him long enough now to see past his egotism, to see behind his mask of self-assurance. There was little that was self-assured about Merrick Ryder. Yes he was a skilled swordsman, yes he had the gift of charm and a handsome face some might have found alluring, but to Kaira saw was just a lonely boy in the body of a man. Not that she would let that hold her back.

'When you're ready,' said Garret as they faced one another.

Kaira merely stood there, waiting. Merrick, with his guard lowered, was goading her to attack but she had been here enough times to know it would not be long before Merrick's impatience forced him to act first. She didn't have to wait long.

He strode forward, his guard still down, but she still didn't move, her wooden sword held loosely at waist height.

As predicted he struck out, feigning low then thrusting high. It was a speculative strike, which she easily parried, but with Merrick she knew to be on her guard. For all his predictability in approach, once engaged he could change his attack in an instant and she knew better than to take him lightly.

Merrick backed away, still smiling. Kaira's feet were firmly planted to the spot, not taking a step back, even when he came in again, this time scything in four swift blows from left and right. Kaira's sword parried each in turn, though she almost misjudged the last one. Could it be that Merrick's skill was improving while hers was not? She dismissed that thought immediately. It would not do to harbour doubt, not in combat. That way only lay defeat.

The rest of the Sentinels were muttering their support now, some for her, some for her opponent. Despite his haughtiness Merrick was popular with his fellows, always ready with a joke, always able to raise a smile. Kaira couldn't help envying that. Though more comfortable now with casual mirth, she was much more guarded about her thoughts and feeling. Still, she had her own supporters. The older Sentinels respected her skill and her discipline, but she knew respect was all she'd get. Merrick was well liked, despite himself.

He moved in again, this time determined to force her on the back foot. She parried his first set of blows easily, then spun, ducking a swing and bringing her own sword in to take him in the ribs. Merrick managed to dance away just in time, much to the delight of the other Sentinels. They were laughing now, excited by the display.

As Merrick skipped away, Kaira took the initiative, following him and unleashing a volley of swings and cuts. Now it was Merrick's turn to parry and dodge, and the sound of their wasters clacking together filled the practice square with a staccato beat.

On they went, trading blows; ducking, swinging, spinning. The click-clack of their wooden swords grew faster. They were both sweating, the chill of the afternoon air doing nothing to cool their flesh. Merrick's arrogant smile was gone, his brow was furrowed, his jaw set. Kaira in her turn glared at him with a steely determination, willing him to make that one mistake that would seal her victory.

They paused a moment to get their breath, eyeing one another with a hunger, comfortable with their game. It was these moments she cherished, seeing Merrick fully alive, sharing the thrill of combat with a true exemplar.

Then they were at it again. This time, as they went through their swift routine of thrust and parry, she saw a gap, the smallest chink in his defence and went for it. It was a reckless move, one that left her own defence open, but with luck he would spot it too late. Her wooden sword cut in, sweeping over his arm, to press against his throat. Had it been a keen blade it would have opened his neck and spilled his lifeblood to the ground. She allowed herself a smile, but Kaira's brief elation disappeared as at the same instant she felt the press of his blade against her stomach. For all she had slit his throat, he had opened her guts. They were both dead.

Merrick grinned as the Sentinels began to laugh, making noises of approval, some even clapping the display.

'Just can't separate you two, can we?' said Garret.

Merrick raised a suggestive eyebrow at that but Kaira shook her head.

They stayed to watch the sparring continue, Merrick chatting easily with the other Sentinels while Kaira stood quietly to one side. Leofric was beside her, seeming to prefer her stern silence over the brash camaraderie of Merrick and some of the others. It wasn't the first time, and she felt some pride that he so obviously respected her skill and wanted to follow her example. He still had a long way to go, but his attitude was promising.

When they were done, Garret gathered them all round.

'A good showing today – I'm seeing improvement. Take a rest, then I want everyone out here at eight bells in full dress.'

Normally by eight bells they would be patrolling the halls and grounds of Skyhelm, but they nodded their assent and went about their business.

Kaira took the time to wash and pray as she always did. Not many of the other Sentinels staunchly observed the faith of Arlor, but she was meticulous in her adherence. She may no longer have been a Shieldmaiden, but she was still the spear hand of Vorena; still a protector of the weak and a tool for her divine vengeance.

Later, the Sentinels gathered in the training square well before eight bells. Garret was already waiting for them.

'Right,' he said, standing in their midst. 'We all know how this works – no hanging around on ceremony. No endless prattling oaths. Kaira, Merrick, step forward.'

Kaira moved up with Merrick at her shoulder. As Garret produced two medallions, gleaming in the torchlight, she knew what this was about.

'Kneel then,' said Garret. 'We haven't got all night.'

Kaira dropped to her knee in an instant, but Merrick was slower about it. More measured. She wondered briefly if he might be having doubts, but when she glanced across she saw he was grinning.

Can't help drawing it out for the crowd. Typical.

Garret crossed to Merrick first; if he was annoyed at the show of reticence he didn't show it. 'Merrick Ryder, do you swear to defend the bearer of the Steel Crown unto death?' He recited the words as though he had done it a thousand times and was bored to the hells with them.

'Aye,' said Merrick, the grin still on his face.

Though Kaira knew that was not the proper response, Garret placed the medallion around Merrick's neck anyway.

'Kaira Stormfall, do you swear to defend the bearer of the Steel Crown unto death?'

She paused for a moment before answering.

Stormfall? Could she accept entry to the Sentinels under that name? Had she the right to be known by it anymore?

Garret shifted uncomfortably. Kaira knew she must give an answer and now was not the time to agonise over a name.

'I do,' she replied, head still bowed.

As the medallion was placed over her head the rest of the Sentinels said, 'Skyhelm, and the queen,' in unison, their voices echoing around the square.

And with that simple ceremony, Merrick and Kaira were full members of the Sentinels.

There was no celebration afterwards, no words of congratulation, no further rites to observe. Kaira found the simplicity of it strangely comforting. Coming from a life of cloistered ceremony and religious fervour it was liberating to be amongst a group of warriors as dedicated to their credo as the Shieldmaidens, but without the constant burden of dogma.

She collected her sword and shield and, with Merrick at her side, took to the wall of Skyhelm to patrol its outer boundary. Merrick was strangely silent as they went about their task, causing Kaira to wonder what he was thinking. Despite his aloofness she sensed he took some pride in the honour that had been bestowed on him. For her own part, Kaira felt relieved to be part of something again.

Yet when she looked south over the city to the statues of Vorena and Arlor, she felt a pang of regret. A tiny part of her still yearned to be over there, training with her sisters. Preparing themselves to face Amon Tugha, now that it seemed he could not be stopped.

And when he finally reached the walls, would they be enough to stop him?

Kaira Stormfall guessed they would all find out soon enough.

FIVE

They were exhausted to a man, each face dour, brows furrowed, jaws set. None of them had signed up to put down their own people like this, to purge an uprising with shield and baton like they were facing a foreign horde. Might not have been so bad if it was only men who were coming at them, but it was women and children too, wild and starving. It was plain to anyone with eyes in their head these people were desperate, that they needed help, but there weren't no help to give. The grain stores needed to be protected and it was down to the Greencoats to do it.

Nobul Jacks had no complaints about that part. He'd put his mark on the contract and had his duty to carry out. He'd done dog-work before; grim and bloody work in the name of the king and the Free States. There'd been no glory in it back then and there weren't none now. Best just get on with the job and hope it didn't haunt you in your sleep.

Rest of the lads weren't handling it so good, though. As they sat beside the huge warehouse amongst dozens of other Greencoats, Nobul could see they were nervous. Hake's eye twitched so hard it was like the whole side of his face had a mind of its own. The old man had seemed to deteriorate in the last few days of scrapping, showing his age more than ever, and Nobul guessed the business at hand certainly weren't helping with that.

Bilgot might try to hide it, but the fat bastard was as scared as anyone. Probably more so. With his darting eyes it looked as though he expected trouble at any minute – and trouble he couldn't handle. For all his bluster and lip he was a bloody coward, but then hadn't Nobul spotted that from the start? The ones as made the biggest noise usually had the smallest stones.

Dustin and Edric made a better show of being brave. They were solid lads and their brotherly bond was a strong one. It was obvious they were scared, though.

The one handling all this the best was Anton. His miserable face never quivered, stayed firm and grim throughout this whole bloody business. If anything, these past few days seemed to have hardened his resolve. Of all of them, Nobul guessed Anton was the one he'd most like to have watching his back – now that Denny was gone.

Just the thought of that stung. Nobul had tried to put it to the back of his mind, but he still felt it down deep. He deserved to suffer though, for what he'd done. It was his fault the lad was dead. Nobul might just as well have thrown Denny to his death and the knowledge of that hurt. Not that it was the only pain he had to deal with, not that it was the only daemon nagging at the back of his head.

Might as well just stack it with the rest.

Serjeant Kilgar watched over them all with that one piercing eye, keeping them in check, bolstering their morale when needed. They'd been together long enough now though, they all knew their jobs. Do as the serjeant says and don't question him. It had worked for them so far, and there had been no casualties to speak of. Even so, they were all still scared.

Nobul knew this weren't even the real fight. The Khurtas were bringing that south with them, and they'd be bringing it screaming and roaring and with a razor's edge. Not that it mattered to Nobul Jacks. Let them come. Let them lay siege, let them try to raze this city to the ground. They'd find there were a few folk ready to stand against them, ready to cut a bloody red line through their middle, and Nobul would be right at the front.

Part of him couldn't wait. Part of him remembered there was trouble enough to deal with here first.

'Looks like rain,' said Anton, glowering up at the grey clouds. He'd said it every day for the past four but there had been no rain as yet, just the miserable sky looking mournfully down on them.

'That's the least of your problems, you miserable bastard,' said Bilgot with that smirk he used to try and mask his fear. No one found him funny but he still took the piss, still made out he was the jester of the bunch. Maybe he'd get the message eventually. Maybe not.

'Never mind any of that,' said Hake, pushing himself gingerly to his feet and gesturing with a withered hand. Nobul saw a young, skinny Greencoat emerge from one of the alleys and run towards them.

'They're coming,' shouted the youth.

Men got to their feet, still weary from four days of guard duty. Kilgar strode to the front, the other serjeant, Bodlin, moving to stand beside him. The young lad stopped before them both, gripping his knees, panting for all he was worth.

'Well?' Kilgar growled.

'They're coming in… through the Rafts…'

'How many?'

The lad shook his head. 'Hundreds, it looks like.'

Kilgar swore under his breath. Nobul sympathised; he was none too happy either. The Aldwark Bridge had been closed off so refugees from the Town couldn't cross the Storway into the city proper, but there was nothing they could do about the Rafts. It was a district unto itself, a flotilla strung across the mouth of the river that connected the old city with the new. There was little they could do to block it short of setting the place on fire.

'Right lads,' said Kilgar, turning to the two dozen of them set to defend the warehouse. 'Time to form up.' They were already moving into rudimentary ranks, but there simply weren't enough of them to defend the whole building. All they could do was plant themselves in front of the huge wooden doors and hope for the best.

Bodlin was barking at his own men, setting them to block two of the alleyways that gave access to the front of the warehouse. The alleys were narrow, so a handful of lads with shields could hold them all day, but it was the main thoroughfare that was the problem. There was no way they'd be able to stop a rabble of hundreds.

It would have been an ideal job for cavalry. A few lads on horseback could easily control a mob – one charge into their midst would see them off good and proper, but every man who could sit on a horse was away north. No one had anticipated needing them for something like this, so the Greencoats would just have to do it the old fashioned way.

Nobul took his place in the rank, right at the front. Right in the middle. It was where everyone wanted him; they all knew what he was capable of. Nobul wouldn't have it any other way, right at the heart, where the violence was worst. Right where he was most likely to get killed. Right where he belonged.

Anton was to his left, Kilgar to his right and Bodlin next along. Nobul was starting to like the other serjeant almost as much as he liked Kilgar. They were both good men who led by example. Nobul had seen enough officers did their business from the back of the field to know a good one when he saw him. But no serjeant, however good, was going to save you if it was your time to go.

In the past few days they'd had crowds come to take the grain, crowds they'd beaten back – but they had never been numbered in their hundreds. A few good officers could never beat those odds. Nobul hoped the young lad had exaggerated. If he hadn't... well, they'd find out soon enough.

After the clamour of men preparing themselves – grasping their spears and batons, adjusting their armour – a brief quiet fell over them. It was as though the whole city was deserted. Everything was calm. Peaceful. It brought back memories for Nobul, old and grim and black. It was always the same. Always the quiet moment before the carnage. A moment to stand and think about what you'd done with your life, what you still had to live for, what you'd miss if it all went to shit. Maybe some men took solace in those final thoughts. Not Nobul Jacks.

As they stood there waiting, a seagull fluttered down and planted itself right in front of them. It regarded the Greencoats from the side of its head, one eye staring, darting from man to fearful man until its gaze came to fall on Nobul, as though issuing challenge. It stared at him arrogantly... balefully. A lad further down the line spat, sending a white gob soaring towards the bird to land a foot away. The gull didn't flinch.

'This what we were worried about?' shouted one of the lads. 'I reckon I can take that bastard on my own.'

There was laughter, some of it too loud, more braying in fear than true mirth. It did little to relieve the tension.

Nobul just watched. Waited.

With a beat of white wings the gull was off, just as the bellowing started. It came from up the street, and they didn't have to wait long before they saw what was making the noise. They'd come armed, carrying sticks, bricks, whatever they could lay their hands on. A big mob, bigger than before anyways, screaming to the sky.

'Here they come,' Kilgar shouted as the rabble filled the street up ahead, advancing like a stinking, unkempt wave. 'Stand firm. Stand with the man next to you…'

He carried on shouting but the noise from the crowd drowned him out. Even standing right beside him Nobul could no longer make out the words over the shouting and yelping of mad hungry bastards come to take some food for themselves. They were starving. Desperate. But that was none of Nobul's concern. His business was to stop them. Oh, and maybe to survive the afternoon – that would be a bonus.

They stopped about five yards in front of the Greencoats. Every one of them yelling, spitting their hunger and fury at the men who stood against them. It would be like this for a while until one of them plucked up the courage to attack. He'd be the one to get the hardest kicking.

Nobul tried not to look at them, tried not to focus on the faces. Seeing just one starving pathetic urchin in this human wretchedness might make him pause, might distract him long enough to get a shiv lodged in the neck. *Don't think of them as people. They're a mob. A mob come to kill and steal.*

As they stood baying, Nobul could feel Anton shifting uncomfortably. The lad was most likely ready to shit. There was no getting used to this, no learning to control the fear, you just had to swallow it up and spit it right back as hot fucking rage.

Someone from the back of the mob threw something through the air. It just missed Nobul, clanking off the helm on one of the lads behind him. Nobul heard him shout out in pain over the noise of the mob. More missiles came – sticks and rocks and what looked like mud but was probably shit. A bottle smashed in front of him, whatever it had contained splashing his boots. Piss more than likely.

A couple of the rioters jumped forward, brandishing their makeshift weapons and snarling like dogs before scurrying back amongst their fellows. Still the Greencoats held fast and Nobul admired their discipline. They were a solid bunch of lads, but this hadn't even started to get nasty yet.

Someone darted forward, pickaxe handle raised high, and tried to smash it over a helmeted head further down the line. Before he could reach his target, one of the Greencoats had stabbed out with a spear, the point impaling the attacker in the shoulder. He squealed and staggered back clutching the wound. Nobul knew it could go one of two ways now – the crowd would get scared and run, or enraged and attack.

Just his bloody luck – they picked the latter.

More missiles rained in, much less shitty and much more solid, and as they came more of the mob lurched to attack. They were battered back by the Greencoats, but suddenly the mob, spurred on by the rush, swept forwards like a tide.

Nobul had a cudgel, old and weathered and held together with steel bands he'd twisted round it himself. It wasn't meant as a lethal weapon but it could be if he chose. As the crowd surged forward all wide eyes and rotten teeth, Nobul picked his target out. It was no use waving your weapon at a bunch of enemies and hoping for the best – chances were you wouldn't hit a bloody thing. You had to choose your target, wait for him to come within reach, then give him the business end of whatever was in your hand.

To his left and right, Anton and Kilgar were hacking at the angry mob. Nobul did the same as three faces leered at him. He swung his arm, fast and heavy, and those faces fell back bloodied and broken. Then, after that initial rush of bodies, they were locked together, all crushed in tight. Nobul had the good sense to keep his weapon arm high above the crowd so at least he could still use it. Most of the other lads were just trapped in the crush, backs to the warehouse with no place to retreat.

With no room to use their fists the throng took to spitting insults, screaming that they were hungry and needed food and the Greencoats should have been ashamed for letting them starve. They pushed forward in a mass of stinking bodies, but with the Greencoats in the way they were going nowhere. In the end they were just a load of bodies squashed together, heaving and shouting.

After a while, after mad moments of crushing bodies and yelled hysteria, the crowd eased off, realising they weren't getting anywhere. Some of the lads put in some half-hearted blows and Nobul could hear screaming from down the line. As they backed off, a pack of rioters managed to grab Serjeant Bodlin and drag him with them.

Nobul sprinted forward, Serjeant Kilgar at his shoulder. One of the mob was kicking Bodlin in the head and Nobul went at him first, rapping the club across his shoulders and putting him down. It didn't deter the rest of the crowd, who were now intent on claiming their prize. If they couldn't have grain they'd take a Greencoat scalp instead. Nobul wasn't having that.

Bodlin reached out, his face a mess, blood covering his mouth and spewing between those teeth which hadn't been knocked loose. Nobul grabbed his arm as he himself came under attack. He could see the man's stick coming at him, but before it ploughed into his head, Kilgar had smashed the man back. The serjeant waded in, cudgel swinging, while Nobul grabbed Bodlin with two hands and pulled him away to safety. More of the lads joined them then. Seeing the mob on the back foot they wanted to give them a little more encouragement to fuck off.

By the time Nobul had dragged Bodlin back to the warehouse doors, the mob was fleeing back towards the Old City.

They collapsed on their arses and sat for some time then, just breathing in the air. A couple of the lads down the line had cuts and bruises, one of them sported a bloody gash to the front of his scalp, but head wounds always looked the worst. Despite losing some teeth, Bodlin didn't look much worse for wear apart from the blood down his front. He was back to ordering his men in no time. It almost made Nobul smile.

'Looks like we've paid back that one we owed you, Serjeant Bodlin,' Kilgar said.

'And then some,' replied Bodlin, winking at Nobul. It had been Bodlin and his crossbowmen who'd got them out of the shit when they were clearing out the Town a few weeks back. Seemed a bit ironic that the folks they'd been clearing it for were most likely the ones who'd just tried to kill them.

There were a couple of rioters lying on the ground, and the lads cleared them to one side, not really caring if they were alive or not. Nobul couldn't bring himself to feel any ill towards them. They were starving after all, only wanted to feed their families, most like. Who was to say whether Nobul would have been amongst their number if the boots were on the other feet? Only difference was he'd have done a damn sight better job.

As he sat, he saw one of the lads peering in through a crack in the warehouse doors, a hungry look on his face.

'Don't even think about it,' said Bodlin and the lad turned round, all guilty like.

'Wasn't gonna, Serjeant,' said the lad, though it seemed obvious he was. Then, after he'd thought on it for a bit. 'But who'd notice if we took just a bit for ourselves? For our hard work, like?'

Bodlin shook his head, but then, with a bloody grin he said, 'Open her up then, lad. Feel free.'

At that, the rest of the Greencoats started showing some interest, moving quick to the warehouse as the young lad pulled up the crossbeam and wrenched open the door. The lads were whooping in delight as they stormed in, but when the dim light of the afternoon illuminated the inside of the building, they soon changed their tune.

The place was empty.

'You didn't think we was guarding the actual stores did you?' Bodlin asked. 'This is just a decoy.' Then he walked off with a smirk, leaving them staring and hungry.

Nobul might have grinned with him. Might have. Instead he just stood there, wondering whether this was the only thing he'd be defending in the days to come. Wondering if he'd be risking his life for some other worthless, empty hole.

As he looked, the rain began to patter down on his head.

'See,' shouted Anton. 'I told you it looked like rain.'

It was the happiest Nobul had ever seen him.

SIX

A knight in the Skyhelm Sentinels. It almost made Merrick Ryder laugh.

Honour. Duty. A uniform.

What in the hells was he thinking?

And now he had a little medallion about his neck, with the crown and crossed swords – just like his father had worn. What more could a boy want?

Kaira, of course, was over the moon about it. On the surface she was her usual quiet and brooding self, but he could still tell she was filled to bursting with pride. And why shouldn't she be happy? She'd been brought up in the Temple of Autumn. Being locked in a citadel, with no company but other brooding knights, surely made this a home from home for her.

He looked over to her sitting atop her bunk, staring at that medallion about her neck.

'Pleased with yourself?' he asked.

She looked up as though she'd vaguely heard him. 'What?'

'Now that we've been inducted? Happy now?'

'Happy doesn't come into it.'

'Proud then? Ready to do your duty?'

Kaira frowned. 'I am ready to serve my queen and my city. To act as the hand of—'

'Oh, this is such horseshit,' he said. 'We're fucking trapped. We're prisoners in a gaol of our own making. This was a shit idea.'

She got up then, staring at him as though she wanted to reach out and grasp him by the throat. But she restrained herself and said calmly, 'It is what it is, Merrick. Live with it.' She turned to leave, then thought better of it. 'Remember, this was your idea. We did this to survive as much as to serve.'

He knew that all right. 'And survive we have.' He gestured at their austere surroundings. 'And look how well we've done for ourselves.'

'Still can't stand to think of anyone but yourself, can you? I thought you might have changed, that you might embrace a chance of redemption.'

That made Merrick smile. 'Have you ever considered I might not want redemption? Not everyone is plagued by guilt, Kaira.'

'Keep telling yourself that.'

She fixed him with a glare that spoke accusation, judgement and condemnation all at once.

Fuck off, would have been his natural response. *Take your judgement and stick it right up your pious arse!*

But of course he didn't say that. Not because he respected her. Not because she might well be able to kick him from one side of the city to the other in her bare feet. It was because she was right.

There were a lot of things Merrick Ryder hated: his father, the Guild, authority, an empty wine jug and no coin. But they all paled into insignificance next to the loathing he felt for himself; for the money he had squandered; for the talent and opportunities wasted. Now he had a chance of salvation and he did was treat it with the usual disdain.

What an utter cunt you are, Ryder.

Before he could begin to argue, begin to tell her that he *had* changed, young Leofric was at the door.

'Captain Garret wants to see you both,' said the lad.

Merrick looked to Kaira but she only shrugged.

'What for?' asked Merrick.

'He didn't say, and I didn't ask,' Leofric replied.

It was obvious the young recruit didn't like him, but Merrick could live with that. The lad was about as interesting as your average provincial pig farmer, so no great loss there.

'We'd best be off then,' Merrick said, standing and straightening his tunic.

His feigned attempt at decorum was met with a silence that continued all the way to Garret, who sat in his courtyard, drinking his tea. Two other Sentinels stood to attention beside the captain and when Merrick drew closer he recognised Waldin and Statton.

As Merrick and Kaira reached him, Garret placed his cup down and regarded them with an appraising eye. 'I have a task for you both.'

For the briefest of moments Merrick was reminded of a warehouse he had once been bundled into. One where he'd been given another task by Friedrik and Bastian. A task that had almost seen him sell a thousand souls into slavery and ended with him almost being killed. He couldn't wait to learn of this one.

'It requires my best swords and it's the most important job in the realm,' Garret continued. 'Could well be the most dangerous too.' He paused, looking at the four of them. It was obvious he was waiting for them to question him, to ask what in the hells could be so perilous. Merrick knew Kaira would say nothing – she'd have jumped from the top of the Tower of Magisters without question, if Garret had ordered her. Waldin and Statton weren't about to speak either and Merrick was damned if he'd make an arse of himself and be the one to open his mouth.

'Our queen requires a guard of the body. A permanent guard to watch over her night and day. Wherever she goes, there you will be. I don't think I need to stress how important this is.'

'No, Captain,' Kaira said, before Merrick could even think to complain. 'It would be an honour.'

Gods, why didn't she just bend down and kiss his arse while she was at it.

Statton and Waldin also made noises of assent, only too eager to volunteer.

'And you?' Garret asked, looking at Merrick, who had remained conspicuously silent.

He smiled back. 'I live to serve.'

Garret didn't seem to see the funny side. 'On two occasions assassins have breached the walls of Skyhelm and tried to murder our queen. Chances are there'll be more attempts. Chances are you'll be called on to offer your lives for her. If you're not up to it, Ryder, say so now and I'll put someone else in your place.'

All of a sudden this was real. Until now Garret had tolerated Merrick's blithe attitude due to his skill with a blade and the debt Garret thought he owed the Ryder family, but now all that was forgotten. Things were suddenly serious.

And perhaps this was the chance Merrick had been waiting for.

'Of course I'm up to it,' he replied, perhaps with a little too much edge.

Garret frowned. 'Don't fuck this up, Ryder. It's your chance to make something of yourself.' The captain stood up and drained the rest of the tea. 'Come with me,' he said. The four Sentinels followed him across the courtyard and through the doors that led into the palace proper.

As a child, Merrick had walked these halls with his father, Tannick. He had shown him the hallowed seat of power within the Free States, explained to him the responsibilities he bore in protecting the king who sat upon it. Merrick had listened intently, awestruck at the majesty of the building, had even hoped he might one day follow in his father's footsteps.

As a man, Merrick was still struck by the splendour of the place, but there was now an edge of resentment. Remembering his father only evoked bitterness, even made a part of him hate this place. The old man had managed to ruin this, even though he'd been gone for most of Merrick's life.

They reached the massive throne room, the Sentinels standing aside as Garret approached. Merrick could see her there on that stone throne. Though he'd patrolled the palace scores of times he'd never been presented to the woman for whom he might have to give his life.

At first glance, Janessa looked every inch the queen; the crown sitting comfortably on her head, her expression composed, regal. But there was still vulnerability there. Was it her youth, or perhaps her beauty, that instantly made Merrick want to protect her? Maybe it was a growing sense of duty.

Ha! Duty? Who are you trying to kid, Ryder? Since when has that meant anything to you. You'll fuck this up like you do everything else.

Merrick tried to put any doubt behind him. He had to make an effort. Had to rise to this challenge. For once. So far he'd treated the Sentinels like he treated everything else – as an inconvenience. Now he had a chance to do something of value. To make amends, achieve something his mother would have been proud of. This was no time to let old doubts undermine him.

Garret stopped before Janessa, dropping to his knee and bowing his head. The four Sentinels did likewise, waiting for her to address them.

'Captain Garret, to what do I owe this unexpected pleasure?' said the queen.

Her voice was kind and lacked authority. It was then Merrick could see through any façade she might have been trying to create. She *was* just a girl sitting on that throne. Not a real queen. Not a leader of men. Just a girl thrown in the river and told to swim. Merrick knew only too well how that felt.

'Majesty,' said Garret rising gingerly as his old joints protested. 'Please allow me to present my four best swords. Statton, Waldin, Merrick and Kaira. Each has volunteered to be among your personal guard.'

That's not exactly true is it, Garret. I don't remember asking to volunteer.

'Please rise,' said the queen, and the four of them stood up. For a moment the queen looked them over with an appraising eye. Then she rose from her throne. 'Walk with me.'

With that she walked across the throne room and right past them. Garret looked momentarily flustered but he followed anyway. Kaira glanced to Merrick but he merely shrugged. It was clearly an unexpected breach of protocol. Merrick was beginning to like Queen Janessa already.

They followed her through the winding corridors, down through the depths of the palace until they came out into the garden. It was all bare trees and bushes. Here and there stood shaped topiary that looked distinctly worse for wear in the chill winter air.

'You can remain here, Captain,' said Janessa, and Garret hung back as the five of them strolled on along a paved route through the garden. Merrick glanced back, and saw a look of furrowed concern on Garret's face.

Best watch your mouth, Ryder, or there'll be the hells to pay.

'How long have you served in the Sentinels?' asked the queen, moving her hand across a bush of dried and darkened lavender.

Waldin and Statton told her of the years they had spent within the Sentinels. When Kaira and Merrick remained in awkward silence, Janessa turned to them expectantly.

'Only a matter of weeks, Majesty,' Merrick replied. Under the circumstances he thought it best he do the talking – Kaira had never been one for easy conversation.

'And yet Garret puts you among my personal guard. He must trust you implicitly.'

'Though I, myself, have not been a Sentinel long, my father served among their number. I often visited the palace as a child.'

Janessa looked at him curiously. 'So you are carrying on a family tradition?'

For all the bloody good it's done me. 'I am, Majesty.'

'Then it seems we are both following in our father's footsteps.'

That thought galled him, more than he could have expected. The idea that he was following that old bastard Tannick Ryder anywhere filled Merrick with sudden revulsion.

'And you, Kaira?' said the queen. 'Why are you such a trusted servant?'

Kaira didn't answer. Her mouth opened to voice a reply but she seemed lost for words, being unused to singing her own praises, especially in front of royalty.

'Kaira Stormfall is a former Shieldmaiden, Majesty,' Merrick interjected. 'And a woman of few words.'

Janessa turned to him, appraising him. 'You are used to speaking for the women close to you, Merrick?' He wasn't sure how to respond. 'I can assure you,' Janessa continued, 'you will not have to speak for me.'

'I would never presume—'

'No, please don't.' She turned, carrying on through the gardens.

As he followed, Merrick couldn't help but be intrigued by her self-assurance. Maybe he had underestimated her. Maybe she had it in her to be a ruler after all.

After some moments of silence Janessa stopped, and stood staring up at a bare tree as she said, 'Would you give your lives for me?'

He hadn't expected such directness, but Merrick already knew the appropriate answer.

'We are sworn to defend the bearer of the Steel Crown unto death, Majesty.'

'I didn't ask you to repeat your oath, Merrick. But since that's your answer, how do you really feel about it?'

How do I feel about it? I feel fucking great. I can't wait to fling myself in front of the spears and arrows that are inevitably heading your way.

'We—'

'We live to serve, Majesty,' Kaira cut in. 'To serve the city of Steelhaven. Serve the Crown. And to serve you. Our feelings were put aside when we made our oaths. We are now dedicated to this task, nothing else.'

Queen Janessa smiled at this. Then shook her head. 'I ask because I would never expect anyone to lay down their life for me. I've never wanted that.'

She looked wistful, as if she was thinking of someone in particular. Merrick knew men had died during previous attempts to assassinate her. From her reaction it seemed the queen felt responsible, and the guilt weighed on her.

'If it's any consolation, Majesty, I've no intention of being killed.'

He'd said it without thinking. Flippant. Stupid. But where he might have expected a reprimand, she merely smiled.

'Neither have I, Merrick,' she said. 'So there we are. None of us will be killed. I could ask for no more.'

With that she made her way back through the garden to where Garret stood. The captain of the Sentinels looked concerned, but the Queen placed a reassuring hand on his arm and said, 'They will do, Garret. A good choice, I think,' before making her way back into the palace.

Garret looked with some relief at Merrick. 'Managed not to mess that up,' he said. 'Well done.'

'Was there ever cause for doubt?' Merrick replied with a grin. Garret just shook his head and followed after the queen.

Later, back at the barracks, as the sky began to darken Merrick and Janessa donned their armour. Merrick's earlier confidence was gone, and he wondered what in the hells he had let himself in for.

He was risking his life for a woman – a girl – he didn't even know. A queen... *his* queen, but what in the hells did that actually mean? Merrick had never been a worshipper of faith or Crown and now here he was, preparing himself to offer his life for someone ordained as his superior.

It smacked of horseshit.

Where was the profit? Where was his angle? His reward for all this? If the other men of the Sentinels spoke true, the assassins that might be coming to kill her were prodigious of strength and unequalled in speed. Skilled beyond the ability of normal men. And here he was, Merrick Ryder, exemplary swordsman maybe, but hardly superhuman, tasked with protecting her.

He glanced across at Kaira and saw she wore her armour with honour, her expression free of doubt or reservation. For a moment, a fleeting second of madness, he envied Kaira her blind devotion, her naïve dedication. What he would have given to be so stalwart in mind and principle.

But he wasn't. He'd never done anything for anyone but himself. Never risked his own neck for friend or family. Never willingly risked his *coin* for someone else, let alone his life.

'Is this the right thing for us?'

He asked the question before he could stop himself. Even though he knew the answer, knew what she'd say, he just had to ask it.

Kaira glanced over at him. No misgivings. No hesitation. 'Yes. This is a duty. Yours as well as mine. You know it's the right thing to do, and that's where your doubt comes from.'

He thought on that for a moment but could make no sense of it.

'What do you mean?'

'Your doubt means you're changing, Merrick. It means you're becoming a responsible human being.'

How very fucking reassuring. 'That's worth getting killed for, is it?'

Kaira shook her head. 'We all die, sooner or later. Would dying for nothing be your preferred way?'

'My preferred way would be living.'

'Yes, you've already made that clear. But one day soon, you might have to make a choice. Might have to offer your life for someone else. You need to decide if you've got that in you. And you need to decide it soon.'

With that, she made her way from the barrack room, leaving the door open for him to follow.

Merrick stared after her. Tempting as the prospect of giving his life for the queen was, he could think of a thousand other things he'd rather be doing with it. But where else was there to go? Out on the streets to wait for the Guild to find him?

No, that was just stupid. He had his sword and his armour and Kaira watching his back. They were in an impregnable citadel in a heavily defended city.

What was the worst that could happen?

As he followed Kaira he began to wonder, if it came down to it, whether he really would sacrifice his life for someone else. Especially when that someone else was a girl he hardly knew.

Merrick could only hope he never had to find out.

SEVEN

It was a dark damp cellar, hidden deep beneath a house in a shitty part of Northgate – though truth be told, all of Northgate was pretty shitty. Rag had learned there were a thousand cellars like this in Steelhaven, the Guild's secret little crap-holes where anything, or anyone, could be spirited away from the world, never to be seen again.

'I haven't got the money, Mister Friedrik. Honest I haven't!'

The words came in a frantic series of pants, spat from a bloody mouth dripping with lies.

Or was he telling the truth? Rag couldn't really say. He must be lying, mustn't he? Otherwise why would they be putting him through this?

Walder was tied to a chair, a single lantern swinging above his head, bathing him in light and surrounding him in shadow like he was the only one in the room – the only one in the world. His face was a mess, his clothes filthy, britches and shirt piss-stained and hanging off him in torn clumps. He was breathing hard, face tear-streaked, desperate, wits shredded to shit. It was a sight that could have turned the stomach of even the most hardened thug, but Rag had seen this a dozen times before – heard the pained cries, seen the beatings again and again. As much as she hated to admit it, she was getting used to it.

A man walked forward into the light and Walder gave a little squeal. Harkas was an evil-looking bastard what never smiled. Without a word he leaned in over Walder, expressionless, just looming over him all intimidating.

The punch came quick and fast, fist stabbing out like a knife from the dark. It hit Walder in the middle of his little paunchy gut, knocking all the wind from him. The noise that he gave out made Rag flinch. It reminded her of a time, years ago, when some of the street lads had caught themselves a kitten. They'd tortured that little thing for what seemed like an age, and Rag had watched them, too afraid to step in, too sorry for the little thing to run away. In the end they'd thrown it in a fire, after they'd snipped its ears and tail off, and the sound it had let loose was a bit like the one Walder was making right now.

When he'd stopped wailing and Harkas had made his way back into the dark he began pleading again.

'I'm sorry… I'm sorry. I wish I knew where it were.' *So did Rag, then this could all be over with.* 'If I knew I'd tell you, Mister Friedrik, honest I would. Please don't kill me, Mister Friedrik. I've got mouths to feed.'

Rag had heard pleading like this before; so many times even she was growing hard to it. *Please don't hurt me, I've got kids. My old mammy's sick with the gout. The wife's in the family way, Mister Friedrik, please let me live.* At first she'd believed every line, felt sorry for every pathetic one of them, but now it was just getting fucking dull. And if *she* was getting bored with it, she was damn sure *he* would be too.

Walder stopped, breathing hard, looking out from the lamplight, straining into the dark. With slow measured steps, Friedrik walked forward.

It never failed to impress Rag what fear such an amiable looking bloke could strike in another human being. She'd been in the Guild long enough now to meet some pretty scary bastards, but Friedrik, despite his little frame and his curly hair and his friendly smile, was scarier than any of them.

'Walder,' Friedrik said casually as though he was greeting an old friend, and not some poor bastard strapped to a chair and bleeding. 'Walder, Walder, Walder.'

Friedrik smiled then, one of his big friendly don't-worry-about-it smiles. All Walder could do was smile back, but Rag could see the desperation behind his eyes. Could see that Walder knew he was walking a thin line and whether he'd live or die would depend on the next few moments.

'I believe you, of course,' Friedrik said, holding up his hands like this had all been some kind of misunderstanding and they could just go out for a beer to make it right. 'You fenced the items for us, like we asked. You took the payment, like we asked. What you handed over to us was a little light, but why would you lie about it?' Walder opened his mouth to speak, but was silenced by Friedrik's raised finger. Rag flinched again at that. If there was one thing guaranteed to piss Friedrik off it was being interrupted. She let out a sigh as Friedrik patted Walder on the shoulder. 'It's all right, mate. Things like this happen. Cut him loose.'

Two lads moved from the dark behind Walder, reaching down and cutting the rope that secured him to the chair. Walder looked around, wide-eyed.

'Is that it then, Mister Friedrik? Can I go now?'

Friedrik frowned. 'Can you go? Yes, Walder, you can go. Just as soon as I've had what you owe.' He held his hand out and big Harkas stepped forward, placing a little knife, handle first, in his outstretched palm.

Walder looked at the blade, the colour draining from his already pale features. He shook his head but didn't say a word.

'It's obvious you don't have the coin, Walder,' Friedrik said. Then he held out the knife. 'So you owe me... ooh... let's say two fingers. Your choice which ones, I'd go for the pinkies if I were you, but I want my fingers. And I want them now.'

Walder looked at Friedrik, then glanced around. There were three other men in the light now but Rag knew there were more lurking in the dark, just waiting for Friedrik's word. Walder knew they were there too.

'Please,' he said, more of a high-pitched whine than a word. 'I can get money. I can get you a—'

'It's too late for that,' Friedrik said, shaking his head. He had a sympathetic look on his face, like there weren't nothing he could do about this. Like it weren't him asking a fella to cut his own fingers off. 'Now, get to it, Walder, we haven't got all day.'

'But... but I can't.' Walder stared mournfully at the knife, then back up at Friedrik.

'Yes you can,' Friedrik replied, the sympathetic look gone now, replaced by a dark expression that spoke no mercy or reprieve. 'Because if you don't, I'm gonna let the lads choose something else to cut off, and whatever they decide I can guarantee you'll miss it more than a couple of fucking fingers.'

Walder knew then there weren't no options left. He stood up from the chair and kneeled down next to it, placing his hand flat on the seat and taking the knife firmly in hand. He gave a last look up at Friedrik, but there was nothing there that would save him.

As Walder began to squeal in pain, hacking at his pinky finger like it was a tough piece of roasted meat, Rag closed her eyes and turned away. He grunted like a pig, and some of the other lads laughed at that. Then the grunting stopped and she heard a clattering sound.

'Gods be damned,' whispered Friedrik in frustration, and Rag turned to see Walder had passed out from the pain and the fright. One of his fingers was bleeding, but still very much attached to his hand.

'Do the honours would you, my dear,' Friedrik said.

At first Rag could barely believe what she was hearing, but when she looked at him, Friedrik was staring right at her, a smile on his face like he'd just asked her to slice him a piece of cake.

'Eh?' she replied, still hoping there'd been some kind of mistake.

'His fingers,' said Friedrik, sounding a bit impatient. 'Come on, we don't want to be down here in this shit-hole forever.'

Everyone was looking at her now. They were just standing there, watching her, waiting. There was nowhere to run to. No way to get out of this. If she didn't do it, Walder wasn't the only one who'd be losing bits of himself.

Rag walked towards the prone body bleeding on the floor. The knife was still on the chair, the blade sharp and shiny in what little light there was down in the cellar.

Ain't no point in waiting on it, girl. Just get along and do what needs to be done. No room for pity or mercy or any of that old shit. Walder's got this coming whether it's you that does it or someone else.

She picked up the knife and knelt beside Walder. His breathing was shallow, but at least he wouldn't be conscious for what was coming. Rag fished in her pocket and pulled out a kerchief. After twisting it she tied it around Walder's little finger and fixed it there with as tight a knot as she could manage. Hopefully it would stop him losing too much blood.

Walder didn't stir as she took his hand and placed it on the chair. Didn't moan or cry out as she placed the knife over his finger. Didn't shout and open his eyes in agony as Rag slammed her hand down on top of the knife, the blade slicing right through bone and flesh.

A couple of the lads laughed at the sight of Walder losing his pinky. Rag fought to keep down the bile that was rising in her throat.

She looked up to see Friedrik smiling his approval. 'And the other one,' he said shooing her on with his hand like he was in a hurry.

Doesn't look like you've got any choice in the matter.

Rag took Walder's other hand and did as she was bid.

The sight of those dead, pink little fingers stayed with Rag for some time after. They stayed with her all the way from that dank cellar, following Friedrik and his hulking bodyguard, to their little tavern. Of course it wasn't a tavern at all, though it had a bar and kitchen and rooms. This was Friedrik's own private lair. Rag had learned quick that Friedrik liked his comforts. He was a homely fellow, truth be told. It was just his habit of hacking bits off people, or having them hack their own bits off, that made him stand out from other blokes.

They sat together, just she and him, as the rest of Friedrik's men milled round in the background. A plate of roasted lamb haunch and veggies sat in front of them, but she found that the thought of Walder had ruined her appetite. All she could do was push that food around with a fork, staring at it like it was the last thing she'd ever want to stick in her gob.

'What's the matter, little Rag?' Friedrik said from a mouth rimmed with grease. 'Not hungry?' She just shook her head. He shrugged. 'Best not let it go to waste. Don't want to upset cook.'

Rag knew that cook couldn't have given a shit whether she ate or not. Friedrik, on the other hand, was a different matter. His amiable act was just that, and at any moment he could become that menacing bastard again, all subdued fury and concealed hate. Not that he'd tried that on with her in the weeks she'd been with him. In fact, he treated her as something of a pet.

She was dressed in the best finery – but not a gaudy dress only fit for the stuffy bollocks in the Crown District. She wore hand-stitched britches, with a silk shirt and embroidered waistcoat. Her shoes, which had taken some getting used to, were waxed and buffed to a mirror sheen, the buckle on the top shining like gold. Every morning she combed her hair like Friedrik wanted and secured it with a silver clasp.

How this had happened, how she had ended up as Friedrik's right hand girl, she couldn't fully explain. Back in that warehouse, when she'd held a knife to his throat and given him no choice about taking her on, she'd thought he would just give her a job pinching on the streets. But it was clear he'd taken something of a shine to her, and there weren't no talking him out of it.

That didn't stop him being a scary bastard though, and in the intervening weeks she'd seen more beatings, stabbings and torture than she cared to remember. Today was the first time he'd made her join in, though. She hoped it wasn't a sign of things to come.

But who was she to complain? Wasn't this what she'd wanted – a way into the Guild? And as much as she hated the way people got treated, it beat the shit out of living on the streets.

Rag picked up her fork and stuck it in a piece of roast turnip, seeing Friedrik smile as she stuffed it in her mouth. She did her best to smile back as she chewed, visions of squealing Walder and his mutilated hands dancing in front of her eyes. She chewed until her jaw ached, then swallowed hard.

'There's my girl,' said Friedrik, going back to hacking at his lamb.

There's my girl.

For all she didn't want to complain, Rag still felt trapped. But what was she supposed to do? Where was she supposed to go now? Back to the street?

No chance of that. Even if she did, he'd come looking for her. And Friedrik *was* the Guild – it wouldn't take him long to track her down.

Fact was she was stuck here, but there was food in her belly, clothes on her back and a roof over her head. What more could a gal ask for?

Maybe a life that didn't involve watching people being beaten to shit?

Well, nothing was perfect, now was it? She was part of Friedrik's crew. Part of his little entourage, for better or worse. Best to just keep quiet and deal with it.

Rag looked around the room, glancing at the other members of their little group. Her new pals.

There was Harkas of course, silent imposing bastard that he was. She avoided him whenever possible, even though he mostly ignored her. It was pretty obvious there weren't nothing going on behind those blank eyes of his, not until Friedrik gave him an order to hurt someone.

There was fat Shirl. A bit useless in all respects, but loyal nonetheless. He'd been the one Rag had stolen the knife from weeks back when she'd given over Krupps' head in that warehouse. She still kept it in a little sheath at her waist. If Shirl was pissed off about it he didn't say nothing. There was no way he'd risk upsetting Friedrik.

Yarrick and Essen were the last two men close to Friedrik. Neither said much, other than to each other, and both had thin faces and broad shoulders, which made Rag think they might be related. She'd never had courage enough to ask, though.

Of course there were more thugs and brutes and snakes and rats loitering around, but they came and went, often sent off on one errand or another that most likely involved someone getting stabbed or robbed or both. Rag tried her best not to overhear lest she learn something she'd rather not know and she found she'd got good at that – ignoring the bad things.

She looked up at Friedrik stuffing his face full of roast meat and vegetables and remembered that day she'd been on top of him, knife to his neck. If she'd stuck it in his throat, right to the hilt, that might have changed something. Walder, for one, would still have his fingers.

Friedrik looked up and smiled, mouth full of food, and she smiled back. Then the door opened.

Two men walked in and Rag knew them before she could even see their faces through the gloom. They were the only two men in the whole of Steelhaven who would have entered this place so brazenly, rather than wringing their caps and bowing their heads in respect.

The first was tall with a strong build, and a thick dark moustache that drooped around a grim, set mouth. His eyes glared with wolfish intent as though he were on the hunt for something. Second fella was slight and gaunt featured, eyes set deep within his skull. Though he was hunched in the shoulders he still walked across the room as though he owned the place.

Rag could barely hide her discomfort as Palien and Bastian made their way nearer. She put down her fork and sat back in her chair, trying to look as insignificant as she could. Friedrik carried on eating as though they weren't even there.

As Bastian pulled up a chair and sat with them, Palien stood to one side, looking on hungrily. It took Rag a moment to realise he was staring at the food on the table as though he wanted to dive right in and devour the lot.

Bastian looked on, watching Friedrik eating with an expression of distaste, though from what Rag had seen of him before now, distaste was just about the nicest of his expressions. When Friedrik gave no sign of finishing his meal anytime soon, Bastian leaned forward just a touch.

'We've found him,' he said.

Rag had no idea who he was on about, but whoever it was they were important enough to stop Friedrik cold. His mouth was open, fork stuck into a slice of quivering lamb. Then he gently placed his fork down and sat back in his chair.

'Where?' Friedrik asked.

'Now that's the problem,' said Bastian. 'Word is he's joined the Sentinels. It appears Garret's taken the boy under his wing – they go back a long way by all accounts. He trusts him.'

'Trusts Ryder? That drunken whoremonger? The man must be a moron.'

'Whatever he is, he's taken that bastard into his employ and granted him all the protections that entails.'

'So what's the problem?'

'The problem is we can't breach the walls of Skyhelm, and the loyalty of the Sentinels is legend. Even if we get access to Garret, to make him an offer, they would never betray one of their own.'

'That is a quandary.' Friedrik sat back, deep in thought.

Whoever this Ryder was the Guild wanted him bad. Rag was glad she wasn't in his shoes. She was sure he wasn't going to last long, no matter where he was holed up.

'We need a spy,' said Palien. Rag turned to see him staring down with those hungry eyes. 'Someone good at slipping in and out of places unseen. Someone who could track his movements, maybe even lure him out in the open.'

'Yes, and I think we know just the person.' Bastian glanced towards Rag and she suddenly felt more uncomfortable than ever.

Friedrik asked the question for her. 'Where would we find someone…?'

He stopped when he saw Bastian leering at Rag.

She looked pleadingly at Friedrik and he began to shake his head. 'No. Out of the question. She's my… my…'

'Your what?' said Bastian through sneering lips. 'Your new plaything? A doll for you to dress up? Well, it's about time she made herself useful. Everyone has to pull their weight, Friedrik, in your crew as well as mine.'

'I said *no*.' Friedrik's expression hardened. It was a look Rag had seen a hundred times before. A look that had made so many men almost shit.

It had no effect on Bastian.

'Well, I say *yes*. She's already proved herself capable. Brought you a severed head, as I remember, and right out of a Greencoat barracks. No small feat for such a little dolly.'

Friedrik continued his glare, but he had no answer for Bastian. He looked at her, then back at his partner, then back to her again.

Rag wanted to speak up for herself, to say something on her own behalf, but these two were the men that controlled the Guild. What in the hells was she supposed to say?

'All right,' said Friedrik finally. 'I'm sure it's well within her capabilities. She can get in, track his movements and lead him into any trap we choose to set. What do you say, Rag?'

All eyes were on her now – the weight of expectation hanging over her like an anvil on a piece of thread.

'Yeah, sure,' Rag replied, before she'd even had time to think.

Friedrik smiled and sat back in his chair. 'See,' he said. 'Problem solved. Merrick Ryder is as good as fucked.'

EIGHT

The mountains were far behind them, their peaks visible above the endless forest that spread out to the south. For five days Regulus had pushed them on through the densely packed trees expecting the enemy to fall upon them at any moment, but they had made it through and out onto the Coldlands of the Clawless Tribes.

This land of rolling hills was strange to them. They saw low stone walls and hedgerows and streams flowing strongly. It was in stark contrast to the endless flat plains of Equ'un, where one might travel for days without sign of water.

Leandran moved up beside Regulus as he stood surveying the land before them.

'We have to keep moving,' said the old warrior with a shiver. Regulus knew the chill air was creeping into his old bones. None of them were used to cold like this, and the venerable Leandran was suffering most.

'I know,' said Regulus, looking back at his warriors. They were all weary. All tired of this ceaseless flight. 'Have we perhaps done enough running, old friend?'

A snaggletooth smile crossed Leandran's lips. 'I'll stand beside you, whatever you decide. You know that.'

'I know.' Regulus patted Leandran firmly on the arm.

With a sigh, he scanned the terrain for a defensible position. There was nothing that might afford them an ambush, no construction that they might barricade. Only hills on whose upper slopes they could sit and await their enemy.

Regulus glanced back towards the forest. It would not be long before their pursuers burst out of those trees. Was there any chance his small band could find the Steel King of the Clawless Tribes before they were hunted down?

Regulus doubted it.

And if they must fight, far better to die making a stand than to be cut down in ignominious flight. As much as he had wanted to escape to the north and restore his reputation, that opportunity had passed.

With a bitter smile he thought of what he might have achieved. The victories he could have won in honour of his father and the Gor'tana. But best not to dwell on that, it would only fill him with sorrow.

'There,' he said abruptly to his warriors, pointing to a hill that looked down towards the forest. 'We'll rest there.'

'Even though they must be right behind us?' said Hagama.

Regulus glared at him with determination. 'Yes. And with luck they will be.'

As they wearily made their way up the hill, Regulus felt Janto Sho's presence at his shoulder.

'We run all this way just to make a stand here, in the cold, in this land far from home?'

'Would you rather we keep running? That we die from exhaustion? Besides, this is as good a place to die as any,' Regulus replied.

Janto barked a laugh at that. 'Aye, you might be right. But what about those tales?'

Regulus shrugged ruefully. How he had wanted to create a legend, to have legends told of him from one side of Equ'un to the other. Then again, perhaps they set too much store by such things.

'They'll just have to tell their stories about someone else,' he replied, without looking around.

No one else spoke as they waited. The day wore on, and while his men rested Regulus kept his eyes fixed on the trees below. Not until the sun had crested the sky, even then bringing little warmth to the day, did their pursuers come into view.

At first there was a single scout, his eyes scanning the ground, searching for tracks. He stopped, tipping his nose to the air to catch their scent, and at that point he saw them waiting. Regulus savoured the scout's look of panic, visible only for a moment before he fled back into the safety of the trees.

'On your feet,' Regulus said, rising and unsheathing his black blade. His warriors did likewise, some of them looking resigned to their fate, though none of them balked at what was asked of them. Regulus felt a smack of pride at that – though his warriors were few they were loyal to the end. He was reassured by the keen glint in Janto's eye. The Sho'tana was obviously eager for this to get underway, relishing the prospect of violence.

They did not have to wait long before several figures strode out of the trees. Regulus had not known how many to expect and didn't know whether to be relieved or not when just twenty broke the tree line. Regulus experienced a brief moment of hope. Though he had only nine, he would have staked his life on the prowess of his warriors.

When he saw who led the hunting party though, Regulus took a blow to his confidence.

At their head stood Gargara, Faro's conspirator in betrayal. It was Gargara of the Kel'tana who had helped Faro usurp the crown from Regulus' father. It was he who had led the charge and killed many of his father's best warriors.

The fierce Kel'tana fixed his glare on Regulus as he led his men up the hill. His eyes dripped hatred, though Regulus had more justification for vengeful fury. Gargara's reputation went before him; his ruthlessness and strength were legend, but so was his hubris and arrogance. For the briefest moment Regulus saw a way he and his men might yet live.

'Gor!' Gargara spat out his name, stopping some feet away flanked by his men, their weapons drawn and claws out. 'My Lord Faro has put the death mark on you. I am here to see it carried out, but there is no need for your men to suffer. Kneel before me and I'll make this quick.'

Regulus glanced at his men who, despite their fatigue, looked on with steely determination. 'My warriors are loyal, Gargara of the Kel'tana. They will stand beside me to the death. I wonder whether you could say the same of yours.'

Gargara tossed his head furiously, his black mane whipping across his face. 'Enough! I am not here to talk. Kneel before me now or every one of you shall die.'

'As will many of yours.' Regulus could see that a number of the men who stood beside Gargara were not so keen on the prospect of battle. Most of them looked as weary as Regulus' own warriors. 'But there is a way of cheating the Dark Walker of his sport. A challenge. You and I, Gargara. Tooth and claw.'

Regulus spat his last words with relish, taunting Gargara with the prospect of a duel. If he had hoped the champion of the Kel'tana might be intimidated he was sorely mistaken as Gargara smiled, his eyes lighting up at the prospect, his white fangs flashing in the sunlight.

'I have killed a hundred pups like you with the claw,' he replied, unbuckling his sword and axe and letting them drop to the ground. 'Torn out a score of throats with the tooth. But yours will give particular pleasure, Gor'tana scum.'

Regulus skewered his black blade in the soft earth. 'Then come,' he said, his voice a hateful growl. 'Here is my throat. Come and take it.'

Gargara charged, churning up the ground between them as he raced up the hill. Regulus waited for him to come, letting his hatred roil inside as his claws sprang forth from his fingertips. He bared his fangs, unleashing a roar that more than matched that of Gargara.

They both leapt at one another on that hilltop, encircled by the warriors of both tribes. With a flurry of claw swipes, Gargara took the initiative. He was a mountain of muscle, his flesh scarred and torn from a hundred battles, his deadly reputation well earned. Regulus was hard pressed to avoid his blows, knowing that a single one could tear open up his flesh. As Regulus ducked those claws, Gargara's head shot forward and he attempted a bite with gnashing fangs. Regulus kicked out, leaping backwards away from the deadly teeth and hot stinking breath of his enemy.

They paused for a moment, facing one another and Regulus crouched low, ready to pounce as Gargara, eyes wide with rage, charged forward once more. With a quick swipe of his claws, Regulus opened his opponent's thigh. He tried a second swipe with his other hand, but Gargara was faster, rending three red claw marks across Regulus' chest. They backed off, stalking each other once more, breathing deeply as their men watched in silence.

Gargara Kel stepped forward and Regulus could see his hate had dissipated slightly, the pain from the wound in his thigh taught him that he fought no pup, but a seasoned warrior. This seemed, briefly, to quench the fury in his eyes. Then, with another roar, Gargara came on again, and Regulus was only too keen to meet him.

The enemies traded quick blows, blood spattering as they cut deep rents in one another's flesh, their grunts of anger growing louder, more frantic. As Gargara launched his head forward attempting another bite, Regulus ducked, lashing out with a claw. Gargara pulled away, but not fast enough – as Regulus tore at Gargara's head, ripping the flesh of his face from nose to ear, a black talon bursting his enemy's eye.

Gargara screamed again, but this time in pain, blood running through his fingers as he vainly tried to staunch the wound. Regulus might almost have smiled, but he knew he was not victorious yet.

He raced forward, keen to press his advantage, leaping for his enemy's throat, but Gargara showed why he was champion of the Kel'tana. As Regulus leapt, Gargara reached forward, heedless of the teeth and claws that had scored great tears in his body, and grasped Regulus by the throat.

Helpless in that grip, Regulus felt his enemy's claws pierce the flesh of his neck as he was squeezed tighter, throttled, driven to his knees. Gargara glared from one baleful eye, seemingly indifferent to the bloody ruin of the other. The smile appearing on his face revealed two rows of razor teeth. Shame washed over Regulus as he imagined those teeth tearing into his heart to consume his warrior's strength. How he would shame his father's memory, shame the Gor'tana with his defeat.

As his vision began to grow blurred, Regulus snapped out an arm, rending asunder the loincloth between Gargara' legs and clamping his black talons around his foe's genitals. Gargara had no time to panic before Regulus closed his clawed grip, tearing them off in his hand and gelding his opponent as he stood on the cusp of victory.

Gargara's high-pitched scream echoed across the hilltops as he reeled backwards, releasing his grip on Regulus' throat. It was all the opening Regulus needed. With teeth bared he flung himself at his enemy, clamping his jaws around Gargara's neck and tearing out his throat. The champion of the Kel'tana collapsed, blood gushing from throat and groin.

Regulus staggered away, staring at the warriors who had pursued them for so many leagues. Then he flung Gargara's bloody genitals onto his dying body.

He was about to tell Gargara's warriors to run, to flee south back to their homeland and tell Faro that someday soon Regulus would come to reclaim the chieftainship of his father's tribe.

But Janto Sho had other ideas.

Whether his bloodlust had been fuelled by watching so vicious a duel, or whether he craved blood himself, the warrior of the Sho'tana gave a roar of his own. With one axe he beheaded a man to his left, and with the other he cleft the skull of the warrior to his right.

Regulus had no chance to offer clemency – the rest of his warriors were quick to battle, young Akkula and the venerable Leandran quickest of all. The men of the Kel'tana were at first taken by surprise, but fast to counter, and Regulus barely managed to retrieve his blade from where it was skewered in the ground before he was set upon by a pair of warriors. He ducked a sword blow from one, severing the leg of the other before parrying the first sword as it came at him again. If his opponent thought Regulus might have been weakened by his battle with Gargara he was sorely mistaken. Screaming his rage, his blood still up from his duel, Regulus pushed his opponent's blade back. The warrior stumbled a step down the hill, dropping his guard just long enough for Regulus to hack down with his sword, splitting the warrior at the shoulder right down to his ribs.

He pulled his weapon clear, and saw that his men had made short work of the Kel'tana. A dozen of them lay dead, the handful of survivors fleeing back towards the tree line as the Gor'tana roared their victory. But it was a victory hard won.

On the ground, amongst the bodies of the Kel'tana were four of his own – Ortera, Felik, Churnik and Theoda. All had been brave and loyal warriors and many had fought alongside Regulus since they were boys. He hoped that they might reach the stars before the Dark Walker knew of their deaths.

Regulus could not bring himself to blame Janto for his rashness – he suspected the Kel'tana would not have spared his men, whatever the outcome of the duel.

Now there were only five left in his warparty, but he would be sure to celebrate his victory as though they were a thousand strong. Leandran was the first to cry out in triumph as their enemies fled into the forest. Regulus was quick to join him and soon all six Zatani were raising their voices in a terrible cacophony.

Later, after the sun had dropped below the horizon and they had lit four pyres for their fallen, Leandran observed the funeral rites. The bodies of the Kel'tana they left to the carrion eaters. Regulus had no desire to hamper their journey to the stars and so all were left with their teeth and claws. All except Gargara Kel.

The champion's corpse was laid out in their midst and Regulus, alongside his remaining men, looked down on it with loathing. They had already stripped him of his fangs, already ripped the claws from his fingertips and cast them to the ground. As victor in their duel, Regulus would receive the honour of being the first among them to feast.

He held out his hand and Leandran placed a narrow blade in his palm. Regulus knelt, slicing Gargara from the ragged open wound at his neck to his navel. With a clawed hand Regulus reached into the chest cavity, rooting beneath the ribcage until his hand closed around his enemy's heart. There was a sucking sound as he wrenched it free, then held it aloft, savouring his victory.

'For the Gor'tana,' he cried, then sank his teeth into the organ, causing the blood of Gargara Kel to stream down his chin. As he swallowed he savoured the taste – the taste of triumph.

As the funeral fires burned, his warriors began to feast on Gargara's corpse. It was late into the night before their hunger was satisfied. In the morning they woke up beside the embers of the pyres, sluggish and still sated. Little was left of the corpse.

Leandran came to join Regulus where he stood, looking out to the east.

'What now?' said the old warrior. 'We got rid of those behind us, but there might be more trouble ahead if we press on any further into the Coldlands.'

'I'm counting on it,' Regulus replied. 'Trouble is exactly what we came here for. Trouble and glory. And I have a feeling we'll find both in that direction.' He gestured lazily towards the east.

'There's trouble enough where we came from. I guess trouble ahead's no worse.' With a wink Leandran went to raise the others from their slumber.

Regulus looked them over: Leandran, lean and old, alongside Janto, dark, brooding and fearsome. Then there was Hagama, Kazul and young Akkula. Five warriors left to stand beside him. Five warriors remaining to help him reclaim the glory of his tribe; to make the Gor'tana great again.

It was a start.

Regulus could only hope there was indeed trouble to the east.

And if not, he swore by the Dark Walker himself he'd be sure to cause some.

NINE

The Lych Gate stood in the far eastern side of Steelhaven's curtain wall. It was housed in a barbican that rose up forty feet, with two figures carved from the stone that flanked it depicting hooded swordsmen. Who these men were supposed to be, Nobul had no idea, but they looked impressive all right, and none too welcoming.

Amber Watch had been posted to gate duty for two days now. It was an easy detail, and Nobul was getting pretty bored. Northgate was dangerous; no doubt about it, but at least there was something to do of an afternoon. Mind you, it beat getting shit and stones flung at you in the Warehouse District, so he couldn't really complain.

The Lych Gate was open from sunrise to sunset, allowing traders to come along the Great East Road from Ankavern, bringing their wares for trade. Watching the sporadic procession go in and out of Eastgate market wasn't Nobul's idea of a good time. Still, there'd be action soon enough. In a few days it wouldn't be farmers and fishermen trying to get through these gates, but a horde of angry Khurtas. Nobul was pretty sure he wouldn't be bored then. He was pretty sure he'd have plenty of things to occupy him. Not getting his head cut off would be chief among them.

A horse and cart rolled up, stopping beneath the massive gate. Nobul stepped forward, nodding at the old geezer sat on its seat, gripping the reins in arthritic fingers. The man didn't deign to nod back. Nobul took the horse by the bridle, placing a hand on its nose and whispering nothing in particular to keep it calm as Anton checked the cart, for what, Nobul didn't quite know. Perhaps there could have been Khurtic infiltrators in there, waiting to leap out, all painted and scarred, weapons dripping venom, ready to murder the first person they saw. Maybe Amon Tugha himself was concealed in there, ready to take on the city single-handed.

Anton finished his check and gave Nobul the signal to let the cart through.

Obviously it was just full of turnips.

No sooner had the cart passed through the gate than Hake yelled something from up on the barbican. The old man was pointing down the Great East Road.

'Riders!' he shouted 'Bloody loads of 'em. And they look tooled up.'

Nobul stared down the road. He couldn't see a thing at first, other than an endless roadway heading on down the coast. Perhaps Hake's eyes weren't all they should have been. Wouldn't be the first time the old man had seen something that wasn't there. But then something did come into view, something flapping on the sea breeze – a pennant.

He was about to grab Anton and rush inside, about to shout for the Lych Gate to be closed when Kilgar joined him, squinting into the distance from his one eye. The first rider was in full view, bronze armour glinting, pennant held high – though they couldn't yet make out what was depicted on it.

'What do you think, Lincon?' said Kilgar still unaware of Nobul's real name. 'Trouble or not?'

Nobul couldn't tell yet, but it was no use taking chances. 'We should close the gate, ask questions from behind the wall. If they're friendly they'll understand. If not, then we won't be caught with our arses hanging in the breeze.'

Kilgar seemed to agree. 'Close the gate,' he barked as they stepped inside. Nobul followed the serjeant up the stone stairs of the barbican to the rampart that looked out on the Great East Road. Hake was still standing there, staring out. Nobul was sure he saw a look of glee on the old man's face.

'Happy about something?' asked Nobul.

Hake's shoulders moved in a silent laugh and he pointed eastward with a bony finger. 'Don't you know who they are?'

Nobul looked out, shielding his eyes against the bright sunlight. Though it was cold, the wind whipping in from the Midral like a breath of ice, the sun was still beating down. From their high vantage point he could see the procession more clearly. The longer he looked, the more pennants came into view and it didn't take too long before he could make out several hundred riders. He couldn't count exactly how many, but they were all armoured, helms gleaming, pennants flapping in the breeze.

'One of the Free Companies?' Nobul asked.

Hake shook his head. 'Look at their flags.' Perhaps the old fella's eyesight wasn't so bad after all.

Even as they came closer, Nobul found it difficult to read the pennants with them flapping in the wind, but he could just make out...

'The Wyvern Guard,' said Kilgar. Nobul saw a smile creep up one side of the serjeant's stern mouth. 'Arlor's Blood, it's the frigging Wyvern Guard.'

As they watched the row of horses advance. Nobul wondered where they had come from. Even he knew the legend of the Wyvern Guard, the fabled order of knights who would come to Steelhaven's aid in its direst need. Well, it was in need now, and no mistake.

Every knight had armour of bronze, a sword at his side, and a shield on his arm emblazoned with the wyvern rising. Their helms were domed, sweeping down at the front over their gorgets. Their armour at shoulder and knee flared out in the shape of a wyvern's wing and each rider's horse wore barding in a similar style. One of them stood out from the rest. His helm bore wyvern's wings and he rode at the head of the column, a huge sword strapped across his back.

Nobul noticed an unexpected figure riding with the knights, a young lad in a brown robe. It almost made him smile to see the boy – he looked so out of his depth riding alongside warriors like these.

Just within the city gates a crowd had gathered, some anxious the barbican had been closed, some just nosey bastards. It didn't take long for rumour of the Wyvern Guard to spread, and the closer the knights drew to the city walls the bigger the throng got.

'This could be a problem,' said Kilgar, looking down at the gathering mob, and he shouted for Dustin and Edric to fetch the High Constable.

By now the head of the column had ridden within the shadow of the Lych Gate. The knight at their head, with his winged helm and huge sword, held up an arm. Almost as one, the column, several hundred strong, came to a halt.

Kilgar looked down uncertainly. He glanced at Nobul, who had no clue what to do. Before the serjeant could say anything the young lad in the brown robe piped up from below.

'Erm… can you open the gate?' he called. 'I think they'll be expecting us.'

It was almost funny, such a young streak of piss speaking for such an imposing column of warriors.

Kilgar turned to Nobul. 'Go on then,' he said through gritted teeth. 'Open the bloody gate.'

Nobul hurried down to pull back the wooden bars that held the gate fast. Within the structure of the barbican there was also a portcullis that could be slammed down during siege, but that had not been used in decades. Wouldn't be long before it would be needed again, he found himself thinking, but the gate was now open, and Nobul was staring at an army of armoured riders, whose leader was looking down at him like shit on his shoe.

Without a word the first knight touched spurs to his steed and the column was on the move once more. As he passed by the young lad in the robe looked down at Nobul and said, 'Thanks,' with an embarrassed smile.

It was then Nobul recognised him. Recognised him from weeks ago in the Chapel of Ghouls, remembered it was that young face covered in dust he'd seen when Nobul had looked up from cradling Denny's body.

Whoever the lad was, he certainly got himself about a bit.

'Right, let's clear a path,' said Kilgar, who had followed Nobul down from the barbican. At that, the lads of Amber Watch began to press ahead through the gathered crowd. Old Hake wasn't much use, but it was work for which Bilgot was uniquely suited as he barged his fat frame through the city folk, shouldering the gawking onlookers out of the way. Nobul, Anton and Kilgar did their best, but it was still slow going as word spread throughout Eastgate and people flocked to see the fabled Wyvern Guard who had returned to Steelhaven once more.

Amber Watch and the new arrivals had almost got through when there was a commotion coming the other way. The crowd was suddenly bundled from the path and Nobul could see Dustin and Edric alongside the High Constable. He had his own retinue of Greencoats and each of them looked on open-mouthed as they saw the parade of bronze-armoured knights working its way through the city streets.

'You weren't lying, were you lads?' said the High Constable as he looked up at the rider leading the column.

The knight looked down from within his winged helm. Nobul could see his neatly trimmed beard and his intense eyes.

'I am the Lord Marshal of the Wyvern Guard, here to see the queen,' he said. And that was all. Again he just sat there looking on expectantly, like he was the Duke of bloody Valdor and they should know to give him the red carpet treatment.

The High Constable looked up agog, clearly unsure of what to do. 'Er ... an audience with the queen might be difficult at short notice,' he replied.

'Trust me, she'll make time for us,' said the Lord Marshal, and Nobul had to agree; she just bloody might.

Before the High Constable could find any more excuses, other figures pushed their way through the crowd, this time Sentinels from the palace of Skyhelm. They looked up unsurprised, as though they had been expecting the Wyvern Guard all along.

'You'll follow us,' said the first Sentinel. 'The palace is—'

'I know the way, son,' said the Lord Marshal, touching his spurs to his horse once more.

Nobul stood back, allowing the knights to ride on past him. He didn't get an accurate count, but there were at least a couple of hundred in the column. Not enough to hold back the Khurtas on their own, but a welcome addition to the city's defences however you looked at it. He hoped he'd be there to see the looks on those savage bastards' faces when they realised they were up against the greatest knights in all the known world.

'Don't see that every day, do you?' said Hake, as they watched the last of the riders disappear towards the Crown District, followed by a gaggle of cheering city folk.

Nobul just shook his head.

Later, back at the barracks, having already put his weapon back in the store, Nobul was changing out of his green arming jacket. Kilgar stood there watching him with his one good eye. It was obvious he wanted to speak, maybe wanted Nobul to ask what he was standing there for, but then Nobul had never been one for starting up conversations.

They looked at one another for a moment and Kilgar took a deep breath.

'Good that they've come... the Wyvern Guard, I mean.'

'Aye, reckon it is,' Nobul said.

Another pause. Kilgar took another breath.

'It's coming, you know. It'll be like the Gate all over again. The piss and the blood. The crying and the screaming. You reckon you're up for it?'

Nobul nodded, though he reckoned this time it might well be worse. At Bakhaus Gate they could have retreated, but here they only had the sea at their back. He could swim well enough, but doubted he'd make it to all the way Dravhistan in one go.

'We'll weather it,' Nobul said. 'We've done it before.'

'Aye that we have. And lived to tell the tale.'

Another pause, but this time Kilgar walked forward, leaning in like he didn't want no one else to hear, even though there was no one else there.

'It wasn't your fault you know,' said Kilgar. 'It could have happened to any one of us. Any one of us could have been there that night. Any one of us could have ended up dying in that place.'

'I know,' said Nobul, not too sure this was a conversation he wanted to be having.

'Denny thought a lot of you. He'd have been glad you were there ... at the end.'

That one stung. Nobul didn't believe Denny *would* have thanked him after leaving the lad to fall to his death. But what was he supposed to say? Was he supposed to open his mouth to Kilgar and tell him the facts? That Denny had been the one who shot his boy? That he'd wanted to punish the little fucker, and when he got his opportunity he'd let him drop from that ledge on purpose?

They said unloading your sorrows on someone else was meant to help. Nobul wasn't convinced. Either way, he had nothing to say he wanted Kilgar to hear. He felt guilty all right, but he reckoned it was *his* guilt to bear, and bear it he would.

Before he had to make up some reply, Anton walked in. Dolorous as always he regarded the pair of them for a moment then began pulling off his jacket and helm.

'Just think on,' said Kilgar, patting Nobul's shoulder with his one remaining arm. 'If you want to talk about it, you know where I am.'

Hells, if Kilgar still had both eyes he'd most likely have given a wink too. Nobul wasn't too sure he liked this side of Kilgar. He'd preferred him when he was hard as stone, a serjeant to be feared. Not acting the priest and confessor.

Kilgar left, and Nobul hung back, giving the serjeant enough time to clear the barracks before he made to follow. By that time Anton had finished with his gear and was leaving too. They walked out side by side, and Anton looked up and smiled. Now that was new. Nobul had never seen so much as a twitch on the lad's lips since the day he'd started with the Greencoats.

Was everybody going fucking mad?

'Er... fancy a beer, Lincon?' Anton said.

This was all he needed. It seemed half of Amber Watch was keen to sit down and have a long chat with him about the great cycle of life.

'No thanks, Anton,' he replied.

Anton looked downcast, became his usual miserable self. Which only made Nobul feel worse. This was supposed to be his mucker, his comrade-in-arms and he couldn't even be bothered to go for a beer with the lad.

What a twat you are, Nobul Jacks.

'Well, all right then. Maybe just the one.' He'd said it before he could stop himself. But what was the harm? It had been months since he'd been for a drink. Months since he'd just sat back and relaxed. Maybe it was about time. Maybe he even deserved it. In a few days he wouldn't have the chance to do much of anything but fight. Best grab the laughs while you could.

'I know just the place,' Anton said, brightening once more. It was a side of the lad Nobul hadn't seen. It was certainly better than the side to Kilgar he hadn't seen – all caring and touchy feely like.

They made their way up through Northgate, past the dilapidated houses, up through the cold streets, the muddy ground frozen almost to stone. It wasn't a bad time of year to walk through Northgate, if any time could be considered good. At least the cold of winter hid the human stink.

The further they went the more Nobul began to wonder if Anton knew where in the hells he was going.

'Sure this is the right way?' he asked.

'Oh, it's not far, Nobul,' he said. 'Just down here.'

'All right. If you say so.'

Anton led them down an alley but it didn't look like a decent spot for no alehouse. In fact it didn't look a decent spot for much of anything, but who was Nobul to complain. It wasn't like Anton was one of the rougher lads. It wasn't like he'd be leading them into some cutthroat shit hole.

As Nobul thought that, he frowned, suddenly realising what had just been said between them. Anton had called him 'Nobul'.

And he'd answered to it.

Before he could speak something hard hit him on the back of the head. It fuzzed his vision and dropped him to one knee, but it didn't put him out.

'Hit him again,' someone said, panicked, desperate that they hadn't knocked him unconscious.

Nobul spun around, dizzy, stumbling, seeing the club come down again. He just managed to raise an arm, felt an impact, grunted against the pain. More feet clattered towards him across the hard earth and knew he didn't have much time. He reared forward, butting the club wielder and knocking him back. But that made Nobul stumble again and by the time he'd righted himself someone had shoved a sack over his head.

They pulled on it, dragging him, tightening the sack round his neck.

'Fucking hit him!' screamed another voice more frantic than the first.

Nobul backed up, shoving against whoever held the sack, trying to smash him against a wall, but he lost his footing. Something hit him in the shoulder, a plank of wood, another club maybe. He growled, getting his mad up, ready for the next blow. When it came he lashed out, feeling his foot hit someone who squealed. He grabbed at the sack trying to get it off.

'Fucking help me!' someone cried from behind. 'He's strong as a fucking ox!'

Nobul's hand grasped a wrist, dragging it forward. The sack loosened about his neck as he pulled someone in front of him, punching out twice, feeling the impact against his fist, hearing a pained wheeze from someone's lungs.

Before he could finally drag the sack off something hit him again, bang across his skull, driving him to the ground.

Last thing he heard was the sound of blows smashing in, pummelling him to…

TEN

She was on her hands and knees, retching up a long string of bile that dangled from her mouth but stubbornly held on, as though it didn't want to break off and fall into the bowl in front of her. Janessa's long red curls hung in that bowl, the strands of her hair splaying in the fresh vomit, but she didn't care.

All she wanted was for this to go away.

Her hand strayed down to her belly. She could feel it had grown, the swollen flesh seeming to have hardened around her middle. It wouldn't be long now until people other than Nordaine started to notice… if they hadn't already.

And what would happen when they did? How would she be greeted at court? Half of them already despised her, coveting her power, waiting for her to fail so they could grab some advantage for themselves. And would the other half remain loyal once they discovered the truth?

The Whore Queen, they would call her. Her courtiers would snigger and gossip behind her back. *Who is the father? Could be anyone — I hear she'll lie with any man who offers her a red rose and some honeyed words. Must be young Lord Raelan Logar's, I heard he was quite the rogue. No, they say it's Leon Magrida's, though she refuses to marry him.*

Yet it was not the courtiers who mattered to her. It was the people of Steelhaven, *her* people, she really cared about.

Would they see this as a betrayal of their trust? Would it make them lose faith in her?

Whore Queen or virgin, her desire to do her best for them remained the same. She must still lead Steelhaven against the tyrant who would see the city razed to the ground; fight for victory – no matter her condition.

Janessa rose gingerly from the floor, and sat back on her bed, relieved that the nausea had abated. What a state she must look – hair dishevelled, sweating like a fat drunkard. Her appearance was the least of her worries, however.

What was she to do?

Should she find a husband, and quickly? Janessa had been determined to rule on her own, but the child inside her put an entirely new complexion on things and now her options looked decidedly slim.

Should she marry Leon Magrida? Would he want her, now she was with child? Or could she attempt to deceive him? What was she even thinking? Leon's views were immaterial – Baroness Magrida would seize any chance to share the Steel Crown, even if it meant her son marrying a three-copper whore.

No.

This was desperation. Why was she even considering marriage to a man she despised? The very thought of it made her skin crawl. She could never give herself to another man while River was still out there… somewhere.

She felt a moment of panic. Was he still faithfully waiting for her? Would he come back? Hold her in his arms once more? Take her away from this place?

Janessa shook her head against the thought.

That was all whimsy. Another life she had dreamed she could have. But it was impossible. Janessa Mastragall could run away neither from Steelhaven nor from her daunting responsibilities.

The worries of giving birth out of wedlock would have to wait. Her armies to the north had been defeated. The Khurtas would be at the gates of Steelhaven within a few short days. Amon Tugha was coming.

Word had reached her that the Wyvern Guard had arrived, though they alone could never be enough to hold off an army tens of thousands strong. The entire city had to fight – its people united against the merciless enemy.

They needed a beacon to rally around, and Janessa was determined to be their light.

Wallowing in her woes would not see the city defended.

Rising with new purpose, Janessa heard a knock at the door. She knew it was Nordaine . Her governess had been more attentive than ever these past few days, but there had been no prattled advice. The older woman knew Janessa had to find her own way.

Janessa allowed Nordaine in. Silently, the governess placed a little food down next to Janessa and began clearing away the bowl of vomit. Every day she brought food, even though Janessa usually refused it.

With fresh water she washed Janessa, wiping away the sheen of sweat on her body. Then she rinsed the vomit from Janessa's hair, before dressing it formally. Finally, Nordaine helped Janessa into the gown she wore for court. It was a plain dress, austere as the room and throne from which she governed.

When ready, Janessa stepped out of her chamber and waiting, as ever, were her Sentinels. Kaira looked stern; always ready to carry out her duty. Merrick was more casual, but he snapped to attention on seeing her.

These two warriors, still new to Janessa, instantly made her feel safe. However the city and her court might judge her, she feared no harm as long as these two were by her side.

They led the way through Skyhelm's corridors and into the main hall where Janessa saw Odaka waiting for her. The throne room had been cleared, not a soul in sight, and Odaka looked troubled.

'What matters of court today?' she asked. 'Where is our usual audience?'

Odaka took a step forward. 'Before any matters of court, Majesty, there is something that requires your immediate attention. To have the customary audience would be inadvisable. The matter is most sensitive.'

Janessa was confused. All matters of state, other than those of the War Chamber, were conducted in public. What could warrant such privacy?

Odaka continued. 'An envoy has arrived from the White Moon Trading Company. I cannot over stress the importance of his visit.'

The importance was certainly not lost on Janessa. The company was affiliated to the Bankers League – a powerful organisation with members from a number of nations across the Midral Sea, which might hold the key to her city's survival. If she could persuade them to back her with their money the Free Companies would fall over one another to flock to her banner.

'I am to deal with him now?' Janessa didn't relish the idea of bargaining over the future of her city, her country, but knew she must. This man would negotiate only with her, would accept no intermediary. This was a duty for her alone.

'He arrived unexpectedly, Majesty, and he has demanded an audience with you immediately.'

This envoy was no king, perhaps not even a noble, but if Odaka was willing to acquiesce to him, he must be powerful indeed.

'Very well,' said Janessa. 'We will speak with him.'

'I will bring him, Majesty. But remember, he will not offer his coin lightly. This could be a long and difficult dance. A game of strategy, so to speak. Accept nothing until we are sure what he wants in return.'

Janessa nodded.

As Odaka left to fetch the envoy, Janessa took to her throne, flanked by Merrick and Kaira. She suddenly felt sick again, but this was nothing to do with the child growing inside her. Janessa knew the man she was about to meet might hold the key to her city's survival. She hoped the price for his aid would not be too high.

Odaka soon returned leading a small procession. Beside him was Chancellor Durket babbling on about the history of Skyhelm and the reason for the throne room's austerity. Janessa hardly noticed either of her advisors though, her attention focused fully on the man they led into the chamber.

He looked harmless enough. Just below average height, with olive skin. He had a headscarf wrapped tight around his head. His robes were black and plain, his hands hidden in their sleeves. As he drew closer, Janessa could see he wore kohl around his eyes giving him a feminine look, though the thin moustache and beard that joined around his mouth showed he was every inch a man.

Behind him walked four men, whom Janessa guessed were his personal bodyguard. They all had identical shaven heads, with matching red tunics and pantaloons that were striking against their dark skins. None of them carried a weapon.

They stopped at the foot of the stairs leading to the throne and Odaka announced, 'Azai Dravos of the White Moon Trading Company.'

Dravos inclined his head, but kept his painted eyes fixed firmly on Janessa.

'Greetings, your illustrious Majesty.' His thick accent dripped with charm. 'Might I say your splendour was much understated. I have met the queens of every nation in the East, but your beauty surpasses that of them all.'

Janessa somehow doubted that, but she smiled nonetheless.

'I am sure you flatter me, Azai Dravos. Welcome to my city. I hope your stay will be a pleasant one.'

'What a magnificent city it is. Would that I could stay longer and sample its many wonders.'

Yes, I'm sure you'd love to stay while my city is besieged. It will be most stimulating.

'But at least you will be able to enjoy the palace? Chancellor Durket will see you and your men accommodated in our finest rooms.'

Azai Dravos smiled, but a look of discomfort flashed across his face.

'I regret that I am unable to stay, Majesty. Now, if we might move on to the purpose of my visit...'

Janessa felt her stomach lurch. He was steering this away from her and she needed to be in control. She certainly wanted his coin, and fast, but she couldn't allow him to dictate proceedings.

'Nonsense,' she said quickly, 'I will not hear of it. Durket, see that our guests are offered all the luxuries the palace can provide.'

'But—'

'I will not hear of it.' Janessa tried to inject an element of command into her words and was pleasantly surprised at the result. 'You have come far. It would reflect poorly on me were you to leave without experiencing our hospitality.'

At first Azai Dravos looked annoyed, but he held Janessa's gaze and smiled his reply. He had played this game many times before.

'On behalf of the White Moon Trading Company, I thank your Majesty for her generosity, and look forward to speaking with her at length... very soon.'

Without waiting for dismissal he backed away with a bow, as did his men. They left with Durket, who continued his prattling as they retreated down the corridor. Odaka moved forwards, nodding his approval.

'That was well done, Majesty. But Dravos will not be put off indefinitely, and neither do we have the time to allow it. I would suggest a private audience when he is more comfortable. The deck is stacked heavily in his favour; he knows we are desperate and he could demand almost anything.'

'Which could be what?'

Odaka shook his head. 'It could be many things: crippling interest on the loan, or maybe future trade deals heavily weighted in his paymasters' favour. He might even insist on a permanent envoy in your court. Until you can meet with him alone and appeal to his better nature, there is little doubt he will not budge on anything.'

'But what can we afford to give? You're right; we have little bargaining room and no time to manoeuvre him into a reasonable deal.' Things were deteriorating by the moment. Must she act the gambler, with the future of her city the stake?

'Ultimately we must be prepared to pledge almost anything to save the city. Any bargain struck with a member of the Bankers League will come with a heavy price. But pay it we must, Majesty.'

'Then there is no choice, is there? A poor hand indeed.'

She spoke to no one in particular.

ELEVEN

He stood at her shoulder, to the left hand of that big stone throne. Merrick had almost laughed the first time he'd done it, the first time he'd stood in that huge throne room protecting their queen. A couple of months back he'd been chancing his arm on the streets: whoring, drinking, gambling. Everywhere he turned people wanted him dead, and he'd been lucky to survive.

Now he was in the great palace of Skyhelm, armoured and armed, a chosen lifeguard of the most powerful woman in the Free States.

Even he had to admit he'd done pretty bloody well for himself.

Kaira stood to the queen's right – stern, implacable almost. It was a duty to which she was wholly suited. Merrick knew that were Kaira called upon to lay down her life for the young girl that sat between them she would have done it without question.

Well, at least that made one of them.

In the past few days he had seen Queen Janessa preside over her court assuredly. This had surprised Merrick at first, but then he hadn't really known what to expect. When he first encountered her she had looked like a naive child thrown in with the sharks, but he had come to admire how she handled things – always calm and diplomatic, always taking a measured approach. Had he been forced to deal with half these greedy, clamouring bastards Merrick was pretty certain he'd have told most to go fuck themselves.

He'd definitely got a bad feeling about the foreigner they'd just seen. There was something about Azai Dravos that Merrick didn't like, and it wasn't just the perfumed stink. He'd been relieved when the bastard left.

With Dravos gone the Sentinels at the entrance to the throne room had allowed in the usual collection of simpering prigs. Merrick hadn't quite worked out which one of them he loathed the most yet, but he was getting there.

Lord Governor Argus of Coppergate stood wringing his hands. He'd already entreated for aid a dozen times, though it had become obvious the Khurtic horde was more interested in making its way south than besieging his city. It was a mystery why he was even here – he'd have been safer cosseted within the walls of his city rather than in Steelhaven. Maybe he was just lurking around for the entertainment. Or to see what fell into his grasping hands as the place crumbled around him.

General Hawke stood nearby. He'd spent the last few days in court, leaving his armies to the north under the command of Duke Bannon Logar. He claimed he was here to oversee the defence of the city walls in readiness for a coming siege, but Merrick could see the old man looked weary. He was most likely here for some respite from the constant fighting – unlike Marshal Farren, who looked as if he couldn't wait to get back to the front quick enough. The leader of the Knights of the Blood was a fearsome individual, his armour proudly bearing the marks of battle. One heavily scarred eye twitched occasionally as if he had something in it. The man made no secret of his disdain for Skyhelm's Sentinels, and he still upheld the old rivalry. Luckily Merrick hadn't been on the receiving end of his notorious temper. Not so far, anyway.

Of course, Odaka Du'ur stood at the base of the stairs to the stone throne, presiding over all the courtly business. Merrick hadn't quite worked him out yet; that ebon face was hard to read. And Merrick was usually a good judge of character. The advisor acted loyal enough, and seemed as intent on protecting the queen as her Sentinels. Whether it was ultimately for his own gain only time would tell.

One character who was easy to see through stood opposite Odaka at the foot of the stair. Seneschal Rogan cut quite a loathsome figure. Why they kept the bastard around was a mystery. If it had been up to Merrick he would have confined Rogan permanently in his torture dungeon well away from decent folk, or at least made him conduct his business from behind a wooden screen. The leader of the Inquisition smiled and made all the right noises, but his manner was too accommodating. Merrick had been on the streets long enough to see through it. No one was that gracious, that selfless – especially someone who tortured people for a living. Every time the slimy bastard opened his mouth it made Merrick's skin crawl, and he found his hand straying to the sword at his side. Janessa often listened to Rogan intently, taking in what he said, but not always acting on his advice. Merrick could only hope it stayed that way.

The gathered courtiers turned their heads as a man walked into the throne room. He was a shaggy affair, furs piled up around his shoulders, bow at his back, axe and knife at his waist. It was difficult to tell his age, his face was weathered like a battered bit of old leather, his hair grey, but he walked with the sureness of a much younger man, despite a slight limp.

He kneeled before the throne and bowed his head as though he meant it.

'Oban Halfwyrd, Warden of the North, Majesty,' he said, his voice as grizzled as his face. 'Come with words from the front, Majesty.'

'Stand, Oban Halfwyrd, and tell us your news,' Janessa replied.

The Warden rose gingerly, and Merrick saw then he showed his age, something cracking in his knee, his breath laboured as he gained his feet.

'Well, it ain't good, Majesty. Duke Logar has ordered a full retreat. It's been three days since we tried to hold 'em at Deeprun Bridge, but we just lost too many men. Khurtic bastards don't give in… er, pardon, Majesty.' He paused, as though cursing in front of the queen was a hanging offence.

'Continue,' she said.

'Ain't much else to tell. Without the Free Companies to help us we've only got bannermen from Valdor, Dreldun and Steelhaven. Just ain't enough. There's the best part of forty thousand Khurtas headed this way and nothing to hold 'em off except prayers and bad language, Majesty. Only a few days till they come knocking at Steelhaven's door.'

He was silent then, looking round as though someone might walk forwards and give him a slap for the bad tidings he'd brought. Instead, Queen Janessa rewarded him with a smile.

'We appreciate your haste in bringing the news, Oban Halfwyrd.'

'Weren't nothing, Majesty,' the Warden replied self-consciously.

He took a step back, readying himself to leave, but not everyone had heard enough.

'Where is Logar now?' demanded a voice. Merrick looked across to see Marshal Farren glaring at the Warden, his scarred left eye twitching of its own accord.

'Er … not five days north, milord. The Khurtas stopped for a bit at Deeprun, doing their burning and pillage. Our army's resting up thirty leagues south of 'em.'

'What numbers are left?' This was General Hawke. He tried to sound as commanding as Farren but failed dismally.

'Might be eight thousand, maybe six. Difficult to say, we didn't have time to count the dead and wounded, what with the Khurtas dogging our heels.' Even Merrick could tell there was bitterness in Oban's words. Whether it was for the loss of comrades at the front, or his disdain for a general who would leave his men behind for the safety of the city, he couldn't tell.

Odaka Du'ur turned to the queen. 'We need to send one of the Free Companies to escort the army back from the front. We cannot risk our bannermen being slaughtered before they have a chance to retreat.'

Seneschal Rogan raised a hand before the queen could reply. 'Ah, that might be problematic.' He spoke with a smile. Even when delivering bad news he had that same simpering smile on his face that made Merrick want to ram a gauntleted fist down his throat. 'The Free Companies have yet to receive payment. The Brotherhood of the Sun and the Hallowed Shields will not raise so much as a finger until they have been paid in full. The Midnight Falcons are threatening to leave the city within the next two days if they are not paid a retainer.'

'Then they must be paid,' said Lord Governor Argus, though what it had to do with him, Merrick had no idea.

'With what?' said General Hawke. 'The coffers are empty!'

This seemed to silence them all for a moment. If the coffers were empty they were all deep in the shit.

'A meeting has been arranged,' said Odaka, 'that will see the Crown's finances flourish. Do not worry on that score. Seneschal, you may inform the Free Companies that payment is guaranteed.'

The Seneschal flashed him that smile again. 'These are mercenaries. They care little for guarantees, I'm afraid. Cold hard coin is all they believe in. It is the only thing that will ensure their loyalty.'

Merrick could see Janessa moving uncomfortably next to him. This was supposed to be her throne room, these were her decisions to make, helped by her reliable advisors, who at the moment were bickering like children.

'If they won't fight for the Crown voluntarily when in its direst need, they should be forced to fight,' barked Marshal Farren. 'We conscripted mercenaries before Bakhaus Gate. We can do it again.'

'We conscripted *former* mercenaries who were citizens of the Free States, Marshal,' Rogan replied. 'The mercenary levies were still paid for by the Crown.'

General Hawke shook his head. 'This is madness. If Cael were here he'd make them fight, whether they wanted to or not.'

Merrick heard Janessa let out a despondent breath at the mention of her father – at the suggestion of her inadequacy. He could see her fingers gripping the stone arms of the throne on which she sat as though she wanted to rise, to shout at them, but something was holding her back.

Merrick suddenly wanted to help her but guessed that if one of her personal guard drew his sword and threatened the room to silence she would not thank him.

'Everything is in hand,' said Odaka. 'The queen is to meet with a financier very soon.'

'Is she?' said Argus. 'How reassuring. And what will she bargain with? What assurances can she give them that their investment will be well placed? This city may well be ash in a few days. Who's going to lend her money? Perhaps we should ask her?'

Argus turned expectantly, and Merrick found his hand had straying to the hilt of his sword. It looked like he bore more allegiance to Janessa than he'd thought. Or maybe he just wanted to draw on this pompous arse and teach him some manners.

Luckily, Merrick wasn't the only one.

'Watch your fucking mouth, bastard.' It was Oban Halfwyrd, who'd gone so far as to draw the knife at his belt.

Argus took a step back, looking for support from the Sentinels who were present. None of them offered any help.

Merrick saw Janessa move forward in her seat, perhaps to demand Argus be punished or that Halfwyrd stand down. He never got to find out which.

Captain Garret entered the throne room briskly, fully armoured, helmet held under his arm. The throne room hushed as all eyes fixed on him. Courtiers scurried out of the way to allow the imposing figure a clear path to the throne. From outside came the sound of marching feet.

Then they entered.

They advanced in ranks of two, bronze armour gleaming, faces hidden behind intricate helms. At their head two knights carried pennants which, on reaching the front of the throne room, the knights displayed so the red wyvern on a green field was visible to all. Behind them the bronze-armoured knights marched in strict unison, over a hundred in all. The knights at the front dropped to one knee, quickly followed by those behind, one by one, like a row of toppled books. Merrick marvelled at their practised discipline.

Four more bronze-armoured knights strode into the great hall. The first wore a massive winged helm and a broadsword strapped to his back. Behind him were two more bronze-clad warriors, one of them wearing the white pelt of some enormous snow beast around his armoured shoulders.

Garret looked on as the warriors stopped in front of the queen, then knelt before her, head bowed. 'Majesty,' Garret said. 'May I present the Wyvern Guard and their Lord Marshal.'

'Your servants unto death, Majesty,' announced the warrior with the winged helm.

There was something about that voice. Something about its commanding tone that Merrick recognised. But surely it couldn't be…

'We were told of your arrival and we are grateful for your aid, Lord Marshal,' Janessa replied. 'I am sure Captain Garret will see to your needs and those of your men.'

'I will, Majesty,' said Garret with a bow. 'They will be housed in the Skyhelm barracks with all the privileges bestowed on my own Sentinels.'

Merrick saw a flash of pride in Garret's features. It was true that everyone knew the legends of the Wyvern Guard – their deeds during the Dragon

Wars, their banishment of the ghouls, the Harrowing of the Blood Isles – but Garret seemed to regard these men as old friends.

'That's it?' said Marshal Farren suddenly, taking a step forward. 'We are to invite these... men to dine at our table without so much as a by your leave? They could be spies of the Elharim for all we know. Who will vouch for them?'

'I will,' said Garret, his words snarled angrily, his disdain for Farren and his Knights of the Blood clear for all to see. But the Lord Marshal of the Wyvern Guard had already walked forward.

'We are here at the behest of the city. Here to defend its people and its queen. Had we wanted to do it harm don't you think you'd already know about it?'

Farren turned impatiently to the queen. 'House them in the city gaols with the rest of the mercenaries. Not in Skyhelm. What have they done to deserve that honour?'

'Indeed,' said General Hawke, a little uncertainly. 'We know nothing of these men.'

'Oh but *we* know of *you*,' said the Lord Marshal. 'We know you let your king be murdered. We know you've both left your armies to the north and come here to hide like rats. Don't talk to me of "honour" when you have none.'

'Watch your mouth, dog!' said Farren, taking a threatening step forward.

The Lord Marshal didn't move but the warrior to his right, the one with the fur cloak, moved into Farren's path, his sword ringing halfway from its sheath.

'One more step and I'll cut that winking fucking eye from your head,' he said. Despite his choice of language in front of the queen, Merrick kind of liked him already.

Farren stared, his eye twitching frantically, but he went no further.

The Lord Marshal stepped towards the queen, and removed the helmet from his head.

On seeing the man's face Merrick felt sick. Felt small. Wanted to piss. Wanted to run. A host of childhood memories flooded back. Of castigation. Of punishment. Of training... endless training... and never getting a fucking thing right.

'Majesty,' said the Lord Marshal. 'My name is Tannick Ryder. Former Captain in the Skyhelm Sentinels. Sent forth almost twenty years since to restore the Wyvern Guard to its former glory. And now I have returned to defend your city and your life. Accept not just my words of loyalty. Accept my sword.'

With that he pulled the massive blade from his back with a metallic ring. Merrick saw Kaira tense across the throne from him, her hand straying to the hilt of her sword as this man drew his blade in front of the queen. But the Lord Marshal only knelt and offered up the magnificent weapon.

Odaka glanced up to Janessa but Merrick couldn't read his expression. Not that he gave a shit what Odaka thought; he was battling his own daemons. Daemons from the past that couldn't be fought with any weapons. Daemons of regret. Daemons of anger. Of sadness and loss.

Once again he was that abandoned and vulnerable child, and the man responsible was right there. The man who should have protected him all those years ago was not ten feet away.

'Lord Marshal Ryder,' Janessa said, standing. 'It is an honour for us to accept you in our city. The Wyvern Guard has always stood beside Steelhaven and the Free States. Always defended its people in their greatest need. Now more than ever do we require your help.'

'Then we will defend Steelhaven to the last, Majesty,' he replied, standing up and sheathing his sword.

After bowing low, he turned, marching his entourage through the corridor formed by his bronze-clad warriors. Garret gave Merrick a knowing nod before accompanying them.

When the two men were gone the Wyvern Guard stood up as one, their discipline something to marvel at, turned on their heels and marched from the throne room. The warrior in his white pelt remained briefly, sword half drawn, staring at Farren, who glared back balefully. When the last of the Wyvern Guard had left the room, the man winked arrogantly at the Marshal of the Knights of the Blood, sheathed his sword and swaggered from the hall.

'There is risk in this, Majesty,' said Rogan as soon as they had left, but Janessa simply raised a hand.

'Enough,' she said. 'Clear the hall.'

At that Odaka ordered the gathered courtiers on their way. Merrick stared on in shock. It must have been plain on his face, for even the queen seemed to notice, though she mistook his expression.

'A fortunate turn of events,' she whispered, as the seemingly endless trail of courtiers left the hall.

'That's one way of looking at it, Majesty,' Merrick replied.

'You don't think so?'

Merrick looked at her, wondering whether to unburden himself. She was his queen and already bore on her shoulders the problems of the nation but...

'I'm sure the Wyvern Guard will fight for you loyally, Majesty. It's their Lord Marshal you shouldn't put your faith in.'

'Why would you say that?' she asked, but then realisation seemed to dawn on her all at once.

'Yes, Majesty,' he said. 'Tannick Ryder is my father.'

TWELVE

Accompanying Queen Janessa from the great hall, Kaira noticed how the queen gripped her fists tight to her sides, her knuckles white. Surely troubled was the last thing she should have been – the legendary Wyvern Guard had returned to the city. This was the most favourable news they had received since Amon Tugha set foot in the Free States. But no, Janessa walked with a troubled brow as Kaira and Merrick accompanied her through the palace.

She did not head back to her chambers as usual, but instead made her way into the bowels of Skyhelm, down towards the War Chamber. There, outside a small vestibule she ordered them to stop. Janessa opened the door, enabling Kaira to see inside. It was a bare chamber with a single plinth at its centre on which sat the Helsbayn, the legendary sword of Steelhaven's kings.

'Wait here,' the queen ordered. She went in and shut the door behind her.

The pair stood there for several moments, before Kaira began to grow concerned.

'What do you think she's up to?' she asked.

'How the fuck should I know?' Merrick replied.

Kaira was used to his terse language but even for him this was harsh. However, it wasn't the time to wonder what was on his mind.

'Should we go in?'

He looked across at her with a frown. 'If she was going to kill herself I can think of easier ways than with a sword. It's pretty difficult to behead yourself with a four foot blade, though I've seen it tried.'

Kaira shook her head in frustration. Merrick was going to be of no help. It was obvious Janessa was concerned about something, but what should they do? She had ordered her bodyguard to stay outside. But Garret would never accept that as an excuse if anything happened to her

Something clattered inside the room. Kaira looked to Merrick, who merely shrugged his reply. It was no good, she would have to enter.

'Wait here then,' she snapped at Merrick, and opened the door.

Inside, Janessa sat on the floor, the ancient sword, the Helsbayn, lay next to her. The queen looked up with tears in her eyes.

'I can't even swing the damned thing,' she said. 'How am I ever supposed to wield it?'

Kaira closed the door behind her and moved forward to help Janessa to her feet.

'You will not have to wield it, Majesty. No one expects you to fight.'

'But my father was a great warrior,' Janessa replied as Kaira helped her up. She dusted down her skirts and glared at the sword accusingly. 'How will I lead my armies if I cannot fight? Why would anyone follow me unless I can lead them in battle?'

'It's true King Cael was a great warrior, Majesty. But not all good rulers must be warlords. You are only as strong as those you gather about yourself, your power is derived from loyalty.'

Janessa pondered on that.

The sword lay there, as though flaunting its illustrious pedigree to the room. Four foot of blade, it had runes etched from tip to base. The hilt was another foot of solid steel, the handle worked in an intricate pattern favoured by the ancient Teutonians, the cross-guard and pommel made of plain unembellished steel.

'I may soon have no choice whether to fight,' said the queen. 'I may have to stand atop the battlements and rally those loyal to me. How can I ask my people to fight in the city's defence if I am safely hidden away in the palace?'

'They would still fight, Majesty. For they also fight for themselves, for their families. For their country.'

'I wish I bore your confidence.'

Kaira knew, though her own loyalty was without question, that the queen was right to have doubts. There were many in the Free States who would gladly have substituted one ruler for another if it meant their survival… or their gain. Even if that would mean serving a foreign master.

Kaira saw hopelessness in Janessa's eyes. She was just a girl, whose courage was faltering.

'Then confidence is what we must build,' said Kaira, stooping to pick up the Helsbayn.

As Kaira gripped it she could instantly feel the dead weight, much heavier than it should have been for a solid steel weapon of that size. How Janessa had even lifted it off the plinth was a mystery. As Kaira tested it in her grip it felt clumsy, unwieldy and poorly balanced. Why a warrior like King Cael had carried such an inferior weapon for so long she could not imagine. It was one of the Nine Swords, said to have been crafted by Arlor himself, a weaponsmith without peer, but such a legend was hard to believe. Despite the Helsbayn's reputation it was nothing more than a cumbersome hunk of metal.

Nevertheless, it was the ancestral sword of the Mastragalls, crafted almost a millennia and a half ago. It was Janessa's by right of birth and if she were to wield any weapon then this would have to be the one.

'Please watch, Majesty,' Kaira said, holding up the Helsbayn and demonstrating the proper form. 'The sword should be gripped in both hands, right hand closest the cross-guard. Hold it close to your body; you can even rest the blade against your shoulder if it's too heavy.' And given the sword's considerable weight Kaira felt sure it would indeed be too heavy for Janessa. 'Lead with your left foot, right foot back. You'll find it better for balance.'

The queen watched intently, though it was obvious she had never been privy to any kind of combat training.

'You try, Majesty,' said Kaira, holding out the weapon.

Janessa took it, and Kaira noted she seemed to handle the weight well. As she tried to mimic Kaira's stance it almost looked as though the sword was lighter in her grip. Even so, her form was clumsy, her stance weak.

'Perhaps we should try with a practice weapon first, Majesty?' said Kaira.

'No,' came the reply. 'I must learn, and you will teach me. This is the sword I must wield, what better weapon to learn with?'

Kaira nodded at the command. 'Very well, Majesty.'

'While you are the teacher you need not keep calling me "Majesty". Janessa will be fine.'

'As you wish… Janessa.'

It felt strange to say, almost disrespectful, but if that was the queen's demand then that was what Kaira would call her.

Drawing her own blade, Kaira took up the defensive stance. She held her sword upright, blade pointed slightly forward. Janessa did her best to match the posture and, to Kaira's surprise, adopted it as well as most novice Shieldmaidens; even managing to hold out her unwieldy weapon at the proper angle.

'That is good,' Kaira said, growing in confidence with her student. 'Perhaps next time we should try this in more suitable clothing.'

Janessa grinned, glancing down at the gown, which covered her from neck to foot. 'Yes, perhaps I should have armour made?'

'Let's not get ahead of ourselves,' Kaira replied, feeling more relaxed with this girl with every passing moment.

'Should I swing?' Janessa asked, readying herself to raise the weapon above her head.

'Perhaps briefly,' Kaira replied, wishing now more than ever that she had insisted on practice weapons. 'But slowly, and keep control of your blade at all times.'

Janessa raised the sword and Kaira cringed, expecting at any moment that the weapon would fall from her grasp and cut a furrow across her head. But Janessa raised the blade as directed, following it up with her eyes.

'Keep looking ahead,' Kaira commanded, memories of barking orders in the training yard of the Temple of Autumn coming back to her in a flood. 'Always watch your opponent, not your weapon.' Janessa's eyes flicked straight ahead, her expression turning from tentative to stern. 'And put your tongue away.' The tip of Janessa's tongue popped back into her mouth.

'This is easier than I thought,' she said with a smile.

'Concentrate,' Kaira ordered. 'Now bring the blade down, firmly but under control. Slower!'

Janessa lowered the blade in an arc, keeping it under control. Again, Kaira marvelled at her strength. Even the most experienced Shieldmaiden would have struggled with the weight of the Helsbayn.

'I think that will do for now,' said Kaira, sheathing her own sword.

'Yes. Thank you, Kaira. That was most enlightening.'

Kaira nodded her reply, then turned to leave the chamber. She instantly realised she should have taken the Helsbayn from Janessa's hands first, but by then it was too late.

It was probably youthful exuberance that made Janessa raise the sword one more time. It was her inexperience and the thrill of combat instruction that made her go for one last swing. Kaira had seen it so many times before in the training yard, when green recruits would get carried away with themselves. It rarely ended well.

Janessa raised the blade, this time faster than before, bringing it down in a sweeping motion that made a whooshing sound as the runic blade cut the air.

Kaira's heart almost stopped.

The blade sheered away half the plinth on which it had been standing and both women watched as the corner of the stone block toppled to the ground, some of it shattering into pieces. They stood in silence for a moment, neither of them quite understanding what had happened.

The plinth was solid granite. No ordinary weapon could have sliced it asunder so easily, and this one was in the hands of a novice, scarcely more than a girl.

Janessa looked at Kaira, the Helsbayn still gripped in her small hands.

Then they laughed.

Kaira walked forward and gently took the weapon from Janessa. Still it felt heavy and clumsy in her grip and Kaira struggled to sheath it.

'I think perhaps we should leave this here,' said Kaira, leaning the sword up against what was left of the plinth.

'I think you may be right,' Janessa replied.

They both left the room, still smiling. Merrick glanced at them questioningly, but neither woman was ready to tell him what had happened.

The two Sentinels escorted their queen back to her rooms where her governess could attend her. They spent the rest of the day guarding their liege, but Kaira never felt it was appropriate to tell Merrick what had happened.

Some part of her was grateful to have shared a private moment with Janessa, which for now she was happy to keep to herself.

Later, when Waldin and Statton had taken over their duty, they had both returned to the barracks. Merrick was silent all the while. Normally Kaira would have welcomed the peace and quiet but she could see he was still troubled as he stared out across the training yard.

'What ails you?' she asked, finding his silence almost as disquieting as his constant chatter. 'You've been acting strangely all day.'

Merrick turned to her, annoyance on his face. 'Did you not hear him? Did you not take note as he announced himself to the court like a noble of the provinces? Tannick Ryder? *Lord Marshal* he calls himself now. How apt.'

Silently Kaira cursed herself for her stupidity. How had she not made the connection? Kaira had been so shocked by the sudden arrival of their new allies she hadn't even thought that the Lord Marshal of the Wyvern Guard bore Merrick's name.

Merrick looked back out across the yard where the Wyvern Guard had trained until sundown, before disappearing into the chambers set aside for them.

'I'm sorry, I didn't realise.' Kaira could barely remember the conversation they'd had weeks before when Merrick had told the tale of being abandoned by his father. 'I never thought—'

'No, well you wouldn't, would you. We have the queen to protect, that's all you can focus on right now.'

'Stop acting the child, Merrick. You're a man grown. I understand it must be a shock, but he's here now. If you have an issue then go over there and speak to him.'

A simple solution, but one Merrick was not ready to try. He merely shook his head, letting out a long petulant sigh.

Kaira found it difficult to understand his problem. She had never known her own parents, having been brought to the Temple of Autumn as an infant. Had she suddenly had the opportunity to speak to one of them she doubted she would have had problems. But then she faced her difficulties head on, unlike Merrick, who took every opportunity to avoid them. Even if it meant running from something right in front of his nose.

'You don't know him,' Merrick said bitterly. 'You don't know what he's like. He's not going to greet me with open arms. We were hardly close.'

'Then why let it bother you? If you hate the man so much then forget he's even here. It's likely he'll do the same.'

Kaira instantly regretted her comment. With Merrick so obviously finding this challenging it had been an insensitive thing to say, but tact had never been her strong point.

'Yeah, forget he's even here. That's a good idea. Right up there with "why don't you stop drinking and join a bunch of celibate knights devoted to protecting the palace with their lives". I'm sure I'll be able to manage it. Just forget the father you haven't seen for eighteen years. The one that abandoned you and your mother to a life of penury.'

'Then go and confront him.' This was beginning to annoy her. She knew that Tannick had indeed abandoned Merrick and his mother, but by all accounts he had left them a generous estate. 'Your paths are bound to cross sooner or later. It's no use putting it off.'

Merrick stared hard at her. Then his expression softened. 'You're right. I should just go over there. Introduce myself. Show him I'm carrying on the family tradition.' He began to smooth out his uniform. 'Show him I'm not a complete failure.'

Before he could move, the door to the chamber opened. Garret strode in, lit ominously by the winking candlelight. Kaira quickly stood to attention, but the captain was focused on Merrick.

'I meant to come earlier, but I've had business to attend to,' he said.

'I'm sure,' replied Merrick, glancing again across the courtyard. 'I was just thinking of attending to some business of my own. He should know I'm here. That I'm still alive.'

Garret cast his eyes at the ground, his mouth moving as though he had something to say but couldn't decide the right way of putting it. 'He knows,' he said eventually. 'He already knows you're here.'

There was a pause.

'And?' said Merrick.

'And he doesn't want to see you.'

'*He* doesn't want to see *me*? Are you fucking joking? He's the one that left.'

'It's come as sudden news, what happened to you, your mother, your estate. And he has other responsibilities now.'

'What the fuck does he know about responsibilities?'

Garret's jaw set and he addressed Merrick sternly. 'It is a great honour to be appointed Lord Marshal of the Wyvern Guard. A responsibility only he could rise to, only he could accomplish. It won't have been easy for him.'

'It wasn't easy for *me*. You know it wasn't. Yes, I've made some poor choices, but that's behind me now. Even though I'm here – even though I'm the queen's personal guard – he still doesn't want to see me?'

'I'm sure he's proud in his own way. There is just too much going on—'

'Fuck him then. Let him play at being the noble knight. He was always more interested in soldiers and horses than he was in his family, anyway.' Merrick turned back to the window.

Garret made to speak again, but thinking better of it he left the room.

Kaira came over to Merrick, but she had no words for him.

'What an arsehole,' Merrick said.

Kaira couldn't bring herself to disagree.

THIRTEEN

T here were few things Waylian had experienced in life that could beat a hot bath. But of all the baths he'd had in his life, this was by far the most welcome. It was as if he were sloughing off the past few weeks of pain and misery; the biting cold, the endless riding, the awful company. All that suffering was drifting away like steam from the water's surface.

Waylian had no idea whose room this was, though from the books and paraphernalia that adorned the shelves it must have been a senior magister. It was unusual indeed that an apprentice like him should be granted the honour of a hot bath rather than a rub down with a damp soapy rag, and in the chambers of a senior member of the Caste, no less. But then Waylian had accomplished a most unusual and dangerous mission.

Upon his return with the Wyvern Guard he had been ushered back to the Tower of Magisters by two Raven Knights sent specifically for the task. Waylian had expected Magistra Gelredida to be waiting for him, but of her there was no sign. Instead he had been guided to a chamber, given food and wine – *wine, oh how he had loved the wine* – and a bath hastily filled with steaming water. There was even perfumed soap.

As he lay there in the water, now murky from the filth of his body, he began to think how easily he could get used to this. Maybe his perilous mission had been worthwhile after all. Maybe he should ask for similar tasks, with ever greater rewards.

Then again, maybe not.

The memory of that cold mountain range gave him the shivers. Just thinking about his close encounter with the jaws of some savage beast made his arse clench in terror. As it turned out, being rescued in such a timely fashion hadn't been the end of his woes, either.

The knight who had saved his life had led him through the snows to a place they called Wyvern Keep. Waylian later discovered the knight's name was Cormach Whoreson, and at the time he had wondered why a knight of such a fabled and noble order would have such an ignominious title. It wasn't until he entered the keep that he learned the Wyvern Guard weren't exactly the heroes of legend they were made out to be.

They were disciplined all right. Constantly training and honing themselves for a war they were eager to fight. But they were also mean-eyed and haughty, staring at Waylian with scarcely masked contempt. They brooked no weakness, either in themselves or others, and they didn't come much weaker than Waylian Grimm.

After what seemed like an age of him waving around his sealed missive and asking to see the man in charge, he got the attention of the Lord Marshal. If Waylian had been expecting any more understanding from him than from the rest of the knights he was sorely disappointed. The Lord Marshal totally disregarded Waylian though he read the letter with interest. When he announced to his men that they would ride to war, the news was greeted with enthusiasm, but Waylian got the impression they were looking forward more to the fighting than saving the Free States.

Waylian received not a word of thanks for risking his life to bring the message. He was all but ignored as the Wyvern Guard prepared to travel the long road south, and he was reduced to begging for food and drink when none was offered. And what he received wasn't fit for a dog – food was in extremely short supply up in the mountains. Such short supply that the Lord Marshal had felt the need to slaughter his prized goats to bolster provisions for the journey to Steelhaven.

The Wyvern Guard went about their preparations as though Waylian wasn't there. He would most likely have been left behind in the empty keep, in the middle of the freezing mountains, had he not insisted to the Lord Marshal that he be conveyed back to the city.

Begrudgingly they had allowed him to accompany them, though on the mangiest horse they had. It was an angry and unpredictable beast, nipping at

Waylian when he least expected it. Perhaps it was just animals in general that didn't like him. Perhaps he was just unlucky.

Either way, the journey back to the city had been almost as traumatic as the journey to the mountains, but he survived it. He had endured and come through the other side, and here he was enjoying the rich rewards.

The Wyvern Guard had arrived in the city – surely Steelhaven's troubles were over? Surely Amon Tugha and his hordes would not stand a chance now? Maybe they'd even call off their attack once word spread they would have to face these fabled warriors of renown.

Waylian guessed he was clutching at straws there. Deep down he knew this was only the beginning. That this bath might well be the last bit of respite, his one last piece of luxury, before the butchery began.

In that case he was determined to get the most from it. Closing his eyes, he sank down into the water, allowing it to come up to his nose, allowing the warmth to consume him.

This was truly the life.

The door to the chamber opened.

Magistra Gelredida walked in and stared at him as he lay there in the bath. Waylian thanked the gods that the filth on his body had rendered the water too murky for her to see his privates – not that she'd have been in the slightest bit interested in seeing those.

'So, you survived.' she said. He nodded, his mouth still beneath the surface of the water. 'I can't begin to tell you how much that fills me with joy.'

To be frank, she didn't look very joyous, but then she never did. Not that Waylian cared either way. She'd sent him on a perilous mission. He'd almost died... more than once. On several occasions he'd cursed her to the hells, and worse.

'Anyway, well done, Waylian. I'm proud of you.'

Oh well, that's all right then. That more than makes up for me nearly being eaten, and having to suffer the company of fierce warriors who would have left me to perish in the elements if I hadn't begged them for help.

'Thank you, Magistra,' he said, his lips barely breaking the surface of the water.

'Don't lie there all day; you'll only go wrinkly. Besides, there is still much work to do and I require your help.'

'Yes, Magistra. I'll be with you presently, Magistra.'

She nodded before leaving him alone in the bath.

He wanted to ignore her, to throw a foul gesture in her wake, to tell her, albeit under his breath, to go and fuck herself for what she'd put him through.

Instead he eased himself out of the water, feeling the chill of the room despite the fire in one corner. He dried himself quickly and donned the fresh robe that had been left for him beside the bath.

You're a mug, Waylian Grimm. Chasing after that woman like a little lapdog. Craving her approval. Licking at her heels until she throws you a bone of appreciation.

He regarded himself in the mirror for a moment. It had been a long time since he'd looked in a mirror and some of what he saw he rather liked. His hair had grown longer – well, there was nothing to cut it with on the trail northwards – and he liked the way it framed his face. His chin and top lip had developed a subtle growth of stubble. He was leaner, his jaw line more prominent. Might some say he was even growing handsome?

Not bloody likely.

No, despite what he'd been through he was still the same old Waylian. Still pretty useless. Maybe that was why she'd sent him. Because he was expendable. Because if he'd died up there in the mountains no one would have missed him.

He was inconsequential. Surplus to requirements.

Yes, the Magistra made noises about needing him by her side, but who didn't need a faithful companion? What witch didn't have her familiar?

Waylian shook his head at that reflection.

'You're a waste of space,' he said to himself, before leaving the room.

He didn't have to go far to find his mistress; she was waiting for him at the end of the corridor. Like a needy pup he followed her as she trudged her way up through the Tower of Magisters. It wasn't until they made it all the way to the magnificent hallway at the tower's summit that Waylian realised they were in store for another audience in the Crucible Chamber.

'I have no doubt that this will be yet another waste of our time,' said Gelredida as two Raven Knights secured the strange bracelets around her wrists that would nullify her powers. 'But we have to try.'

The great doors were pulled open and Waylian followed her inside. It was as though nothing had changed. Each of the five pulpits loomed like ancient standing stones, and behind them awaited the five Archmasters.

Waylian's eyes swept over them: Hoylen Crabbe, dark haired and severe; Crannock Marghil, his ancient face peering down over thin eyeglasses; Drennan Folds, his hirsute features set in a permanent state of rage, his eyes, one blue and one white, furious as ever; Nero Laius looking amiable, though Waylian had seen him demonstrate his power first hand and knew he was not to be taken lightly; and finally young Lucen Kalvor, who might perhaps be the most dangerous of all.

As Gelredida came to stand before them, Drennan Folds leaned forward, shaking his head, his impressive chin whiskers quivering as he did so.

'Here again?' he said, his furious expression softening to one of feigned amusement. 'Have we not already given you our answer, Gelredida? Or do you come on another matter?'

'No, Drennan,' she replied. 'I have come once more to ask that you all see sense. Amon Tugha will not stop until Steelhaven is ashes. The Wyvern Guard have already come down from their mountain holdfast to defend us. With the aid of the Tower of Magisters there is no way the Elharim could breach the city walls. There is nothing to fear if you stand beside the defenders of this city. Do nothing and you will all surely die.'

'You cannot say that with any certainty,' said Crannock Marghil, peering over his spectacles with rheumy eyes. 'There is no way you could be sure of the outcome were we once again to pool our powers in defence of the Free States.'

Gelredida shook her head. 'I know the consequences were you all to sit on your hands, Crannock. It would mean your doom, and the doom of every man, woman and child within the walls of Steelhaven.'

'You have had our answer, Red Witch,' said Hoylen Crabbe. 'We are neutral in this.' He glanced down, as though his words had shamed him, yet maintained the perpetual frown about his brow. 'We sympathise, but there is too much at stake.'

'What, Hoylen?' said Gelredida. 'What could be at stake? What could matter more than the safety of this city? The safety of the queen, her people? What is it that you all fear...?' She paused, looking at them all in turn. Then she nodded as though realising the reasons for their cowardice. 'He has truly cowed you all – the great Archmasters, the Crucible, scared into inaction by a single Elharim prince. You are the greatest casters in all the known world! Where is your courage?'

Her shout echoed from the top of the chamber.

None of the Archmasters responded.

Gelredida took a step closer. 'Drennan,' she said, almost pleadingly. 'There is no love lost between us, but surely you can see we must fight?' He would not look at her. 'Hoylen.' She took a step closer to the stern Archmaster. 'You helped me before, helped me save this city, this land, from the Aeslanti. If that was worth anything you must help me now.' He only shook his head and she moved on. 'Crannock, look inside yourself. You know we cannot trust the Elharim. You know I'm right.'

The old man reached up a quivering hand and pulled the eyeglasses from his face.

'We appreciate everything you have done for this city, and not just in recent times,' he said. 'Your strength and your wisdom have been invaluable to us. But we cannot act.'

She took a step back, her fists clenching in her red velvet gloves, the ones she had taken to wearing so many weeks before when Waylian had left for the Kriega Mountains. 'Cowards! Cowards all of you! I wonder if you'll even find the breath to defend yourselves when the Elharim outcast comes for your heads, for he will brook no rivalry to his power, mark me. He will not suffer any of you to live.'

'Have you finished with your doomsaying, woman?' said Lucen Kalvor, clearly tired of Gelredida's chastisement.

'Not yet,' she replied, and she stared at the young Archmaster until he could hold her gaze no longer. 'I would have you think on this for a time. Think on your fate should you do nothing. Then I would have you vote.'

'But we have already given you our answer,' said Crannock.

'I think some of you may change your minds as the horde nears the gates. And I would give you each the chance to reconsider.'

'We can vote right here and now,' said Hoylen Crabbe.

'No. It is my right as a member of the Caste to demand a vote, and at a time of my choosing. And I choose five days from now.'

There was silence.

Waylian wasn't familiar with the protocol involved, he was not yet a member of the Caste, but it appeared Gelredida spoke true. The Archmasters regarded one another before Drennan said, 'Very well. Five days from now, but our minds are already made.'

Gelredida looked back and smiled. 'I am confident good sense will come to you all in the end.'

With that she turned to leave. Waylian was once again fast on her heels.

They walked from the Crucible Chamber, and Gelredida led the way back through the tower to her room at the top of those winding stairs. Waylian had remembered her chamber being spick and span when he left so many weeks ago, but those weeks must have been troubling for Gelredida. Now the room was a jumble of parchments and books. Quills, ink and other paraphernalia were scattered across her large desk, every shelf and surface strewn with one piece of clutter or another.

Gelredida sat in her chair and steepled her fingers.

'There is much to do, Waylian,' she said, clearly deep in thought.

'Then I'll leave you in peace, Magistra,' he replied, turning to go.

'No, Waylian. I mean there is much for *us* to do.'

'*Us*, Magistra?'

A smile crept across her face. If he didn't know better he'd have sworn there was a trace of sadism in that smile. Hadn't she already put him through enough?

Clearly not.

'I have bought us some time. Nothing more. The way things stand the Archmasters will never agree to put their weight behind Steelhaven's defence. They are frightened of what they might lose. They must be persuaded there is more to fear than this warlord.'

'But what could they possibly fear? And what does that have to do with us?'

Or, more to the point, with me?

'We have five days to put our case across. Five days to persuade our illustrious Archmasters to come to the right decision. Of course we don't need this to be unanimous – three in favour will seal their compliance – but let's not hedge our bets.'

'I don't understand.'

'No.' She rose to her feet. 'But then you don't have to. Trust, Waylian. Trust is all you need. And to do exactly what I tell you. Come,' she said, leading him out of the room.

Waylian began to think it wouldn't be long before she got him a collar. A nice studded one. Or maybe something with jewels in; gemstones for the Magistra's favourite pet.

They made their way down through the Tower of Magisters, down below the entrance hall, down into the bowels of the massive construction. The stairs wound down, guarded here and there by imposing Raven Knights. The passages down below twisted in a labyrinthine pattern and Waylian soon found himself hopelessly lost.

Eventually, Gelredida led them through a creaky wooden door into a musty chamber. It was freezing, and lit scantly by tall red candles. An old man seated in one corner looked up suddenly from his dusty old tome as they entered.

'You're here,' he said in surprise. Gelredida didn't answer, merely waiting there as the man closed his book. 'I'll be off then,' he said despondently, walking past Waylian and, with a shrug of his eyebrows, leaving the room.

Waylian might have felt sorry for the man, but he'd had more than his share of being treated like shit by the Red Witch, so it was a bit much to expect any sympathy from him when someone else was on the receiving end.

As he focused through the gloom and saw what awaited them in the chamber, his shoulders sagged. Not again. Hadn't he had his fill? Just how much death was one person supposed to endure?

Gelredida moved to the table at the centre of the chamber. With a flourish, she pulled back a grimy white sheet to reveal beneath the desiccated corpse of an old man – or what could have been an old man, it was almost too far-gone to tell.

She looked up at him expectantly. 'The instruments for dissection are on that table over there.' Waylian looked round to see a selection of blades, saws and callipers glinting in the candlelight. 'Be so good as to bring me the filleting knife and we'll begin.'

No! No I won't. I've had enough of this and I've had enough of you and your bloody unreasonable expectations. Do your own dirty work from now on, you old witch!

'Yes, Magistra,' Waylian replied, and looked along the row of instruments for the sharpest knife.

FOURTEEN

With every new day the air seemed to grow colder. The further they trod through the lands of the Clawless Tribes the more hostile the elements seemed, the wind howling in their faces as though screaming at them to turn back, to abandon this folly. Regulus and his warriors had hunted much game – deer, wolf and the like – and taken to donning their hides to shield themselves from the cold. Kazul, cowed by the weather and in no mood for hunting, had satisfied himself by slaughtering some docile beast with a curly white pelt. It had not even attempted to flee as he leapt upon it. The cries it made in its death throes had been brief.

Of the Coldlanders they had seen little. Small settlements dotted the landscape, and it had been difficult for the warriors to resist their natural urge to fall upon those wooden huts and pillage them for what they had. But this was not where they would wage war. Not yet anyway.

'How much further?' said Akkula, as they crested a hill looking down on a wide valley. 'This wind chills my bones.'

Regulus would have admonished him for his complaint if he hadn't been so cold himself. This land seemed determined to freeze them where they stood and only through a massive effort of will did they keep moving ever onward.

'You will be warmed soon enough, young Akkula,' Leandran replied. The old warrior must have felt the cold more than most, but he complained the least. 'When we offer our spears to the Steel King he will unleash us upon his enemies with all the rage of an inferno. Then you can warm yourself in a pool of our enemy's blood.'

Hagama and Kazul growled their assent, but Leandran's words did nothing to spur Akkula's spirits. He pulled his hide cloak about him all the tighter and took on a sullen expression.

'There,' said Janto suddenly, dropping into a crouch and pulling one of the axes free from his belt.

Regulus and the rest of the warriors fell in beside him, keeping low and scanning the valley ahead. In the distance they could just make out a procession of Coldlanders moving towards the west. They looked a sorry band, labouring under their packs and pulling carts behind them, their young at their heels as they trudged along the road.

'What do you think?' said Leandran, glaring down. 'Do we avoid them?'

Regulus shook his head. 'No. We will greet them. We need to know if we are heading in the right direction to reach their capital and their king. It will not serve us well if we have to wander this frigid land for many more days.'

'And if they won't speak to us? If they flee?'

'They will speak to me,' Regulus said. 'I know their language. I will go alone.'

'No,' said Janto. 'I will go with you … just in case.'

'In case what?' Regulus gestured to the pitiful line of figures. 'They look about ready to drop. I am hardly in any danger.'

Regulus could see Janto wanted to say more but thought better of it. Yes, Janto wanted to accompany him, wanted to watch his back, but simply to serve his own ends and free himself of his obligation.

'The rest of you should hide yourselves. We don't want to alarm these people.'

His warriors understood. Regulus skewered his sword in the ground and made his way down into the valley, briefly losing sight of the travellers behind a copse of trees.

When he reached the bottom he stood to the side of the road, his hood drawn up to cover his dark features. As he waited, Regulus thought hard about the best way to approach these people without alarming them. He was a foreigner after all; his appearance alien in this land of pale diminutive folk, their teeth and claws only good for chewing grass. It was understandable that they should fear him. But he had come to serve their king, to offer his sword in their defence. Surely they would understand that.

And if not, he would make them understand.

The procession came into view along the path at the side of the trees. At the front was a man pulling a small cart. He looked sorrowful, the child at his side looking sorrier still. Regulus took a step forward, his palms showing in the sign of peace.

The man screamed.

He backed away, almost falling over his cart as he pulled his child close to him – Regulus couldn't tell whether it was son or daughter; the Coldlanders mostly looked alike to him – but it too began screaming. At first the sound was annoying, then alarming as it spread down the sorry row of travellers. Panic gripped them as they saw him standing there blocking their path. Regulus tried to calm them, tried to explain, but his words were lost in the din as they ran shrieking into the trees or back down the path.

To pursue would only have distressed them further. Perhaps this would be more difficult than he thought. If the sight of a lone Zatani was enough to send a dozen of them fleeing in terror, what fear would he and his warparty inspire when they arrived at the capital?

Before he made his way back up the hill Regulus heard a quiet voice from down the path. He slowly made his way along the trail of abandoned carts and packs until he found an old man, kneeling on the cold earth. His eyes were tight shut and he was mumbling a hasty prayer to the heathen gods of the north.

'Do not be afraid, old one,' Regulus said in the Coldlander tongue. He tried to make his voice as soft as he could, but it seemed to make the old man say his prayer that much faster, as though the speed of his words might deliver him from his doom.

'I am not here to do you harm, old one. I carry no weapon.'

The old man opened one eye, looking up as though a weapon was the last thing he feared, tears streaking his face. Regulus tried a smile, but it only made the old man's eyes open the wider.

Gently, Regulus reached down and raised the old man to his feet.

'I would talk with you, old one. Nothing more.'

The old man shook at the knee, but he held Regulus' gaze. 'I'm an old man and in no mood for tricks, lord of devils. If you aim to kill me do it quick.'

Regulus almost laughed. If he'd wanted the old man dead he would certainly not have toyed with him first.

'You have nothing to fear. I come to your lands to help. Not to hunt.'

The old man's brow creased in confusion, his patchy flesh wrinkling about his face.

'You aren't gonna eat me?'

Regulus looked down at the emaciated figure, wondering if there was any meat on his bones at all.

'No, old one. I am not going to eat you.'

At that the old man seemed to calm a little, leaning back against one of the carts. Regulus briefly wondered why these people lugged their own belongings and did not use slaves or beasts of burden, but he had more important questions to ask.

'Is this the road to the capital?'

'Aye,' said the man. 'About thirty, forty miles that way – to the east – lies Steelhaven. That's where we've come from. Soon be flooded with Khurtic bastards and we didn't wanna be there when it was.'

'Your chieftain, your king. He lies within?'

The old man looked up with sadness in his eyes. Then slowly shook his head. 'King Cael's been dead these past two months. Since before winter set in. Murdered by that bastard Amon Tugha and his Khurtic scum.'

Regulus felt his heart drop. This was grave news indeed. He had wanted to offer his blade to the Steel King, the victor of Bakhaus Gate. Such a man might have appreciated the gesture, but now that all seemed lost on the winds.

'Who has his seat now?' asked Regulus. 'Does a son take his place?'

The old man shook his head. 'He had one daughter. She sits on the throne now.'

'A daughter?' Regulus could barely take in the old man's words. 'A woman sits upon your throne? Wears your crown?'

The old man nodded. 'The queen, yes.'

This was impossible. Regulus could hardly kneel before a female, less still offer his fealty and his blade. His warriors would never follow him, even if he could bring himself to stoop so low.

'You all right?' asked the old man.

'I am, old one.' But he knew he wasn't.

Everything he had hoped for had suddenly crumbled to so much dust. Every reason for him fleeing north, coming to this cold, frigid place, had been blown away in a breath.

'C... can I go now?'

Regulus barely heard the old man's words as he turned and made his way back up the hill to where his warriors waited.

'Well?' asked Leandran..

'Make camp,' was all Regulus could say.

'Why here?'

'Because I order it. And build a fire. I am getting sick of this cold.'

'We'll be seen for miles,' said Janto.

'By who?' Regulus replied, spreading his arms and gesturing to the four horizons. 'More peasants? They're hardly going to put up a fight – they can barely raise their chins.'

There was no more argument. As night fell they built their fire from what wood they could find and hunkered around it, wrapped in their furs.

The news that King Cael had been killed was not taken well, especially when they discovered who was his heir.

'We must turn back,' said Janto, almost enraged. 'We cannot serve some... chieftainess.'

'They call them "queens" in the Clawless Tribes,' Regulus replied. 'And we would be warriors, fighting for her and our honour. We would not be serving her.'

'Even so,' said Leandran. 'We have come north to build a fearsome and glorious reputation. What will our enemies in Equ'un say when they learn we act at the behest of a female?'

If Regulus had been hoping for support from the oldest and wisest of their number he was sorely disappointed.

'When they hear of our victories in battle, of the deeds we have done, it will not matter in whose name we have done them. We are here to fight for the Coldlanders. If this Amon Tugha is mighty enough to defeat the Steel King, then slaying him would be a deed of legend.'

'I have a better idea,' said Janto, staring into the flames of the campfire. It gave a daemonic look to his dark features – all blue eyes and fangs. 'We bend the knee to this Amon Tugha instead. We fight for him against the Coldlanders and their *queen*. Surely that would bring us the most honour? Not to bow to some woman who wears her father's crown?'

'No!' said Regulus, rising to his feet. 'I came north for glory. To fight for the man who freed us from bondage, not start a war with his spawn. Battling women is the way of the Kel'tana, of the Vir'tana. That is not my way. I will offer my blade to the daughter of the Steel King. You must each decide now whether or not to follow me. There will be no shame in a refusal.' Regulus stared at them each in turn. 'What say you?'

There was a pause as they all thought on it.

'I reckon we've come this far,' said Leandran. 'No use in turning back now. One chief's as good as another.'

Akkula nodded beside him. 'I'm with you.'

Hagama and Kazul added their voices in support.

Regulus turned to Janto who still stared into the fire. 'If you wish to turn back south I release you from your life-debt,' he said.

Janto looked up slowly, glaring from where he sat, his blue eyes blazing in the firelight. 'Whether I'm released from my debt is not up to you. I'm released when the debt is paid. Where you lead, I must follow.'

Regulus nodded. He had known this all along, but thought it best to give Janto the illusion of choice.

'Settled then. We go east and offer our spears to the queen of the Coldlanders.'

Janto suddenly reached for his axes. Regulus laid a hand to the hilt of his blade, thinking the warrior had decided to abandon his debt and attack after all. Then he caught a scent on the cold night breeze. It was a raw scent, almost imperceptible, but it was no animal.

The rest of his warriors rose, facing outwards from the fire and brandishing their weapons. Then slowly, almost casually, a figure strode into the light.

He was a Coldlander, a beard about his face, dark hair running down and into the furs he wore on back and shoulders. His hands were held down by his side, palms flat, facing out in the Zatani display of peace. He carried no weapons, yet did not seem to fear Regulus and his warriors.

Janto made to move forward but Regulus laid a hand on his arm, feeling him tense at the touch.

'Lower your weapons,' Regulus commanded. 'This man comes in peace.'

The Coldlander stepped to within a yard of Regulus, then stopped.

'I speak your language not well,' he said in broken Equ'un.

'Then it is fortunate I speak yours,' Regulus replied in the Coldlander tongue.

The man smiled, relieved that he had been understood rather than attacked. 'That's a rare skill for your kind. The name's Tom. Some call me the Blackfoot, Warden of the South and servant to the Free States and its ruler.'

'I am Regulus of the Gor'tana.'

'You are far from home,' said the Blackfoot.

'And you are a brave man to enter our camp without weapons.'

The man smiled. 'Oh, I have weapons, back there somewhere.' He nodded back into the darkness. 'Don't reckon they'd have done me much good against the six of you though, so I thought it best to leave them behind and show I intend no harm.'

Regulus placed his black steel sword down by his side and his warriors seemed to relax.

'Come, Tom the Blackfoot. Share our fire.'

With that the warriors squatted by the fire, continuing to rub the warmth into their limbs. The Coldlander sat with them, his small frame dwarfed by those of the Zatani.

'Tell me,' asked Regulus. 'What makes a lone man of the north walk into a camp of Zatani warriors?'

Tom glanced around at the six massive figures. 'I'm a Warden of the Free States. It's my job to make sure no one's up to mischief on our lands. When there's a dozen terrified peasants running through the wilds with tales of black devils abroad, it's my job to look into it.'

'Do you think we are "up to mischief", Tom the Blackfoot?'

Tom shook his head. 'You boys are miles from home. Miles inside Teutonian lands. I reckon if you were gonna cause mischief it would have happened already, but there's been no word of any killing. Does lead to the question though – if you're not here for a raid, what are you doing here?'

Regulus smiled. 'We are outcasts looking for a new liege lord. Now that your king is dead we will make for your greatest city and offer ourselves to your queen.'

If Tom was surprised at such a bold statement of intent he did not show it.

'Steelhaven will welcome all the mercenaries it can get right now. But you should watch yourselves, if that's your intention. That city's dangerous enough, but I imagine when you turn up it'll get a sight more dangerous. Foreigners are treated with suspicion, especially now. The place takes no prisoners, and there's a trick or trap waiting around every corner to snare the unwary. You might find you don't exactly get the welcome you were hoping for.'

'Then we will face it as warriors, Tom the Blackfoot. And show how strong the Zatani are in battle.'

'I bet you will. But it's not always what you're facing that's the problem. Oftentimes you'd be better served watching your back.'

'Sound advice much welcomed. I hope that you have countrymen in Steelhaven as willing to show us such kindness.'

'I hope so, too,' Tom replied with a wink. He rubbed some warmth into his hands. 'Well, good luck to you, Regulus of the Gor'tana.'

He stood up, and when Regulus stood up beside him, he towered over the small man. With a nod to the rest of the warriors sat by the fire, Tom the Blackfoot was gone into the night.

'So, what did he have to say?' asked Leandran.

Regulus stared into the dark after the man for a moment before answering.

'He said there is glory to be had in Steelhaven. He said we will be welcomed as brothers and celebrated as the noble warriors we are. He said we should not tarry, for our destiny awaits.' With that Regulus took up his sword. His warriors took it as their cue and they all got up, ready to move on into the night.

He could see the fire in their eyes now – their need to fight, to find glory, to wade in victory. It made Regulus proud and eager for battle.

As the sun rose they could not move fast enough towards the east.

FIFTEEN

This was ridiculous. And dangerous.

Rag could've lived with the ridiculous bit – she'd seen plenty of that in her time – it was the dangerous part she weren't too keen on.

It seemed easy on the face of it: walk into the barracks, find a bloke called Merrick Ryder, report back to Friedrik for further instructions. What could be simpler?

As she stared up at the palace of Skyhelm, soaring upwards like some fairy castle, Rag decided there were lots of things could have been bloody simpler.

It had been easy enough getting into the Crown District this time around. The last time she'd seen Krupps bribing one of the Greencoats at the gate to get in. This time there weren't even any bribes to pay. She was in the Guild now – they practically owned the Greencoats, and all she'd had to do was stroll up, plain as day. The guards at the entrance didn't so much as look at her, opening the gate and letting her in as though she'd been expected. They didn't even check the wooden tray she was carrying, didn't pull back the muslin sheet draped over the top to take a look at what lay underneath. Rag had almost burst out laughing at that – Greencoats letting her stroll right into the Crown like she was some la-de-da lady of leisure.

Once inside it weren't hard to find the palace – it stood taller than any other building, but once she made it to the wall that ran around its edge she began to have doubts. The barracks of the Skyhelm Sentinels stood to one side of the palace, guarded by two knights in silver, their faces hidden behind full helms, nasty looking swords in their hands. Weren't no way this was gonna be easy.

But Rag had a job to do, and do it she would. She was in the Guild now, just like she'd wanted. It was time to prove to Friedrik she weren't just there for window dressing, weren't just his doll to dress up and play with.

The thought of Friedrik made her stop in her tracks. Did she even want to please him? Over the past weeks she'd realised what a mad bastard he was. How cruel and mean, just for the sake of it. If she'd known what she was getting herself into, would she have tried so hard to join the Guild in the first place?

Who are you kidding? Course you would. It's all you've ever dreamed of, and it's a damn sight better than pinching for coppers and sleeping on the roof of an alehouse.

Just thinking about those days, those long gone days of cold and hunger, made Rag strangely homesick. She tried to put the thought away, tried to tell herself it weren't her home anymore, yet somehow she was missing it. Missing her boys most of all, even Fender, though she knew that were stupid. She had a place with regular grub and a roof over her head, she was looked after, she belonged to a proper crew. It was her new family now, the family of the Guild. But then, it weren't exactly the kind of family she'd wanted. At least on that roof with Chirpy, Migs and Tidge she'd never had to watch someone having their fingernails pulled out.

Bollocks! That was the past. This is the present. Pull yourself together, Rag, and do what you've been fucking told.

Even if she did have to stand witness to some horrible shit, it was be better than acting mother to a bunch of street rats. It was *her* what got looked after nowadays. She got cared for like she'd always wanted. Had people watching *her* back. Now was the time to earn her keep and all she had to do was get herself into that barracks and find some bloke called Ryder.

She gripped her tray all the tighter and walked towards the guards bold as brass. When she got close she put a big smile on her face. Rag knew she wasn't the prettiest thing a bloke might have ever seen, but there was a lot could be bought with a smile. Make yourself look harmless and it disarms people. If you're no threat they're likely to treat you a lot nicer. Well, that was the plan, anyway.

She'd find out soon enough if it worked.

Rag stopped in front of the two guards. They stood like statues, their swords gripped at their chests, blades pointing upwards. For a few moments she just looked at them, waiting. Neither one made a move.

With a flourish Rag pulled the muslin cloth aside, revealing the tray of goodies beneath. She had an assortment of treats – potted eel from up the Storway, fresh scallops cooked in the shell with a pastry top, smoked fish rolled in egg and breadcrumbs, little meat pies with dried fruit on. Friedrik's cook had spent almost a whole day preparing the lot. He was a miserable bastard at the best of times, but Rag had to admit he could put together a decent spread when he wanted to.

She let the tray just sit there for a few seconds, allowing the smell to waft upwards. One of the knights looked briefly towards his companion. Then the other one leaned his sword up against the entryway to the barracks and removed his helmet.

If Rag expected him to start filling his face though, she was sorely mistaken.

'Where did you get this lot from then?' he asked.

She hadn't been expecting questions.

'Erm… my uncle makes 'em. Gets his fish fresh every day.'

'There's a food shortage in the city and you're wandering around with a tray handing it out for free? You're expecting us to believe that are you?'

This wasn't going at all well. Maybe they hadn't thought this through properly. Maybe she should have come with wine instead.

'Came direct from the palace kitchens,' she answered. 'Just what we had left over.'

'Palace kitchens? Who in the palace ki—'

'Oh, leave it out will you,' said the second Sentinel, removing his helmet. 'These smell bloody lovely.'

He placed his sword down and reached for one of the scallops. Rag moved the tray away from his grasping hand.

'Just one each,' she said. 'These have to go around the rest of the barracks.'

She let him take what he wanted. The second Sentinel eyed her suspiciously, but only long enough for her to flash him another smile before he too gave in to the temptation and took one of the pies. As they both dug in, she wandered past them, holding the tray high, like it was the most normal thing in the world.

Through the entrance was a courtyard, surrounded by barrack rooms. Around twenty blokes stood in the middle of the square, stripped to the waist, practising with their swords. Rag watched for a bit, spellbound. She'd never seen soldiers act with that much control before, their swords moving as one, each cut and thrust timed to perfection. She was more used to dirty brawls on the streets, biting ears and pulling hair and gouging eyes. Best she'd seen someone use a blade was years ago down near the Rafts, and that had happened so quick it was over before it began. This was like watching a dance, only with less music and more danger.

'What the fuck do you want?' said a voice to her left, and she snapped her head round to see a tall fella looking down at her. He wasn't bad looking, or he wouldn't have been if he weren't frowning. He was stripped to the waist like the rest but he had the pelt of some great white beast draped across his shoulders. His bare chest was visible, all scarred and muscled, and Rag had a bit of trouble dragging her eyes away from it.

'Been sent with some food,' she said, holding up the tray.

He kept his eyes locked on hers, but reached out with a hand and took some potted eel. Held in that gaze she almost dropped the tray and made a run for it, but without another word he just turned and walked away.

Rag let out a sigh, before moving around the edge of the courtyard. There were more warriors watching from the sides and she walked over to them.

'Got some goodies from the kitchens here,' she said, trying to sound confident, like there was nothing out of the ordinary about a girl wandering the barracks with a tray of food. The group of warriors glanced across at her, none of them saying a word in reply. One reached out and took a pie, but the others never made a move.

Now she was here, Rag started to wonder how in the hells she was going to find this Ryder. How was she supposed to start that conversation?

Oi, lads! Anyone know Merrick Ryder?

Why do you ask?

Erm... because he's pissed someone off in the Guild and I've been sent to bloody find him.

Yes, that was sure to grab her some attention, and probably a sharp knife in the ribs.

Rag was going to have to come up with something, and fast. She'd thought this might be one of those times when being ignored was a good thing, but that wasn't turning out too well. Maybe it was time to be the centre of attention.

The soldiers at the middle of the courtyard had finished swinging their swords, and another batch of around twenty were readying themselves to take up their positions. Rag walked out onto the courtyard, right in front of them, holding out her tray for all to see.

'Come on then,' she said with a grin. 'Get it while it's going. I haven't got all day.'

Some of the warriors looked at one another in confusion. Others tried ignoring her, but Rag was determined to have none of that.

'What's the matter? You're not telling me you ain't hungry, all that bloody sword swinging. You must be bloomin' famished.'

This raised a smile from a couple of them, and one even strolled over, sword in hand, and plucked a pie from her tray.

'Any good?' she asked loudly as he took a bite.

He just nodded his reply, too busy chewing to talk.

Another of them came forward, and before he could take something from her, Rag looked him up and down and gave a whistle.

'Ooh, you're an 'andsome fella, and no mistake,' she called out, trying to sound like one of the street girls from Dockside. 'I could take quite a fancy to a big strong bloke like you. What's your name then?'

Well, it seemed as good a place as any to start. Friedrik had told her what Merrick looked like – average height, brown hair, handsome – and this bloke seemed to fit the bill. Problem was, so did half the other lads in here.

'My name's Hennar,' said the warrior, plucking a piece of fish from the tray. 'And you don't look old enough to have had your blood yet. So take as much of a fancy as you like, but I'm not interested, girl.'

With a shake of his head he popped the food in his mouth, then walked away.

That didn't really work out to plan, now did it?

'Hey lads, these are good,' said the soldier who had taken a pie. Next thing, Rag was swamped by sweaty half-dressed warriors, all reaching out to take a piece of food. In no time she was left holding an empty tray.

That was it; she was left with nothing, standing in the middle of the courtyard. As the soldiers began to line up to begin their training she slunk to the edge of the square. No one was watching now; it was as if she were invisible again.

Stick to what you know, Rag. Don't bring attention to yourself.

Gently she placed the tray down so it leaned against the wall, then she moved towards the nearest door of the barrack building. She had no idea where she was going, or what she was looking for, but there just might be some clue somewhere – she might overhear some crumb of gossip that pointed her in the right direction. By all accounts this Merrick Ryder was a big-mouthed bastard, so surely it wouldn't take long before she heard word of him.

Inside was a long empty room lined with uncomfortable-looking wooden pallets. From the look of them she'd have got a better night's sleep on the roof of the Bull, but thankfully those days were well behind her.

She crept further into the room, checking the bunks for any names that might have been written on them. In the past weeks Rag had done her best to learn her letters, Friedrik had insisted on it. She'd already had some schooling back in the old days before her mother had abandoned her for some smooth talker from Silverwall, and it hadn't taken much to pick it up again. Looking around though, there was not so much as a pair of initials written on anything.

As she made her way through the building Rag began to feel that old fear creeping up on her. What if someone came? What if she got caught creeping around in a soldiers' barracks? She'd have some questions to answer then all right.

Don't be soft, Rag. Concentrate on your business. Whatever this lot might do to you for snooping will be a sight nicer than what Bastian and Palien will do if you fuck this up.

Rag balled her fists. She'd been through worse than this. Weren't nothing to be done about it, so best get on.

The door at the end of the room led into a little chamber with desk and parchment and ledgers. Her heart beat a bit faster as she moved forward with a quick glance to the little round window that let in the only light. No one could see in, and outside she could just hear the sound of soldiers running through their swordplay, swinging and shouting as they went about fighting their invisible enemies.

She turned her attention back to the desk. Opening the ledger she stared at the neat script and silently she thanked Friedrik for those long boring days of teaching her what the letters meant.

In the first ledger was a list of supplies going back months – food and weapons and the like. Rag moved on to the next book; a diary of some sort. She looked back through the entries, seeing it was a list of the comings and goings, realising that the lads outside swinging their swords like there was no tomorrow were most likely the Wyvern Guard. Whoever this diary belonged to was definitely pleased at their coming, writing about how grateful he was that the city was practically saved. Whoever the diary belonged to was also particularly happy about the return of his old friend Tannick…

…Ryder!

Rag breathed out, thinking for a second she'd found her man, but then it weren't Tannick she was after, it was Merrick. Perhaps they were related. Brothers maybe?

Frantically she flicked back through the pages, seeing if there was any more word of him, but she hadn't gone back more than a couple of pages before something moved behind her.

She stopped, placing the book down and slowly turning at the noise. There, standing in the doorway, was a woman. She was big, must have stood a good six feet tall, her shoulders broad as a bloke's, the look on her face as grim as any fighting man Rag had ever seen.

'Looking for something?' said the woman, her voice deep and hard, like no woman Rag had ever heard before.

As a matter of fact I am. A fellow named Merrick Ryder. Have you seen him?

'I'm… er… lost,' she said, and realised how fucking pathetic that must have sounded.

'Really?' She said it like a question, but Rag could tell by the look on her face she already knew the answer.

Rag was floundering. 'Yeah, can you show me the way out? I need to be off. My uncle's waiting for me.'

The woman stared intently like she was hunting for the lies and could see them plain as the nose on Rag's face.

Then they stood there, just looking at one another. All at once Rag's nerve gave out. She was trapped in here, weren't nowhere to go, nor nothing to say that would see her free of this.

A tear welled in one eye then began to trickle down her cheek. If she'd have planned it – if she'd have wanted to cry, put on an act – she'd never have managed, but this was real. She was in the shit and she knew it.

'Why don't you tell me why you're really here,' the woman said looking into her like only the truth would do.

Rag couldn't see that she had much choice about it.

SIXTEEN

T he girl was lying to her. During Kaira's many years teaching young acolytes in the Temple of Autumn there had been times when girls in her care had tried to fool her, to make excuses, to rely on their feigned naivety. Kaira could see deception now in the eyes of this girl.

Young and simply dressed, she had looked innocuous enough handing out food in the courtyard. But Kaira had watched as she crept into the barrack room, had followed her as she entered Captain Garret's study chamber. This was no lost waif. There was something going on here and Kaira wanted to know what.

'Ain't got nothing to tell,' insisted the girl, lifting a hand to wipe away a tear. Was it a real tear or part of an act? Kaira guessed the latter.

'Maybe I should just call the Greencoats. Have them deal with you.'

'No,' said the girl, too quickly. Clearly she'd had run-ins with the Greencoats before.

'Why shouldn't I?'

'There's… just no need. I have to go, my uncle will be waiting.' She seemed desperate, like a cornered animal. Her eyes darted to left and right but there was nowhere to escape.

'Who is your uncle?'

The girl paused. Thinking fast, devising her story. Kaira let her think a while.

'He… he works in the palace.'

'Where in the palace?'

'Kitchens.'

'What's his name?'

'F… Henrik,' she said, mouth twitching at her error.

'F-Henrik,' repeated Kaira, finding herself enjoying this a little too much. 'Come on then. We'll go and see him together.'

'No.'

The girl stood rooted to the spot, another tear starting down her face. As much as she was putting on a brave show, she obviously knew the game was up. The girl was scared, exposed – Kaira felt a sudden pang of guilt that she was enjoying watching her squirm.

'Sit down.' Kaira gestured to a chair beside Garret's desk.

The girl obeyed, watching Kaira warily, as though she might attack at any minute. Kaira remained standing, thus reinforcing who was in control here.

'What's your name?' Kaira asked.

Another pause.

'Rag,' the girl replied.

'Rag?'

'Yeah, Rag. Am I lying about that too?'

Kaira guessed from the girl's sudden anger that she wasn't.

'All right, Rag. My name is Kaira. And I know you're not lost, so you may as well tell me exactly what you're doing here.'

Rag looked up defiantly, angry that Kaira had doubted her when she was actually telling the truth.

'I don't have to tell you shit,' she said, sloughing off her pretence of innocence. 'Go get the fucking Greencoats. I don't care. Nothing they'll do to me will be worse than…'

Rag look as though she had said too much, said something she didn't want Kaira to know. Was this girl in trouble? It roused Kaira's natural instinct to protect the weak, but she had to be careful – the girl could well be stronger than she made out. If Rag really was in trouble it was Kaira's duty to help, but the last thing she wanted was to be made a fool of.

'Worse than what?' Kaira said gently. 'Has someone threatened you? Are you in danger?'

That brought a wry smile to Rag's face. 'What do you care? I don't know you. You don't know me. Let's just keep it that way.'

'If someone wants to harm you, I can protect you from them.'

Rag gave a little laugh. 'Lady, you can't do shit. No one can protect me from them. And who says I want protecting anyway?'

Kaira looked into those fierce little eyes. Despite her protestations it was obvious Rag really did want someone to protect her. Behind that brave face there was a sadness, a defencelessness.

'We all need protecting, in our own way, even if some of us can't admit it.'

Rag just shook her head and stared down at her lap.

'Why don't you tell me why you're here?' Kaira asked gently. Rag shook her head but the tears were coming now. Kaira tried giving her a smile. 'You can trust me. You can tell me the truth. I promise no harm will come to you.'

'*I* can trust *you*?' said Rag. 'How do you know you can trust me?'

Good question.

'Let's say that, on occasion, I like to put faith in people. I let them try to make the right choices.' Her memory flashed back to that day weeks before, when Merrick had taken up his sword and freed a warehouse full of slaves. He had done that because Kaira's faith in him had led him to make the right choice.

'How has that worked out for you so far?' Rag asked.

Kaira shrugged. 'Let's just say I've had mixed results.'

Rag was frowning, as though weighing up whether Kaira could be worth confiding in. Eventually she made her decision.

'I'm just here to find someone,' she said. 'That's all. Nothing serious or nothing.'

'Who were you sent to find?'

Rag paused, as though holding onto her one final bit of information, as though giving up this last thing would leave her completely vulnerable.

'Bloke by the name of Merrick Ryder,' she said with a sigh.

Kaira stopped breathing.

There could only be one reason Rag was here for Merrick. This girl had been sent by the Guild, most likely Palien himself, eager for his revenge. But Kaira had to be sure.

'Tell me, Rag. Who sent you to find this man?'

'Just...' Rag couldn't answer. She had already said too much.

'I thought we were going to trust one another. I promised no harm would come to you, and I will keep that promise. In return you have to tell me who sent you.'

'It was... Look, it's nobody you'd know. Nobody important.'

'Someone asked you to break into the barracks of the Sentinels and they're not important? They sound important to me, Rag.'

'It was a man I know.'

'His name?'

Rag shuffled uncomfortably in her seat, opened her mouth to speak then thought better of it, shook her head, then sighed.

'His name is Friedrik.'

Kaira felt disappointed. She'd been hoping it was Palien. Hoping it was the Guild, but it was most likely just someone Merrick owed money to.

'What does this Friedrik want with Merrick Ryder?'

Rag looked guiltier than ever. 'Don't rightly know. But Friedrik's one of the fellas what runs the pickers and pinchers and the rest, so it can't be for anything good.'

'The pickers and pinchers?' said Kaira.

'Yeah,' said Rag, as though Kaira were somehow dense for not understanding. 'You know... the Guild.' She whispered her final words as though someone might be listening.

All Kaira could do was stare.

The Guild.

This must be him – this was the man Kaira had been hunting, the man she had been sent from the Temple of Autumn to track down and bring to justice. And her one link to him was a girl off the streets.

'What you staring at?' demanded Rag.

Kaira realised her eyes had been locked on Rag all the while.

'Nothing,' she replied. And it *was* nothing. Her mission for the Temple of Autumn was long past; she had turned her back on all that. She had a new life and she was no longer beholden to the Shieldmaidens and the Matron Mother.

Even so, something in Kaira wanted to find this man, to bring him, kicking and screaming if necessary, to the stairs of her temple. To shout out the Matron Mother, to tell her she had succeeded in the task given, and on her own terms.

Besides that, it was obvious this man wanted Merrick for nothing good. Kaira could not simply stand by and let the Guild find him. Though they were safe within the boundaries of the palace, they could not stay inside its walls forever. It was only a matter of time before the Guild would make their move. And if they found him they would most likely find her, and it was doubtful they'd greet her with smiles and hugs of friendship.

Kaira Stormfall was not the type to wait for the trouble to come to her. If there was a fight to be had she would take it right to the enemy's door.

And this urchin – Rag, the street rat – was the key to it all.

Kaira looked down at the girl, still deciding if she could trust her. Perhaps she had no choice. Was she to torture her for the location of the Guild's leader? Hand her over to the Inquisition and let Seneschal Rogan use his own inimitable methods? Not likely. Even if Kaira could have allowed such a thing to happen to a young girl, there was no guarantee Rogan wasn't already in the Guild's pocket.

'Do you know what the Guild intends to do with this Merrick Ryder?' Kaira asked.

Rag shrugged. 'They didn't say.'

'What do you think they'll do?'

This time there was no shrug. Rag had every idea what they'd do.

'Nothing good, I'll wager,' the girl replied.

'And you're happy with that?'

Kaira could see Rag weighing that up. She clearly understood the implications of her actions.

'No,' she replied. 'No I'm bloody not. I've…' She stopped herself.

'You've what, Rag?'

The girl's brow furrowed into a frown and then her face crumpled. 'I've had enough of watching what they do to people. I've had enough of seeing the misery they cause folks. The things they make people do… I only wanted to join up 'cos I was sick of living day to day with nothing to eat and no roof over my head. But they… they…' She looked down at her hands, squeezed together all white-knuckled, on her lap. 'All I wanted was somewhere to belong. But I don't belong with them. I'm just not like them.'

Kaira took Rag's hands in hers.

'I can help you,' she said with a smile. 'I can protect you from them. Give you a new life if you want it. But you have to help me first. Do you think you can you do that?'

Rag nodded. How could she turn down the prospect of a new life away from Friedrik and his vicious ways. 'What do you want me to do?'

'This man Friedrik. I want him. And I need you to lure him out so that I can get him.'

Rag understood. 'All right,' she said. 'But how am I going to do that?'

'He's after this Merrick. If you tell him you've managed to infiltrate the Sentinel barracks, you'll gain his trust. Say you can lure Merrick out but you'll need more time. Persuade Friedrik to meet you at a certain time and place when Merrick will be outside the palace. That is when I will strike.'

'All right,' said Rag. 'I can do that.'

She stood up and wiped her eyes dry. Kaira placed her hands on the girl's shoulders.

'I can trust you, can't I, Rag?'

Although Rag's nod seemed genuine enough, Kaira hoped that Vorena was watching and this girl's lament about the Guild was indeed genuine.

'How do I get them to believe me?' Rag asked. 'To believe me enough to do what I say?'

Kaira thought for a moment. It would certainly help the girl to persuade Friedrik and the Guild to follow her if she had something to back up her words.

'Take this,' Kaira said, removing the Sentinel medallion from around her neck. 'As a show of trust. It could also help you to convince this Friedrik that you have been successful; that you have found the man he's looking for. Tell him it belongs to Merrick Ryder.'

Rag took the shiny steel medallion and ran her thumb across the face of it as though the crown and swords emblazoned there might rub off.

'Thanks,' she said, putting the medallion round her neck and tucking it inside her shirt. She took it a little too easily, tucked it away rather too deftly, and again Kaira had fleeting doubts. But what choice did she really have?

She guided Rag out of the barracks, across the courtyard and out onto the street beyond.

'I'm counting on you, Rag,' Kaira said as they stood in the shadow of Skyhelm.

'I know,' the girl replied, and walked quickly away.

Kaira watched her go, hoping her faith would be justified. Only time would tell.

As for Merrick – did he have to know about this? That the Guild had not forgotten about him and were even now planning to kill him? No. He had enough to worry about right now.

Kaira would see this through on her own.

SEVENTEEN

I t started raining just before nightfall. Kaira had come to relieve him of duty at the queen's chamber door and all Merrick wanted right now was to indulge in the luxury of sleep. These past days at the queen's side had not allowed him or the three other Sentinels the usual amount of respite. They barely had enough time to eat and shit before they were once again on duty. Not that Merrick would have complained – this was his time to shine, to prove himself.

And is that what you want, Ryder? To shine? To show your devotion to the Crown and make your father proud? Or are you fooling yourself? Nothing's changed, has it, Ryder? You're still the same useless bastard, only now you've got a shiny suit of armour to strut around in.

Making his way through the gates of the barracks he could hear men shouting as they trained in the courtyard beyond. So far he'd managed to avoid the Wyvern Guard, which was fine by him. All they seemed to do was practise, practise, practise. Training themselves to a physical peak, honing their sword skills or beating the shit out of each other just for the fun of it. Merrick had been forced to train hard upon joining the Sentinels, but had never been subjected to anything like this.

The courtyard was full of men stripped to the waist, the rain glistening on their bodies in the lantern light, steam rising off them as they exerted themselves in the cold evening. Two men with canes walked up and down a line of warriors who were performing push-ups. Every man did them in unison. Any man who dropped behind the pace received a whack with the cane.

Despite his fatigue, Merrick was tempted to watch a while from the shelter of the eaves. Part of him envied these men their strength and dedication. Though he was a consummate swordsman who had endured his share of gruelling training, Merrick doubted he would respond well to being beaten. He'd most likely have told them where to shove their bloody canes.

That had always been his problem – too independent, too headstrong. It was an attitude that hadn't served him well over the past few years, and having someone else making his decisions might have been a good thing. But, you had to play the hand you were dealt the best you could. No use crying over it.

'Impressive aren't they?'

Merrick turned to see a grizzled-looking man standing at his shoulder. His hair and beard were close-cropped, his nose a broken mess. From his age and demeanour, and the fact he wasn't sweating like a pig with the rest of the Wyvern Guard, Merrick guessed he was one of the Lord Marshal's lieutenants.

'They're certainly good at push ups,' Merrick replied. 'Though being beaten with a stick would motivate most men.'

'Lord Marshal Ryder believes in obedience at all times. Pain is a good reminder of that. Most of these lads have been training under him for years. Long, hard years learning the spear and sword. They're as disciplined a bunch of men as you'll find in all the armies of the world.'

Merrick knew well how much Tannick Ryder loved his discipline, though he had always been spared any physical chastisement as a child. He guessed he had his mother to thank for that.

'I'm Jared,' said the warrior. 'The Lord Marshal's second.'

'Merrick,' he replied, thinking it best to leave it at that for now. No point admitting he was a Ryder – he was in no mood for the inevitable inquisition that would follow.

'Merrick?' Jared asked. 'Funny – Lord Marshal used to have a goat called Merrick. We had to slaughter it for rations before leaving the Kriega Mountains. He was ever so upset about that.'

A goat?

A fucking goat?

'Some people do get attached to their pets,' Merrick replied through gritted teeth. *Shame they don't feel the same for their families.*

Out on the rain-soaked courtyard the warriors of the Wyvern Guard had changed from press-ups to sprinting. Each man carried one of his fellows on his back and ran the thirty-yard length of the square before they swapped over.

'Since there's going to be a fight the likes of which no one's seen in centuries,' said Jared, 'we have to be prepared. Strong. Fast. Or at least stronger and faster than the enemy.'

'I see you're taking no chances on that score.' One of the cane wielders was thrashing a pair of sprinters who had fallen behind.

'Aye. Those Khurtic bastards will take some beating, but we'll be ready for them. Anyway, might soon come the day when we have to fight shoulder to shoulder. Hope you're ready too.'

'As I'll ever be,' Merrick said, though he wondered if he really was ready. Defending the queen was one thing – standing on the wall of the city and waiting to be attacked by a horde of angry Khurtas was quite another. 'But I certainly feel a lot safer knowing you'll be by my side.' He feigned a smile at Jared, who flushed with pride.

'Ha,' said the warrior, slapping a heavy hand on Merrick's shoulder. 'It'll be an honour. The Wyvern Guard and the Sentinels, side by side once more. The tales will last long after we're dead.'

'I'm sure they will.' *And let's hope that's not for many, many years yet.*

The warriors in the courtyard had finished their sprints and were standing to attention. One of them placed a finger to his nostril, snorting snot into the rain. As he did so one of the cane wielders slashed him across the back. Without flinching he spun round, snatching the cane from the man's grip and snapping it across his knee.

Merrick recognised him from days earlier in the throne room. He'd been the one wearing the white animal pelt that had faced off against Marshal Farren of the Knights of the Blood.

'Bloody hells,' said Jared to himself, as things looked like they might escalate.

'Seems some of your men haven't quite got that message about discipline,' said Merrick, suppressing a grin.

Jared took a step forward as the two Wyvern Guard looked like they might come to blows, but before he could speak a voice barked from the shadows at the edge of the courtyard.

'Whoreson!'

The men froze where they stood, but the two warriors still glared at one another.

Merrick watched as a tall bearded figure walked into view. His stern visage was unmistakeable in the scant light. Tall and imperious in his armour, Tannick Ryder strode over to where the two men confronted each other.

'It's always you, Whoreson. If you weren't so bloody good with a blade I'd have put you out in the snow years ago.' Whoreson stood to attention. 'All brawn and no brains. Well you're lucky that's what we need right now. Assume the position,' Tannick ordered. 'The rest of you watch, and watch closely. I'll brook no dissent. No argument. No disobedience.'

Whoreson strolled to the centre of the courtyard and dropped to his knees. Merrick could see something in his face; something in his eyes… could he be looking forward to what was coming?

Merrick leaned in to whisper in Jared's ear. 'Interesting name, *Whoreson.*'

Jared grimaced. 'His name's Cormach. Whoreson's just a nickname. Best swordsman we've got, but he bloody well knows it. This ain't the first time he's taken a caning and I doubt it'll be the last.'

Tannick signalled to the other man who held a cane. The man walked forward and looked a little nervous. 'Nothing personal,' he said, before he raised the cane and struck. It made a wet slapping sound against Cormach's soaked back.

'Again,' said Tannick.

The man began the flogging, whipping the cane through the drizzle-filled air and striking again. Merrick counted twenty strokes. Each time Tannick Ryder repeated, 'Again,' the cane struck hard and true.

Merrick was amazed at how Cormach took every blow, and with each strike the corner of his mouth turned up in a bigger grin.

'Enough,' said Tannick finally, reaching for the cane. 'Remember this well; I don't fuck around. You are all made of mountain rock. You're all heartless bastards, fed on blood and steel. None can stand against you because *I* have made you invincible. You are *mine* alone, my sons and brothers both – the Wyvern Guard. Never forget that.'

Tannick looked down at Cormach Whoreson, still kneeling in the rain, then brought the cane down with a final mighty slash. It split in two against his back, one end flying off into the night. Cormach fell forward, then righted himself. As he did so he looked up at Merrick, catching his eye for the briefest of moments. Merrick didn't know the man from a bag of nails yet he was sure he could see hatred in that look. What in the hells he'd done to offend this man he had no idea.

'Get some sleep,' Tannick shouted, flinging away the remains of the cane. 'Be ready for training tomorrow.'

Obediently the warriors of the Wyvern Guard made their way into the barracks. One of them tried to help Cormach to his feet but the man shook off his hand and, after rising unsteadily, followed the rest inside.

'See you later, friend,' said Jared with a quick salute.

'And you,' Merrick replied with a casual salute. 'If you need some stronger sticks I'll have a look in the stores for you.'

Jared frowned at the joke, then followed his men. Tannick Ryder, however, remained standing in the middle of the courtyard.

Merrick watched from beneath the eaves, sure he was concealed, not daring to move lest he give his position away. But the longer he stood the more his unease grew.

'Did you enjoy the show?' Tannick asked.

Merrick looked to left and right. There was no one else in the courtyard besides Merrick and his father. *Clearly not as concealed as I thought.*

Tannick turned to look at Merrick. The rain beat down on his armoured shoulders, and his hair and beard were drenched. Merrick, for once, was speechless.

'Cat got your tongue, boy? This is what you wanted, wasn't it? The big reunion? Well, I'm here, so say what you've got to say and we can both be done with it.'

Memories from childhood came rushing back to him. All those days of admonishment and scornful glares. Of never being good enough. Of feeling useless. A disappointment.

At last he had the chance he had waited years for, and now it was in his grasp he had no idea what to do.

Almost involuntarily Merrick stepped forward and he was out in the light, feeling the rain tamp down against his head, feeling it wash down his face and the back of his neck and into his armour. All at once it was as though the rain had washed away any reluctance to speak up for himself.

'It's been a long time,' he said.

As good a start as any.

'Yes, it has,' Tannick replied. There was no emotion in his voice, no notion of regret or paternal feeling, but what had Merrick expected?

'Too long,' ventured Merrick. This time Tannick gave no reply. Clearly he didn't share the sentiment. 'I assumed you didn't want to see me.'

'I didn't. But since you're here now, let's get this out of the way. So what have you got to say?' Good to see his father still had that inimitable charm.

Merrick had plenty to say. Years of pent up frustration just boiling up, waiting to explode, but he couldn't find the words. He had to say something. Had to grasp the moment. He couldn't just stand there getting piss wet through.

'How have you been?'

That was a bit more pathetic than he'd been going for.

'The question is: how have *you* been?' said Tannick. 'But you don't need to tell me, I've already been informed. You're a drunkard and a gambler and a whoremonger. You left your mother to die while you spent her fortune and ended up on the streets. Is that about right?'

You fucking left her to die, you bastard! You were the one that abandoned us! You were the one who rode off into the night like a bloody thief!

'I'm not like that anymore,' Merrick said. The voice that came out of him was hardly his own. It was the voice of a child. A lonely child with no father and a sick mother. A child that simply wanted to be loved, accepted, reassured

.

'No? You're not like that anymore? I suppose you wear the armour of a knight well enough. It's a step in the right direction, I suppose.'

'I protect the queen,'

'Really? You stand beside her as she carries out her duties. You're as much a proven bodyguard as the tapestries on her wall. Whether you're capable of protecting anything remains to be seen.'

I rescued a warehouse full of slaves! Hundreds of people would be in bondage if not for me. All right, I put them there in the first place, but I did end up saving them from a fate worse than death, and at particular risk to my physical well being.

But he could never explain that to Lord Marshal Tannick Ryder.

'What do I have to do to prove I've made a man of myself?'

Tannick considered that. 'There'll be time aplenty to prove yourself when the Khurtas come. Maybe even before that if I hear right. The queen is in constant danger. Assassins, they say. And I believe there's a few in her own court wouldn't mourn her death. She might even have to rely on you to save her. You up to that, boy?'

'I'll do my duty,' Merrick replied.

It wasn't a lie. *Was it?* Either way he hoped his father believed him.

'We'll see,' said Tannick. 'We'll just see.' Without another word he turned and walked back into the barracks.

Merrick watched him go as the rain beat down.

EIGHTEEN

I t took Rag until nightfall to make up her mind. She had sat on the steps of the Sepulchre of Crowns, looking down the Promenade of Kings for hours before the rain started. Then she made the long walk back as the dark set in, still thinking.

That woman, Kaira, had been all right. She'd seemed straight up enough, given Rag no reason to question if she was telling the truth. When she said she would protect Rag it was like she meant it.

Thing was – you couldn't be kept safe from the Guild. Not even the Sentinels could protect Rag. The Guild had eyes and ears everywhere. There was no place she could hide where they wouldn't find her. And if they thought she'd betrayed them it would mean the end of her – and it wouldn't be quick.

As she walked back to Friedrik's alehouse, soaked through to the skin, Rag decided that all the wishing in the world would never change anything. She had only wanted a normal life, but it was never going to happen. Best to just make of this one what she could.

Once inside the tavern she saw Friedrik was waiting for her by the hearth. They were all stood around – Harkas, Shirl, Yarrick, Essen. Even Palien was lurking there by the fire. He was eating off a metal plate, his knife scraped along it all shrill and nasty, setting Rag's teeth on edge.

'Well?' said Friedrik eagerly as she entered. 'Is he there? Did you find him?'

She nodded, and a big fat smile opened up on his face.

'Can I get dry?' Rag asked, and Friedrik looked at her all apologetic like.

'Of course.' He looked around at the lads standing idly by, his expression changing from glee to annoyance. 'Shirl, you useless bastard, get her a towel.'

Shirl scurried off and Friedrik ushered Rag nearer the fire. Part of her was grateful of the warmth. The other part didn't really want to be so close to Palien and his knife, but she reckoned she was safe enough with Friedrik there.

'Did you see him?' asked Friedrik when they'd sat down. 'Did you lay eyes on him?'

'Yeah, course I did,' she replied. 'Good looking fella, never shuts up.'

Of course that was the description she'd been given in the first place; she wouldn't have known Merrick if she fell over him in the street, but her answer was enough to make Friedrik smile and nod.

'That's the bastard! Good girl, Rag. I knew you wouldn't let me down.'

And Rag was pretty sure what would have happened if she had.

Shirl came back with a towel and Rag dried her hair. When she'd finished she saw Palien glaring over at her.

'How do we know she's telling the truth?' he said.

'What do you mean?' said Friedrik.

'How do we know she's not just making things up? That she didn't just sit there in the Crown District stuffing her face full of that food your cook made and now she's stringing us along to cover her tracks?'

Friedrik looked at her questioningly, but didn't say anything.

Rag looked away and into the fire. 'Suppose I'll need to prove it then,' she said, and just left that in the air. From the corner of her eye she could see Palien looking frustrated, waiting for her to carry on.

'Well?' he said when he couldn't stand the silence no more.

Rag reached into the top of her shirt and pulled out the medallion. She took it from around her head and handed it to Friedrik. He looked it over for a while, then smiled before handing it to Palien.

'Think you owe someone an apology,' Friedrik said.

'She's a fucking street thief,' said Palien. 'She could have got this anywhere. It's no proof.'

Rag was ready to argue, but Friedrik took the medallion from Palien's fist and handed it back to her.

'What do you want her to do, bring Ryder's head back on a stick? This'll do as proof enough because I fucking say so.'

Palien didn't look happy but knew when to keep his mouth shut.

'I didn't steal it from him, neither,' Rag said. 'He gave it me.'

This made both the men stare at her. She let it hang there, enjoying the moment.

'He what?' asked Friedrik.

'He gave it me,' she said suddenly shivering. 'We had a good chat. I think he liked me.'

Friedrik turned and shouted over one shoulder, 'Get some more fucking wood on this fire.' Then he looked back at Rag.

What was she supposed to say now? That she could lure Merrick out? Get him into the open?

And then what?

This woman Kaira would do her thing but even if she managed to kill Friedrik, the Guild would still know it was Rag who'd betrayed them. There was no way she could ever be safe if she went along with that woman, no matter what she'd promised.

'Weren't nothing much,' she continued, unsure of what to say next.

Before she could go on, Shirl came back with a bundle of wood. He wasn't three yards from the fire when his foot caught on the rug and he went tumbling forward, spilling the pile on the floor close to Friedrik's feet.

'Clumsy bastard,' said Palien, like Shirl had done it on purpose.

Friedrik didn't say nothing. He just bent down and picked up one of those logs. At first Rag thought he was going to throw it on the fire, but he didn't. That little man with the curly hair and the amiable expression turned on Shirl as he picked himself up. Friedrik brought the log down on his back with a dull thump. Shirl squealed, falling back down as Friedrik raised the log once more. Rag watched Friedrik hit him viciously again and again. Each time Shirl gave a squeal of pain. It was like watching a piglet get beaten to death.

Rag was beginning to feel sick. How much longer could she watch this kind of shit? Someone had to stop it. Someone had to put a bloody end to this.

'I can lure him out into the open,' she said all of a sudden.

Well, that's fucking torn it.

Friedrik stopped, log raised up in his hand, Shirl cowering on the ground, whimpering.

'What?' asked Friedrik.

'I can get him to leave the palace. I can probably get him out of the Crown District too.'

So much for not betraying the Guild. Looked like that Kaira woman would be able to trust her after all.

Friedrik smiled, lowering the log and letting it drop. He looked down at Shirl as though he'd just seen him for the first time. 'What are you doing down there?' he asked. 'Go stand somewhere I can't see you, and stop making that frightful noise.'

Shirl struggled to his feet, hands clutching his sides, face twisted in pain though he didn't dare say a word in complaint.

Friedrik turned to Rag. 'Well, why didn't you say that in the first place? How are you going to get him out in the open, then?'

She shook her head, thinking fast. Friedrik had talked about this Merrick long and loud and she tried desperately to remember something that might help. He was a drinker, a womaniser, a… gambler.

'I told him my uncle owned a gambling den. I made out they were amateurs, that anyone with any nouse would be able to fleece them easy. He swallowed it, couldn't wait to find out where it was. I played all cagey like, told him I'd get my hide whipped if I told. I reckon another couple of visits and I can get him to follow me to Northgate and you can nab him. Hells, I reckon I could get him to follow me to Silverwall if he thought there were enough easy coin waiting.'

Friedrik looked at her, taking in the words. If she was wrong about Merrick, or what she thought she knew about him, this could turn out bad for her. Much worse than a beating with a log.

'You know every day I'm finding more to like about you, Rag.' Friedrik smiled, and she smiled back. 'Don't you think she has excellent potential, Palien?'

Palien paused, his knife close to his mouth, some meat skewered on the end of it.

'She's a veritable fucking prodigy,' he said, before popping it in.

'Glad you think so. You won't mind giving her some coin then, will you? I haven't got any on me and it's obvious she deserves a reward. Don't you agree?'

Palien stopped mid chew and shot Rag a hateful glance, but it fell from his face as Friedrik turned expectantly. Plastering a smile to his lips, Palien dipped into the coinpurse at his side and produced two gold crowns.

'Don't spend it all at once,' he said as he slapped them on the table next to Rag. Gently she slid the coins into her hand, keeping her eyes on Palien, just in case he got any ideas with that knife of his.

'What are all these logs doing on the floor?' said Friedrik as though he'd forgotten all about beating Shirl to shit.

Rag cringed. Shirl was bound to get another kicking if Friedrik went off on one again. Mercifully, before that could happen the door to the alehouse opened.

Two figures struggled in through the door, soaked from the rain. They were dragging a body in between them, someone big and heavy, hands bound behind them and a sack over their head. Harkas slammed the door shut and moved forward to help with the body.

'Ah,' Friedrik said. 'Our guest has arrived. Although rather late, I think.'

Both the men carrying the load looked up like they was sorry. Rag could understand that; she wouldn't have wanted to keep Friedrik waiting either.

'We was gonna bring him last night,' said one of the men with no front teeth. 'But he was still knocked out and he's a right lump. The two of us would have struggled to carry him all the way without being seen.'

'Never mind,' Friedrik replied. 'You're here now. Yarrick, open up the cellar, there's a good chap.'

As Yarrick scuttled off, Rag marvelled yet again at Friedrik's sudden change of mood. It was always like this – one minute wondering if he was gonna stab you in the eye, next if he was gonna plant a kiss on your cheek.

The men dragged the body after Yarrick. Rag could see that whoever was under the sack was moving, but none too fast. Friedrik strolled after them, glancing at Rag over his shoulder.

'Come along,' he said. 'You won't want to miss this.'

Rag was pretty sure she *would* want to miss this. She'd been here a dozen times before. It was like Friedrik wanted to show off to her – like she'd be impressed by his cruelty. She knew better than to refuse, however, and followed him as they dragged the body out to the back of the alehouse.

A trapdoor led down some squeaky stairs into the dark. As Rag followed Friedrik down, someone lit a lantern that illuminated the cellar. The place was massive, at least a hundred feet long. In the middle was a pit six feet deep and twenty wide – a dirty hole for dirty deeds. Though Rag hadn't yet witnessed what went on down here every now and again, she knew it was a nasty business. There were fights in that pit; that much was obvious, and Rag had an inkling that not everyone who went in came out alive.

They dragged the body over to one of the wooden props and undid the rope binding its wrists. Then the one with the missing teeth chained its hands to the prop. They all stood back, just looking.

For an awful moment Rag wondered if this was Merrick Ryder – if they'd actually managed to catch him – and in moments Friedrik and Palien would find out she'd been lying all along.

When Friedrik pulled the sack from over the body's head, Rag didn't have time to be relieved it wasn't him, because she recognised the face that glared up at them.

He looked at the men surrounding him, his face a battered mess, one eye swollen and half closed, lips and nose rimmed with dry crusty blood. Rag knew him despite the sorry state of his face. Lincon, he'd said his name was. She remembered how nice he'd been to her after Krupps had almost killed her. He kept her safe, gave her water for her parched mouth. She still felt guilty that she'd cut off some bastard's head and then run from those Greencoats before she'd had a chance to thank him.

Well, there was no way she was gonna thank him now.

'Nobul Jacks,' said Friedrik like he was greeting an old mate. 'How good of you to join us. I think you already know why you're here.'

Nobul? Hadn't he called himself Lincon before? Either way, it didn't matter – it was definitely him; Markus' old man.

Palien leaned forward, though not too close, like at any minute Nobul would savage him with his teeth. 'Not so fucking clever now, are you?' he said, sneering all the while.

Nobul stared back, hate burning in his eyes.

'Did you think you could just finish off two of my best collectors and there'd be no repercussions?' Friedrik asked. 'That we'd never be able to find you? We're the Guild, Nobul. We have eyes everywhere. Young Anton's been one of ours since he was a boy. He's been waiting for the opportunity to draw you out for weeks.'

Rag could see Nobul's brow furrow at the mention of 'Anton'. Whoever he was she reckoned he'd be in deep shit if Nobul ever got out of here, but that didn't look too likely right now.

'Now, I know what you're thinking,' Friedrik continued. 'You'll be tortured to death, body dumped in the Storway never to be seen again? Right?' He cupped an ear as though Nobul might give him an answer. 'Wrong. I've got something much more entertaining in mind. Big strong chap like you, bulging at the shoulders, good in a fight, if rumour is to be believed. Why would I waste an opportunity like that?'

Still Nobul didn't answer and Palien gave him a sharp kick to the legs.

'Be grateful, bastard,' Palien said. 'I'd have gutted you and thrown you to the fucking fish.'

'Careful,' said Friedrik. 'Mister Jacks has a tough few days ahead of him. What days he has left, that is. We wouldn't want to see him injured before he's had a chance to perform.'

With that Friedrik shot Nobul a grin, then signalled for the rest of them to follow him back upstairs.

Rag was about to join them when Nobul caught her eye. He looked at her from beneath a dark brow and she couldn't tell whether he recognised her. She would have spoken but couldn't think what to say.

Hello, remember me? You saved my life once. Any chance I can return the favour?

With the tiniest gesture Nobul shook his head. Rag backed away. Maybe he did recognise her after all.

'Come along. Rag,' Friedrik called from the top of the stairs. 'Don't want to be down there all alone with the dangerous animal, do you?'

She hurried up the stairs after him.

Yarrick slammed the trapdoor closed behind them as Palien and Friedrik went to sit back beside the fire to discuss their plans. Rag didn't want to listen, didn't want to have any part of this. She was already in well above her head. Nobul, or Lincon, or whatever his name was had helped her once, but what in the hells was she supposed to do for him now? He was caught, landed like a bloody fish. If she crept down there later and let him free no amount of smart chat and bullshit would cover her tracks. She owed him, but there weren't a damn thing she could do.

Rag followed Yarrick into the kitchen where she heard hard and fast breathing from one corner. Essen and Harkas stood over fat Shirl. His shirt was off, rolls of fat bulging over his hairy waist. The lads were staring down at his back and from the look on Essen's face what they saw weren't too good. She walked closer, watching them.

'He's made a right mess of him,' said Essen. 'What do we do with him?'

Yarrick shook his head. 'He needs a surgeon or an apothecary.'

'Who's got the money for that?'

Shirl looked up, his face a sweating red mass. 'Friedrik's got coin.'

'Like he's gonna pay for you,' said Yarrick. 'Why don't you go and ask him, see if he doesn't just finish you with another log.'

'It... hurts,' said Shirl. He looked in a bad way and it was obvious he'd only get worse if no one helped.

Rag fished in her pocket, feeling for the two crowns that Friedrik had made Palien pay her.

'Here,' she said, taking out one of the coins. 'This'll do, won't it?'

Yarrick, Shirl and Essen all looked at her as she held that coin out like it was some wondrous treasure. Even Harkas eyed her funny, like there was some trick to it.

'What do you mean?' said Essen.

'What do you think I mean? Take the fucking money and get him sorted out.'

Yarrick and Essen glanced at one another, then back at Rag.

'Why?' Shirl asked in between laboured breaths.

Rag stared at them like they had heads full of sawdust. 'We're a crew, ain't we? We all got to look out for one another.'

Yarrick shook his head. 'Yeah, but you're...'

'What?' she said, getting annoyed that they were questioning her generosity. 'Friedrik's little pet? Fuck off, Yarrick, and take the money.'

He didn't need any more persuading, reaching forward and plucking the coin from her outstretched hand.

With some difficulty, Essen and Yarrick picked up Shirl and struggled towards the door. As they bundled him outside she thought she heard one of them utter their thanks.

Rag felt good about that for all of about a heartbeat before she realised Harkas was staring at her. He looked down from that big hard head, his arms folded across his broad chest. She looked back, wondering what was going on in that brain of his – or what he had in place of a brain. Then she nodded at him as though they were mates now – as though they were crew.

It was worth a punt at least.

And Harkas nodded back.

Rag left the kitchen then. She should have been pleased with herself that she'd done some good for once. But all she could think of was a bloke chained down in the cellar that she couldn't help, and no amount of crowns was going to get him out.

NINETEEN

The rain had stopped a little before dawn leaving the palace gardens sodden. Janessa loved the smell of the trees and grass after the rain, though only in the summer months. In summer, when the heat of the sun warmed the gardens, rain only intensified the sweet aroma of flowers and blossoms. Now, as winter was drawing in, all you could smell was mud. Nevertheless, she stood in the garden, furs pulled tight about her shoulders, and waited.

Azai Dravos being late to their meeting didn't surprise Janessa. Already he was playing his game, manoeuvring his pieces. They both knew that Janessa was in the more vulnerable position; her king had already been taken after all. Normally that would signify an end to the game, but Janessa was determined to prove the queen could be just as powerful as anything else on the board.

Merrick and Kaira stood nearby as they always did. For once, their presence didn't make her feel safe. This was a battle she would have to fight alone. There would be no sword and shield here, though the fate of the Free States might well depend on how the next few moments went.

Strangely, Janessa felt an overwhelming need for a weapon at her side. From the first time she had lifted the Helsbayn she had gained a comfort from its weight in her hands. If ever there was a need for it, surely it was now. For a fleeting moment she imagined wielding it in battle, charging at her enemy, blade held high, rallying her troops to her side.

Don't be ridiculous. You are untrained. As if fighting men would rally to an untested girl.

Smiling at her foolishness, Janessa moved close to one of the statues in the garden. It depicted a handsome warrior, princely in his beauty. She had always liked it, even as a little girl, and had often wondered which of Steelhaven's monarchs it depicted, though no one had ever been able to tell her. Now, as she stood in its shadow, she found herself hoping he would watch over her as she bargained with the man who might hold her city's fate in his hands.

Dravos' bodyguards appeared first, their matching red tunics almost gaudy against the muted colours of the leafless trees and topiary. They glanced about the gardens for any possible threat, then positioned themselves to ensure that when Azai Dravos appeared he could walk safely between them.

The envoy followed his bodyguards at a leisurely pace. He wore a black scarf tied tight around his head and a black robe billowing from shoulders to ankles. Dravos smiled as he approached, his olive skin glistening slightly in the sunlight. The dark liner about his eyes accentuated their piercing greenness, giving him something of a feline look.

He stopped before her, smiling and bowing low, all the while keeping his green eyes upon her.

'Majesty,' he said. 'I must thank you again for granting me an audience – and in such pleasant surroundings. Skyhelm's gardens rival any I have seen in all the palaces of the East.'

'Thank you,' she replied. 'I hope your stay so far has been satisfactory. You and your companions have been well cared for?'

'Like kings.' He beamed at her, his teeth bright white against his tanned skin. 'I have feasted in the palaces of sultans and emperors, and never before have I been treated as generously as I have at Skyhelm.'

She smiled graciously at his compliments.

All right, let's dispense with the fawning pleasantries.

'Azai Dravos, I am a plain speaker, as was my father. You well know what danger threatens my nation and its capital. You also know I require a substantial sum to defend them adequately. The Bankers League is in a position to offer that sum. I trust you are authorised to finalise dealings in this matter?'

If Azai Dravos was surprised at her directness he did not show it.

'I speak for the White Moon Trading Company and have also been given dispensation to represent the Bankers League in this matter, Majesty.'

'Good. Then let's to business.' She had to find out what he really wanted. Go on the offensive; make her demands and wait for him to counter. 'We will require one million crowns, half in coin, the rest in notes of credit guaranteed by the Bankers League.'

She watched Dravos' reaction, but he gave away nothing. She had already discussed with Odaka and Chancellor Durket the needs of the treasury. A million crowns would be adequate to defend the city – provided it was delivered quickly. They had very little time. If coin could not be made available, notes of credit would suffice to secure the support of the Free Companies. Hopefully, with them on side, they would be able to turn back Amon Tugha and his Khurtas.

Dravos smiled warmly.

'The Bankers League is able, and willing, to provide the sum you request.'

Janessa felt a sudden wave of relief wash over her but stayed on her guard. For him to accept so quickly she knew there would most likely be some substantial caveat attached to his terms.

'That is welcome news,' she said, keen to press her advantage. 'The Crown can offer to pay interest to the—'

'No,' Dravos interrupted, the smile now gone from his face. 'The Bankers League will pay the loan in full and with all haste. We will require full repayment within five years, but no interest will be levied.'

He paused. Janessa knew he was waiting for her to ask the question, to enquire what his demands were. She had already said too much by immediately offering to pay interest. Let Dravos show his hand now. Let him make his final move.

The silence ran on until it was obvious she would not be the one to break it. Dravos smiled at her stubbornness.

'My associates will require lands and title in Ankavern,' he said finally. 'The Princeling Moaz Bayek of Jal Nassan hopes to settle in the Free States and establish a trade route across the Midral Sea from Fleetholme to the Eastern Lands. We will also require the reestablishment of the embassy of Mekkala within the walls of Steelhaven, with all the sovereignties, religious provisions and immunities that entails. In addition there are several mines around the city state of Silverwall we will require ownership of – representatives of the White Moon Trading Company have already sent prospectors to determine their future viability and are more than happy with the potential yield.'

When he had finished he stared straight at her. Janessa looked back into his deep green eyes, trying her best to give no sign of her emotions.

Ankavern, though part of the Free States, was its own province and able to determine its own trade deals. If she tried to impose the sale of its lands there would most likely be a revolt. How would she fight that off after the costly endeavour of ridding her country of the Khurtas? Likewise, Lord Governor Tyran of Silverwall would never hand over any of his lucrative mining interests. As for an embassy – Janessa was under no illusions that it would simply be a front for whatever schemes the Bankers League wanted to pursue within her capital. A base from which they could plan and plot and ultimately cause mischief.

There was no way she could agree to any of this, and Azai Dravos knew it. So what did he actually want?

Perhaps it was time to find out.

Janessa smiled at Dravos, then moved from beneath the shadow of the statue –it hadn't brought her any luck so far.

'When my father succeeded to the throne and became master of Skyhelm he had these gardens renovated,' she said, gesturing to the now bare trees and the cold stone statues. 'He found solace here, and I would play at his feet as he considered the difficult decisions of state.' Dravos made to speak but Janessa carried on. 'My father had the luxury of time. I don't share that luxury, Azai Dravos. Time is the least of my commodities. So why don't you stop wasting it and tell me what you really want.'

Dravos bowed, but again never broke off his gaze. 'Apologies, Queen Janessa. Old habits are hard to shirk and I have been a broker in the cutthroat arenas of the East for many years. However, you have spoken candidly to me, so I will return the courtesy.'

He stepped closer then; much closer than Janessa would have liked. She could smell the spicy musk of his clothes and it almost made her head spin.

'I represent Kalhim Han Rolyr Mehelli. He is owner of the White Moon Trading Company, amongst other interests, and is one of the five masters of the Bankers League. In return for the money that should see you and your city saved from the Elharim warlord, he requires nothing less than your hand in marriage and all the lands and titles that come with it.'

Azai Dravos had at last played his endgame. It was indeed a devastating move but Janessa would not declare her defeat yet, not when so much was at stake. Instead she smiled, the genial smile so often affected by aspiring courtiers. She hoped it was a smile that gave nothing away.

'I am most flattered by the offer,' she said, hoping to buy enough time to formulate a counter offer, but Azai Dravos was not a man to be diverted.

He stepped in closer, his dazzling smile gone, the green of his eyes seeming to darken a touch. 'My master will not be refused in this,' he whispered. 'There is no alternative. Declare your betrothal, or your city and every soul within it will burn.'

Janessa wanted to step back but she found herself rooted to the spot, held in that ever-darkening gaze. She wanted to reject his terms right there, to tell him she would never consider gifting her hand to a man she had never met. That she was queen of all the Free States and she would rule it alone until her dying day.

But she didn't. Something in Dravos' eyes held her tight.

As she looked into them she began to think that perhaps this was not such a poor idea after all. Perhaps this Kalhim was a good match. He was a powerful merchant prince after all – one of the richest men in three continents. What would she have to fear anything with such a man at her side?

As she stared into his eyes, Azai Dravos suddenly held out a hand. She was aware that his open palm was straying towards her belly. There was a twitch of surprise across Dravos's brow, his mouth turning up slightly at the corners.

Something moved inside her, roiling as though it were suddenly gripped by terror. She wanted to back away, wanted to shield her stomach, but she felt like she was caught in a net, unable to move, unable to defend herself and the life within her.

'Majesty, are you well?'

Janessa suddenly stumbled backwards, realising it was Kaira who had spoken.

'Yes,' she replied, still looking at Azai Dravos, who was now smiling back at her as though nothing were amiss.

Kaira took Janessa by the arm as she tried desperately to compose herself.

'My apologies, Azai Dravos,' she said. 'I must return to my chamber. Be assured you will have your answer very soon.'

Dravos bowed low and Kaira helped Janessa across the gardens. Her stomach felt taut and rigid, and for a moment she was gripped with panic about her child's health.

Merrick and Kaira helped her to her chamber, and by the time she reached the door, her head had seemed to clear.

'Bring me Odaka,' she breathed as Kaira helped her onto the bed. Merrick hurried from the chamber to carry out the queen's demand.

Janessa laid a hand on her stomach. She was relieved that everything seemed back to normal, but the memory of Azai Dravos' words – and his strange eyes – was at the forefront of her mind: *There is no alternative. Declare your betrothal, or your city and every soul within it will burn.*

'Should I fetch the apothecary, Majesty?' Kaira asked.

Janessa shook her head, then forced herself to stand, gripping one of the posts of her bed to assist her.

Her head was reeling. This was supposed to have been her moment to shine, to show her mettle, to stand up for her city and her country. She had only succeeded in showing how weak she was. Azai Dravos had gained the upper hand and her only choice now was whether or not to marry some foreigner to save her people from the Khurtic hordes.

Odaka opened the door to the chamber. When he saw Janessa was in distress he ordered Merrick and Kaira to leave, demanding they tell no one about this.

Janessa read the concern on Odaka's face – he knew that she had failed utterly, that she had tried to act as a true monarch and had been found wanting.

'I don't know what to do,' she said, her voice as small and hesitant as it had been when she had first taken her father's crown and declared herself the Protector of the Free States. 'Dravos demands my marriage to his foreign master. He will give us what we need to save the city and the Free States in return for my hand.'

'A complicated situation,' Odaka replied. 'Especially now.' He glanced down to her stomach and she understood his meaning immediately.

She laid a protective hand on her belly. 'How long have you known?'

Odaka paused, as though he were somewhat embarrassed. 'Not long. But there is little that happens within these walls I am not aware of.'

Of course he would know; little got past Odaka Du'ur. That was why her father had entrusted the running of the kingdom to him.

She sat down on the bed. Part of her was relieved that he knew, part of her ashamed. Janessa was surprised when Odaka sat down on the bed beside her and gently took her hand.

'There are important decisions to be made,' he said. 'I will help you in any way I can, but I am no longer regent and the final decisions are yours alone. Are you able to make them?'

When Janessa looked at him she saw compassion in his eyes. She would have embraced him, but knew that would not be appropriate. Though Odaka was a man she could confide in, he was not her father. Already he bore more than his share of state responsibilities. She could not burden him further,

'I am able,' Janessa replied. 'Azai Dravos made his demands clear – a marital union with his master in return for the wealth we need.'

'What was your response?'

Janessa thought back to Dravos's eyes, to the feeling in her belly when he had moved closer. Was her revulsion because she was with child or... something else?

'I said I would need to think on it.'

'As you should,' said Odaka. 'But this might not be as cursed an offering as it seems. A swift union and consummation will explain away the child that grows within you. Your heir will still be a noble of the Free States and inherit the throne. No matter who its named father is, we both know they will be of noble lineage.'

Janessa realised Odaka's mistake immediately. He assumed the life growing inside her had been put there by Raelan Logar. Right now she did not feel able to disappoint him with the truth.

'But what of my people? What of their fealty if I were to marry some foreigner with no claim to the Steel Crown?'

'If you do not seal this bargain there may well be no city, no Free States, left. Do you think the people would rather have a foreign king by marriage, or an Elharim tyrant by conquest?'

Janessa knew the answer, but still could not bring herself to admit it. This was what she had tried so hard to avoid from the start. She had rejected Raelan and Leon for the love of another man; a commoner, a killer. Now it seemed she must wed some wealthy foreigner she had never seen, solely for purposes of state.

'I will need to think on it further,' she said.

Odaka stood up. 'Then I suggest you think fast, my lady. The child within you grows by the day. The hordes to the north draw nearer even as we speak. Whatever decision you make I will follow, but you must make one. And soon.'

With that he left her alone. Janessa stared after him, absently placing a hand to her belly.

Could her city be saved without the aid of the Bankers League? If she rejected Azai Dravos' offer, she would still have to explain the birth of an illegitimate child. Should she choose Leon as husband instead? She was sure his mother would jump at the chance and never question the legitimacy of the grandchild.

Whatever her choice, it had to be a swift one.

Amon Tugha was fast approaching and it seemed there was nothing that would stop him.

TWENTY

Nobul had no idea how long they'd kept him down in the dark. Then again, it wasn't the dark that bothered him. It wasn't even the fact they'd kill him eventually, and they *would* kill him, any simpleton could work that out. It was just a matter of when and how.

What hurt him most was being helpless to do a fucking thing about it. That he was going to die helpless as a pig on the butcher's block.

He hadn't realised how much he'd had to live for until they caught up with him. For too long Nobul had wanted to punish himself for what happened to his son. He'd wanted to put himself through shit to try and cast off the guilt that hung round his neck like an anvil. But now he was here, now they'd got him and the punishment had started, he knew that wasn't really what he wanted.

What Nobul Jacks really wanted was retribution. To hurt someone. To cause pain. To destroy.

Those old days of blood and slaughter in the levies, when he'd waded through guts, deafened by the screaming – that had been when he'd felt truly alive.

Nobul didn't want to be punished – he wanted vengeance.

But it looked like fate had robbed him of that one, showing him its arse as it ran on by. Didn't look like he had a shot at revenge anymore. Didn't look like he had a chance at much of anything now.

It was a shame. He'd have loved to get his hands on Anton. That miserable little bastard had it coming. How much coin had they paid him? What had they promised him to be their man in the Greencoats? If Nobul ever got out of here he'd make sure Anton regretted the day he'd ever heard of the Guild. But then the chances of him ever getting out of here in one piece were pretty slim.

There was a creak of wood, a deadbolt snapping back, and Nobul instinctively drew his legs up, tensing his shoulders trying to make himself as small as possible. He didn't know how long he'd been chained to the post but he felt the aches and pains of it. He knew what was coming and the tighter a ball he made of himself the less of a kicking he'd have to take.

Light crept into the cellar and he squinted through it, hearing someone coming down the creaking stairs. Eventually he could make out a face he recognised.

'Rise and fucking shine,' said the figure through the gap where his front teeth should have been. He placed the lantern and the bucket he carried down on the ground, then gave Nobul a vicious kick. 'You're on soon. Waiting's over. Been sent to clean you up.' Before Nobul could react, Toothless picked up the bucket and doused him in freezing cold water.

Nobul gritted his teeth against the shock, breathing hard as his heart suddenly pounded against his chest. Toothless moved behind him and pulled him up on his feet. His arms were still chained to the post, but he gave one last tug anyway – one last pull to see if he could free himself. It was never going to happen.

'There,' said Toothless. 'Awake now are we?'

Nobul didn't answer, just stared with hate at the bastard's ugly face. Without warning Toothless hit him in the gut. It wasn't the hardest or most accurate he'd ever had – a good gut punch could knock the air right out of you – but it still hurt.

'I asked a fucking question,' said Toothless. 'What have you got to say?'

Nobul grinned. He showed his bloody teeth through his split lips.

'I'm gonna kill you,' he replied.

Toothless took a step closer, but not too close. Nobul expected another punch to the gut, but Toothless just smiled back.

'*You're* the fucking dead man,' he said. 'Tough, though, I'll give you that. Must have been to have killed two of Friedrik's enforcers. They were good men by all accounts. Two of the best. You must have some big bollocks to have gone against the Guild like that. Or maybe you're just frigging stupid.'

Nobul stared back.

'Been talking about you a lot upstairs, they have,' Toothless continued like this was some cosy fireside chat. 'Word is you had a boy as got killed. They say it were an accident but we both know it weren't.' He moved a little closer, almost close enough for Nobul to reach out and bite the fucker, but he was too intent on the words to try. 'Those Greencoats what shot him were trying to catch a killer, an assassin. And who do you think sent that assassin?'

Nobul had a pretty good idea. He'd thought about it long and hard. Wasn't a crime committed in the walls of Steelhaven that didn't have the mark of the Guild on it somewhere. This only confirmed a suspicion he'd had for a while now.

'That's right – we sent him. His mark was some merchant called Constantin. He'd took what wasn't his, what belonged to Friedrik. And if it weren't for him, your boy might still be around. It's a shit one, and no mistake. I'm sure Friedrik's frightful guilty about it. I'm sure he wants to make amends.' Toothless glanced at the pit behind Nobul. 'Guess that's why he's giving you a fighting chance.'

Denny had been the one that killed Markus, Nobul already knew that, but the lad had done it by accident, only trying to do his job. The real reason Markus had died was because this Friedrik had ordered a hit and it had gone wrong. And now Nobul was about to die himself, to be slain by the very man who was the cause of his son's death.

Toothless went back up the stairs giggling to himself, and it wasn't long before other figures started to come down through the trapdoor. Some carried torches, others held flagons of ale and bottles of wine. There were men and women, laughing and joking, groping each other drunkenly. It soon looked like half of Northgate was there.

It didn't take long for the cellar to fill up with the buzz of chatter and a haze of smoke from their pipes. Nobul was right next to the pit – they'd certainly given him a decent view. Whether that was intentional or not he didn't know, but it didn't put him at his ease any.

Before long there was a shout at the far end of the cellar. Some fat bloke was standing on a barrel trying to get everyone's attention.

'Ladies and gentlemen,' he shouted. 'I know you're all here for the main event, but first we have a little warm up contest to get you in the mood.' A cheer went up from certain parts of the crowd. 'Now, for your delectation, we have a prime example of the pugilistic arts. Our first contender plied their trade in the cellars of Coppergate for five years before moving up to the big time. It's their third fight in Steelhaven, and some of you'll remember the mess they made of their last opponent. That's right, you know who it is – it's the scourge of the Iron Pits, the hammer fisted daemon, Gnasher Arys!'

The crowd began to cheer and boo as a path opened up. Nobul was expecting some thickly muscled brute – all broken nose and knuckles – but that's not what came. A woman strutted in through the haze. She was broad about the shoulders, her hair greased back in a topknot. When she reached the side of the pit she grimaced at the onlookers, revealing a row of yellowing teeth, sharpened into nasty looking points.

'Who could be mad enough to face her in the ring?' the fat bloke continued over the jeering. 'What kind of woman could care so little for her personal safety that she'd take to the pit with a beast like that?'

He paused, waiting for the answer. Someone chanted something that Nobul couldn't quite make out and before long that person was joined by another voice. Soon the whole crowd was calling the name – *Lady Pain* – over and over again. Another gap opened up and this time the woman who appeared didn't look like any lady Nobul had ever seen. She was almost as big about the shoulders as he was, a leather corset holding in her girth all the way up to the bosom. Her hair was shorn short, nose smashed in, jaw jutting like it didn't take any shit.

'Yes, you know it,' shouted the bloke. 'Lady Pain – Princess of the Pit, Mistress of the Melee, Baroness of the Brawl, undefeated in twelve contests!'

The two women stood at either side of the pit eyeing one another, letting the anticipation build within the crowd. The man on top of the barrel watched them, a smile growing wider on his face as he felt the atmosphere in the cellar growing. Then, without anyone's say so, the two women jumped in.

Nobul couldn't see nothing then. The revellers surrounded the pit, staring down, their cheers and jeers filling the cellar with a deafening racket. Every now and again he heard grunting as the pair went at it. The spectators would occasionally give a groan or a roar as one or the other of them struck a violent blow or maybe bit something off the other. Coin was bandied around the edge of the pit as several shills ran their books on who'd win. Nobul could only watch all that shouting and wonder if he'd get cheered or booed or spat on when his turn came. And he knew his turn was coming sooner or later. Only question was what sort of bastard he'd be fighting.

There was a scream that went on a bit too long. It silenced the crowd for a moment before everyone surrounding the pit erupted as one. Once the cheer had subsided, some people started laughing, a few turned away with a grimace. Nobul could see several were spotted with blood that weren't their own.

The man took his place on the barrel once more.

'Ladies and gentleman,' he shouted as one of the women crawled unsteadily from the pit. 'Our victor this evening is Gnasher Arys.'

The spectators began to clap in appreciation as the woman rose to her feet, mouth dripping with blood. Nobul doubted any of it was hers. Her right eye was closing and she clutched a hand to her ribs, but she still smiled in her victory.

'Let's hear it for the gallant loser,' shouted the fat bloke as Lady Pain was unceremoniously dragged from the pit. No one seemed too bothered about giving her a clap. She looked like her fighting days were over.

Nobul wasn't that bothered either. He had his own problems to think on. Mercifully he didn't have to stew on them for too long.

Almost as soon as they'd carried the woman out and the crowd had gone back to its chatter, the announcer climbed on top of the barrel once more. He clapped his hands, grabbing the attention of his audience and hushing them into silence.

'Well, ladies and gents, now's the time you've all been waiting for: the main event. A one-time opportunity to witness what has not been seen within the walls of this city for a hundred years.' He pointed over to Nobul, and all eyes turned. 'A death sentence to be carried out before your eyes.' One of the ladies clapped in glee as someone began to mess with the chains binding Nobul to the post. Any thought he might have had of making a break for it were dismissed by the sharp end of a blade against his throat. When he looked he saw it was the curly-haired one – Friedrik – who was holding it.

'You'll put on a good show, won't you, Nobul?' he asked, as two big ugly bastards unchained him from the post, but then quickly secured his hands behind him again. 'There's a lot riding on this. And I've got a reputation to keep.'

Nobul didn't answer as the two thugs manhandled him to the edge of the pit. All he could think about was how good it would be to get his hands around Friedrik's throat right now. But he forgot that as he looked down into that big hole.

'So without further ado,' shouted the announcer. 'Let's get on with the dogfight.'

There was no time to wonder what he meant by 'dogfight' before Nobul was shoved down into the pit. Neither was there any time to try to make a graceful landing as he went sprawling in the dirt, his shoulder crunching awkwardly.

Nobul stood up, feeling the first spark of the pain, letting it feed the rage a little. The edge of the pit was surrounded now with jeering onlookers. Someone spat at him and missed, but Nobul wasn't too bothered about that. He was more concerned with the iron grille set in the wall. From behind it he could see something thrashing and snarling, spitting its fury at the bars.

'Remember,' shouted a voice, and Nobul looked up to see Friedrik looking down with a grin, waving his knife like he was conducting an orchestra. 'It's not the size of the dog in the fight… it's the size of the fight in the dog.'

Nobul wanted to tell him to go and fuck himself with his little knife, but before he had the chance someone pulled the grille up.

A hundred pounds of angry pit bull came tearing at him. Its ears were pinned back to its head and strings of slaver covered its snout. Nobul just about had time to back up to the wall of the pit before it leapt at him. He ducked, rolling away and came up on his feet but the pit bull was already after him. From above came the sounds of people cheering the dog on, willing it to tear his bollocks off.

He took a step towards it and kicked out, but the beast was faster, ducking his foot and lunging at his outstretched leg. It bit at his thigh, but got more of his trews than the flesh of his leg. Nobul tottered as it pulled backward, its thickly muscled haunches doing their best to drag him over, but all it managed to do was rip away a mouthful of cotton and some of his leg with it.

The crowd roared in appreciation of first blood, and Nobul gritted his teeth against the pain. He had little time to spit his curses before the dog was at him again, this time aiming for his ankle. Nobul jumped back, doing a stupid fucking dance around the pit as the animal tried to take another lump out of him. There was laughter from above, a shrill woman's laugh that only served to make him angrier, and as the dog came in again he stamped down. His boot hit the pit bull's head and it gave a yelp, scrambling back before attacking again.

It jumped at him and Nobul twisted, not quite far enough. Jaws clamped around his arm pulling him off balance and the weight of the pit bull sent him sprawling. It let go, and Nobul knew what was next – it would be after his face. He tried to twist away, but the dog was too fast. It went for his throat, but only got his ear. As the beast ripped half his lobe away Nobul grunted at the searing heat of it and could hear the snarl right down his earhole.

Fury bubbled up in him.

Fuck this bunch of bastards and their jeering. And fuck this dog.

Nobul kicked out with his legs as the dog reeled back with his ear. Before it could come in again his head shot forward and he bit down – his teeth clamped just over the pit bull's eye. There was a pained squeal as Nobul brought up his knee, driving it into the dog's ribcage. It howled again as a rib cracked. Scrabbling away in panic, the dog ripped its eyebrow away from Nobul's jaws and fled to the other side of the pit where it slunk in fear and pain.

Nobul staggered to his feet, spitting out the dog's flesh and heaving in a laboured breath. The pit bull cowered, whining in one corner and the crowd's noise seemed to subside for a moment. There was shouting from above and someone bundled their way through. Another snarl and there, at the lip of the pit, was someone big and grim, holding another fucking dog on another bloody chain.

'Get in there,' he commanded, wrenching the chain from round its neck. It needed no more encouragement, jumping in and coming on as ravenous as the first had been.

Nobul's mad was up now. He had tasted blood. Had raw flesh between his teeth. There was no fear – this was battle, plain and simple. Kill or be killed.

Nobul rushed at the dog, heedless of its slavering jaws. It leapt at him, aiming for the throat and they smashed into one another, both of them going down, writhing in the dirt, snarling and biting and screaming. The dog bit his shoulder and he sank his teeth into its paw. It yelped, wrenching its limb away, but Nobul was in no mood to let it escape. As they rolled around on the floor of the pit, even with his hands behind him, he somehow managed to tangle the chain fastening his wrists around the dog's throat. It struggled in his grip, trying to escape, chewing at his forearm as Nobul arched his body and squeezed the chain tighter. He gritted his teeth, pulling with all his might. The dog strained every muscle taut, desperate to escape.

The revellers looked on in disappointed silence when the pit bull finally went slack in his grip, tongue lolling from its mouth like a raw slice of steak.

Heaving in ragged breaths, the pain starting to leach into the wounds the dogs had left, Nobul rose to his feet. They all looked down at him now, every face seeming disappointed. He wanted to remember all those faces, wanted to keep them in his mind's eye so later he could find every one of them and make them pay for what they'd watched.

Not much chance of that, though. So maybe he'd best give them something else to remember him by.

The first dog still cowered in the corner of the pit and Nobul walked towards it as it whined in panic. It had nowhere to go, nowhere to run.

'You cunts want a show?' Nobul yelled. 'You want to see a fucking dogfight?'

The pit bull yelped as he struck it with his boot and tried to make itself smaller and smaller as he kicked it again and again. It didn't even try to defend itself or make a run for it as he slammed in with his boot, grunting, spitting blood, eyes wide, seeing nothing but hurt and pain and death. Before long the dog wasn't moving no more.

Nobul turned back to the crowd to scream at them that he'd won, that he didn't die so easy, when someone threw something over his head.

In a moment he'd been wrestled to the ground and his legs bound. There was nothing he could do but just lie there and wait to be kicked to death just like that dog. But it didn't happen.

They just left him lying in that pit with the two dead fighting dogs, as the sound of the disappointed onlookers slowly drained away.

TWENTY ONE

Magistra Gelredida's requests were often cryptic. Despite the time he'd spent with her, Waylian could find it difficult to decipher much of what she asked of him. It was strange then, that, on this occasion, she had given such clear instructions for his tasks.

Waylian had been ordered to the Northgate Orphanage for Boys, in whose care was a certain Josiah Klumm. Upon finding the boy Waylian was to present his documents of adoption to the proprietor and accompany the lad to a house in Dockside.

What could be simpler?

Only as Waylian made his way north through the city streets did he begin to think that perhaps this task actually wasn't quite so simple as it had first seemed.

When last he'd trod the streets of Northgate he'd been in the company of his mistress and two Raven Knights. Now, alone, he was conscious of his vulnerability to the depredations of beggars and thieves. At every corner there seemed to be someone watching him, assessing him for the kill. He'd tried pulling his hood up to try to blend in, but that only reduced his field of vision, making it easier for someone to creep up and cosh him over the head, then drag him away to do Arlor knew what...

Get it together. You've survived the road to Silverwall. Battled beasts in the Kriega Mountains. Travelled league after league in the company of hard-bitten warriors. Surely the streets of Northgate are a piece of piss.

Two young boys chased one another across the street in front of him, their mother shouting at them from a window above. If two young lads like that could play in these streets, surely he was safe enough. So Northgate was rough, no one could deny that, but it wasn't as if there was a murderer on every corner.

Feeling a little more at ease, Waylian carried on. His mission was for the good of the city, or so he assumed. He could brave the dangers of Northgate for that. If he didn't feel safe on Steelhaven's own streets how was he going to react when the Khurtas got here? Hide under his bed and wait for them to finish with all the rape and pillage?

Waylian had already proved his mettle more than once; surely this was nothing by comparison. Hells – he'd saved the city from an infestation of ravenous ghouls and come out the other side unscathed.

Well, almost unscathed.

It was time to step up and finally prove himself, to Gelredida, to his fellow students, hells, maybe even to the Crucible. A fire was about to consume Steelhaven, a horde bent on slaughter and destruction, and Waylian had to play his part to avert the city's annihilation. He trusted Gelredida, even if he didn't always understand her actions. She had the city's best interests at heart and he would do his utmost to aid her in any way he could.

So, when he finally found the orphanage, Waylian began to wonder what in the hells this could have to do with the safety of the city.

It was a plain square building surrounded by a high stone wall. The roof was covered in ancient slates, some skewed dangerously as though they might fall at any moment taking a dozen of their fellows with them. Waylian wouldn't have housed pigs in there, let alone children.

He pushed open the black iron gate and walked inside the grounds. Stairs led up to a rotting oak door and as he took them he began to wonder if he was in the right place. The whole building looked just about ready to fall down. But then, this was Northgate where most of the buildings were in some state of disrepair. The place was still hard for Waylian to stomach, coming as he did from Ankavern, and the little town of Groffham with its affluent community of artisans and shopkeepers. It was a far cry from the sprawling hive of Steelhaven.

Girding himself for what he might find inside, Waylian raised the brass knocker and banged on the door. There was a bit of a wait, in which he rehearsed in his head how he'd introduce himself, how he'd display some of his magisterial authority. How he'd express his newfound courage.

When the door opened all that seemed to fade.

The man who stood there was huge, his gut hanging out from under a woollen shirt and dangling over his stripy britches. So faded and stained was the material that the stripes were barely visible, but Waylian tried not to dwell too long on the man's nethers – although dwelling on his face wasn't much better. His head was bald but for a crown of long lank hair that hung down past his ears in greasy locks. His teeth protruded over fat wormlike lips and here and there about his chin sprouted wisps of a ginger beard.

Waylian would not have put this man in charge of a scabrous donkey, let alone orphaned children.

'Mister Fletcher?' Waylian asked, all his former composure now fled.

'Who wants to know?' growled the man, his bloodshot eyes staring accusingly.

'I've been sent from the Tower… of Magisters.' Waylian feebly presented the sealed parchment Gelredida had given him.

Fletcher took it in one fat, sweaty hand and looked down at it, then up at Waylian, wrinkling his nose in suspicion.

'What's this about?' Fletcher looked tense, like he was unsure whether to fight or flee, but then Waylian didn't know which he wanted to do right now either.

'I've come to take charge of one of your orphans. Josiah Klumm?'

At that Fletcher seemed to relax some. 'Oh. Why didn't you say so? Come in then.' He turned and waddled off into the building.

The narrow corridor led into a massive hall. Rows of tables lined the chamber and sitting at them, busy with their labours, were scores of boys. Some looked almost in their teens whilst others were not that much older than toddlers, but each one was hard at work. It dawned on Waylian why the master of this place was called Fletcher, for each of the boys busied himself making arrows. Some whittled the shafts, while others fletched or affixed arrowheads. From the speed and industry they were displaying it looked as if they were trying to supply every unit of archers in Steelhaven.

'I know what you're thinking,' said Fletcher, gesturing to his charges. *What, that you're a profiteering bastard who makes coin from the labour of infants?* 'And no, they don't like it in the Trades Quarter. But they can go shit. District commissioner says I can run my business any way I like and I've got the paperwork to prove it. Keeps these little fuckers off the streets anyway – so you could say I'm doing Northgate a service.'

Fletcher tousled the hair of one of the younger lads as he went by. The boy looked none too keen on being touched by those greasy hands, and Waylian couldn't blame him.

'So, is Josiah here or not?' Waylian asked, only too eager to conclude his business and be on his way.

'Dunno. Have to check, won't I.' Fletcher walked through the hall to a back room.

It appeared Fletcher didn't even know the names of the children in his care. Seeing how they were being used, Waylian also guessed that the man couldn't have cared less about any of them.

In the back room Fletcher grabbed a weathered ledger from a shelf and slammed it down on his desk raising a billow of dust. He opened it near the middle and began to paw it with his fat fingers.

'Krumm, you say?'

'No, Klumm,' Waylian replied. 'Josiah Klumm. I believe he's around thirteen or fourteen.'

Fletcher turned a couple of pages until he found the one he wanted.

'Ah yes, I remember now. Tall lad. Never said much.' He looked up from the ledger. 'He left a couple of years ago.'

'A couple of years? Where's he gone to?'

Fletcher consulted his ledger once more. 'It says here someone from the Artisan's College in the Trades Quarter took him. That's all I've got.'

This wasn't the news Waylian was hoping for. It appeared the first part of his mission was about to end in failure.

When back on the street Waylian thought about his next move. Gelredida had sent him to Northgate with two tasks. So far he'd failed in the first – but he wouldn't report that just yet – not before he'd at least had a go at the second.

It was getting dark by the time Waylian found the other place in Northgate Gelredida had written down. An indistinct house on an indistinct terrace, the only thing that stood out about it was the pitch-coated lintel above the door. It had the word 'Apothecary' scrawled across in white spidery script.

Waylian paused at the door, glancing up and down the street. It was deserted. An apothecary located in this part of town was unusual in itself, but such a merchant should have been inundated with requests for tinctures and salves to remedy the numerous maladies caught from the insalubrious goings on around here. They should have been queuing down the street, but no – not a soul in sight.

Perhaps it was closed.

When he pulled the chain next to the door Waylian could hear a bell jingling inside. He didn't have to wait long before a hatch in the door snapped back. A pair of piercing eyes stared at him through the iron grille.

'Yes?' The voice was deep, the word breathed out long and slow.

'Hello,' Waylian replied, starting to feel just a little nervous. 'I've been sent from the Tower of Magisters with a... erm... request.'

A pause as those eyes regarded him unblinkingly. 'What is the nature of this request?'

'Can we talk inside?' Waylian asked.

The hatch snapped shut and there was the sound of keys in mortice locks and the sliding snap of deadbolts being pushed open. The door slowly creaked open to reveal a tall man with dark, immaculately coiffured hair who duly moved aside to allow Waylian in. As soon as he stepped into the dark room the door was closed behind him and Waylian began to wonder if he should have stayed out on the street after all.

'What can I do for you?' said the man, lighting several more candles from the one he held in his long fingers.

'I've brought a list,' said Waylian, clutching the parchment Gelredida had given him to his chest.

'I am to provide the items on that list?' asked the man, stepping behind the counter that filled one end of his apothecary's shop.

'Er... yes,' Waylian replied.

As the newly lit candles began to illuminate the room, Waylian could see it housed shelf upon shelf of phials, jars and other alembics. Herbs sprouted from tiny clay pots and stood alongside ready-made poultices and noctums. On the wall behind the counter were row upon row of tiny drawers, each bearing its own neatly written label. Waylian couldn't make out any of their names in the wan light, but he had no doubt this man knew what every one contained.

'Could I see the list?' he asked, holding out his long hand. Waylian found it almost mesmerising, like a gigantic spider unfurling itself on its web.

'No,' Waylian said, a little too loudly. 'I mean… I'm supposed to read it to you.' Indeed, Gelredida had been most specific about that.

The man smiled. 'Very well. Read away.'

Waylian squinted at the list through the gloom. 'Erm… lugroot?'

The apothecary smiled. 'Yes, I have lugroot,' he replied, turning to his left and reaching out a long arm. Deftly he flicked open one of the many drawers behind him and pulled out a chunk of vegetable matter, placing it down on his counter with reverent care.

'Dogweed?'

The apothecary pointed with that long arm of his. 'Shelf over there,' he said, but his assured smile was suddenly gone. Waylian moved to the shelf and reached up to something that looked like a small bundle of straw. 'No, to the left.' Waylian plucked a small pot from the shelf in which sat a flower reminiscent of a dandelion. Carefully he placed it on the counter next to the lugroot.

Waylian looked back to his list. 'And do you have essence of clove?'

'Of course,' replied the apothecary, who was now frowning. 'Who sent you with this list?' he asked as he rummaged beneath his counter.

'I… er… can't exactly say,' replied Waylian. Gelredida had given him strict instructions to keep his mouth shut about that and he'd bloody well stick to them.

'My name is Milius, by the way,' the apothecary said, placing a phial down on his counter. 'What's yours?'

With that he extended his hand towards Waylian.

'My… erm… Waylian,' he said, grasping that huge hand. It was like grabbing a tree branch, and he was struck with a sharp spike of panic as it closed around his own. He looked back to his list and the last item on it. 'Just one more thing. Do you have any shade grass?'

The apothecary – Milius – closed his grip tighter around Waylian's hand and stared at him with dark eyes.

'You know I do, young Waylian. You know very well.'

'Do I?' Waylian asked, trying to pull his hand free, but it was locked tight in the apothecary's grip.

Milius stared for what seemed like an age, unspeaking, unmoving. Waylian felt fear creeping up on him like a mugger in the night; he dare not look away, dare not try to extricate himself from the apothecary's hand.

Then Milius relaxed, released him and took a step back. 'You know I've got just the thing for you,' he said, turning and disappearing through a doorway behind his counter.

Waylian wasted no time – he wasn't about to hang around here any longer, it was time to bloody scarper while the scarpering was good.

He backed up to the front door, keeping his eyes fixed on the dark opening Milius had disappeared into. His hand fumbled with the doorknob but it was stiff and difficult to turn. His fear and panic grew at the prospect of being trapped in here and he grasped the doorknob with both hands, pulling with all his might, gritting his teeth with the exertion. To his relief the stiff door scraped open, revealing the night- darkened street beyond.

'Where are you going?' asked a voice behind him. Waylian turned to see Milius holding two cups of steaming liquid. 'I've made us a brew.'

A brew? From this freak of nature? You must be bloody joking!

'No thanks,' Waylian replied. 'I've just remembered… I've got to go and… feed my fish!'

With that he was gone, leaving the apothecary and his unwholesome brew far behind him.

So much for helping save the bloody city. Right now Waylian could only think about saving himself and, though he knew his mistress would be displeased by his only partial success, that would just have to do for now.

TWENTY TWO

R egulus had never seen anything so magnificent. The tribes of Equ'un were nomadic by nature; their only settlements built from hide, bone and mud. Altars to the gods of the skies were constructed from stone and rock but the largest only rose to ten or fifteen feet. They did nothing to prepare him for the sight of the city.

Steelhaven was like a mountain newly conjured from the earth, rising up along the edge of the coast to stand defiant against the sea and sky. Its walls rose high and straight as though carved from bare rock. Within were high towers, like stolid giants facing off against one another in a vast arena of stone.

When they were close enough, Regulus halted his warriors on a rise to watch the city. A steady stream of people was filtering into Steelhaven from the north, and from his vantage point Regulus could see magnificent ships with sails of many colours cruising into the harbour from the south.

'I have never seen such things,' said Akkula, gawking at the vast harbour. 'Surely the gods must have had a hand in this.'

Leandran barked a laugh. 'What the Clawless Tribes lack in strength and ferocity, they make up for with their ingenuity. This is not the work of gods but of men.'

Leandran was the oldest of their number and had travelled widely throughout the grasslands of Equ'un. But Regulus doubted even he had seen anything like this before.

'So how do we approach, my lord?' Leandran asked.

Regulus stared down at the city, at its vast walls and the soaring towers beyond. 'We will walk up to the city gates and present ourselves,' he replied.

'I thought perhaps one of us might go ahead and announce the coming of a Zatani chieftain.'

Regulus shook his head. 'No, Leandran. I am no chieftain. We are merely warriors offering our spears to the city's cause. But fear not. One day we will return to Equ'un as heroes, with the reputation to match.'

'And I believe you, but shouldn't we at least be cautious?'

'Cautious we will be, old friend, but what choice do we have but to present ourselves at the gate? It's not as if we'll be able to hide ourselves amongst the rest of those Coldlander travellers.' He gestured to the steady stream of bodies filtering through the city gates.

There was no more talk. As much as he had been warned of the danger there was only one way to approach, and that was to forge ahead. Besides, Zatani warriors did not creep and cower in the shadows. They fought with their heads raised, roaring their fury to the sky, facing adversity unto death.

Regulus pulled the cloak from his shoulders, flung it to the ground and strode towards the city. His warriors did likewise, following the leader of their tribe as they had done for so many leagues. Regulus hoped he was worthy of their trust, that he was not leading them to certain death.

The stone paved path beneath their feet ran east until it came to a bridge that crossed a wide river meandering down from the north. To the south of the bridge, on the western side of the river, was a ruined expanse of ramshackle buildings. They looked ancient, yet Regulus could see men, women and children moving within the sprawl. Across the bridge stood a huge gate from which another wide stone pathway led northwards.

As soon as Regulus and his five warriors had set foot on the bridge they heard a cry go up. Their approach had been seen by spotters along the city's vast wall and, as they made their way over the bridge, they could see warriors in green moving frantically to intercept them. One was screaming for the gate to be closed, while another shouted for reinforcements.

'Hold steady,' Regulus said as they reached the centre of the bridge. 'We are here as allies, not enemies.'

Though his warriors obeyed his words, Regulus could sense unease, particularly in Janto, whose hands strayed dangerously close to the handles of his twin axes.

At the gate there was more frantic movement – a woman screamed and travellers were bundled aside as more warriors in green came flooding out of the city. They positioned themselves at one end of the bridge, longspears held out in a phalanx. Regulus almost laughed at their display. Had he wanted to pass his warriors would have barely drawn breath before these Coldlanders were dead.

When they were within ten yards, Regulus lifted an arm signalling the Zatani to stop. He strode forward and stood before the row of spears, regarding the nervous men who held them.

'Fear not,' he said. 'I have come as a friend and ally. Not an enemy.'

Several of the men looked on in amazement. 'Fuck me – it speaks,' said one of them, momentarily lowering his spear.

'Yes, I speak. And I would parlay with your queen. I would offer her my sword.' Regulus grabbed the hilt of his black steel blade and shook it in its scabbard, which only served to spook these men further.

'It's a trick,' said one of the men.

'Not a very good one, if it is,' replied another. 'Just wandering right up to the gates like that.'

'Well, what do we do?' added a third.

By now another warrior in green had come to stand behind the men. He looked Regulus over with a keen eye. This one looked older than the others, his face scarred and weathered.

'You're mercenaries?' the man asked.

Regulus was familiar with the term – roving warriors who fought for the material rewards of battle, rather than loyalty to chief or tribe. He supposed that, as an outcast, mercenary was the closest these Coldlanders would understand to his current status.

'I am. And I would fight for the glory of this city.'

The man gave a wry smile. 'There may not be much glory in the days to come, but we're in no position to turn away warriors willing to fight. Even if they are… well… foreigners. Let them through,' he told his men. 'We'll escort them to the Seneschal. He'll know what to do with them.'

'We're just letting them into the city?' said one of the men.

'Do you think it's better we let them wander the countryside?' said their leader.

There was no more argument. The spearmen raised their weapons and allowed Regulus and his men to cross the bridge. The green-garbed leader walked them through the vast city gate and his men moved along beside them. Regulus could see they were nervous, gripping their spears tightly; but they had nothing to fear. Soon they might find themselves fighting side by side – then they would see the wisdom of allying themselves to Zatani warriors.

Once inside the gate Regulus and his men looked on in awe at the buildings that towered above them. The ground beneath their feet was roughly spotted with stones that made a crude pathway between the dwellings that stood to either side. Each stone construction rose up and seemed to lean over like the boughs of trees, forming a corridor of rock like the sides of a steep valley. They scarcely registered that the people milling about were staring at them Zatani with wonder and fear.

Regulus' warriors soon arrived at the gates to another massive construction. It rose up mournfully, reaching for the grey skies above. More of the green-coated warriors awaited them and Regulus began to feel an uneasy sense of foreboding. The warning he'd been given by Tom the Blackfoot suddenly came back to him.

'Stay your hands,' he said to his warriors in their own tongue. 'But be wary.'

They needed no further prompting and Regulus could see each picking his own target – a man who would immediately die if they were suddenly attacked.

From within the tower came a lone figure, dressed in a plain grey robe. The hood was drawn back and his face showing he was slim, even for a Coldlander, and he regarded Regulus with interest.

'Greetings,' he said to the Zatani. 'Word has it you are ready to join battle with Steelhaven against the horde advancing upon us?'

'I am Regulus of the Gor'tana. Come north to win glory for my tribe.'

The man smiled, but seemed suitably underwhelmed by Regulus' statement. 'Yes, I'm quite sure. Please, follow me.'

He led the way towards the vast tower, and Regulus followed. They walked through the grounds and into the dark interior where fires were lit along the walls. Regulus suddenly felt trapped; he was a warrior of the open plains, used to sleeping under the stars and the watchful eyes of his gods. In such a place as this he may as well have been interred beneath the earth.

'I have come to offer my sword to your queen,' he said, his sense of unease growing. 'Where do you lead us?'

The man in grey turned and smiled. Regulus had little experience with the Coldlanders of the Clawless Tribes, but they certainly seemed to smile a lot. Regulus was unsure what this one had to be so pleased about.

'I am Seneschal Rogan – advisor to Queen Janessa of Steelhaven. It is my honour to meet and receive all those who would fight for the city. Mercenaries are to be housed here, where they can be properly... cared for. These will be your quarters.'

'But I must offer my sword to your queen.' Regulus was finding it difficult to hide his frustration, and his warriors could sense it. Hagama gripped his spear in both hands as though ready to attack and Janto rested his hands on the handles of his axes, his eyes scanning the dark for signs of danger.

'I am afraid that is out of the question,' said Seneschal Rogan, leading them out into a cavernous room. 'The queen does not meet with mercenaries.'

The room was huge and lined with tables. Around several of them were men dressed in all manner of colours, some of who glanced over with interest.

'We are not mere mercenaries,' said Regulus slowly, wondering if this Coldlander was finding it difficult to understand him. 'We have travelled many leagues to be here, suffered much hardship. Faced much danger to fight for this city. We are warriors of the Gor'tana, tempered on the battlefields of Equ'un. Your city faces danger and I intend to turn the tide of battle in your favour. I will not be treated as a common slave. We *must* be presented to your queen.'

Regulus could see the unease had spread to the guards of this place, and they stood by nervously. He had raised his voice, and all eyes had turned to him, watching and waiting for any threat of violence. But Seneschal Rogan continued smiling, untroubled by Regulus' outburst.

'I can see you are seasoned fighters, but you are not the only ones who have pledged their service to the Crown.' He gestured down the hall towards the men who sat within. Regulus could tell these were warriors but he was sure he had no rivals here. 'You have two options. Join the rest of the mercenaries and receive your pay alongside them, or leave the city.'

'Mercenaries,' Regulus said, chewing on the word. As he did so he realised he was no longer a prince of the Gor'tana. No longer honoured among his tribe. What right did he have to be presented to this Coldlander queen? He was nothing more than an outcast, a sell sword who had forfeited his honour. There was a chance that he could regain that honour though, if he did not squander this opportunity through his own hubris.

'Very well,' he conceded. 'If that is what we must do.'

'Excellent,' said Rogan. 'Now, just one more thing: your weapons. You will need to hand them over.'

Regulus looked to his men. None of them would be ready to surrender their arms and he was in no hurry to do so himself. Must it be done? Might this be the kind of trick Tom the Blackfoot had warned him about?

Glancing down the vast hall Regulus noted that none of the men bore a weapon. Perhaps this was the way of the Coldlanders.

'They want us to hand over our weapons,' Regulus said in the Zatani tongue.

'Never,' Janto growled, eyeing the nearest green-coated guard. The man took a step back, gripping his spear the tighter.

'It could be a trick,' said Leandran.

Regulus nodded. 'I know. But we have come so far. We cannot turn back now.'

Though it pained him to do it, he slowly took his sheathed sword from his belt and handed it to Seneschal Rogan. Leandran then handed over his spear, quickly followed by Akkula. Hagama and Kazul were next. Only Janto remained, his hands on the handles of his axes. All eyes were on him now, and Regulus knew any future glory hung on whether this unpredictable warrior would allow himself to be cowed by these lowly Coldlanders.

Silently, the warrior took the axes from his belt. For a fleeting moment it looked as if he would bury one of them in the head of the nearest guard, but instead he spun them in his hands, offering the handles.

As they were taken from him, Rogan bowed. 'The queen thanks you. I can assure you she is grateful for your pledge of allegiance. Now, please eat. You said that to come here you have travelled far.'

Regulus saw that food was being brought into the hall. His men looked on hungrily; slaver dripping down Akkula's chin as he eyed the meagre offering.

When Regulus signalled permission the Zatani moved swiftly to fall upon the food. Regulus looked back to Seneschal Rogan.

'Take care of those weapons. We'll want them back soon,' he said.

'You will have them back,' Rogan replied, still bearing that smile. 'The enemy is close.' With that he smiled once more and left.

Regulus watched him go. Encompassed by dark walls and foreign warriors, he wondered which enemy Rogan was referring to.

TWENTY THREE

I t wasn't often Merrick found himself frequenting Crown District taverns. He was more used to the hovels of Northgate where you needed to wipe your feet on the way out, or the earthy, musky, fishy dens of Dockside, where the whores had thicker beards than the men. This place was like a sweet breath of air – all polished wood and crackling fire, with the stuffed heads of assorted game glaring down at him as he drank. Merrick might even have gone so far as to say that this was the best tavern he'd ever been in – if only the wine hadn't been so bloody expensive.

Of course, the company wasn't too great either; Merrick was all alone at the bar. He'd never been able to stand his own company that much. Being on your own wasn't healthy; it made you think. And Merrick was in no mood for thinking.

He'd made a fool of himself in front of his father, though that was hardly surprising; he made a fool of himself on a daily basis. But he'd so wanted old Tannick to be proud of him.

Who are you kidding, Ryder. You're a drunken ass. You're selfish and vain and you'd stick it in anything that flashed you a smile. Hells, you'd fuck the crack of dawn if you could get up early enough. Why would anyone show you anything but contempt?

Merrick stared down at the goblet in front of him, then drained the dregs and slammed it down on the bar. He looked across the tavern, his vision starting to go a little fuzzy round the edges. This was the best kind of drunk

– enough to take the edge off, but not too much to have him reeling around spewing vomit everywhere.

He knew he'd fucked up. He was supposed to be on duty, supposed to be protecting his queen, but here he was, back to his old tricks. He'd tried to stay sober, tried to do the right thing, but it simply wasn't working. Now he'd let Garret down, let Kaira down… he'd let the bloody queen down. Just one big, long list of failures. Why would anyone think well of him?

What bloody good was he, after all? He could barely look after himself, let alone the queen of the Free States. Garret should have put him on latrine duty, not safeguarding the most important woman in Steelhaven. Then again, he'd probably have fucked that up too; covered himself in shit and piss most likely.

What was he good at anyway? What could he do better than anyone else? That wouldn't involve people criticising him, or judging him, or looking down on him?

'Drink?'

Yes, that was probably about it.

Merrick looked up to see the barkeep staring at him. He had a half empty bottle of wine in his hand.

'Why not,' Merrick replied and slid his goblet across the bar. The barman filled it almost to the brim. 'Why don't you have one yourself?'

The barman looked sheepish. 'I probably shouldn't.'

Merrick glanced around the empty tavern. 'Why not? Expecting a rush?'

The barman looked across the empty tavern and shrugged. He took another goblet from a shelf and filled it with what remained in the bottle. Merrick held his up and they clinked them together before taking a swig.

'Here's to quiet days,' he said.

'To quiet days,' the barman replied. 'Though I'm not sure how many of those we have left.'

'Not many, I'll wager. So we may as well make the best of it.'

The barman nodded in agreement, though he didn't seem entirely sure. 'I should have left this place when I had the chance,' he confided.

'Why didn't you?'

'I have responsibilities,' he replied. 'People that rely on me.'

Responsibilities? Merrick knew about those all right and he was beginning to realise what a total pain in the arse they were. He had responsibilities that required his attention right now, but they somehow seemed unimportant next to his current woes.

There you go again, Ryder – always thinking about yourself. But then you're the most important man in Steelhaven. Nobody else has as much on his shoulders as you, do they?

'You've got family here?' Merrick asked quickly, keen to clear his head of the daemons of his conscience. 'Wife? Pups?'

The barman shook his head. 'No, nothing like that. But my old man's frail and can't travel. I have to stay and look after him.'

His old man? Bet he was a kindly old duffer too. Bet he'd always been there – a mentor, a confidante, a shoulder to cry on.

'You two must be close then, if he's the reason you've stuck around here for the Khurtas to arrive. That must be nice for you.'

The barman shot him a quizzical look. 'Close? You must be fucking joking. The old bastard's a millstone around my neck. I'm only hanging around for my inheritance. If I leave now I've got no chance of getting my hands on it.'

A smile of understanding spread across Merrick's face. 'I'll drink to that, friend,' he said, raising his cup before realising it was already empty. The barman grabbed another bottle and opened it, filling both goblets.

'What about you then? What's your problem?' asked the barman.

'What makes you think I've got a problem?' Merrick replied.

The barman looked at him knowingly. 'I've seen your kind a hundred times – drinking alone, when the rest of the city is going to the hells in a handcart. It's like you don't care. I'm guessing a woman.'

'As much as I've had woman trouble aplenty – and you could say I've still got it – that's not why I'm here.' He looked at the barman, wondering whether or not it was worth the trouble of unburdening himself. But sometimes strangers were as good as priests for letting out your inner daemons – and they made you feel less guilty afterwards. 'Let's just say I've got troubles with my father too.'

'Really? I bet mine are worse,' said the barman.

'I'll take that bet,' Merrick replied.

'All right then. Ten coppers says the troubles I've got with my father are worse than yours.'

'You're on,' said Merrick, offering his hand, which the barman keenly shook. 'You first.'

'Well, let's see,' said the barman thoughtfully. 'He can't shit nor piss on his own and he can barely feed himself. He pretends to be getting forgetful but he remembers where his coin's hid, all right, and he's got no intention of letting me in on that. All his assets – the house, the furniture, his stake in his business – are all tied up and if I don't do exactly as he wants I'll get nothing. How's that sound?'

'Sounds terrible,' said Merrick. 'But I reckon I've got you beat.' He sat back, with a smug look on his face. 'I hadn't seen my father for about eighteen years – since he upped and offed – then he turns up out of the blue. Not only does he act like nothing's happened in between, like he's just been out for an afternoon stroll, but he also has the good graces to point out to me just how disappointed he is with how I've been living my life. It's not like he just abandoned me and my mother – he has to condemn me for how badly I've done since then.'

The barman looked at him as though assessing his words. 'Is that it?'

'Yes,' Merrick replied. 'What else do you want?'

'So you've never had to clean his shit up off the floor?'

They looked at each other for several moments before they burst out laughing.

'You've got me there,' Merrick said, fishing in his purse for the coins. 'Here.' He slid the ten coppers across the bar. 'Hire yourself a maid.'

They both laughed long and hard.

'Here's to fathers,' said the barman finally, raising his cup.

'To fathers,' said Merrick. 'May they not burden us for much bloody longer.'

They clinked their goblets then drained them.

Merrick placed his cup back down on the bar, expecting it to be quickly refilled, but the barman was looking over towards the door. Someone had walked in. Merrick immediately felt on edge. As much as he hated to admit it, when he was outside the palace grounds he didn't feel safe. It was dangerous being here, but he needed some respite. Just a little time away from the duty and the obligations. What harm could it do?

Well, it could get you stabbed in the fucking back by some assassin from the Guild, if you're not careful.

Slowly he turned, half expecting to see some knife-wielding Guild bruiser coming at him with murderous intent. What approached across the tavern was nowhere near as ugly, but no less threatening.

Kaira stared at him as she approached. Her brow was furrowed, her eyes accusing. Merrick had seen that look before and knew it was no good thing to be on the other end of it, but he'd had enough wine not to care. He just offered her a weak smile as she walked to the bar.

'Drink?' he said, waggling his goblet as though teasing a dog with a bone.

Kaira slapped the goblet from his hand. It clanked off the bar, splatting the wood with dregs and causing the barman to take a step back.

'Are you out of your mind?' she said.

Funny you should ask – I've been wondering the same thing for days now.

'Oh, calm down, will you. Take a load off.' He gestured to a stool nearby.

'Take a load off? Are you insane? We have a sacred duty. The queen trusts us, and here you are drunk. Will you never learn?'

Merrick rounded on her. What right did she have to come in here and bark at him like he was some child? He'd had enough of being told what to do.

'Fuck you, and your fucking queen. I've had just about—'

She cuffed him round the head. Not hard enough to do any serious harm, but enough to knock him off the stool and send him reeling.

'What the fu—'

She cuffed him again, this time with the other hand and he slid the opposite way. He felt himself getting angry now. The red mist descending, and the wine he'd drunk didn't help any.

Kaira tried again, but this time he lifted an arm and blocked her, staggering away and righting himself.

'What are you doing, woman?'

'I'm trying to knock some sense into you.'

'Sense? I've eaten shit for weeks. Done my duty. Paid for my sins and now my father turns up out of the blue and it's like I'm nobody. You have no idea—'

'I have every idea. You're feeling sorry for yourself. The world is against you. We could be killed at any second and for no reward. I understand the notion of responsibility is a new one for you. I get that seeing your father again is difficult. But there are more important things at stake here than your feelings.'

'Fuck off! What the fuck do you know?' he screamed. 'You know nothing about me or my father or fucking anything.'

She came at him again. He blocked the first blow but she hit him with the second. It slammed him back against the bar, his rib cracking against the wood. It only made the anger within him burn more brightly.

Merrick struck out. He'd never hit a woman before, but then Kaira was hardly your typical woman. She was a warrior born. He'd already seen her cut through half a dozen men like wheat. Merrick was sure as shit she could take a punch.

Unfortunately she took it better than he expected.

The blow hit her cheek, turning her head for an instant. Then she hit back. This time when she struck him Merrick could feel the weight behind it, the intent. He'd rattled her and no mistake. So maybe she was human after all. And maybe she could even be beaten.

Merrick went for her. He'd had enough wine to make this seem almost sensible, but not too much to make him a stumbling fool.

He put his head down, bowling into her and knocking her back. There was a scrape of the table legs on wooden boards and a chair fell over. Then she grabbed him and flung him aside. He smashed into more furniture, its clatter echoing through the empty tavern as he went sprawling.

As he scrambled to his feet he saw her coming at him, eyes like a wolf after its prey. He picked up a chair and threw it at her head. She deflected it with her arm but it put her briefly off balance, and then Merrick struck.

What he lacked in brawn he more than made up for in cunning. He'd been in enough bar fights to know there was no place for honour. And if you couldn't win by foul means, there was no one going to make it bloody fair.

He took her around the hips, powering through with his legs and lifting her off the ground. They both slammed to the floor with him on top and he immediately tried a punch to her face. Kaira's arms came up quick to block the blow, then her legs. She wrapped them around his neck, impossibly fast.

It was as if he was watching all this happen to someone else only he was the one taking the beating.

Merrick managed a pathetic throttled sound as she squeezed his throat shut with her powerful legs. Panic hit him then as he realised he'd lost his edge. This was all he needed – to be beaten up by a woman in a bar… again.

As she squeezed tighter, his vision closed in. He desperately patted her thigh in submission, and she loosened her grip, letting him free. He scrambled away, raising his arms. 'All right! All right, I give in. You're right; I'm stuck here feeling sorry for myself when I should be carrying out my… duty.' The word almost stuck in his throat.

Kaira breathed hard as she stood staring at him. There was no less loathing in her expression but at least she wasn't trying to pummel him into the floorboards anymore.

'It's as simple as that, is it?' she said. 'Just an apology and a smile and everything's forgiven?'

Merrick rose to his feet, dusting off his britches. 'What more do you want? That's all I've got. Take it or leave it.'

'I want you to commit. Either that or leave – run away. You cannot go on giving yourself to this task half-heartedly. Sooner or later it will get someone killed.'

He wanted to argue that point, but part of him knew she was right. The longer he wallowed in self-pity, the more chance there was that the worst would happen. What was he even doing here drinking himself into a stupor, just when he thought he'd left all that behind him?

Maybe his father was right, after all. Maybe Merrick had spent his time hating the man for his scorn, when his father had been right about what Merrick was all along.

Take the offer and run away. Leave this place; run as far as you can.

And yet he couldn't. The only thing keeping him alive was the Skyhelm Sentinels. There was no way he was about to throw that away.

Was this his one last chance to redeem himself… again? To get it right?

'All right, you win,' he said. 'Let's go.'

He turned to the barman, who was standing as far back in the corner as he could conceal himself. With an apologetic look Merrick fished in his coinpurse for a gold crown. He put it on the bar, hoping it would be enough to cover the damage he and Kaira had caused, then he quickly left the tavern without a word.

The street air made his head spin, but Merrick did his best to keep control of his faculties. As they made their way back to the palace he began to feel a strange sense of guilt and… was it shame? Maybe he was learning after all. He could only hope he'd have a chance to make amends, and in the meantime nothing would go wrong.

TWENTY FOUR

T he mural was hardly ancient, yet the paint was already crumbling and its image had faded in places. It had been rendered hastily over a decade earlier, and not by the most gifted of painters, but Janessa took solace in it, nonetheless.

The depiction of Bakhaus Gate took up an entire wall in one of Skyhelm's many feasting rooms. To the left side of it the Aeslanti were depicted in all their ferocious glory, bedecked in slate grey armour, serrated weapons gleaming, teeth and fangs bared at the enemy. Janessa had to trust the artist's impression that they were so frightening to behold. She had never seen one of the savage beast men of Equ'un and from their depiction on the wall she was sure she never wanted to.

On the right side was an image of her father leading the massed armies of the Free States. The nine flags flew high and proud, carried by heroic looking standard bearers. Beside the king's destrier stood the noble form of the Black Helm, wielding his mighty hammer – the champion of Bakhaus Gate, warrior without peer, Arlor reborn.

If only he were here to aid her now.

Time would tell if Steelhaven was to have new heroes. Men and women of valour on whom she could rely to deliver the city from destruction. Should Arlor see her triumphant, Janessa would be sure to have a more robust depiction of that victory emblazoned on the wall.

'We have one just like it at our keep in Touran.'

Janessa turned around at the voice. In the shadows of the room she could just make out a figure.

As he stepped into the light she let out a sigh of relief.

Leon Magrida smiled, then offered a sweeping bow.

Janessa had wanted to be alone for a while, wanted to take some solace in her father's glorious victories of old, and had told her guard to wait outside. How Leon had slipped past them she had no idea.

Despite his presence being a gross infringement on her security, she returned his bow.

'My lord, you startled me.'

'Apologies, Majesty. I was already in the room when you arrived. I too like to gaze upon our nation's history. It stirs the heart, does it not?'

'Yes,' she replied. 'It certainly does that.'

'Your father was truly an inspiration. As I am sure *you* will be in the coming days of battle.'

'Your words are kind, Lord Magrida. I can only hope to muster a scrap of my father's strength and loyalty in the hard times ahead.'

Leon took a step forwards, looking closer at the mural as though examining it for imperfections, of which there were clearly many.

'He had the foresight to gather about him men of power and wisdom. I imagine you will do the same.' He turned to her and smiled.

Janessa smiled back. Surely he couldn't be suggesting that she choose…

'Fear not, Lord Magrida. I already have wise counsel at my disposal. Loyal men who have the city's best interests at heart.'

'Of that I am sure. But you can never have too many loyal servants at your side.'

Or, apparently, too many preening fops.

'Indeed,' she replied, and took a step away from him before she had realised what she was doing.

'I would be only too happy to put my experience at your disposal,' he said, taking a step towards her and closing the gap she had placed between them.

'Your experience?' she asked.

'Yes, Majesty. I have been trained in lordly manners and the arts of war and culture from an early age.'

Not if your mother's to be believed. She thinks you're a dullard.

'I am sure, Lord Magrida. And should I require your... expertise, I'll be sure to call upon it.' She took another step back.

'Please do.' He smiled, moving forward once more.

She considered him then, standing before her, offering himself in so gracious a manner. He looked almost presentable, his black doublet fastened tight to the throat, his trews tucked into a pair of shiny boots.

Had she somehow underestimated him? Had she judged the man from his poor reputation without giving him the chance to show his true self?

If his mother was to be believed Leon Magrida was a pup not yet fully trained. 'Not a perfect choice,' she had said. But it had turned out that no one was. Not Raelan. Not even River.

Leon would one day be a powerful man, Baron of all Dreldun and Steward of the High Forest. She couldn't go on simply ignoring him. One day, when all this was over, she would have to govern the Free States and repair the damage done by the Khurtas, and she would need every ally she could get. She might not be prepared to marry him, but there was no point in rebuffing the man simply for the sake of it.

'Lord Magrida,' she bowed. 'I thank you for your pledge. I'll be sure to call upon you in the future. Perhaps sooner than you think.'

He smiled his thanks. She had expected a final bow, but instead he took yet another step towards her.

Was he about to try to kiss her? Had she given him the wrong impression?

The door to the feast hall opened, and framed in the light from the room beyond, Janessa could see one of her Sentinels.

'Majesty, your presence is required,' Waldin announced.

Janessa turned to Leon, who, she was relieved to see, had now decided to keep his hands to himself. 'If you'll excuse me, Lord Magrida.'

'Of course, Majesty,' he replied with a bow.

As Janessa left the room she thought she saw something in Leon's eyes – was it disappointment? Regret at a missed opportunity? Did he really want to aid her? Or had he merely wanted to press for her hand in marriage?

Janessa dismissed the thought and followed her Sentinels. There was enough to burden her already without letting Leon Magrida add to those woes.

As they made their way through Skyhelm they were joined by Chancellor Durket, who had been lurking in the corridor like some worrisome troll.

'He says he won't wait any longer,' said Durket, eyes wide with panic.

His distress did nothing to put Janessa at her ease but she hid her discomfort.

'I assume, Chancellor, we're talking about the representative from the Bankers League?'

'Erm… yes, Majesty. Apologies, Majesty, but he is most insistent. Azai Dravos says he wants your answer today or he is leaving the city. I don't even know what the question is, but he seems most keen to have it answered.'

'Very good, Chancellor. Then an answer we will give him.'

But what could she possibly tell him? That yes, she would marry some merchant prince? Or no, she could never offer her hand to such a man? She needed Odaka by her side, now more than ever. Though had he not already told her this was a decision she alone could make?

From Durket's discomfort she had expected Azai Dravos to be in a frothing fit of rage, but instead he stood in the hallway, calmly awaiting her arrival. He even managed a smile as he saw her.

She remembered the last time they had met, and how uncomfortable she had felt under his gaze. This time she would ensure her Sentinels remained close. For his part, Azai Dravos kept a respectable distance, though his own bodyguard, in their robes of red, stood not far from him.

'Azai Dravos,' she said. 'I understand you are eager for your answer?'

The man bowed. 'My apologies, Majesty, but my master, Kalhim, is an impatient man. And perhaps you are not in a position to tarry either?'

'You're right, of course. It seems time is a commodity neither of us can spare.'

She felt Durket squirming beside her, wringing his sweaty hands and moving from foot to foot. It made her want to slap him.

'May I assume your answer is "Yes"?'

Janessa looked at him, at those green eyes and that white smile. What was her answer? Choose yes, and she would have mercenaries to help defend the city, but ultimately it would be a city influenced by a foreign hand. Refuse, and there might indeed be no city to rule.

'I am sorry, Azai Dravos, but the answer is no.'

But then it had to be. Her father had fought to unite the Free States and she was his only heir. She could not betray his legacy by gifting the kingdom he had fought so hard for to a merchant from the Eastern Lands. Had she said yes she may well have gained ten thousand swords but the trust and love of her people would have been washed away into the sea. It wouldn't matter whether Steelhaven was razed or not – she would have given away a kingdom to save a city.

Azai Dravos took a step forward. His smile was gone now. Durket shrank from the man, but Janessa stood her ground, taking strength from the warriors that stood at her shoulders.

'My master will be most disappointed. And he is not a man used to being spurned.'

'I am sure he will accept my decision,' Janessa said. 'Now if you'll excuse me...'

Before she could withdraw Dravos was right in front of her. How he had moved so fast she couldn't tell, almost as though he was possessed of some preternatural speed. Durket and her Sentinels took a step back, taken by surprise, but Janessa was held by that green gaze.

'No!' Dravos demanded. 'You will listen, girl. My master has made an offer you *cannot* refuse. Without his aid you are damned. This city is damned. The unborn child that grows within you is damned.'

How could he know? What witchcraft was this?

Janessa tried to step away but she was locked in place, held by Dravos' piercing eyes.

'I... I cannot...'

But he is a man of wealth and power. A man used to governing a kingdom of his own, if the reputation of the White Moon Trading Company was to be believed. Would it not be a strategic match?

'You will say yes,' demanded Dravos, staring intently into her eyes.

Something shifted inside her, and she again placed a protective hand on her belly.

Janessa knew that she was being manipulated. It was obvious Dravos' charm was not all in his smile. Was he some kind of sorcerer? Was he even now casting some glamour on her?

'No,' Janessa barked, pulling her gaze away and stumbling back.

The spell broken, her Sentinels rushed forward, Janessa watched as they drew their swords and Durket scrambled desperately out of the way of any possible violence.

Azai Dravos did not move as the Sentinels drew on him. Did not move as they advanced. Did not move as one of them raised his sword to strike.

He didn't need to.

There was a flash of red as one of Dravos' bodyguards moved in. He was unarmed and clad in only a simple cloth tunic, but there was no fear in him as he faced the armoured knight. As the sword came down the bodyguard caught the knight's arm, twisting his body and sending the Sentinel crashing to the ground. His fist came down again and again, a bare fist that pummelled the faceplate of the knight's helm, denting it more and more with each swift blow, only stopping when the knight was no longer moving.

By now the second Sentinel had charged in, but two more of Dravos' men had moved to intercept. One swept his leg low, smashing it into the knight's knee and knocking him to the floor. The second kicked out, his heel thudding into the Sentinel's helm and sending him sprawling.

Janessa staggered back, staring at the downed knights. She could hear Durket whimpering somewhere in the shadows, mumbling to himself in fear. Before she could flee, Dravos was in front of her again. He took her arms in his powerful hands and shook her.

'There is no one here to protect you, girl. You have only one option.'

Janessa, desperate to avoid that gaze, turned away from the green eyes, but Dravos slapped her across the face. It was an open-handed blow, strong enough to send her reeling to the ground.

She could taste blood on her lips. The room spun around her and for a moment she was fearful, not for herself but for the life inside her.

What was she to do now? Who would come to her aid?

No one. No one is coming. You have to get out of this yourself, stupid girl. Did you think you would be protected forever? Did you think every knight of legend would come running at your beck and call?

Janessa looked up, seeing a door in front of her and she realised where she was. This was the reliquary chamber, where the Helsbayn was kept on its plinth. If only she could reach that sword she would give good account of herself.

She tried to stand, stumbling towards the door behind which her sword stood. From the corner of her eye she could see Azai Dravos following her.

'Where are you going?' he asked, seeming amused by her defiance. 'There is nowhere to run. You cannot escape me, child.'

Janessa reached the door, pushed it open and fell into the small chamber. On its plinth stood the Helsbayn, the fabled sword that had been wielded by her ancestors in so many victories. Janessa reached out, but before she could grab the blade Dravos had her by the wrist and forced her to look at him.

His touch burned and she refused to cry out in pain but as she was caught in Azai Dravos' baleful gaze she could not turn away.

'Your persistence is admirable, but futile. You will promise yourself and your throne to my master whether you want to or not. You cannot resist. You *must* yield to my will.'

His hand seemed to be searing into Janessa's flesh. His eyes bored into her soul. She wanted to scream but no words would come. The urge to beg for respite was almost overwhelming, but even as the sorcerer's powers tore into her she somehow found the strength to resist.

I will not beg. I will not yield. I would rather die.

Her defiance suddenly seemed to frustrate Dravos, and he frowned in consternation. 'You cannot disobey me. I am an acolyte of the Sha'kadi. A priest of the Black Light of Horas. You will submit to my will.'

'The hells I will!' Janessa screamed, spitting in Dravos' face.

As the spittle ran down his cheek his only response was to look down at Janessa and smile.

She could feel herself weakening, her vision darkening, filling with images of strange horrors. She would never be able to resist and she knew it. Ultimately Dravos would win.

It was too late now. Too late for her, for the city… for her child. No heroes were coming. No one would save her.

The world began to darken, and she wondered if there would ever be light again.

As her mind faded, she seemed to see the image of a man's face… a beautiful face, marred on one side by a crisscross of scars.

She knew him from long ago. It seemed important somehow… but for the life of her she couldn't work out why.

And as the dark began to consume her she realised she no longer cared…

TWENTY FIVE

Mandel Shakurian closed his eyes and listened to the sea crashing against the cliffs. It was a sound that usually filled him with peace and made his troubles seem to fade. But today Mandel remained troubled.

He was a Prince of Keidro Bay, Third Lord of the Serpent Road, Master of Ghulrit Island and High Overseer of the Spice Web. By far the wealthiest of his peers he lived in a coastal manse that was all but unassailable. It sat on the easternmost promontory of the island, looking out towards Dravhistan, and was surrounded by walls reaching forty feet towards the sky. Sheer cliffs made it impossible to reach from the sea, and only a single gate, guarded day and night, allowed access from the land. Mandel Shakurian should have felt secure in his holdfast. But he did not.

His troubles had started weeks before with the news that Bolo Pavitas had been murdered in Steelhaven. Not surprising news in itself, Bolo had always been reckless and his early demise expected, but it had heralded a slaughter never before seen in Keidro Bay.

Five Lords of the Serpent Road lay dead. Five of Mandel's fellows – all men of wealth and power. Pirate kings, surrounded by veritable armies, killed in their homes, on their ships or even in the street. And there was no pattern to the murders; two had been killed silently in the night, the others murdered along with dozens of their guards. The warlord Amon Tugha must have unleashed all the assassins of the Riverlands to cause such mayhem in Keidro Bay, the very place the Lords of the Serpent Road were supposed to be safest.

Curse Amon Tugha to the Underworld, and curse the day the Lords of the Serpent Road had ever entered into a bargain with him. It had seemed a good deal at the time – the pirates would provide a fleet of artillery ships and the men to sail them in return for a supply of prime Teutonian slaves, much sought after in the Eastern Lands since the abolition of the slave trade in the north. Naturally, after the death of Bolo and the loss of all those slaves, the bargain had been annulled… or so they had thought. Now it could not be clearer that Amon Tugha was still determined to have his ships.

'No!' said Mandel aloud, opening his eyes and looking out onto the turbulent sea.

He would never give in to the demands of some Elharim outcast. He was Mandel Shakurian, wealthiest of the Lords of the Serpent Road. He had not reached his dominant status by crumbling at every threat of assassination.

His manse was a virtual fortress, manned by forty of the most savage warriors in the known world. Many had been bought from the fighting pits of Mekkala, with a few from far-flung Kaer'Vahari. He had bolstered their number with enslaved tribesmen bought from the warlord beast-men of Equ'un – these warriors, though scarred and demoralised by their enslavement were yet formidable fighters, and they would obey his every whim.

The other Lords of the Serpent Road had been careless, had not taken the threat seriously enough. Mandel would not make that mistake. He had made himself safe here. There was nothing to fear. Yet still he could not rest.

He breathed deeply, sucking up the sea air and trying his best to put such thoughts away. Something to take his mind off it, perhaps?

Food? Mandel patted his substantial belly. *Perhaps not.*

Whores? But no, not that diversion for the moment. Mandel had more than slaked his thirst for women over the past days of strife. Besides, there was no telling what guise Amon Tugha's assassins might come in. He must be wary of strangers, must keep himself surrounded by men he knew he could trust.

Music perhaps?

Mandel Shakurian relaxed just a little. Of all the pleasures he indulged in there were none he relished so much as music.

He walked to the huge oak cabinet that took up one wall of his chamber. With his heart aflutter he opened the six doors, each intricately carved with scenes of merriment and debauchery. Inside was an array of musical instruments from the four corners of the known world: a harp, from Kaer'Vahari, its frame carved to resemble a swan; war pipes from the snowy wastes of Golgartha, their sound as wicked as the barbarians who had crafted them; a black polished lute reputed to have been played by the Sword King Craetus himself; drums from the tribes of the Aeslanti, said to be made from human hide; and an array of others. Mandel looked at his collection with pride.

As a boy he had been trained in many arts and had become an accomplished musician before moving into the spice trade. But as much as he loved music, he had always loved money more, making it an easy choice to become a merchant rather than a minstrel. Nevertheless, Mandel often still played for the sheer pleasure of it.

He strolled in front of the instruments, wondering which to pick. The lute looked the most attractive to him and he reached out a hand for it.

A loud bell began to ring.

Mandel recognised it instantly – the alarum.

An intruder.

But it couldn't be. Not in his impregnable citadel. Nothing short of an army could break in. It must be some mistake… a false alarm?

Nevertheless, Mandel locked his chamber door and slid across the three bolts that would secure him inside. As he backed away he stared at that door, wondering what was coming from the other side. Whether it would be able to smash its way through. Whether it would simply wait him out.

A scream echoed across the rooftops of the manse.

And the bell stopped ringing.

Mandel looked around him. He had to defend himself. There must be something in his chamber he could use as a weapon. But Mandel Shakurian was no warrior. He had no need for weapons. That's why he surrounded himself with bodyguards. That's what he paid good, honest gold for.

Another scream, followed by voices shrill with panic.

It appeared his good, honest gold might well be going to waste.

Mandel moved to the cabinet, grabbing the black lute by the neck and brandishing it threateningly... or as threateningly as he could manage. He knew he must look pathetic, but the feel of the sturdy wood in his hands reassured him somewhat.

More shouts from outside, the clashing of metal. The scream of someone falling from a great height suddenly cut short by a sickening thud.

He was breathing heavily now and had a sudden urge to piss. This was intolerable, but what was he to do?

Perhaps he could bargain. Perhaps gold would get him out of this. It had always worked before. There was not a man in all the continents of the world who couldn't have his loyalty questioned by the promise of riches. It was how Mandel had risen so high. Bribery had always been his weapon of choice, followed only when necessary by threats of violence and blackmail. It had always worked before.

A thudding at the chamber door made Mandel jump, and he let out a pathetic squeak.

They were here. They had come for him and he had no one to protect him.

Another rap at the door.

Mandel tightened his grip on the lute. He wondered ruefully if this was it; the ending of his song.

'My lord? Are you in there?'

Mandel let out the breath he had been holding at the sound of Dahlen, his equerry.

Another insistent knock. 'My lord? Please let me in.'

Mandel moved forward, then stopped. What if Dahlen was being held at knifepoint? What if the assassins who had invaded Mandel's home were waiting on the other side of the door?

Dahlen knocked again. 'Please, my lord, we must get you out of here.'

'How do I know this isn't a trick?' Mandel asked, trying desperately to subdue the quaking in his voice.

'My lord, please, we don't have time for this. We have to leave while we still have the chance.'

Mandel considered his options. Stay inside until the intruders were able to break down the door, and he was dead. Or, if he opened the door and it was a trick, he was dead.

His only chance was to trust Dahlen.

Mandel slid back the bolts and opened the door, expecting to be faced by murderous assassins.

Dahlen looked fearful – terrified even – but Mandel could have hugged him. At his back were three of the fiercest looking men Mandel had ever seen, but they were *his* men. Loyal to the core. Ready to give their lives for him.

'Come, my lord,' said Dahlen. 'We must hurry.'

Mandel didn't argue, following his equerry out into the corridor. The three bodyguards surrounded them, two at the front, brandishing their swords warily, one at the back, an axe in his ebon-skinned hands.

As they moved through the manse towards the only entrance gate, Mandel was met by an appalling scene. The bodies of his men lay sprawled about the place amongst broken furniture and smashed ornaments. Blood daubed the walls, corpses stared blank-eyed and it was all Mandel could do to avoid their accusatory gaze.

With racing heart, Mandel moved through the house with his men until they reached his feasting hall in the centre of the building. There were no windows here, the only light in the chamber coming from the ornate candelabras that lined the room.

A sudden groan drew Mandel's eyes through the gloom to where one of his guards was propped against the wall. Blood was oozing from the man's mouth, and his hands were holding in a sausage-string pile of entrails that hung from his slit guts.

'We're nearly there, my lord,' said Dahlen, sounding as panicked as Mandel felt. The equerry turned to give a reassuring smile, but instead his eyes widened in terror. Mandel spun round and saw that the bodyguard bringing up their rear was no longer there.

Something cut the air swift as an arrow, and with a clang one of the candelabras tumbled, extinguishing its candles and plunging part of the room into darkness.

The remaining bodyguards brandished their weapons, but found nothing in the shadows. Still Mandel moved up beside Dahlen and the two men clung to each other in fear, at any moment expecting a horde of savage cutthroats to come rushing from the black and hack them to pieces.

Another clang, and a second candelabra fell. The room darkened further. Something moved to Mandel's right and without hesitation one of his bodyguards stepped bravely towards it.

Behind them the second bodyguard grunted and lurched forward, a knife buried in his back.

'Good gods...' cried Mandel, but never got to say more before the final candelabra toppled to the ground, plunging the chamber into total blackness.

Mandel clung to Dahlen for dear life as they stumbled through the dark, towards the far door and the main gate of the manse. And all the while Mandel clutched his lute, feeling his heart beating, wanting to scream, wanting to beg.

Ahead of him Dahlen fumbled in the shadows, a door handle turned, a latch snapped opened and there was sudden light. Mandel all but fell over his equerry in his haste to leave the blackened chamber behind him, and they both staggered out into the reception hall.

Mandel turned, expecting an assassin to come rushing at him from the dark, but it was his last bodyguard who staggered forward through the doorway. A bloody stream welled from a great gash in his throat. He did not walk far. Dahlen screamed with terror as he pulled Mandel after him and across the chamber. The reception hall in Mandel's manse was magnificent to behold, constructed to demonstrate the opulence of his home and the wealth he bore. Marble pillars filled the room, hewn to resemble vast tree trunks with vines twisting about their pure white boughs. The walls were lined with mirrors, making the room seem truly enormous, but Mandel had no time to admire his reflection now. The mirrors only served to multiply the corpses strewn in Mandel's path.

'Almost there, my lord,' Dahlen gasped as they reached the front door of the manse. The equerry fumbled with the ring full of keys at his belt until he found the right one to thrust into the lock. Mandel's fear began to subside with the prospect of escape.

Dahlen flung open the door, revealing the courtyard beyond and the main gate at the far end. It stood open; in its shadow two dead guards lay awkwardly in pools of their own blood. But Mandel made no attempt to run across the courtyard. He stood stock still as he felt the cool metal of a blade press itself to his throat.

As he turned, Dahlen's eyes widened with terror. He could see the assassin and the knife held to his master's throat.

'Dahlen?' said Mandel, though he wasn't exactly sure what he wanted his equerry to do.

Then a voice, so close that Mandel could feel the breath of it on his neck. 'Run away'.

Two simple words in the Teutonian tongue. Dahlen stared for the briefest moment as though he couldn't believe his luck, then he began to move away.

'Dahlen, don't leave me here,' begged Mandel, but his equerry was already stumbling across the courtyard.

'I am truly sorry, master,' he cast over his shoulder as he fled through the gate.

Mandel stared in terror as his 'faithful' equerry abandoned him to his fate.

'Close the door,' whispered the voice.

With his free hand, Mandel pushed the large door of his manse closed. In the other he was still clutching the black wooden lute, though he doubted it would do him any good now.

Once the door was shut, the assassin removed his knife from Mandel's neck. 'Turn around,' he ordered.

Mandel turned slowly, wondering what kind of monster Amon Tugha had unleashed. He was certainly not expecting the youth that faced him. Though his clothes were drenched in the blood of Mandel's men and one side of his face was marred by a crisscross of scars, he was not the beast Mandel had imagined. The assassin was barely more than a boy, his features strong and, despite the scars, handsome. But when Mandel looked into his eyes he saw no mercy there, no remorse. They were eyes that had seen death on a scale Mandel could only dream of and he knew he was staring into the face of his killer.

'Get on with it then,' he said, sick of the waiting. He would not be toyed with, not be made to suffer further. If he was to die it would be on his own terms. He had not risen to such a level of wealth and power by being craven every time he was threatened with death.

The assassin, however, shook his head. 'No, Mandel Shakurian. I have not come here to kill you.'

Then what? You've come round to bandy words over tea and sweetcakes? Because I'm not sure murdering an entire cohort of my bodyguard was quite necessary if you have!

'I don't...'

The assassin fished inside his grey tunic and, in a hand slick with blood, produced a piece of parchment. 'You will sign this,' he said, offering the paper, 'or you will have this.' In his other hand he showed the well-used blade. There was little doubt as to his meaning.

With a quivering hand Mandel reached out and took the dog-eared piece of vellum. He scanned the neat script, written in the Merchant's Cant of the Eastern Lands. It contained the particulars of their original promissory note to Amon Tugha, detailing the fleet of ships they would provide, the mariners set to sail them, the artillery they would transport and the mercenaries to use it. At the bottom of the paper, scrawled in red ink by shaky hands were four other names – the surviving four Lords of the Serpent Road – Lyssa of Tul Shazan, Lord Kurze, Halcion Graal and Javez Al Kadeef. Of the remaining lords, only his signature was missing.

'But...' Mandel didn't know what to say. He had been the first to suggest they stand up to the Elharim tyrant, but it was obvious his fellow lords had all succumbed to the warlord's persuasive messenger.

'You will sign this, or you will have this,' the assassin repeated.

Mandel stared at him, into his young face with those cold eyes that spoke an experience beyond their years. For a fleeting moment he wondered if this was one of Amon Tugha's Elharim assassins, an immortal killer from the far north. Not that it mattered. If this was only a man it was clear he could kill Mandel just as dead as any immortal.

'I have no quill or ink,' Mandel said, for it was obvious he had no choice in this.

In one swift movement the assassin pulled something from his sleeve and stabbed forward. Mandel gave a yelp as it pierced the flesh of his forearm. Then the assassin held the object out before him. It was a long thin needle of metal, one end tapered like a quill and now thickly coated with Mandel's blood.

With a shaking hand Mandel took the metal implement and signed his name on the parchment, noting his own mark was just as spidery as the rest. Once it was done, the assassin took the parchment and quill from him and secured them within his tunic.

'This will not be forgotten,' said the scarred killer. 'Any betrayal will not be forgiven.' Mandel nodded compliantly before the assassin said, 'Turn around.'

Without a word, Mandel obeyed.

He stared at the wood of his front door for what seemed an age. At any moment he expected the assassin to stab him in the back or slit his throat, but no such killing blow was struck. When he found the courage to turn around, the assassin was gone.

Shaking at the knees, Mandel opened his front door, allowing the light of the sun to bathe him, feeling the relief well up inside. He stepped out onto the courtyard, stood amongst the corpses of his bodyguard, and noticed the lute he still held in his hand.

A lot of good it had done him.

He let it fall to the ground with a discordant clang. Then he picked up the fallen blade of one of his guards.

He needed to find his equerry, Dahlen.

Mandel would enjoy teaching him the meaning of loyalty…

TWENTY SIX

Kaira watched as Merrick collapsed on his bunk, still fully clothed. She had been furious. She was *still* furious, but now wasn't the time to sort that out. Merrick began to snore as she donned her armour and strapped her blade to her side.

She had asked Statton and Waldin to stay on duty when it had been hers and Merrick's to carry out. Though Merrick would be of no use she could at least allow one of them some respite. If Garret found out what had happened there would be the hells to pay and no mistake. But Kaira would face any consequences as she faced all things – head on. It had been more important that she find Merrick, to stop him sliding back to his old ways. There was a good man, somewhere in there, but he was prone to bouts of self-pity. Kaira had saved him once, but did not know how often she could keep doing it.

She rushed from the barracks and through the corridors of Skyhelm. By now the queen would be in her bedchamber and with luck Kaira would be able to relieve Waldin or Statton before anyone was the wiser. At this time of night the corridors of the palace were deserted, yet she had a feeling of disquiet. Was it her guilt? She felt as though the ancient tapestries and the grim portraits of kings long dead were looking down at her in judgement. Was she ashamed that she had abandoned her post to find Merrick?

Kaira made her way towards the reliquary, just beneath the upper chambers. On opening the door she saw a sight that made her heart almost stop. Two Sentinels lay on the ground, their helms stoved in. Neither was moving.

She drew her sword and moved forward, suddenly startled to see Chancellor Durket crouched in a corner. Tears streaked his face and he bit down hard on his knuckles as though desperate to suppress his sobs.

Kaira opened her mouth to ask what had occurred, but cursed herself instead as she heard a movement in the shadows to her left. She barely had time to dodge out of the way as the attacker struck.

Kaira ducked the blow and staggered back into the centre of the chamber. Focusing with difficulty in the dim torchlight she could make out four men surrounding her. They wore tunics of red, their faces expressionless, but she still knew their intent. They wanted her dead.

These foreign bodyguards might be unarmed, but they were clearly dangerous: the fallen Sentinels were testament to that, and Kaira had no time to wonder why they had suddenly turned on the knights of Skyhelm. Two rushed her at once and the fighting began.

Kaira's sword swept in low and swift, hacking off a leg at the knee but as the red-clad bodyguard fell she was hit from the side. Despite the armour she wore from neck to foot the strike still shuddered through her entire body as she was knocked aside. There was little time to recover before another warrior leapt at her. Kaira rolled to the left, towards where Durket cowered, as her attacker's foot came down, smashing into the tiled floor and sending shards flying.

Chancellor Durket let out a yelp and scrambled some distance away from the combat, as quickly as his waddling frame would allow.

In an instant Kaira was on her feet, with another assailant rushing towards her. She swung high, but he ducked, impossibly fast, and hit her in the gut. There was a dull thud as her breastplate bent inwards and she was flung back. She lost her footing, falling to one knee, the air driven from her lungs. Whilst on the ground she had just enough time to note the first of Dravos' bodyguards was crawling silently across the chamber in search of his severed leg, before the other three were on her.

She kicked out at one, sending him sprawling back, then rolled aside. Before she could rise to her feet another blow to her shoulder sent her reeling. On instinct she turned, guessing the third assailant would be coming at her.

It paid off, and her sword struck out, piercing his tunic and entering his chest through the ribcage. The warrior stared at her silently, no sign of pain or emotion. Then he grasped her sword by the hilt and pulled it from her grasp as he fell dead.

The last two bodyguards gave her no respite, running in once more as she stood unarmed. Kaira knew well the fighting arts, but whether she would be a match for these devils was another matter.

One struck in with sequence of lightning fast punches. It was all Kaira could do to duck and dodge them. She twisted away, but found herself backed up against a pillar. The second guard came from nowhere, his arm moving almost too fast to see. Kaira danced out of range just in time, and the warrior's fist smashed into the pillar, cracking the masonry.

Kaira brought her armoured foot down against his knee, driving him to the ground, then twisted her fingers in his hair and smashed his head into the pillar twice in quick succession. It was enough to drop him, but Kaira scarcely had a chance to revel in her victory before the final guard struck in with a flat palmed strike. His blow deflected off her gorget, catching her cheek and sending her off balance. It was like being hit with a warhammer, and only by the grace of Vorena did it not take her head off her shoulders.

She staggered, raising her arms to parry a kick which knocked her backwards. Her foot hit something and she stumbled, falling on her backside. She just had time to register she had tripped over one of the prone Sentinels, before the last warrior leapt at her, his foot aimed for the kill.

Kaira reached out, her hand grasping one of the fallen blades, then she rolled, swinging the sword round in an arc as she rose, praying silently that her aim was true.

The body hit the ground with a thump as its head bounced across the reliquary floor.

Kaira took a breath, surveying the scene of carnage, before walking purposefully to the last of the bodyguards, who had by now reached his severed leg and was staring at it with mute fixation.

Her execution blow was swift and final.

'Impressive,' said a voice, though it sounded far from impressed.

Kaira turned to see Azai Dravos standing at the edge of the chamber. On her knees at his side was Queen Janessa and Kaira tightened her grip on the sword held at her side.

'What is the meaning of this?' she demanded as she took a step towards him. 'Have you gone mad? That is the queen of the Free States.'

Azai Dravos glanced down at Janessa and smiled. 'Not anymore,' he said. 'Now she is *my* queen.'

'Daemon!' Kaira spat, raising her weapon and advancing on him. But as she glared with hate at the man she suddenly slowed. Caught in those green eyes of his, Kaira no longer wanted to do him harm. In fact she found herself feeling better disposed to him with every passing breath.

'Not quite a daemon,' said Dravos. 'But I do have certain talents. Talents that have allowed me to break your young queen's spirit. I would have preferred to persuade her the old fashioned way. I find coercion so much less stressful to my faculties, but it appears she is strong willed. Though, not quite strong willed enough. She is with child, you know. And out of wedlock.' He shook his head admonishingly. 'I imagine that would normally cause all kinds of problems, but I have a solution to that particular quandary don't I, my dear.'

He patted Janessa affectionately on the head. For such an insult Kaira should have run the bastard through, but instead she lowered her sword to her side.

This was witchcraft, pure and simple. This man was a sorcerer of some considerable power and he now had her under his spell as well as the queen. There was little Kaira could do.

Or was there? Could she dig deep for the strength to resist him? Could she call on powers that were greater than his?

'You will never get away with this,' Kaira said.

For I am the spear hand of Vorena.

Dravos only smiled. 'Oh, but I already have. You see she is quite under my spell. As are you. But don't feel bad. You won't suffer for long.'

She is my courage in the darkness. A bright flame. A beacon for the lost.

Kaira felt her hand loosen on the blade until finally she let it fall, clattering to the floor. Dravos walked forward, staring all the while with those green eyes. She was forced to return the gaze, no longer be in control of her body, but there was some part of her mind still free.

In her service I am resolute of thought and purpose.

From his robes, Dravos pulled a wickedly curved dagger. 'It seems such a waste,' he said holding it up. 'But it will cost me dearly to keep your queen in check. I can hardly go about controlling the both of you. It's a very complicated business, but I won't bore you with the details.'

A defender of the weak, an instrument of righteousness honed and tempered in battle, ready to strike down the enemies of my gods and my king.

Dravos ran the blade down her cheek, and Kaira was powerless to stop it. She could feel a trickle of blood run down to her chin, dripping onto her gorget.

In that moment she knew her death was imminent, and she summoned up the will for one last defiant act.

'Vorena is strength,' she spat.

Azai Dravos raised his eyebrows, then burst out laughing.

And for the briefest of moments his eyes blinked.

Kaira's fist snapped out, hitting him square in the face and bursting his nose. He fell onto his back and she didn't hesitate, stooping to pick up the fallen sword and raising it for a killing blow. As it swept down to cut Dravos in two he mumbled something beneath his breath. In a burst of green dust he was gone, just as her blade struck the empty floor.

The sword was still ringing in her grip as Kaira stared, unable to believe what she had just seen. Then something struck her from behind. It was a swift blow, quick but not deep, as Dravos' dagger found a gap in her armour between breastplate and tasset. Though the cut in her hip wasn't deep, the shock of it made Kaira cry out. She swung her sword around, but Dravos had disappeared once more, green dust the only thing to signify he had been there.

On her guard now, Kaira waited for him to reappear. This was devilry of the most heinous kind. Dravos had to be destroyed and at the first sign of him she would strike.

A figure flashed green in front of her, but before she could react Kaira felt a cut between vambrace and gauntlet. This time it was deep, striking across the back of her wrist and causing her to drop her blade once more. Before she could stoop to pick it up, Dravos appeared once more, to slice his curved blade across the back of her knee.

Kaira growled in pain, falling to the ground. This time Dravos did not disappear in a cloud of green smoke but stood staring down at her. She tried to move, tried to grab him, but with her wrist slashed and her leg wounded she could not even stand.

'Brave indeed,' said Dravos. 'But futile.'

Holding her once more with that green gaze, he stepped forward brandishing his dagger.

'Your death will be swift,' he said, reaching towards her throat with his dagger. 'I will allow you that mercy. And who knows, perhaps one day they will build a statue in your hon—'

A foot of steel burst from Dravos' chest. The green light in his eyes paled and a look of confusion crossed his face.

At once the glamour was broken, and Kaira could see someone standing behind him. Someone brandishing the sacred sword – the Helsbayn.

In a single swift move, Janessa pulled the blade from Dravos' back and swung hard, slicing his head from his shoulders with ease. Body and head toppled to the ground.

For a long moment the queen stared down at the sorcerer, hate in her eyes, then she spat on his body.

Her shoulders suddenly sagged, and Janessa fell to her knees beside Kaira.

'I'm sorry,' she said. 'I'm sorry.'

It pained Kaira to hear the words.

'No,' she replied. 'This is my fault. Majesty, forgive me.'

Somewhere in the background, Durket managed to heave himself to his feet and scramble off as fast as his girth would allow.

'What he said was true,' sobbed Janessa. 'I am with child. I am lost.'

Janessa's tears were coming fast now, her sobs heavy and yet she still clung to the hilt of the Helsbayn.

Kaira gently took the sword from her grip. There should have been some propriety, some boundary of respect, but Kaira saw only a girl now, not a queen. A child whose life had been threatened, and not for the first time. A young woman who not only carried the weight of a kingdom, but also an unborn child, and with no mother, father or husband to help her carry her burden.

Despite the pain in her wrist, her face, her knee, Kaira put her arms around Janessa and held her close.

'You are not lost, child. I am here.'

She held Janessa there until Odaka eventually came rushing into the reliquary, accompanied by a dozen Sentinels. He surveyed the corpses within the chamber for the briefest of moments, then knelt beside the queen.

'Majesty, Chancellor Durket told me what happened. I am truly sorry; I should have predicted something like this. I should have been here.'

Janessa wiped her eyes then climbed to her feet. 'No, Odaka. The blame is mine.'

Kaira struggled to her feet too, helped by two of her brother Sentinels. 'I apologise, Odaka. I should have been by her Majesty's side. The blame for this is entirely mine.'

Odaka regarded the corpses of Dravos and his men. 'It seems you were here just in time. Your wounds require attention. I will see that this mess is cleared up.'

As the Sentinels helped her from the reliquary, Kaira cast one last look at Statton and Waldin, lying silent and still on the ground. They had been serving here because of her dereliction of duty, and the burden of that suddenly stung as deeply than the cuts to her flesh.

Back at the barracks the palace surgeon tended her wounds. Kaira said nothing as her wrist, knee and thigh were bound and the cut to her face was cleaned. None of the wounds was particularly deep, though she would be useless with a sword for a few days, and could well be limping a while longer. Nonetheless, she was desperate to fulfil her duties.

She had let down Queen Janessa. Whilst trying to save Merrick from himself.

Well, no more. Kaira had risked enough pandering to the man's moods and remorse. She had failed miserably in her duty to others. From now on Merrick Ryder could look after himself.

As she had expected, once dawn broke she and Merrick were summoned by Captain Garret. He was seething with rage.

'Well?' he said. 'Where were you? It was supposed to be you two on duty.'

Merrick glanced toward her. She knew she should have confessed, but somehow she still felt loyal to him.

'It was my fault,' Kaira began. 'I should—'

'No,' said Merrick. 'It was my fault. I left the barracks and Kaira came to find me. I was getting—'

'Enough!' Garret interrupted. 'I don't want to hear it. It doesn't matter anyway. If I weren't so short of men I'd have you both flogged and thrown on the streets. And you.' Garret was standing in front of Merrick now, their noses almost touching. 'I've been far too lenient with you. I let you treat this like a fucking country jaunt and you've taken the piss once too often. You need to think, lad. Think whether you want to stay or not, and if you don't you can be on your merry way.'

'I do want to stay,' Merrick replied without hesitation. 'I know that now. I have a duty to perform. Now more than ever.'

This seemed to calm Garret somewhat. 'Very well. But that's your last chance.' He waved his hand. 'You're both dismissed.'

'Waldin and Statton?' Kaira asked, before they left. 'How are they?'

Garret looked grave. 'Waldin hasn't regained consciousness.' Then he paused, as if unable to say more.

'And Statton?'

Garret merely shook his head.

Kaira clenched her fists as she turned to leave. They walked back across the courtyard and Merrick began to speak.

'Look, I'm sorry—'

'Save it,' she snapped. 'I'm not interested.'

'But—'

She rounded on him, her fists balled, ready to fight him again, despite the aches and pains that wracked her body.

'We are finished, Ryder. Garret is giving us a last chance to redeem our honour. Together we will carry out our duties to protect the queen. Other than that, you do not exist to me. Is that understood?'

She left him standing in the courtyard without waiting for a reply.

TWENTY SEVEN

Magistra Gelredida hadn't seemed at all perturbed by Waylian's setbacks on the streets of Northgate. It was almost as though she'd expected it. But instead of scolding him for his incompetence, she merely gave him another task to do.

He'd told her about the orphanage and the children forced into labour by Fletcher. She'd seemed unconcerned by their plight and more interested in Milius the apothecary. Waylian had been dreading telling her what happened; that he'd fled into the night rather than be murdered by some bastard poisoner, but it was as though she knew what would happen.

'Never mind,' she'd said. 'These things are to be expected.'

These things are to be expected?

A few short weeks ago, had Waylian told the Red Witch he had failed in one of her assigned errands, he would have been on privy duty for a month. He was beginning to wonder who this woman was he'd found on his return from the Kriega Mountains. She showed tolerance, understanding, and was even measured in her assessment of him.

But then, Waylian had changed as well. He was stronger, more determined... brave even? With the coming of war everyone had to change. Perhaps Gelredida had changed most of all.

This was a perilous time and if she did not find some way of persuading the Archmasters to join in the fight then the city might well be lost. How

Waylian was helping with any of this was a mystery, but who was he to argue with the Magistra?

He sat at his desk. It was an all too brief respite before he was to be sent out on his next task, and Waylian coveted every moment to himself. On the desk was a book and a piece of parchment. He fingered the small square of paper, looking at the addresses written there. Gelredida had told him this was his next task – travel to the Trades Quarter, find Josiah Klumm and take him to the safe house written on the reverse of the note.

What could be simpler?

Waylian had a feeling *anything* could be bloody simpler. The tasks given by his mistress were never as straightforward as they first seemed and often put him in grave peril. If he admitted it to himself though, Waylian was starting to quite enjoy the danger.

Yes, he'd whined and moaned when he thought he was going to be eaten alive by some mountain beast, but who wouldn't? Looking back on it, he had felt no small thrill in those mountains. A thrill at least the equal of that day in the Chapel of Ghouls.

Waylian was important now. He mattered and he was doing something good, something valuable. Even if he didn't exactly know how or why.

He looked back at his desk and the thick tome that lay open on it. The script written on the pages in thick black ink was neat, some of its syntax archaic, but Waylian found himself understanding the gist more readily than any other book he'd had to read. *Authority of the Voice* it was called. No esoteric title, not even the name of its writer emblazoned on the front in silver leaf.

It contained entire chapters on how to break the Veil and tap into the magick that could unleash vast cosmic power with a word. Waylian was only too interested in what it could teach him. By unveiling the secrets of this tome he could turn men's minds. Shatter their sanity. Bend their will to his every whim. With a word he would be able to wither plants, change the weather or send messages with the birds.

The thought excited him more than he could express, but Waylian didn't think for a moment that he was close to being able to bring down the heavens with a whisper. For now he would have to satisfy himself with something easy.

In front of him on his desk was a little mirror. Waylian had never been a huge fan of his reflection, though in recent days he wasn't quite as dissatisfied as he used to be. Nevertheless, it didn't stop him trying to shatter it with a word.

Since the Chapel of Ghouls, since the day he had defeated Rembram Thule, he had wanted to recapture the power he'd felt. A single word, a word he couldn't remember, had saved his life that day.

Gelredida had suggested he read up on the talent, rather than practise it, but Waylian knew that soon he might need the powers of magick once more. His life might depend upon it. He couldn't very well face the Khurtas with nothing more than a frown and garlic-flavoured breath.

After much study, Waylian had found the word he wanted in the book. *Avaggdu* was the destroying word. It was used to trick the Veil into transforming inanimate objects. Into smashing them or twisting them or turning them into something else. Considering the potential dangers, Waylian thought it best to start with something small.

He said the word, while staring into the mirror.

'Avaggdu!'

All the mirror did was stare back.

Well, what were you expecting on the first go?

'Avaggdu,' he said again. This time more forcefully. This time with a different inflection.

Still nothing.

The instructions within the book had said it was nothing to do with emotion or need, but proficiency with the Channeler's Art, whatever that bloody meant. Clearly he needed more practice, but then how had he managed to manifest the ability when he'd been about to die? It couldn't have just been coincidence, could it? Surely there must have been some emotional connection, something to do with his fear?

He stared at his reflection again. 'Avaggdu,' he repeated, this time trying to do it without thought or feeling.

Still nothing, but this time on saying the word there was a strange feeling of nausea in his stomach. Rather than fight it, Waylian let it grow in his belly. It was uncomfortable for sure, yet not wholly unpleasant.

'Avaggdu,' he said again.

This time as he stared at his reflection a bead of blood blossomed from his eye. The mirror bowed, bending his image, twisting it into something foul.

There was a bang at his chamber door.

Waylian jumped, quickly raising his sleeve to dab away the blood on his face. The feeling of nausea abated only to be replaced by one of revulsion at what he had done. This wasn't right. There was an overwhelming sense of wrongness about the whole thing, but then wasn't that what magick was all about?

Another rap at the door. Someone was insistent.

'Coming,' he said, rising from his desk and moving to the door.

He opened it, half expecting Gelredida come with another task for him, so the two men who stood there were something of a surprise.

The first one Waylian recognised. He was short, with a mop of grey curly hair. Nero Laius had an open and friendly smile, so unlike most of the other Archmasters.

'Hello, Waylian,' said the Master Diviner. 'May we come in?'

'Yes,' Waylian replied, stepping aside and allowing the two men to enter his chamber.

The second figure had to stoop below the lintel as he entered, his black armoured shoulders almost touching each side of the doorframe. He held his helmet in the crook of his arm, revealing a stern face topped with a shock of short white hair. As he strode by his eyes surveyed Waylian, then the desk, his bed, the window, the ceiling – scanning the room as though for any sign of danger.

'You've met Marshal Ferenz, of course.'

Waylian tried to swallow but he found his throat was drying up with each passing moment. 'Er… no, I don't think I've had the pleasure.' The man didn't offer a hand to shake, and Waylian wasn't about to offer his own. Of course he had heard of the Marshal of the Raven Knights, but thankfully never had the need to speak with him.

'Please sit down, Waylian,' Nero said, sitting himself in the chair beside Waylian's desk.

The only place left was his bed, and Waylian obediently sat on it. His feather mattress had never felt so uncomfortable. For his part, Marshal Ferenz stood in front of the door and glared.

'Er… what can I do for you, Archmaster?'

Nero smiled at that, as though Waylian had just made a joke. Ferenz didn't seem to find it particularly funny.

'It's more about what *I* can do for *you*, Waylian,' Nero replied.

Waylian's eyes flitted from Nero to Ferenz, from the amiable to the imposing. 'I don't understand, Archmaster.'

'Oh, come now, young Waylian. Surely Magistra Gelredida has told you what an interest the Crucible had taken in you? It's common knowledge you're a student with great potential. A talented prospect for the future.'

'Er… no. She's not mentioned it.'

Nero looked shocked. 'I can't believe she would keep such a thing to herself. But then she's never really seen eye to eye with the Crucible, has she Ferenz?' The Marshal of the Raven Knights shook his granite head. 'Well, if she's not told you what promise you've shown these past weeks, please allow me to rectify the situation. Word is you're a student of great diligence, admired by your peers and tutors alike. You helped defeat a great evil at the Chapel of Ghouls, one that might have destroyed us all. You've travelled north to the Kriega Mountains taking word to the Wyvern Guard so that they might travel in defence of the city, at great risk to your person. Overcome much adversity, risked your life for the innocent citizens of the Free States. You're a hero, Waylian, and it's about time you were recognised as such.'

'Thank you,' said Waylian, doubtfully. 'But I'm sure Magistra Gelredida appreciates me in her own way.'

'Oh, I'm sure she does. That's why she's got you traipsing halfway across the city on this errand or that.'

How could he know about that? Waylian's tasks for the Magistra were supposed to be kept secret.

'They're not so much errands…' said Waylian, desperate to cover his tracks. 'Come now, Waylian.' Nero sat forward in his chair, those little eyes of his holding Waylian in their steely glare. 'I am the Keeper of the Ravens. Master of Divination. There is nothing that happens in the Tower of Magisters, or indeed the city, which I do not know about. Isn't that right, Ferenz?'

The Marshal of the Raven Knights nodded his head, his eyes glaring at Waylian all the while.

'I can assure you, Archmaster, there is nothing untoward—'

Nero held up his hands, and Waylian stopped.

'I'm sure there isn't, Waylian. I'm sure it's all completely innocent. Harmless chores for your mistress. But then… what if it isn't?'

'I don't understand,' Waylian said. But part of him did understand. Part of him knew exactly what Nero was talking about.

'You're loyal, and that's to be admired. In fact it's one of the reasons you're so well thought of amongst the Archmasters. But sometimes blind loyalty can be used against you. Isn't that right Ferenz?' The Marshal made no move to reply. 'Sometimes you lose focus. Sometimes by the time you realise what has happened you're in far too deep to get yourself out again. Do you get my meaning?'

Waylian nodded, even though he wasn't exactly sure he did. Was Nero suggesting Gelredida was putting him in danger? He already knew that, but it was for the good of the city. Wasn't it?

'I understand, Archmaster. But I can assure you I've just been sent out on a few harmless tasks. Nothing that need concern you or the other Archmasters.'

'Of course,' Nero replied. 'But how long do you think these "tasks" will remain harmless? You're not the first apprentice Gelredida has sent running off to do her bidding. She's had apprentices do her dirty work before and it rarely ends well for them, does it, Ferenz?' The Marshal shook his huge head. 'I'm only thinking of you, Waylian. Which is why I'd like us to be friends. It's why I'd like you to work for me.'

'I… I don't… I can't…'

'Oh, but you can.' That smile again. A smile that seemed to put Waylian at his ease. What was it with this man? 'Gelredida is in her twilight years. Her sky is darkening, whereas mine is just beginning to grow bright. Do you want to align yourself with the future, or be dragged down by the past?'

'I… er…'

'You have great things ahead of you, Waylian. You will have powerful friends. Don't be blinded by your loyalty to one old woman. She is a danger to you. A danger to us, to everyone. You must not let her destroy you as she has done so many others.

'No… I can't…'

'Yes, you can, Waylian. You must.' He was locked in that gaze now. Those eyes boring into him. Soothing him yet compelling him all at once.

Nero was right – Gelredida was the past. If Waylian ever wanted to make anything of himself he had to side with the Archmasters.

You're being used, Grimmy. By Gelredida, by Nero, by everyone. You're a useless pawn in a shitty game. Stand up for yourself for once you spineless son of a…

'No,' Waylian replied. 'I'm sorry, Archmaster, but I just can't help you.'

Nero sat back in the chair, a look of dissatisfaction clouding his once-smiling face. 'That's unsatisfactory, Waylian. Very unsatisfactory indeed. I thought we could be friends. I thought we could help one another, but obviously that's not the case. Marshal, please explain how important it is that Waylian does as we ask.'

Ferenz took a clanking step forward, massive in his black armour; each plate intricately crafted to resemble a raven's wing. He stared down at Waylian, his face looking as if it had been hewn from stone with a daemonic chisel.

'Listen here, you little shit,' he said, as though barking at soldiers on the parade ground. 'We don't have time to fuck around with the likes of you.' He leaned over Waylian, his chin jutting forward, the veins in his neck straining against the muscular flesh. 'The Archmaster has made you a very generous offer. More generous than I'd ever give the likes of you. It would serve you well to accept it.'

'I… er… yes but…'

Nero had come to stand beside Ferenz now. The Raven Knight towered over him, but Waylian was somehow more afraid of the Archmaster than he was of the imposing warrior.

'Don't make this difficult, Waylian. There is only one way this will end if you do. Don't make me have to force you.'

That strange feeling was creeping back into Waylian's gut. The feeling he'd had whilst trying out his words of power. A wave of nausea engulfed him.

Was this fear? Was he even gaining some kind of masochistic thrill from this? What the fuck was wrong with him? Something was boiling inside. Something was stirring like molten iron in the pit of his stomach.

'*No!*' he bellowed, rising to his feet.

To his surprise, Ferenz and Nero each stepped back, the Raven Knight almost backing up to the chamber door. Nero regarded him with a furrowed brow, but he seemed more confused than angered.

The two men glanced at one another, unsure what to do next since it was clear their attempts at intimidation had failed.

'That's most disappointing, Waylian,' Nero said finally. His voice was quiet, almost weak sounding. 'But if that's how you feel, there's nothing we can do, is there Marshal?'

Ferenz shook his head, his confidence clearly reduced.

Waylian didn't quite know what to say as Nero fumbled at the door handle. Ferenz just looked on with confusion as Nero finally opened the door and they both left, slamming the door behind them.

As soon as they'd gone Waylian walked to his desk and sat down. His heart was drumming against his chest and he looked down to see his hands were shaking.

Should he tell the Magistra about this? That he'd been approached by one of the Archmasters and told to betray her? She had enough on her plate to deal with right now. The last thing she needed was Waylian burdening her with yet more problems. And he'd handled it well enough, hadn't he? Told those two exactly where he stood?

That creeping sense of nausea was still filling his stomach and Waylian looked down at the book.

Authority of the Voice.

Had he just manifested some kind of magick?

That was an Archmaster and the marshal of the Raven Knights. If they'd wanted to beat you around your bedchamber until you bled and then make you thank them for it, they could have done.

Couldn't they?

Waylian looked into his little mirror. What he saw made him cry out in shock and stagger back, tipping his chair over.

The glass in the frame was cracked, the mirror now resembling a spider's web.

No, this couldn't be. Was he finally getting it? Was he beginning to learn his Art?

His stomach turned. The knotted feeling in his belly twisted. Waylian was struck with the sudden and uncontrollable urge to shit.

He barely managed to unlace his britches and grab his bedpan before his back end opened up in a flood. Waylian squatted, holding his arse cheeks open as the watery contents of his stomach splashed the pan. By the time he was done it was all he could do to lie on his chamber floor surrounded by stinking brown water.

As Waylian lay there, one thing seemed to be quite evident – if he was beginning to learn his Art, he was more than suffering for it.

TWENTY EIGHT

The revelry had gone on for three days. Friedrik had laid on wine and ale to apologise to his guests. Something to do with the dogfight not turning out quite the way he'd planned.

Rag had no idea what had gone on down in that cellar and she was none too keen to find out. She'd spent the last three days keeping her head down while people fucked and fought in every corner of the tavern. She'd never seen anything quite like it before. Of course she knew what happened late at night on street corners. She'd lived long enough to see some dirty things, but this was very different.

People were going at it three or four at once, men and women sometimes not caring what was stuck where or in who. As everyone got drunker and drunker it just got worse and worse. Part of Rag wanted to run away, as far as she could. The other part, that curious little part she could never quite get rid of, wanted to stay and watch, no matter how sickening it got.

In the end people started to wander off and the crowd thinned out a bit. Rag had no idea who the people left were, but they must have been in Friedrik's good books. Wasn't often he extended a welcome like this. Wasn't often he extended a welcome at all unless he saw something in it for himself.

When there were only around a dozen people left in the tavern, the rest of Friedrik's lads turned up. No sooner had they arrived than Yarrick and Essen went about tidying the place like they were housemaids or something. Neither of them looked particularly happy about it but they didn't complain. But then nobody ever complained when Friedrik told them to do something. Harkas just stood around looking scary and Shirl moped in a corner. He looked a lot better than when Rag had last seen him, but he still looked like someone had kicked the shit out of him and no mistake.

'You all right?' Rag asked as he limped in and sat himself in a chair all gentle like.

'I'll live,' Shirl replied.

Before she could ask more, Friedrik walked out of the kitchens, chewing on something cook had made. The smell of food wafted out and Rag felt her stomach grumbling.

'Right, I have things to do,' said Friedrik. 'You'll keep the rest of my guests entertained until they're ready to leave, won't you, Rag?'

She nodded, though what he meant by 'entertained' she had no idea. Looked like they were making their own entertainment to her.

'The rest of you make sure this place is cleaned up by the time I get back.' Yarrick looked up from his sweeping and Essen mumbled his agreement as he grabbed a handful of tankards.

Friedrik walked out of the tavern. Where he was going at this time of night, and with no bodyguards, Rag had no idea, but then she weren't going to ask.

She was more concerned about what they'd done to the bloke in the cellar.

Surely Nobul, or Lincon, or whatever his bloody name, was dead by now. Still, there was a niggling little voice at the back of her head telling her he might not be. There was only one way to find out, she supposed.

When no one was looking at her she moved to the back of the tavern. The cellar door was open and it was black as the hells down there. A couple of candles were burning on a shelf, and Rag took one in each hand before taking the stairs down. The candlelight didn't pierce very far into the dark, but it was enough for Rag to see by, and she remembered the layout well enough to not trip over anything. That was the last thing she wanted down here.

It didn't take her long to find him, and when she did part of her wished she'd not come down here at all. He was still chained to that same post next to the pit. His head lolled forward, his clothes torn, his hair matted with blood.

Rag moved towards him, wary of what she'd find. She was half scared he'd be dead, half scared he was still alive. Maybe it would be a mercy if he weren't breathing.

Gently she placed the candles down by his legs and crept forward, stooping low. His chest was moving in a shallow rhythm, breath coming all ragged.

'Nobul?' she said.

At first he didn't move and she thought maybe he hadn't heard, but then he slowly lifted his head. His face was a mess, blood crusted on his nose and lips, one eyeball all red where the other was white, and one of his ears had the bottom torn off.

She didn't know what to say. Didn't know what to do.

And then he smiled.

Blood was all stuck to his teeth and gums and it looked like someone had used his face to hammer in a nail, but still he smiled at her.

Rag shook her head, feeling the tears coming at what they'd done to the man who'd saved her life those weeks back.

'Sorry,' was all she could think to say. Not that it was her fault, but part of her still felt responsible. She should have tried to get him out of here when she had the chance. But then how could she have?

'Ain't your fault,' he said.

'I should have tried to help you.'

Nobul shook his head. 'This is nothing to do with you, lass. Why would you risk yourself for me?'

She moved closer. 'It's me. Rag. Don't you recognise me?'

He looked at her, his eyes tracing the features of her face. 'Don't reckon I do. Should I?'

'Few weeks back you got me out of the shit. Bloke was gonna kill me and you came along with your Greencoat pals and did for him.'

As she spoke she saw recognition dawn on his face. His eyes widened, then he smiled again like they were old friends meeting up after a long time apart.

'You're the girl that disappeared. Took that fella's head with you too, if there's any truth to the rumour.'

Rag was hit with a sudden bite of shame. Yes, she'd taken that head – it was her ticket into the Guild. How different would things have been if she'd just left it there?

'I… There were reasons for that. It weren't as strange as it might have seemed.'

'Well,' said Nobul. 'I reckon you did what you did because you had to. And it wasn't like that bastard didn't deserve it.'

'Yeah, he did. But this has all turned to shit. I'm not one of them,' she gestured back up the cellar door, hoping Nobul would get the gist of who she meant. 'I don't even want to be here.'

'You and me both,' said Nobul. 'But we can't always get what we want. Take my advice, lass, and run away. Far away. As far as you can get and don't look back.'

That was always an option. But then, where would she run? She'd just be on the streets again, only in a city she didn't know.

'I can't go. There's things I have to do here first. People I have to see about. Responsibilities.'

But was there? Yes, she'd made a pact with that woman Kaira, saying she'd bring Friedrik to her. Then again, she didn't owe that woman nothing.

There was other people, though – Chirpy, Migs, Tidge – people she cared about, people she was liable for. They had to be looked after and she'd promised herself she would.

'Nothing wrong with responsibility,' Nobul said. 'You just got to pick the right people to be responsible for. Those people worth it?'

'Yes,' she replied. 'They are.'

'You gotta think about yourself as well though, lass. You're a survivor and no mistake, but sooner or later you're gonna have to look out for yourself.'

She nodded at that. He was right: she did have to look out for herself. And she might have to do some more pretty shameful things to survive. But she had to live with herself too, and that would always be the hardest part.

Rag had done some things she struggled to live with. From now on she was gonna try to make sure she made it easy for herself.

She moved to the post Nobul was leaning up against and checked the chains that bound him. His wrists were manacled. There had to be a key somewhere.

'I'll be back soon,' she said, standing up and heading back to the stairs, leaving the candles beside him.

She climbed out, squinting in the light. In the tavern the fire was burning bright, one of the lads must have chucked a load of logs on it while she was down in the cellar.

There were still a dozen of Friedrik's 'guests' lounging around, and Yarrick and Essen were busy tidying, with Shirl and Harkas looking on.

Rag walked up and grabbed the broom from Essen's hand. 'You lads might as well get off,' she said. 'I'll finish up here, no point us all hanging round, is there?'

Yarrick looked at Essen, then back at Rag. 'But Friedrik said—'

'Friedrik told me to look after this lot, not you. It's all right. Not much left to do round here.' The lads looked at each other like they wanted to go, but thought they might take a beating like Shirl had got. 'What? You lot not got places to be?'

Again Yarrick looked to Essen and this time they both shrugged at one another.

'Cheers, Rag,' said Essen. 'Owe you one.'

With a wink they set off for the door. Seeing them leave, Shirl struggled to his feet and followed. Only Harkas remained.

Rag tried to ignore him, carrying on with the sweeping like he wasn't there, but she could see he was staring at her while she worked. Did he know that she was up to no good?

She stopped and looked up at him. Despite his grim expression, she smiled. 'You can go as well you know. Not gonna be any trouble now is there? Look at them.' She gestured around at the bodies heaped around the tavern in various states of undress.

Harkas kept staring at her, and for all her fear she stared back, that smile still on her face. For a moment, it looked like Harkas was going to speak, but then, without a word, he walked out of the tavern.

Rag let out a sigh as the door closed behind him, then she propped the broom up against the bar.

Now where's this bloody key?

If Friedrik had it on him, and there was every chance he did, she'd have no chance of getting Nobul out. But maybe he'd left it with one of this lot.

Rag padded quietly around the room. Most of the bodies lying in the shadows she didn't recognise. Men and women were tangled together in a mass of flesh, the stink of sex and booze wafting off them. Some of the searching was easy, since there was clothes discarded all over the place, but no matter how many pairs of britches she rifled though, there was still no key. Just when she was starting to think she'd have to search through every slumbering body she saw a face she recognised.

He was lying in the corner, a wine bottle in his hand. She remembered him from when they'd first brought Nobul into the tavern. His mouth was shut, but Rag knew inside that snoring gob of his the front teeth were missing. It was this one that had chained Nobul up in the first place. Her heart started to beat a bit faster.

She knelt beside him, taking a quick look around the room to make sure no one was watching, then reached for his belt. He was breathing even enough, snoring heavily, and from the look of the half empty bottle of wine beside him he wasn't gonna wake any time soon. There was a knife at his belt and beside it a pouch for coins. Deftly Rag unbuckled the pouch and fished inside. She let the few coppers in there slip through her finger until she found what she was looking for. When she pulled the key out she almost shouted with glee.

As she stood, the bloke snorted in his sleep, the bottle slipping from his grasp and clattering to the floorboards. It rolled along, spilling its load as it went, and Rag froze where she stood, waiting for everyone to leap up and catch her in the act.

No one moved.

Rag made her way back to the cellar as quiet as she could, her heart cracking along at a gallop. Something was telling her this was madness. That she'd given her loyalty to the Guild. That this was betrayal, plain and simple, and she'd suffer for it in the end. But Rag had already betrayed Friedrik. What difference would this make?

When she made her way down into the cellar, one of the candles had gone out. By the light of the remaining one she moved behind Nobul and slid the key into the lock of his manacles. There was a satisfying click as they opened up.

The chains fell to the floor and Rag moved round to the front. Nobul was still sitting there, head lolling.

'You need to run now,' he whispered, before she could give him a shake to see if he was conscious.

'I need to run?' she said. 'Think you're the one should be doing the running, mate.'

'No,' Nobul said, using the post to pull himself to his feet, lifting his big bulk from the ground like a mountain rising up from the earth. '*You* need to run. Because when I get myself together, I'm gonna go up those stairs and kill every fucker in this building.' He turned to her then, and fixed her with a look she'd remember till her last breath. 'If you're still here, you'll probably end up dead with them.'

Rag looked at him and saw that he didn't look half dead no more. There was an evil light in his eyes, the nastiest twinkle she'd ever seen. She knew he meant what he said.

Without another word she turned and ran for the stairs. She didn't care about making noise now, just about running. When she got up the top it crossed her mind to warn the people left inside – to tell them there was a madman on his way and they should get themselves out.

But they'd made their own beds. They'd come along at Friedrik's say-so and they'd drunk his wine, watched his fights and fucked his whores.

Now they'd just have to take what was coming.

TWENTY NINE

He was hurting. Not like in the old days, when the hurt was good and it fed his rage. This was a new hurt. Deeper. Like a fire down inside, and the only thing that would put it out would be the killing.

Nobul hadn't wanted to frighten Rag, she'd saved him after all, but there was no way she'd want to see what was coming. And he might well have kept his promise and done her along with everyone else he could find. Best if she was far away from here.

There was a dim light coming from the hatch in the ceiling and Nobul took a step towards it. There was a numbness running through his whole body – even the dog bites had stopped hurting. He was hungry and thirsty and he'd spent too long in a dark hole not moving a muscle. A voice inside told him he needed help from an apothecary, but there was work to be done first. It would be messy work. The kind most men would shy away from. The kind Nobul Jacks was born for.

Each step he took towards the light became more assured. Every inch he drew closer to the hatch he was filled more and more with a sense of purpose.

Time to forget the pain. Time to forget your aches.

You know what fucking time it is.

The stairs creaked a little under his weight. His hand gripped the chain still manacled to his right hand and he twisted it around his fist so it wouldn't make a noise. Best not let anyone up there know he was coming for them. Might ruin the surprise.

At the top he could hear someone whistling. Nobul crept up and peered over the lip of the hatch. There, silhouetted in a doorway, was a naked man taking a piss out onto the dark street. Where his clothes were was a mystery, but he wouldn't need them anyway. Not where he was going.

As Nobul pulled himself out of the cellar, he wondered if this man had watched him in that pit with the dogs. Wondered if he'd had a good old laugh. Cheered with the baying crowd or spat on him as he fought for his life. As he threw the chain over the man's head and tightened it around his throat, Nobul realised he didn't give a fuck either way.

Credit to the bloke – he gave a good old struggle for his life, but in Nobul's grip he had no chance. At first the man clawed at the chain about his neck, his feet kicking out as he tried to get purchase, but Nobul only tightened his hold, lifting the man off the ground. Then he did that little dance hanged men do when they're trying to run from the noose. When he could sense the end was near, he forgot about the chain and tried to reach Nobul's face, clawing for an eye. It did him no good.

The man went slack. Nobul held him there a while, just to make sure he wasn't faking it, and then lowered the naked corpse to the floor.

For a moment he stared out through the open door. It was dark, the chill of the night blowing in like the breath of winter. He could walk away now, take his freedom. There would be time for vengeance later. It was the sensible thing to do.

But when have you ever done the sensible thing?

Nobul closed the door. He turned the key that was still in the lock, then took it out and tossed it into the cellar.

Carefully Nobul opened an internal door. Wouldn't want to spook anyone. Wouldn't want to let the whole place know he was coming.

A wave of warm air hit him as he entered a tavern. A fire crackled in one corner, and there was a bar covered in empty tankards and bottles.

He walked across the room, past the slumbering bodies that lay all around. Someone stirred as he walked by but didn't wake. When he reached the other side of the room, Nobul slid the deadbolts across the door, then picked up a chair and wedged it under the handle as tight as he could make it.

Wouldn't want anyone running off before the revelry had ended, would he? And Nobul knew damn well how much this lot liked a bit of revelry.

Before he could decide where to start, Nobul's eye fell on someone sleeping next to the bar. His head was leaning to one side, and he was breathing noisily.

As Nobul recognised him he felt his heart begin to beat faster. Shivers of excitement crept down the back of his neck.

He'd made this bastard a promise. Time to keep it.

In his right hand he twisted the chain tighter round his fist, while his left reached out for the bastard's shirt. As he pulled him off the floor, Toothless opened his eyes, letting out a bark of protest. Nobul slammed him back against the bar and held him there, giving his eyes a chance to focus.

Toothless looked confused, angry, then scared as he looked into Nobul's blooded face.

'Wakey wakey,' said Nobul.

Toothless opened his mouth to reply – to beg, or perhaps to snarl his defiance. Nobul smashed his chain-wrapped fist into Toothless' open mouth. The man squealed as the side of his face erupted in a gout of blood, what rotten teeth he had left flying out of his head.

'What did I tell you?' Nobul growled, smashing his fist into Toothless' face again before he could answer. 'Can't remember, fucker?' Nobul hit him again and Toothless sagged against the bar. 'I told you I was gonna kill you.' He picked his victim up in one fist, bringing his face close. 'And I always keep my promises.'

Nobul let Toothless sag, his head lolling back on the bar. The bastard brought up his hands weakly, pleading for mercy. Nobul brought his fist down, smashing Toothless' head into the bar top. Again and again he pounded that head, pulping it, cracking it, breaking it. Each blow rang out across the tavern, and behind him Nobul could hear people waking to the sound of murder.

Good! Let them watch this. Let them see what is in store.

Long after Toothless had stopped moving, Nobul let the body slip to the floor. He should have been satisfied at that. Seeing this bastard dead should have been enough.

But it wasn't.

A woman screamed. There was a commotion, furniture scraping on the floor, someone running for the exit.

Let them run.

He turned in time to see a naked man coming at him, arm raised, a long black piece of iron in his hand. There was time to see the fear in the man's bleary eyes before Nobul stepped forward with a crushing head butt. It stopped the man in his tracks, the metal falling from his hand. Another butt of the head and the man fell at his feet.

Nobul stooped to pick up the metal. It was a poker, still warm to the touch, and it felt good in his hand. He raised it, smashing the solid iron into the man's head where he lay. A scream went up from a woman. Nobul turned and walked towards her. She carried on screaming, rooted to the spot.

Was she another witness to the dogfight? Did he fucking care?

He smashed the chained fist into her mouth and she fell back stunned. Another punch to the side of her head and he felt her skull crack.

People were running from him now, some cowering, desperate to hide. But there was nowhere to hide, not from him.

Nobul turned to the front door. Half-dressed figures were fumbling at the chair and the deadbolts he'd secured there, frantically trying to get it open. Nobul was across the tavern in a bound, raising the poker. A few nights before they'd been laughing and jeering and waiting for him to die. Now they were just a screaming mass of bodies, ripe for the kill.

Blood splashed his face as he struck. He could taste it on his lips, warm and familiar. He punched out with his fist, the chain biting into his knuckles, and it felt good. It stoked the fire, teased his hunger, and there was only one thing that would see him full.

It didn't take long before there was nothing but corpses lying before the door. Broken and torn.

He span on his heel, hungry for more, and scanned the rest of the tavern. As he walked across the room he heard a whimper from beneath a table and flung it out of the way. Someone cowered beneath it, his face tear-streaked and screwed up in terror.

'Please,' said the man, holding up his hands for clemency.

Nobul stared down, remembering something through the mist, suddenly thinking there was one other bastard who had it coming.

'Where's Friedrik?' he growled.

'I don't know. Hells, I'd tell you if I did, honest I would,' pleaded the man. 'For Arlor's sake, please show me some mercy.'

But there was no mercy here.

Nobul brought the poker down so hard he heard the skull crack. Before the man fell Nobul stabbed out, shoving the iron into his eye, hot blood squirting onto his hand.

There was noise from the back room, as the rest of the revellers banged against the door, screaming for help.

Nobul took his time as he stalked them, a smile creeping across his lips. What was fucking wrong with these people? They'd come here for a killing. Wasn't that what he was giving them?

As he entered the backroom there were more screams and desperate shouts. One of them had the guts to attack, and Nobul almost laughed as the man came at him. He was holding something in his hand, a club or a table leg, and Nobul raised his arm as the weapon came down. The pain as it struck only fed the fire. One quick punch to the throat and the attacker was down, clutching his neck, gasping his last on the floor.

Nobul stooped and picked up the cudgel. His eyes were wide, his mouth was stretched open in a death's-head grin. He went about his grim work with satisfaction.

The screaming and banging didn't carry on for long. There was some pleading in there too but the noise and the faces all seemed to twist into a blur of nothing. When it was over, when his arms were tired from the killing, Nobul was almost disappointed.

He stared at the corpses. They'd been no challenge. Though he was breathing heavy it had been nothing to finish them.

The cudgel dropped from his fingers as he made his way back through the tavern to the front door. The chain unravelled from his fist and dangled from his battered hand as he pulled the chair aside and unlatched the deadbolts.

When Nobul opened the door he half expected a bunch of Greencoats to be waiting for him. Or in the least a gang of Guild enforcers.

There was no one – just him and the night.

As he stepped out he staggered, the fatigue of the past few days finally catching him on a single gust of night air. He had no idea where he was – most likely somewhere in Northgate. The street was deserted as he stumbled along it. A dog barked at him from a side alley. Someone closed their shutters with a sharp bang as he staggered past.

Nobul didn't care who saw him. His clothes and flesh were torn, his breath ragged as he stumbled along. The chain at his wrist jangled like a plague bell as he walked.

Bring out your dead. Bring them out for burning! The Lord of Crows is here!

At any moment he could stumble into a Greencoat patrol, but Nobul didn't care. It wasn't like those murders were going to be reported. He'd killed a bunch of punters in a Guild tavern – they were never going to call the authorities to investigate. They'd want to sort that out by themselves and they'd be after him soon enough.

Well, let them come. They couldn't do anything worse than they'd already done.

The further he went the more Nobul's feet dragged. He could feel himself going hazy at the edges, but he fought against it. If he fell here in the street there was no telling who would find him. He had to find somewhere safe – to rest, just for a little while. Gather his strength. Plan his next move.

Nobul lost his footing and fell to the ground. It was wet and cold and for a moment it brought him to his senses. As he rose once more he keenly felt every ache and pain in his body. His legs were like lead, his arms two slabs of meat dragging him down.

There was a door at the end of the street. Was it a door he recognised? Was it even a street he recognised? As he approached it he tripped on the step, falling forward against the hardwood door. There was a knocker above him and he reached up. It seemed so far away, and the dark was closing in. If he could reach it before…

He couldn't see. It was bloody dark and bloody cold and bloody loud and there was something on his head.

Nobul reached up and adjusted the helm. What he saw made him want to pull it back down over his eyes.

The valley rose high on both sides like it was reaching for the sky. In the middle, two massive statues met each other – warriors locked in eternal combat.

Bakhaus Gate.

Beside Nobul stood an army, men on horseback, banners of all colours tattered and blowing in the breeze. They chanted a name over and over, raising their swords and shields

243

and bellowing their defiance. At the other end of the valley, growling and roaring, the sound echoing like the end of the world, was their enemy.

Nobul tightened his grip on the hammer at his side. How were they supposed to win this? What were they supposed to do against such a ravening horde?

Then he heard what the men around him were chanting.

Black Helm! Black Helm! Black Helm!

Eyes started to turn his way like they were looking for him to lead them. Eyes wide in fear and fury. They wanted him to head the charge. Into that mass of metal and teeth.

Nobul was glad of the helmet. It masked his fear. He lifted his hammer. It felt heavy. So heavy he could hardly lift it, let alone swing it.

A hand patted him on the back. Another gave him a push. One reluctant foot after the other, Nobul moved forward. A horse whinnied at his ear. His tread got faster. Voices began to shout encouragement.

Let them lead the fucking charge then. Let them throw themselves at the bastard enemy.

He was trotting now, moving with impetus. The hammer gripped in two hands. He was shouting, but he couldn't make out his own words over the noise. The enemy started to move. Charging on, bounding ahead in their grey armour, blades raised, mouths gaping wide, fangs bared.

He was going to die here. He was going to be torn apart and he didn't care.

'Come on, you bastards!' he screamed.

The monstrous wave engulfed him.

His eyes flipped open to the bright morning and he'd have sat bolt upright if he had the energy. Or the will.

Instead he just lay there, wondering where the fuck he was and who'd dressed his wounds.

Nobul raised his right hand. The manacle was gone, leaving a raw red band around his wrist. His knuckles were bandaged and he clenched his fist, wincing at the pain. The flesh was torn and battered but at least none of his knuckles were broken.

Gingerly he raised a hand to his ear. Half of it was missing but the wound had been stitched. He could smell the sour tang of liniment. Someone had tended to him with expert care.

With no small effort, Nobul managed to swing his legs over the bed. He was naked, and looking at his body he realised how battered he'd been over the past few days – scarce an inch of his skin had escaped the black bruising that covered him.

But he'd had his reckoning for that, hadn't he? He'd done his killing till there was no more killing to be had. Though there was one more would die before long.

Friedrik.

Nobul would be sure to pay that cunt a visit soon. And it wouldn't be as quick an end as he'd granted those poor bastards back in the tavern.

'You're alive, then?'

Nobul looked up to see her standing in the doorway. Her gaunt frame was barely visible in the shadow, and until she took a step into the room he didn't recognise her.

'Fernella? How did…?'

He stopped, and stared at the old woman he'd not seen since the day he laid his son Markus in the ground.

'You got here last night. Scratching at my door like some little mouse. I barely recognised the Nobul of old. But looking at the state of your fists, I reckon that Nobul's here after all.'

He looked down at his hands, thinking about the killing they'd done, and smiled.

'Aye, I did some things last night. Things you don't want to hear about.'

'No, I reckon I don't. But by the looks of it, some things have been done to you too. They deserve what they got?'

'Does anyone get what they deserve?'

Fernella shrugged. 'I suppose not.' She gestured to a chair that had fresh clothes piled up on it. 'Get dressed. You can't stay here. Got children downstairs, don't want them seeing you in that state.'

Good old Fernella. Mouth as blunt as a hammer. Heart as big as a lion.

He dressed as quick as he could, though it was a bit of a struggle putting the shirt on. A bit tight around the chest too, but it would do.

Downstairs Fernella was pottering in her kitchen. She'd been right, there were half a dozen kids sitting at her kitchen table. Most of them looked up at him, fearful of what they saw, and just like she'd asked him he went straight for the door.

'You want it back yet?' she asked as his hand grasped the door handle.

'What?' Nobul replied.

'The box you give me. You want it?'

He shook his head, the haunting shadow of last night's dream playing on his memory. 'Not right now.'

Fernella laid a hand on his arm. 'Suit yourself, lad. I'll keep it until you're ready.'

'Don't rightly know if I'll ever—'

'No. Don't say that. The man you were. The man who came back last night. Soon enough this city's gonna need him. You understand me? He could do some good.'

Nobul looked at her wrinkled face and those eyes that had seen so much.

'Aye, maybe,' he said.

He opened the door and walked out into the street.

THIRTY

The tension had been building since they'd arrived. The threat of violence had never diminished, but so far none of the Coldlanders had made a move on Regulus or his warriors.

He had learned there were three tribes within the oppressive building. Each had a fanciful name that seemed to relate little to their history and deeds. Regulus could only hope these men could fight as well as they could name themselves. Somehow he doubted it.

Nevertheless, he and his warriors were careful to watch their backs, heeding the words of Tom the Blackfoot well. It was clear these mercenaries held little love for the Zatani.

The Zatani awoke in their cell – a bare room with a single window looking out onto the city. As ever, when Regulus led his warriors out into the vast hall they were the first of the mercenaries to appear. The Zatani were craving daylight, and a lack of it had made their sleep restless and short. It had been days since they had seen the sun, and they were suffering for it. Hagama and Kazul had grown increasingly agitated, taking their frustrations out on the younger Akkula. More than once Regulus had been forced to scold them for it. Leandran seemed to be handling their confinement well, though he had been all but silent since they had come to this place. Janto too, was silent, but that did not serve to put Regulus at his ease. The unpredictable warrior could explode into violence at any second which was the last thing they needed – at least until they faced a real enemy.

Having left their cell, they took their places at a table in one corner of the great hall. The Zatani were used to sitting around a fire under the stars on the open plain, but they had soon grown accustomed to the Coldlander custom of hunkering around a table. As the other mercenaries began to join them, the atmosphere in the hall darkened.

The Midnight Falcons wore night-black livery, their leader a hulking brute who little resembled a bird of prey. They sat at the opposite end of the hall, making no secret of their disdain for Regulus and his warriors, though none were brave enough to speak of it. Regulus put their number at almost fifty. Not even their strongest looked a match for his weakest.

Next to come from their darkened cells was the Scarlet Company in tunics of red. These numbered fewer than the Midnight Falcons, perhaps thirty warriors led by a dark-browed veteran, his white hair pulled back from his head in a topknot. He regarded Regulus with unmasked hatred.

Finally the Hallowed Shields arrived – their emblem of a quartered shield on each of their chests – taking their place close to the Zatani, but only because there was nowhere else to sit. Almost a hundred warriors, and word was they had more fighting men housed elsewhere. Their leader was young but confident, and Regulus had rapidly grown sick of his arrogant smile. How he would have liked to challenge this one, but Regulus was bound to the accord he had made with Seneschal Rogan and was determined he would not be the one to break it.

The hum of chatter filled the hall, and Regulus and his warriors sat around their table in silence. There was no hunt to plan, no strategy to formulate, so why all this talking? Regulus disliked these Coldlanders all the more for their incessant need to waggle their tongues.

With little fanfare, a cauldron of broth was brought in. The other mercenaries quickly stood and formed a line, but Regulus and his men had no need to join it. Rogan had been happy enough to satisfy the Zatani's specific needs.

On a platter, held between two of Rogan's slaves, came a modest pile of meat. The slaves dumped it unceremoniously on the table amongst the Zatani and left as fast as they could. Regulus regarded their meagre and unappetising fare. It was scraps, far from fresh, and flies were already beginning to gather about it.

'This is shit,' said Kazul.

Hagama nodded in agreement.

Unabashed, Leandran and Akkula reached forward to take their fill. Janto sat back, his appetite clearly fled.

'Eat,' said Regulus. 'We need to keep our strength. There will be fighting soon enough. Once the enemy comes and we have tasted our first victory there will be meat to fill us all.'

Kazul reached forward reluctantly and took a hunk, more bone than meat.

'How much longer do we have to be caged here?' Hagama said. 'I'm sick of this place.'

'As are we all,' Regulus replied, fast losing patience. 'But I believe it will not be long. Now eat.'

Hagama glared at the pile of greying animal carcass before digging in. They ate quickly, taking no relish. They were hunters all, used to the warmth of a fresh kill. They were not carrion eaters other than in times of famine. But Regulus guessed a famine was exactly what they had to endure. For now.

As they ate, Regulus could hear the Coldlanders talking. 'Animals' they called the Zatani, 'beasts' or words Regulus had never heard before, though their unpleasant meaning was clear. He ignored them. His warriors could not speak the Coldlander tongue and it was best they did not know what was being said about them.

Once they had finished, Regulus sat back and waited. He tried to block out the noise from the mercenaries, concentrating on the sound of Leandran sucking the marrow from a bone, but it was no use. He was under no illusions: he and his warriors were trapped in here with a rabble that might turn on them at any moment.

The morning wore on, and the Coldlanders began to drink their infernal brew. Regulus understood little about this habit. He had learned their drink was potent, a poison of sorts that sometimes sent them into a rage. He could understand such a thing's value in battle, but in times of repose? And what was its use when it often sent them into a stupor, or caused them to fight amongst themselves, and with no skill – only stubborn ferocity?

The day drew on, and Regulus felt his sense of unease growing.

'Look to yourselves,' he warned his men, as the Coldlanders became more raucous, some of them bursting into song.

His warriors focused on their surroundings. Though they had no weapons Regulus was sure they'd be a match for these men.

'What is it?' asked Leandran.

'Just keep your eyes open,' Regulus replied as the song became more noisy and aggressive.

Slowly he stood up. He knew they needed to get outside, even if just for a little while. They couldn't be expected to remain inside here indefinitely. He had to find one of their guards, gaolers, whatever name they used, and take their leave of this place.

Before he had moved two paces, one of the mercenaries in the livery of the Scarlet Company staggered forward.

'Where are you going?' he shouted. Some of his fellows heard and stopped their bickering to look on with interest.

Regulus did not answer.

The man leaned forward with a smile. More of the Coldlanders were looking on now. Some had clearly been awaiting such a confrontation.

'Come on,' said the man. 'I know you can understand me. I've seen you speaking our language.'

Regulus took a breath, trying to remain composed. He could sense his warriors stirring behind him.

'I seek no trouble,' he said. 'I have come to serve your queen.'

'My queen?' said the Coldlander. 'She's not my queen – I'm from Stelmorn. I'm here for the money, but if you want to fall to your fucking knee in front of her, feel free.' Some of the others laughed.

Regulus regarded the man, bottle in hand, staggering on his feet. How could he even call himself a warrior? What pride did he take in himself? Where was his honour? But then, he only fought for coin – something Regulus would never understand.

He took another step, but the man moved into his path.

'What's the obsession with the queen, then? Not got one of your own?'

There was no way Regulus was about to explain himself to such a cur. He could feel the claws at his fingertips begin to twitch, his jaw tightening. Behind this man, more red liveried warriors stepped forward.

'They probably ate her,' said a man at the back of the group.

'Yeah, they'll have fucked her first, though. That's all those black bastards know about.'

Regulus knew he was being goaded. He must not bow to it. If he lost control, it could jeopardise everything.

'You seen much battle then, darky?' someone shouted suddenly.

Regulus felt his stomach tighten. He clenched his fists, letting his claws dig into his palms.

'What are they saying?' asked Kazul from behind him.

The tension was growing. Regulus knew he had to do something to take the fire out of these men's bellies, but what?

Walk away?

No, Regulus Gor could not do that.

'Yes, I have seen battle,' Regulus said, raising his voice. 'I came north to wield my blade on behalf of your king. The man who set my people free.' The Coldlanders quieted at the mention of their late leader. 'Even though he is dead, I will still fight beside you to defend his lands. For my father's honour and for that of your queen.'

The Coldlanders looked at one another uncertainly.

Before he could think of more to say, the leader of the Hallowed Shields walked forward. He smiled at Regulus.

'You see,' he said, speaking to his men. 'I told you there was nothing to fear from them. They are here as our allies.'

'Like fuck they are,' shouted someone from the crowd.

'What are they saying?' Kazul said again, more agitated.

The leader of the Hallowed Shields looked up at Regulus and winked. 'You're right,' he said. 'We'll soon be fighting side by side. We should be friends.'

'What's he saying?' Kazul stood up, and Janto rose to his feet beside him.

Regulus was about to tell them to sit down again, that this man just wanted peace, when the leader of the Hallowed Shields reached behind his back.

'Let's drink to our new-found friendship,' he said.

'Weapon!' Kazul shouted, darting forward.

Regulus leapt in the way as the Coldlander pulled, not a weapon, but a tin flask from his belt. The man staggered back from Kazul's attack, but Regulus was fast enough to stop his warrior as he leapt with teeth bared.

But he was not able to stop Janto.

At the first sign of trouble the warrior hurled himself at the nearest group of mercenaries. They staggered back under Janto's onslaught as he tore with his claws. Blood flew as Regulus looked on, unable to rein back his warrior.

Before he could attempt to calm them, shouts of alarm and anger went up from the gathered mercenaries. Though unarmed, and facing the fearsome Zatani of the Gor'tana, it did not stop them. They surged forward. Regulus went down under a wave of bodies. Fists pummelled his face and he could hear yells of anger. In the background his warriors roared their defiance as they too joined the fray.

Regulus threw the first Coldlander aside, trying to gain his feet, but two more leapt at him. He was loath to strike them, one blow from his claws would tear out a throat and he was here as an ally, not an enemy. He tried to speak, to talk sense, but blows rained in at him. The Coldlander mercenaries were incensed, and elsewhere Regulus could hear his warriors were not fighting with restraint. Screams of pain echoed through the hall, joined by cries of unfettered rage.

He should not have allowed his warriors to spend so much time incarcerated in this place. They were men of the wild, hunters of the plains. It was only a matter of time before they would unleash their pent-up urges.

A Coldlander came at Regulus, screaming in fury. In his hand, there was a flash of steel. A weapon. They were all supposed to be unarmed but this man had smuggled a knife in with him.

The time for appeasement was over.

Regulus snarled, throwing off the men who were trying to hold him down. With a swipe of his arm he rent the flesh of the knifeman from jaw to eye. As his face came away, the man screamed, dropping his weapon and falling to the ground.

Seeing their fellow so savagely mutilated, some of the mercenaries dropped back. One was brave enough to rush forward but Regulus grasped him by the throat, raising him high, with his legs kicking helplessly for purchase.

'Gor'tana!' Regulus cried. 'To me!'

Immediately his warriors disengaged from their enemy and came to stand beside him – Leandran was breathing heavily, Kazul, Hagama and Akkula all stared wide-eyed, and eager for more. Janto was the last to pull himself away, his mouth dripping with blood.

Regulus surveyed the carnage – men lay dead and dying, blood was strewn on the floor of the massive hall.

Before Regulus could order his men to retreat, there was a commotion in the entryway. More soldiers in the green livery of the city guard rushed in – Regulus counted thirty of them – all carrying polearms, all looking determined.

He could have ordered his men to fight, but to what end? Against unarmed mercenaries they were more than a match, but armed warriors were a different matter.

Janto moved to attack, but Regulus grasped his shoulder, digging his claws into the warrior's flesh.

'Enough,' he said. 'We've done enough.'

He dropped the mercenary he held to the ground where the man lay gasping for air.

The soldiers surrounded them. As Regulus showed his palms in sign of peace, he glanced at the dead and dying that lay all around them.

This would take some explaining.

THIRTY ONE

Merrick had fucked up. Again. It was something he'd grown used to over the years – making a mess and living with the consequences, over and over – but this time he felt an unusual compulsion to make amends.

The queen had almost been murdered, one of his fellow Sentinels had been killed, another gravely wounded.

He should have been there. Should have protected her from Dravos and his bodyguards. Should have drawn his sword and cut that bastard's heart out the minute he laid eyes on him.

But then it would be you lying dead. It would be you cold in the dirt. You'd be a hero all right, but not doing too much bragging – so count your lucky stars and stop fucking moping about it.

Merrick glanced up from beneath his helmet. Kaira and Janessa stood in the centre of the small courtyard. It was a quiet spot, away from the main quarters of the palace; somewhere they wouldn't be disturbed. The queen held her ancient sword in two hands and Kaira was coaching her. Apparently Janessa had lopped Dravos' head off with it, and Merrick had to admit she was rapidly growing proficient with the weapon, despite how huge and unwieldy it looked.

But she'll have to grow proficient with it, won't she, Ryder, because you're about as useful a bodyguard as a shaved fucking monkey.

His hand tightened on the sword at his belt and his eyes flicked to the two entrances to the courtyard. He'd found himself acting more vigilantly since the attack, even though he knew it was too little too late. Waldin lay dying and the other one – *damn, what was his bloody name?* – was already in the dirt. Merrick knew the blame for that lay squarely on his shoulders.

He watched as Kaira demonstrated a sequence of strikes with a stick. Her wrist was heavily bandaged and she moved stiffly. But then she had reason to – she'd been grievously wounded defending the life of the queen. Yet she was still here on duty.

Not like you – always pissing and moaning about one thing or another: 'Father doesn't love me', 'Mother's dead and I've spent the family fortune on whores and booze', 'All my friends want to kill me', 'This jacket doesn't match these frigging britches'.

Little wonder she hadn't spoken to him since.

What had he expected? Kaira had given him enough chances. Offered him opportunity after opportunity to prove he'd changed. In the end it was easier to prove that Merrick Ryder wasn't the changing kind.

A door opened onto the courtyard. Merrick's hand went to his sword and he took a step forward. When Garret appeared he let out a sigh of relief, but was on his guard again when he saw the captain was not alone.

Behind him strode Tannick Ryder, flanked by several of his Wyvern Guard. They marched forward to stand before the queen, who lowered her blade as they approached.

'Majesty,' said Tannick, dropping to his knee. His men did likewise.

'Lord Marshal,' Janessa replied. 'To what do I owe this intrusion?'

Garret stepped forward as Tannick and his men rose to their feet. 'Apologies, Majesty. This is my doing. I informed the Lord Marshal of the attempt on your life. He demanded to see you.'

Janessa looked over at Tannick. 'I appreciate your… concern, Lord Ryder, but as you can see, I am quite well.'

'Yes, Majesty, but for how long?' Tannick replied. 'It is clear your bodyguard are not up to their task.' He punctuated that with a glance in Merrick's direction. 'I must insist you allow my men to watch over you.'

'I have every confidence in my Sentinels, Lord Marshal. They have guarded Skyhelm and its occupants for centuries.'

'But Majesty, with many of their number away from the city, this castle is not as well protected as it should be. Especially now, when a thousand enemies would gladly see you dead. I must insist.'

'My bodyguard is more than sufficient, Lord Ryder.'

'But your most senior knight is wounded.' He gestured to Kaira who, though she stood proudly, was obviously not at her best. 'The rest are untried.' He didn't gesture in Merrick's direction, but the insinuation was obvious.

'I have every faith in them,' Janessa replied.

'Then, if it please your Majesty, let me put that faith to the test.'

Garret moved forward. 'Tannick, this isn't what we discussed.'

The Lord Marshal ignored him. 'Let me show you how easy it would be for a skilled assassin to cut through your men.'

Queen Janessa glanced over at Merrick.

This was like all his worst nightmares come at once; his father judging him wanting, the queen defending him when she had no reason to.

'Lord Ryder, I can assure you—'

'If you please, Majesty. I can prove him wrong,' said Merrick.

The words had slipped out. Something in the back of Merrick's mind had crept forward and taken control. Something that wanted to prove to his bastard of a father that he was worthy of the family name.

Janessa looked at him, then the Lord Marshal. 'Very well. If you deem it necessary, then my man will fight you.'

Tannick nodded. 'Thank you, Majesty. Though it won't be me he's fighting.' He turned to his men. 'Cormach, strip down.'

Merrick looked on as one of the knights shrugged off the animal pelt on his shoulders and began to take off his armour. Jared, the man whom Merrick had spoken to a few nights before, moved forward to help.

Garret walked up beside Merrick, shaking his head. 'This is bloody ridiculous.'

'Don't worry about it,' Merrick replied, handing over his helmet. 'I've got this.'

'Have you?' Garret asked as he began to unbuckle the vambrace at Merrick's forearm. 'That's Cormach Whoreson. Tannick's best sword.'

'I know who he is; I've already seen what he can do to a stick.' For the briefest moment Merrick heard that stick break over Cormach's back again, and almost winced at the memory. 'But how good is he against a sword, and a man who knows how to use it? These Wyvern Guard have been living in the mountains for years with nothing to fight but goats and hill men. I've trained in the blade yards of House Tarnath. I've—'

'Don't underestimate him,' said Garret, before Merrick could go through his full list of achievements. 'The Wyvern Guard are legendary swordsmen. If your father's trained them, they'll be the best.'

Merrick looked over at Cormach Whoreson, now stripped to the waist. His body was covered in scars; he looked as if he'd been chiselled from stone and he was giving Merrick the hard stare. Merrick had spent enough time on the streets to know the difference between someone feigning toughness and a genuine hard bastard.

Cormach was most definitely the latter.

A flash of doubt suddenly clouded his confidence but Merrick pushed it away. He'd been trained by Lord Macharias himself, he knew the sixty six *Principiums Martial*... well, maybe now wasn't the time to go over all that again. Fact was he had something to prove here, and he was damn sure he'd do it.

Garret took the rest of Merrick's armour off before announcing, 'I'll send for practice swords.'

'No need,' Tannick replied. 'Real ones will do the job just as well.' He looked over at Merrick. 'Unless your man objects.'

Garret was about to speak when Merrick stepped forward. 'He doesn't.'

He unbuckled the sword belt at his waist and drew his weapon from its sheath. The blade felt good in his hand. For a moment he was invincible, like a hero of legend, baring his chest to the enemy, blade in hand, with nothing but his skill to keep him alive.

Then Cormach drew his own sword.

He held it with a confidence Merrick could never have matched. Hells, it almost looked a part of his body. Merrick was keenly aware that his own bare torso, though not in bad shape, was nowhere near as taut and honed as his opponent's. The open air of the courtyard suddenly began to feel chill, as though it were seeping through his flesh and into his bones. Could Cormach actually be the better swordsman?

Put those thoughts from your head, Ryder. Your father's standing there, and he's waiting for you to fail. It's time to put the fucker right.

Merrick gave a glance across at Kaira. She was watching impassively. There would be no encouragement there. She probably wanted to see him fail as much as the rest of them.

Both men walked to the centre of the courtyard. One of the Wyvern Guard shouted, 'Come on, Whoreson,' but was silenced by a glance from Lord Ryder.

Merrick wondered if they'd get the shout to begin. From Cormach's impassive stare, he guessed they already had.

Strike first, strike fast, strike hard, strike last. That was the way he'd been taught at the Collegium. No better time to try it than now.

Merrick stepped in, bouncing off the balls of his feet, his sword sweeping in a blinding arc. Cormach didn't even blink, just brought his blade up and struck at the blow, knocking Merrick's sword aside with such strength it almost put him off balance.

He bounced back, out of range, but Cormach hadn't even tried to follow through with a counter. The man just stood there, staring as though this whole thing bored him.

Merrick circled, with Cormach watching but not even keeping his guard up. What a conceited bastard. Didn't he know there was only room for one arrogant swordsman in this city, and that was Merrick Ryder!

Again he moved in, his sword low, aimed at the groin. Again Cormach parried. This time Merrick didn't retreat, but cut in high, but it seemed Cormach could read him before he even knew what he was about to do, and he parried the blow, making Merrick's sword ring in his hand.

Anger began to well up inside. This fucker was toying with him. Showing everyone how much better he was. And to top it all Tannick was watching, smug in the knowledge his man was the better fighter, confident that Merrick was going to lose.

He's always said you were a useless bastard and now you're proving it. Don't just fucking stand there – show him he's wrong.

Merrick let out a growl of frustration as he attacked once more. In the back of his head, Lord Macharias was shouting at him – *don't lose your temper, anger only makes you sloppy* – but he didn't care. These arseholes needed showing that they could spend all the time they wanted in the mountains, humping goats and inbred tribeswomen, but here in the big city they really knew how to fight.

His sword swept in, cutting the air with a hum. It was a feint, and as Cormach brought his blade up to parry, Merrick changed its direction, aimed at his opponent's knee. Casually, as though he knew what Merrick was about to do, Cormach lifted his leg, stepping away from the strike.

Merrick didn't stop, hacking down, gripping his blade in both hands. He grunted as Cormach shifted his own sword, parrying the low blow. Their blades were locked together, Merrick forcing his down with two arms, Cormach holding it off with one. They looked at one another, Cormach impassive, showing no signs of strain.

He's laughing at you. It might not look it, but on the inside he's pissing himself.

Merrick grunted again, this time holding back none of his frustration. His sword swung left and right, a vicious onslaught, heedless of the damage he might do if he scored a hit, but each blow was snatched from the air by his opponent's blade. And every time Cormach didn't bother to counter, parrying each blow as though he was practising with a child.

'Enough, Cormach,' Tannick shouted. 'Finish it.'

As Merrick hacked in again, Cormach parried, but this time he twisted his blade. It hooked under the quillon of Merrick's sword and sent it spinning across the courtyard. Before Merrick could think what to do next, Cormach stepped in and butted him on the bridge of his nose.

Merrick went down hard, his vision flooded. As he floundered on the ground he could taste blood and snot as it ran freely from his nose and into his mouth.

A razor edge pushed his chin up and, through watering eyes, he saw Cormach looking down. The man didn't gloat or smile in his victory, but stared blankly, awaiting further instructions from Tannick.

The old man wouldn't dare to give the order to strike a deathblow in front of the queen… would he? Right now Merrick wouldn't have minded, and nor would he have put it past the old bastard.

'An impressive display, Lord Marshal,' said Janessa, walking up beside Merrick. 'I think I've seen enough.'

'Of course, Majesty,' Tannick replied. 'Cormach – to me.'

The one they called Whoreson took his blade from Merrick's throat and backed away towards the waiting Wyvern Guard, who looked on in amusement.

Merrick raised a hand to his throat. There was blood.

Best be grateful it's only a nick. He could have killed you at any time.

'Don't feel bad,' said Tannick, as Garret helped Merrick to his feet. 'Cormach's my best. You never stood a chance.'

It didn't make him feel any better, but then that wasn't the reason Tannick said it.

'Your Wyvern Guard are clearly skilled in the art of combat, Lord Marshal,' said Queen Janessa. 'But this changes nothing.'

'But, Majesty, your Sentinels are not able to protect you.'

Queen Janessa glared up at the imposing knight. Merrick took some solace in the fact that Tannick seemed a little cowed by her.

'Yet I am not dead, Lord Marshal. It appears they've been doing something right.'

'I must insist—'

'That will be all.'

Queen Janessa's voice was raised and Tannick could respond with little else than a deep bow.

'Of course, Majesty.'

Without another word Tannick Ryder turned and left the courtyard, his Wyvern Guard following close behind. Cormach was at their rear, not even deigning to glance at Merrick. Not that Merrick minded. If he never saw that bastard again it would be too soon.

'That will be all for today,' Janessa said to Kaira. 'You may walk me back to my chambers.' Then she looked at Merrick. He had expected at least some degree of disappointment but there was none, even though he'd let her down so badly… again? 'You should get yourself cleaned up,' she said.

With that, she and Kaira left the courtyard.

Merrick wasn't sure whether he'd wanted Kaira to offer him scorn or sympathy, but she didn't bother either way. It didn't seem like anyone gave much of a shit, but then Garret offered him a kerchief to dab his bloody nose.

'Tannick was right; you shouldn't feel bad.'

Merrick shrugged. 'You did warn me, I suppose.'

'I tried. But you don't take advice from anyone, do you?'

Garret didn't wait for an answer. He too walked away, leaving Merrick half dressed and bleeding in the chill of the courtyard.

Right now, that felt about as much as he deserved.

THIRTY TWO

O n any other day Governess Nordaine's capacity for chatter would have driven Janessa to the edge of her wits. Not today, though. Today she was grateful for the woman's prattle. It helped drown out the thoughts in her head, the hateful memories of Dravos; how he'd violated her thoughts, his sickly eyes staring into her soul.

Though he was dead, his shadow seemed to haunt her. She should have felt vindicated, should have been proud, but she could not bring herself to revel in her victory. At the time she had been thrilled by the experience; the feel of the weapon in her hand, the satisfaction of it pierce Dravos' chest, the sound of his head hitting the floor. The Helsbayn had seemed to almost sing as she wielded it.

Now all that remained was a numbness.

Or is it a yearning? Do you wish to wield that sword again? Do you need to feel its weight in your hands as its edge hacks more flesh, bringing you further glory?

Janessa blinked away such thoughts as she stared out of the chamber window. Nordaine saw to her gown, tightening the ribbons of her bodice very gently, taking pains not to pull too hard around her belly. Below the bodice a skirt billowed outward in an attempt to hide the fact that Janessa was thickening at the middle. The dress could do little about her bosom, which threatened to pop out over the top of her neckline, but a well-placed scarf would suffice to hide it. Fortunate, then, that it was the start of winter, the air colder, the nights growing longer.

The door to her chamber opened and Kaira stood waiting.

'They are ready, Majesty,' she said.

Janessa just nodded. A bond had formed between the two of them and they had grown closer still after Dravos' attempt to… how could she describe it?

To control you. To take over your mind. To remove you from the game altogether and place his master on your throne.

Whatever had been his intention, he was gone now. His body and those of his men had been spirited away by Odaka, and most likely thrown in the Storway with the rest of the city's filth. How she would explain his disappearance had played on her mind, though she felt she owed the Bankers League no explanation. The man might have been their representative but he had come with his own agenda at the behest of his ambitious master. Once Janessa had rid the Free States of Amon Tugha she would have revenge for the attempt to ensorcell her. Kalhim Han Rolyr Mehelli of the White Moon Trading Company would not escape the consequences of his actions.

Janessa made her way to the dining hall, Kaira walking ahead of her, Merrick behind. He had been silent since his duel in the gardens and she had thought it best not to press him on it. Despite the man's defeat she still trusted he would do his best to defend her. Despite the dedication of her bodyguards, it had been weeks since Janessa felt truly safe. Though she knew her guardians would lay down their lives for her, it did little to calm her nerves.

She had been so determined all those weeks ago. On the day of her coronation she had stood looking out at her city and vowed to be a strong, a courageous ruler. Now, with the child inside her, with not just her own life at stake, that courage seemed a distant thing.

As she entered the great feast hall, Janessa was struck at how empty it was. Where once had sat courtiers, aldermen, stewards, magistrates and other men and women of state, there were now just three figures. The table looked ridiculous with so few people at it – and all sitting as far from one another as they could manage.

Janessa couldn't blame the sycophants of court for deserting the palace. They didn't have to be there. They didn't have to stand by while the city fell. Better that they should run anyway – they were useless to her.

The three rose to their feet as she entered, bowing as she approached the table. After taking her seat she bestowed a gracious smile on each of them.

Seneschal Rogan produced a smile in return, never letting his mask slip. Baroness Magrida was equally proficient at affecting the proper airs, though it looked as though her face might crack from the effort. Chancellor Durket looked suitably uncomfortable, and whether he was still in shock from the recent attack on Janessa, or whether he was as eager to flee this place as the rest of her court, it was difficult to say.

As they sat, servants carrying platters appeared and the first course – a meagre bowl of honeyed oats – was placed before each of them. Durket looked down at the paltry fare with a disconsolate look, but as Janessa took up a silver spoon and began to eat, he did likewise.

'I trust your Majesty is well?' said Rogan.

Janessa noted he hadn't touched the food before him. She smiled as though everything were perfectly normal – as though the enemy wasn't almost at the gate, as though assassins weren't trying to kill her, as though foreign powers weren't trying to usurp her throne.

'Of course, Seneschal,' she replied.

Though he said nothing further, she knew he was after something. Did he know what had happened? Only Odaka, Durket and her Sentinels knew about Dravos. They had taken great pains to ensure the incident remained a secret, but she conceded it was Rogan's job to discover things others would rather stay hidden.

Janessa turned her attention back to the bowl in front of her. Despite being almost drowned in honey the oats tasted bitter, but Janessa ate though her appetite was lacking.

She had no real desire to converse with her dinner guests, but it was far preferable to the uncomfortable quiet that descended over the table once they had finished the porridge. She looked up at the Baroness, who was dabbing her mouth with a napkin.

'So your son, Lord Magrida, will not be joining us?' Janessa asked, instantly regretting her question. How would Isabelle take to her showing interest in Leon? Hopefully not as a sign Janessa was interested in his hand.

'He is unwell,' the Baroness replied with a smile. 'Though if he were here to sample the food on offer I doubt he'd feel much better.'

'Many people within this city will not be eating at all this evening, Baroness. We should be more grateful for what we have.'

'Of course,' Isabelle replied. If her feathers had been ruffled by the rebuke she didn't show it. 'It's only fitting that we should suffer along with the masses.'

Her insincerity was barely masked.

'We are far from the brink of starvation,' Janessa replied.

'Quite so,' Isabelle said. 'And some of us need to keep our strength up.'

What did she mean by that? Surely she couldn't know...

'I... I'm quite sure...'

Isabelle smiled. 'I meant that with the trouble to come, you will need to have your wits about you. Facing the northern hordes in a weakened condition would not serve you well, Majesty.'

'Indeed. But I am sure I will be strong enough to face what is coming.'

'I envy you your confidence. If only we could be so certain of victory.'

'If you are afraid of defeat, Baroness, I can see to it that you are conveyed far from Steelhaven before the Khurtas arrive. You and your son.'

Still Baroness Magrida sat and smiled. 'I wouldn't hear of it, my dear.' *My dear?* 'Leon and I are determined to see this through. To offer you any and all support.'

And what support would that be? Your son lounging around in his bed all day leering at the housemaids or you following me through the corridors with your judgemental eye?

'We are most grateful for it, Baroness,' she replied, raising her glass of water in a mock toast.

Isabelle raised her wine in return and took a sip, all the while keeping her eyes fixed on Janessa.

As the next course arrived – chicken stuffed with lemons on a bed of turnip – Odaka entered the room. Silently he took his place to the right hand of Janessa.

'Apologies for my tardiness, Majesty.' With that he glanced towards Seneschal Rogan, who ignored the look, though Janessa was sure he noticed.

'Of course, Odaka. I am sure there is much to which you must attend.'

The tall warrior didn't answer, merely gazed at Rogan, who looked up from picking at his chicken.

'Anything we need concern ourselves with?' the Seneschal asked.

'You know it was.' Odaka continued to glare across the huge dining table.

Rogan looked back calmly. There was no love lost between these two, but then Janessa had known that for a long time; not least because she could sense Rogan manoeuvring himself for power.

Before her father's death she had only trusted Odaka, and Rogan had been all but invisible. Now with King Cael gone it seemed the Seneschal of the Inquisition was trying to make himself invaluable within Janessa's court. Whether she valued him or not, she felt she needed all the advisors she could muster in such trying times, and so far Rogan had not seen her wrong.

Odaka, however, did not share her view.

'It appears there has been an incident in one of the gaols,' said Odaka. 'There have been fatalities.'

Janessa looked to Rogan, who shrugged. 'Unavoidable really, what with so many fighting men cooped up in one place.'

'You put Zatani warriors in a gaol alongside mercenaries,' said Odaka, his voice low and menacing. 'What did you think would happen?'

'I won't pretend to understand what prejudices you might hold against a rival tribe, but they were willing warriors. What should I have done with them? Let them roam the city streets?'

'You should have turned them away at the gate. They are not men but beasts of the wild. Bred only for killing.' Odaka raised his voice. Janessa couldn't remember when she had last seen him lose his veneer of calm. 'Now three mercenary companies are threatening to leave the city and the Zatani are in cells.'

Rogan held his hands up in a placatory manner. 'I can hardly be blamed for the attitude of mercenaries. Word is they're leaving because we have nothing to pay them with, not because of some brawl. Isn't that right, Chancellor?'

He looked over at Durket, who froze, his partly chewed food filling his bloated cheeks.

'We...' Durket managed through his full mouth.

'Apparently our would-be saviour,' Rogan continued, 'the representative from the Bankers League, has gone missing. We can only assume he left on the first boat back to the East, taking his promise of financial aid with him.' He looked at Janessa expectantly.

Did Rogan know what had happened with Dravos and his bodyguard? Not even Durket could have been so stupid as to tell him.

'We were unable to come to terms,' Janessa said quickly, before Durket finished what was in his mouth and said something stupid.

'Yes,' said Rogan. 'That's what I heard.'

That's what you heard? And where did you hear that, Seneschal Rogan? From one of your rats, hiding out in the eaves?

Janessa stood, the tartness of the lemons suddenly making her feel ill. That would be all she needed, to throw up all over the feasting table.

'If you'll excuse me,' she said. Everyone at the table rose to their feet as Kaira moved to her side.

She tried to hold herself steady as she walked from the room. Merrick opened the door to allow her to leave, while Kaira stood beside her all but propping her up. Janessa was thankful for the support.

When she reached her bedchamber she sat heavily on her bed, her responsibility weighing on her.

'Are you well, Majesty? Do you need water?' Kaira asked.

Janessa shook her head. 'I'm just light headed, that's all.'

Kaira sat beside her. 'Is it the child?'

Janessa smiled. Few people knew she was with child and she was thankful for that. Of those who did, Kaira was the one she trusted the most – she had risked her life to save Janessa; almost died for her.

'No, the baby is well.'

The door opened and she heard Merrick telling someone they had to wait, before the imposing figure of Odaka pushed his way inside

'It is fine, Merrick. Please.' She beckoned Odaka to enter as Merrick closed the chamber door behind them.

Kaira stood as the regent entered, recovering her veneer of discipline. Now, it was Odaka's turn to look concernedly at Janessa. It almost made her laugh, their fear for her. The city was on the brink of attack and here they were concerning themselves with one lightheaded girl.

She stood up. 'I am fine. Azai Dravos is dead. Nothing of him or his insidious sorceries remains. My only regret is we were unable to secure his master's coin before he died.'

'Indeed,' Odaka replied. 'Without it we will lose the support of the Free Companies.'

Janessa went to the window that looked out upon a city that might soon be razed to the ground.

'It's my fault,' she said. 'Were I not with child, perhaps Dravos would not have tried to take advantage. Perhaps he would have played straight with me. It has cost us everything.'

'No, Majesty,' said Kaira. Janessa was surprised. Though in private they spoke often, her bodyguard never voiced her opinions in front of others, especially not Odaka. 'Dravos knew what he was doing from the start.'

'She is right,' said Odaka. 'There was nothing that could be done. No outcome other than his death or your enthralment.'

'Then we should be resigned to our fate,' said Janessa, still staring out on the city.

'No, we should not. Every man, woman and child in Steelhaven is prepared to defend its walls. Your father's bannermen will be back in the city soon. They will bolster our ranks.'

What's left of them.

'Thank you, Odaka.'

She wanted to say that she was confident they would put up a valiant fight. That with such brave and loyal warriors victory was assured. But Janessa knew that a valiant fight would not be enough to hold back what was sweeping down from the north.

THIRTY THREE

Waylian had never set foot in the Trades Quarter before and it certainly wasn't what he'd expected. It hardly qualified as a 'quarter' for a start, squirreled away as it was between the Crown District and the Storway River. He'd anticipated bustle and verve, streets alive with the sound of ringing hammer and humming saw, the air on fire with rich aromas.

Fact was, the streets were all but deserted and stank as bad as the rest of the city. He passed a brewery that stood beside a tannery, and the mixture of smells almost turned his stomach. A blacksmith honed horseshoes beside a cooper crafting barrel rings, and the sound of their duelling hammers made such a discordant din he was forced to cover his ears.

He had difficulty navigating the narrow streets. It was only as he was beginning to feel he'd trodden every lane and alley of the Trades Quarter that he found the house he was looking for.

It was a narrow building, stretching upwards in between a weaver's and a chandler's. Unlike most of the dwellings in this part of the city it seemed well constructed; its stonework was uniform, the wood of its door recently varnished, the knocker and handle polished to a sheen. On the wall beside the door was nailed a brass plaque, embossed with the words: *Sequeous Qale – Scribe*. Waylian had to stop himself from punching the air in relief. Instead, he merely knocked three times.

After what seemed like an age, there was a jangling of keys and the door opened a crack, a thick chain snapping taut to stop it. The mournful face of an old man appeared. His features drooped with age, and grey hair fell to his chin. On his pointy nose sat a pair of spectacles, the thick lenses making his eyes look enormous.

'Yes?' asked the man.

'Sequeous Qale?' said Waylian.

'I am. And what can I do for you?'

'My name is Waylian Grimm. I've been sent from the Tower of Magisters. Your apprentice, Josiah Klumm, has been summoned on urgent business.' Waylian held out the sealed scroll Gelredida had given him.

Sequeous took it in his gnarled fingers as Waylian passed it through the crack in the door. With some difficulty the man broke the seal and unrolled it. Waylian watched as the old man cast his huge eyes across the letter. When he had finished he looked up, then slammed the door in Waylian's face.

That went well, Grimmy. You appear to be excelling at this kind of business! Magistra Gelredida will be so proud.

Waylian breathed a sigh of relief as he heard the chain rattle on the other side of the door, and Sequeous opened it. The old man said nothing, just turned and shuffled on down the corridor, allowing Waylian to follow.

The house smelled musty and old, every surface seeming to wear a layer of undisturbed dust. The corridor was lined with bookcases from floor to ceiling, each shelf stuffed to the gills with ancient leather-bound tomes. Where there was no room on the shelves, Sequeous had piled the floor high with yellowing scrolls and parchments of varying sizes.

Waylian followed the old man into an adjoining room. Light filtered in through four windows, lancing through the musty air. Four study tables sat in a rough square, islands in the midst of yet more books and parchments. At each of the tables sat one of Sequeous' apprentices, head bowed in studious observation, quill scratching away with calligraphic precision.

Three of the apprentices were withered and stooped, peering over their labours in a parody of the old men they would one day become. They would end up looking much like their master sooner rather than later. Only one of them still looked his real age. He was young, broad of shoulder, wide of jaw.

'Josiah?' Sequeous said, and the largest apprentice looked up from his parchment, quill appearing tiny in his huge hand. The boy gave no answer, just sat with a blank expression on his face. 'This is a messenger from the Tower of Magisters. You are to go with him.'

Josiah nodded obediently and walked over. Waylian noted how tall he was, how broad. It was a physique more suited to a squire of the knightly orders, where such burgeoning strength would be trained and honed, rather than wasted in an old man's study.

'Hello,' said Waylian.

The boy only stared back as though he'd just been asked some tricky riddle.

'Off you go, Josiah. You shouldn't keep the magisters waiting.'

The boy complied obediently, and Waylian turned and led him to the front door like a cow gone to milking.

When Sequeous had slammed the door behind them, Waylian turned to Josiah. 'Nothing to worry about,' he said, trying his best to reassure the young lad. 'I think they need scribes at the Tower, that's all. They'll just be trying you out. It's an excellent opportunity, by all accounts. Though if you'd prefer to stay here with Master Sequeous I'm sure they'll understand.'

But Waylian wasn't taking Josiah to the Tower. Gelredida had given him strict instructions to take the boy to another address in the city.

Josiah just regarded Waylian with his deep-set eyes. They no longer looked vacuous, and instead were regarding him with keen scrutiny. Waylian had to admit – it unnerved him a bit.

The Tower of Magisters was roughly north-east of the Trades Quarter, but Waylian took them south. The boy seemed placid enough at first, but any hope Waylian might have had that Josiah would come along quietly were soon dashed.

'Where are we going?' the boy asked suddenly.

'Just a slight detour,' Waylian replied. 'Nothing to worry about.'

'That's the second time you've said that.'

'Said what?'

'"Nothing to worry about." You've said it twice now. That kind of makes me think I *do* have something to worry about.'

'Well...'

'What's going on here?' Josiah's voice rose. He seemed to become more threatening. Waylian was acutely aware of the size difference between them – Josiah could easily thump Waylian into the ground.

'I've just got to make a quick stop off. Won't take long.'

Josiah stared at him, as though searching for any sign of deception in Waylian's face. All Waylian could do was look back until finally, the big lad seemed satisfied.

'All right then,' Josiah said, calm once more. 'Let's go.'

They carried on walking until they reached the north end of Dockside. The sea air was chill there, a cold wind blowing in from the Midral Sea, twisting its way through the alleys of the district. As surreptitiously as he could, Waylian checked the slip of paper in his hand and the address written on it, hoping he would find the second address more easily than the first. Too much dawdling might reveal the fact he had no idea where in the bloody hells he was going.

Fortunately, the streets of Dockside were easier to navigate than the Trades Quarter, and Waylian soon found the address. He fumbled in his pocket for the key to the little house and let them both in.

Inside the air was fusty, and the cobwebs draped over the furniture were thick as lace and it obvious no one had been here for weeks. Gelredida had told him to bring Josiah and wait for her to meet them, but how long would that be? How was he supposed to force this giant of a boy to stay if he didn't want to?

'Just take a seat,' said Waylian, dusting off a chair with his hand. 'Won't be long.'

He was relieved when Josiah did as he asked, but then wondered what in the hells he was going to do next.

Perhaps some scintillating conversation, Grimmy. You know – the sort you use to charm the ladies into your bed and the birds from the trees.

'So, a scribe?' said Waylian, with no idea what else he should talk about. 'Must be an interesting line of work.'

'Not particularly,' Josiah replied, glancing around the room as though it were daubed with shit. Waylian could understand that – calling this place a hovel would have been overstating it. 'It's pretty boring really.'

'But old Master Sequeous seems nice enough.'

'He's a cantankerous, doddery old fool, and the sooner he keels over and dies the better.'

'But it must be better working for a scribe than making arrows for some slave driver.' Waylian couldn't help feeling a pang of regret as he remembered those helpless orphans in the Northgate slum.

'I suppose,' said Josiah. 'But only marginally.'

And now Waylian was stumped. It was clear Josiah didn't give a toss about Sequeous, or about how lucky he'd been to escape the squalor of Fletcher's orphanage.

He glanced at the door, willing Gelredida to arrive. The moments seemed to spread out, growing ever more uncomfortable. With every passing breath Josiah seemed to get more fidgety until he could contain himself no longer.

'Look,' he said, rising from his chair. 'I'm not waiting round here all day.'

The confines of the small room emphasized how much he towered above Waylian. 'But... it won't be much longer,' Waylian replied, his fear of failing Gelredida still outweighing his fear of Josiah.

'Not really my problem. Give my regards to the magisters, won't you.'

He moved towards the door, but Waylian moved to block his way. The ridiculousness of Waylian trying to stop his huge adversary was not lost on him.

'Maybe we could talk some more,' he said, desperate to delay Josiah. 'What was life like back in the slums? Must have been difficult for you.'

Josiah's brow furrowed. 'It was just about as shit as you'd imagine. But what I'm bothered about is how you know where I came from? Who told you I was from the slums? Who told you I used to be one of Fletcher's boys? If you're just looking for apprentice scribes how do you know about my past? And why are you so interested in me?'

All very good questions, Josiah. Wish I could answer them.

'It's... erm...'

'Get out of my way.'

Josiah looked determined. Waylian was going to blow it again.

'No. You can't leave yet.' He tried to muster all the power and authority becoming of a magister. He most likely sounded like a petulant toddler. 'We have to wait here for someone. Then all your questions will be answered.'

'Fuck that,' Josiah replied, reaching past Waylian for the door handle.

Without thinking, Waylian grabbed his wrist. It was thick, and he could hardly get his hand around it, but that didn't seem particularly important as Josiah regarded him with fury.

A hand snapped forward and grabbed Waylian by the throat, slamming him up against the door.

'You going to stop me then?' growled Josiah. 'What are you going to do?'

Waylian wanted to be both defiant, and apologetic. Unfortunately, neither option was possible with his throat constricted as it was.

Rage and humiliation welled inside and, for a fleeting moment, he thought he was about to manifest some kind of power – that power he'd felt in the Chapel of Ghouls, and when Nero and Ferenz had come to his chamber to intimidate him.

Before that could happen, Josiah flung him out of the way. Waylian landed hard, hitting his head against the wall. Real anger bubbled to the surface. Not magickal, not infused with power, just cold hard rage.

'*I said no!*' he screamed, as Josiah grabbed the door handle again. With a strength that surprised him, Waylian rose to his feet then flung himself across the room. His arms wrapped around Josiah's neck and he hung there, his feet dangling as the big lad tried to shake him free.

He held on as Josiah staggered across the room making a pathetic choking sound. Josiah's big hands worked to pull Waylian off, but to no avail. There was no way Josiah would escape, no way Waylian was going to disappoint his mistress again.

Josiah stumbled, then toppled over, falling on a broken chair, which shattered into pieces beneath them. The air was punched from Waylian's lungs, forcing him to release his victim.

He flailed his arms, vainly trying to grab Josiah's shirt, but the big lad had already rolled away and risen to his feet. Waylian stared into those murderous eyes as Josiah looked down.

'I'll fucking kill you,' Josiah growled.

Waylian's hand scrabbled around beneath him until it closed on something hard. As Josiah came forwards Waylian rose to his feet, swiping what turned out to be a chair leg across Josiah's head. The big lad went down like he'd been shot with an arrow.

The chair leg felt unbelievably heavy in Waylian's hand and all he could do was stand there and stare at the body in front of him.

Shit, what have you done? You've fucking killed him. Gelredida's going to skin you alive for this.

He dropped the chair leg to the floor, and quickly squatted down beside Josiah. The lad's head was bleeding and he was out like a snuffed candle. Waylian moved closer, relief washing over him as he felt Josiah's breath on his face.

Before he could even begin to think his way out of the predicament, the door to the little house opened.

Gelredida walked in and casually closed the door behind her. She regarded Waylian, kneeling as he was over the body of Josiah Klumm, with curiosity.

'What do we have here?' she asked.

'It's... er... not what it looks like?'

'Really?' She raised one white eyebrow. 'Because it looks as though you've killed the boy I sent you to fetch.'

'He's not dead, Magistra. He's just... er...'

'Having a nap?'

'He tried to leave. We fought and I... hit him with a chair leg.'

'How very resourceful, Waylian.'

'I didn't mean to. It just—'

'Never mind.' She pulled out a length of rope from inside her robes. 'It's saved me a job anyway. Tie him up and put him in the cellar.' She flung the rope to Waylian. 'Make sure he's gagged. We don't want him screaming the place down when we leave.'

Waylian stared at her for a second, then at the rope. 'You mean we were going to keep him prisoner here all along?'

Gelredida smiled. 'I wasn't going to ask him nicely. By all accounts he's quite a stubborn, wilful jackass. Just like his father.'

'Who's his—?'

'Enough questions, Waylian. Rope. Cellar. Chop chop.' She punctuated her last two words with a swift clap of her gloved hands.

Waylian put his mind to the task and tied Josiah as tightly as he could. As he flipped the door to the cellar open and peered down into the dark he did wonder what the lad had done to deserve such a fate. Was it his place to ask? Gelredida seemed in no mood to answer questions, though she'd taken Josiah's unconscious condition better than he expected.

Just do as you're told, Grimmy. It's probably best if you don't know. You don't want to end up the one in the cellar, do you?

As Gelredida watched impatiently, Waylian dragged Josiah's unconscious form into the darkness.

Maybe he'd ask her all about it later.

Maybe he'd just keep his mouth shut.

THIRTY FOUR

As she got to the top end of Slip Street, Rag couldn't work out whether she'd missed this place or not – the filthy streets, the ramshackle houses, the girls calling for punters. It was weird – there were the same faces, the same sights and sounds, but now it somehow felt different. Or maybe it wasn't different; maybe it was exactly the same and it was her who had changed.

You don't belong here no more. You should never have come. Never look back – it only leads to pain. Why don't you just turn around and go back to the Guild? That's your family now. That's where you belong.

But Rag didn't turn around. How could she?

She carried on walking down the street, a sack thrown over one shoulder, tramping through the mud like she'd never left this place. When she saw the Bull ahead of her she got a heavy feeling in the pit of her stomach. Her pace slowed and she came to a stop, just staring up at that roof.

What if they hated her for leaving? What if they threw things and spat at her for deserting them?

What if they didn't?

Only one way to find out what they'd do, and she hadn't walked all the way here for the good of her health. Tightening her grip on the sack, Rag crossed the street and made her way up those rickety stairs, the wood creaking like it was gonna give way beneath her. She'd done it a thousand times before, but she'd never been so scared as she was now.

When she made it up over the lip of the roof she expected them to be waiting, arms folded, evil looks in their eyes. But despite the noise she'd made on the way up, there weren't no one waiting. Just that little shack made of planks sitting on the flat roof.

Rag walked across the rooftop, taking no pains to be quiet. As she got close to the shack she could hear voices talking, fast and low.

'Getting fucking colder,' said one.

'I know it's getting fucking colder, and there ain't nothing to be done about it,' said another.

'We should get a fire going.'

'You fucking get a fire going.'

They were voices Rag recognised, but something was different about them. They weren't carefree like they used to be. It weren't no light-hearted banter. Now there was a hard edge to the squabbling.

She peered inside. Chirpy, his once smiling face now mournful, sat staring at the empty ashes of a dead fire. Little Tidge had grown; but grown lean, and his face had a wolfishness to it like he'd seen one too many bad things. What concerned her most was the sight of Migs curled up on the floor, his long hair matted to his head.

'What's going on, shit stains?' she said, expecting them to turn around and laugh or shout… or something.

The lads didn't even flinch, just looked up at her blankly. She could have been anyone – could have been a Greencoat come to turf them off the roof – it was obvious they didn't care.

Rag squeezed herself into the shack and took a seat on the makeshift bench. She tried a smile but couldn't take her eyes from Migs lying on the floor.

'What's wrong with him?' she asked, reaching out a hand and touching the clammy skin of his cheek.

'Fuck do you care?' Tidge replied.

Chirpy nudged him. 'He's got some kind of fever. We don't know what to do about it. We ain't got coin for no apothecary.'

'So you've just left him lying there – no blanket or nothing?'

'We ain't got one. What we supposed to do?' said Chirpy.

'What about Fender?' Rag asked. 'Where's he?'

Both the boys shrugged.

'Not seen him for weeks,' said Tidge.

Rag placed her sack down on the makeshift bench and knelt down beside Migs.

'All right, little mate?' she asked. 'How you feeling?'

He looked up and tried a little smile that turned into a grimace and a cough.

'What's in the bag?' asked Tidge as Rag wiped Migs' clammy forehead.

'Have a look,' she replied.

As she wondered what to do about Migs, the other two rummaged through the sack, finding the lukewarm pie and the bread she'd brought. There was a small bottle of ale too, but the lads were too busy crowing over the food to notice it.

'Make sure it's shared equal,' Rag said, as she fished around in her shirt pocket. Her hand rested on a gold crown – the only money she had left – and for a second she wondered if now was the time to use it.

What are you gonna keep it for? It's not like you've got expensive taste in frigging clothes, is it? Migs is in need. Do the right thing.

She turned to see Chirpy and Tidge already with full cheeks. For a moment she could have scolded them for their greed, but she'd been the wrong side of starving enough times herself, and knew all too well how it made you forget your manners. Not that these two little buggers had any manners in the first place.

'Listen, and listen good,' she said. 'Migs needs medicine, and you're to get it for him, understood?' Before either of the lads could protest she held up the gold crown. Both of them gazed at it as though it were all the gold in Queen Janessa's treasury. 'This'll be enough. Don't let the apothecary scam you. Just tell him Migs has a fever and you're willing to pay for anything what cures him.'

Chirpy nodded, but Tidge was still staring at that gold crown. Rag thought it best if she let Chirpy take charge of it, and flicked it to him. He snatched it from the air and had it away up his sleeve in a heartbeat.

'You're not back to stay then?' Tidge asked.

'No, I'm not,' she replied, and felt an unexpected twinge of regret at the words.

'You just left without a word. Didn't even say goodbye.'

'I know,' Rag said. 'But there were things I had to do. Things I had to take care of alone. I thought Fender would be looking out for you, but it looks like he lied about that.' *And not for the first time.*

'We can take care of ourselves,' said Chirpy.

Rag glanced around the little shack that looked more rotten than ever.

'Yeah, it looks like it.'

They just sat then, nothing more to say. The lads kept eating – had most of the pie and bread. Rag was pleased when she didn't need to remind them to save a portion for Migs. When they'd finished she stood up, gave them each a nod, and made her way out of the shack.

'You coming back?' asked Chirpy, as she made her way over the roof and towards the stairs.

Well, are you? Will you even bother to come back and see if Migs is okay? There's a tough winter coming, and worse if the Khurtas get through that wall. Are you gonna come check on them, or are you just gonna look to yourself?

'Aye, I'll be back,' she replied, not looking over her shoulder. Not wanting Chirpy to see the same lie on her face as he heard from her lips.

How could she promise to come back? She already had enough to deal with. Hells, she might not even be alive tomorrow.

Maybe you should have told the truth. Maybe you should have let them know they ain't going to see you again. That you only came out of guilt and it hasn't made you feel no better.

But she couldn't do that neither. She was just a coward and she knew it. Only bothered about herself. She'd spent years looking after a crew of lads and look where it had got her – screaming for help on a rooftop while one of them bled his last out through a hole in his throat.

They were better off without her. Better off fending for themselves than getting mixed up with Rag and her shit. And it was shit all right – following her round wherever she went, stinking her up good and proper.

Who are you trying to kid? Don't try to pretend you're protecting them. You're running away, just like last time.

Rag stopped at the end of Slip Street and took a glance back. If she never saw this place again it would be too soon. Saying that, what waited for her elsewhere might not be much better.

As she made her way through the streets towards Northgate, Rag began to get that heavy feeling in her stomach. If Slip Street had held daemons for her, there was a tavern somewhere on her route that held trouble ten times worse, and no mistake.

She'd let that man Nobul go free. What kind of payback would there be for that? Would Friedrik know it was Rag what let him out? Would he be waiting with something sharp and pointy just for her?

Only one way to find out.

The thought of running away crossed her mind, though it was only fleeting. She'd learned how to survive in this city, and that was all she knew. How would she live outside it? Find a job in some backwater village? Get work on the land?

Rag the farmer? Do me a fucking favour.

Friedrik's tavern was quiet when she reached it. The street was dark – no lamplighters would be along this end of Steelhaven any time soon, and she paused at the threshold.

Last chance, Rag. Take it or leave it.

Rag turned the door handle and walked in.

She had no idea what she'd been expecting. *Anger?* Certainly. *Uproar?* Probably. *Carnage?* Yeah... but not like this.

The place looked smashed to pieces. There were corpses everywhere, many of them naked. The lads were doing their best to clean up; Yarrick and Essen were carrying a body to one corner where there was a pile of the dead. Even Harkas was helping, wiping blood off a tabletop with a soiled rag. Shirl, still looking worse for wear, stayed out of the way, too injured to help and too scared to leave.

Rag looked across at the shadow standing in front of the dying fire. All she could see was his back as he stared into the dying embers.

Rag wanted nothing more than to run. She should have taken that chance, should have fled when she was outside and the going was good, but she was here now. Had she brought all this about? All those people dead – and because she'd let Nobul go.

He'd warned her too – told her if she fucking hung around she'd end up dead just like them. And she'd believed him... mostly. She couldn't have expected this though, could she? Surely it weren't her fault?

Slowly she crossed the tavern to where Friedrik was stood. She didn't say nothing, just stood behind him. Rag knew better than to interrupt him when he was lost in thought. Shirl and his bruises were enough of a lesson not to get on the wrong side of Friedrik. But then there was every chance she'd already got on his wrong side. Only question was, would she be able to lie her way out of it?

'Where the fuck have you been?' Friedrik said, not looking round from the fire. Rag couldn't tell if he was angry or not, there was neither joy nor menace in his tone.

'I... I ran away,' she replied, not knowing what else to say. 'When it all kicked off I ran away into the night and I was too scared to come back.' If she tried half-truths maybe he wouldn't sniff out the lie in what she was saying. She'd already proved she weren't no good at lying back when that woman Kaira caught her. No use chancing it now.

'The lads said it was your idea they leave. Your idea the place was left unguarded. I said it couldn't be true, that you'd never be so stupid.'

'Yeah, I did say that, but I didn't think—'

'You didn't think?' Friedrik turned round, and she could see his face was grave, like he'd just been to a funeral. Or a dozen funerals, all at once. 'Do you expect me to believe that? It's something I'd believe of Shirl or Essen or Yarrick, but not you. You're always *thinking*, Rag. Always one step ahead – that's why I like you. That's why I keep you around.'

'I just meant... I didn't think there were no danger.'

He stared at her, those eyes burning deep like he could see through the lies. 'Well, clearly there fucking was, because it's like a butcher's shop in here. Rare cuts lie all around. Chop chop chop.'

As he punctuated his last three words with three slices of his hand, Rag swallowed.

'It all just happened so quick. I had to get out. There weren't nothing I could do.'

'It happened so quick? Yes, I'm sure. A deadly man, our Nobul Jacks. But I'm wondering; how did he manage to get loose? Know anything about that?'

Rag thought hard. What could she say? What did Friedrik think she knew?

'That toothless bloke,' she said. 'He was taunting the fella in the cellar. Couldn't keep away. I told him to leave well alone, but he just wouldn't. Maybe he dropped his keys.'

'Really?' asked Friedrik, looking genuinely interested. 'How clever of you to work that out when I never even mentioned he had a set of keys. How would you know that?'

You and your fucking mouth, Rag.

'Just a guess. How else would it have happened?'

Friedrik glared at her. It was obvious he knew. Obvious he was just dragging this out for the show.

'Where is he?' Friedrik asked, finally.

'Who?'

'Nobul Jacks. The man in the fucking cellar.' He was talking through his teeth now; she'd seen it a dozen times – always just before he stuck something into someone and they screamed and screamed, but he carried on sticking like he couldn't hear their pain.

'I don't know. I just ran. I ran away.' She could feel tears welling in her eyes. Behind her the lads had stopped with their business and were watching what was happening. Rag knew she'd get no help from them.

'Where did you run to? Back to his house? He must have been in a bad way, Rag. Did you see to his wounds and then come back here? Where the fuck is he?'

'I don't know, I swear it.'

Friedrik reached out and grabbed her arms. His fingers dug in deep and she almost cried out in pain. Almost.

'You've been gone all night and all day. Where have you been? Tell me now or I'll—'

'I went to find Merrick!' she shouted. 'That Merrick Ryder fella, like you wanted.'

Friedrik's brow softened all of a sudden. 'What?'

'I ran and I was on the streets and I didn't know what to do and I knew you'd be angry and I went to find that Merrick and he's meeting me later.'

Friedrik let go of her, a smile taking over his face. 'Why didn't you say that in the first place?' he asked. She stared at him, at his smiling face, wondering what kind of mad bastard just changed on a coin toss like that.

'Well? What are you waiting for?' he said. 'Lead the way.'

THIRTY FIVE

Kaira waited in the dark. Leofric and Oswil were in their positions at either end of the alleyway, standing in the shadows, cloaks pulled tight about them. Without their armour, all three looked like any other street scum sheltering from the winter cold. It was a risk to be out here unprotected, but they couldn't chance spooking their quarry. She would have preferred to bring more men, but too many might have given the game away. Besides, she was sure the three of them could handle a bunch of Northgate thugs.

Not that she was even confident they would need to. There was every chance this was a fool's errand and the girl Rag wouldn't show. Kaira had fully expected their first meeting to be their last.

She had placed trust in the girl at the time– what else could she do? – but always remembered Rag was a child of the streets. In the few days since Kaira had let the girl walk from the Sentinels' barracks she had lost all hope of seeing her again. It had been a surprise, then, when Rag suddenly appeared in the night, breathless and fearful. She said the time was right, that she would fulfil her part of their bargain and all she wanted in return was beer and bread and maybe a pie. Kaira had seen to it she had all those things, fully expecting the girl to gorge herself, but instead she had placed the items in a sack. Before she left, they'd arranged this meeting place – a dead end street in Northgate.

As Kaira stood, waiting on the word of an adolescent waif, she began to feel more and more foolish. Kaira was quick to trust, perhaps too quick, that much was obvious. As a Shieldmaiden she had put all her faith in the Temple of Autumn, in the Matron Mother, in the Exarch. Since then she had learned that her faith had been misplaced, that perhaps the Temples of Arlor and their figurehead, the High Abbot, were as flawed as any other institution. For years she had served as a tool, obeying the word of her superiors without question, even when her own feelings might have swayed her otherwise.

Now, as she stood in the cold, it seemed that blind trust had led her astray once more.

Merrick should have been there – he was, after all, the bait – but Kaira couldn't stomach being near him. In the past she had risked everything for him, even gambled her life to save his, and what had she got in return?

Nothing.

Still he wallowed in self-pity, finding solace at the bottom of a tankard. Still he cared only about himself. Only now it was worse. His father had returned and Merrick had to deal with his deep-rooted resentment. Not that he faced it head on, like a warrior should. He shied from it, hid from it like a craven. She had seen him fight well enough, and his sword hand was strong. If only his heart could be the same.

To the hells with him anyway. His wallowing had caused Statton's death and opened Queen Janessa up to sorcerous powers. She would rely on him no longer.

The sound of voices alerted Kaira to someone entering the alleyway. She forgot all about Merrick as her hand strayed to her sword – though she knew that was folly. Her wrist still ached from the wound Azai Dravos had inflicted. She might well be able to draw the weapon from its sheath but she would have been near useless with it.

'How much farther?' asked a voice in the distance.

'Not far now,' came the reply. Kaira's heart beat faster. She recognised the voice.

As Rag walked into the scant light Kaira saw she led a group of men, five in all, of varying sizes. Instantly Kaira's eyes strayed to the biggest of their number, identifying the greatest threat.

Once the group had reached the midpoint of the alleyway, Kaira stepped out into the light of the moon. Rag halted in front of her, but said nothing.

'What's going on?' said one of the men, as they stopped behind Rag.

Kaira watched, assessing the group, giving them a chance to reveal which of them was their leader. As she did so, Leofric came up behind them and Oswil appeared from an alley to the right, both with swords drawn.

The biggest of the bunch looked down at the man to his right, unsure of what to do. The man he looked at, a short fellow whom Kaira had marked as no danger, stepped forward.

'Gentlemen,' he said, relaxed, calm, unafraid. 'It's clear you have no idea who I am, so I'll give you the chance to leave quietly. Because I have pressing business, I'll forget this little transgression, just this once.'

As he spoke, the men around him reached for their weapons – knives, clubs, though none of them carried a sword.

'I know who you are,' Kaira said pulling back her hood.

By now three of the men had squared off against Oswil and Leofric. The biggest of their number just gaped dumbly at Kaira.

'You know who I am? Either you're insane or lying,' said the little man. 'I'm Friedrik. As in Bastian and Friedrik? Of the Guild? I assume you're robbers or killers, so you'll no doubt have heard of me. And you will no doubt realise you'll have nowhere to hide unless you piss off out of my way right now.'

'Your men are free to leave,' Kaira replied. 'I only want you.'

Kaira stared at the little man, Friedrik, but remained aware of the hulking thug standing next to him. Even as Friedrik signalled with his hand, even as he said, 'Harkas, do the honours,' she still stared at Friedrik.

The brute strode towards her, his silhouette blotting out the light of the moon. As he reached out with a huge hand Kaira struck. Her sword hand might have been injured but her left was as strong as ever. And one hand was all she would need.

Before he could reach her throat Kaira grasped that big hand, twisting it at the wrist. She forced the bull of a man to his knees and he grunted, his other hand coming up to grab her. A sharp twist made him grunt again and think better of it. He could only grasp at his wrist as it teetered on the brink of snapping.

Friedrik's remaining henchmen made their move, attacking with little style or skill. Leofric swatted the club from one man's hand with a deft swipe of his sword. Oswil parried a stabbing knife and struck out with his pommel, breaking his opponent's nose and sending him sprawling. The one that remained, a fat man who looked like someone had already given him a beating recently, dropped his knife and held up his hands in surrender.

'What now?' Friedrik asked, seeming more amused than perturbed at the easy besting of his men. 'Are we all to be slaughtered?' The prospect didn't seem to bother him one bit.

'You will come with me,' she said.

'Will I?' Friedrik replied.

Leofric took a step forward, the flat of his sword connecting firmly with the back of Friedrik's head. He was driven to his knees, his hands coming up to that mop of curly hair. Kaira expected him to moan, or at least to beg, but when he looked up she saw he had a smile on his face.

'Looks like I will,' he said, giggling, though Kaira couldn't see the joke.

She glanced at the rest of his henchmen. They seemed a sorry collection. For a man like Friedrik, a man in charge of most of the illicit business in the city, they were a wholly inadequate bodyguard.

'The rest of you can run or die. The choice is yours,' she said, still holding onto the big man's wrist. If any of them were going to offer any trouble it would be him, so better the rest were gone before he was allowed the chance to get up.

Without a second thought for their leader, the three thugs fled down the alley. Kaira looked at the one on his knees.

'What about you?'

He gazed at her for a while, assessing his chances, before giving the smallest of nods.

Kaira released his wrist. He slowly rose to his feet until he towered over her. Kaira half expected him to launch himself forward, throwing his life away for one last chance to rescue his master. Instead, he walked after his fellows, down into the shadows of the alleyway, with not so much as a second glance at Friedrik.

So much for loyalty among thieves.

'Shall we?' Kaira asked.

Friedrik climbed unsteadily to his feet. 'I suppose we shall,' he replied.

Leofric and Oswil took Friedrik by the arms and marched him on into the dark. As Kaira followed behind, Rag appeared at her side. As soon as Kaira had confronted the group the girl had disappeared. Kaira admired her skill for concealment – she guessed it came in handy in her line of work.

'There's no reason for you to follow anymore, Rag. I think your work is done.'

'Where am I going to go?' the girl replied. 'I've started this now, may as well see it through.'

'If you come with us what you see might not be pretty.'

'You think it'll be any worse than the shit I've seen already?'

Kaira guessed it wouldn't be, though how ugly things would get was yet to be seen. Much of that depended on Friedrik.

It was near dawn when they got back to the barracks. The place was all but deserted as they conveyed him to the cells. Kaira could have handed him over to the Greencoats, but she had learned enough to know they could not be trusted, not with a man as important as this. If word spread that they held one of the masters of the Guild he would be dead or fled within the day. Better that she kept her hands on him for the time being.

Why there were cells in the barracks of the Skyhelm Sentinels Kaira had no idea. Perhaps because of some age old tradition that military or political prisoners be kept there. Perhaps because of something more sinister. Whatever the reason, Kaira was thankful for it.

Friedrik was sat in a chair, his hands bound behind him. Leofric and Oswil stood outside the door and Kaira was grateful for their discretion. For a fleeting moment she had considered waking Captain Garret. He should, after all, be informed of what type of guest had arrived, but Kaira wanted some time alone with Friedrik first. She'd been hunting this man for a long while. Had failed in her task to find him once. It was one of the reasons she had turned her back on the Temple of Autumn. She was curious to know the man responsible for much of the suffering in this city.

As she stared at him, Kaira wondered what to say. What could she say? She had never interrogated anyone before. Kaira Stormfall was a warrior, a protector. She was no inquisitor.

'Is this where the torture begins?' Friedrik asked.

Kaira turned, opening her mouth, wanting to tell him to be silent, but she could find no words.

Was it where the torture would begin? Was this where she would beat him? Cut him? Slice off his extremities?

That is not you. That has never been your way. It's not likely you will start now.

'I will ask you some questions,' she replied.

'Questions?' he said, his lips turning up into a smile. 'How utterly tedious. Surely it's time to send in the boys, let the fun begin?'

What was wrong with this man? He couldn't really relish the thought of being tortured… unless of course it was all bravado.

'Where is the Guild based?' said Kaira. 'From where do you organise this city's criminals?'

Friedrik laughed. 'Really? That's all you can come up with? Some dull question you know I'll never answer? Do be serious, dear, and stop wasting my time.'

'I will have an answer to my question,' she said, standing before him, holding him in a steel gaze. A gaze she had used on the battlefield, a gaze that had made veteran warriors crumble.

Friedrik just smiled again. 'Am I meant to be intimidated? By a woman? Is this some kind of joke? I'm guessing a real interrogator will be here in a minute to put me to the question, while you go off and fetch the tea. That's it, isn't it?'

Kaira's fists clenched, her teeth grinding together. She had bloodied men for less.

'Where? Tell me or I swear by Vorena I'll—'

'You'll what? You'll pull out my fingernails? You'll cut out my eyes? Then get the fuck on with it, because listening to you going on, girl, is giving me a stinking fucking headache.'

She hit him, hard in the gut, without thinking. Her wrist suddenly blazed in pain as she felt the stitches pull tight. Kaira gritted her teeth against it, not wanting to show any weakness in front of this man, but she needn't have bothered. Friedrik was doubled over, gasping for air. But as she took a step back and as he laboured for breath, he slowly looked up, eyes wide, revealing a glint of the insane as he forced his mouth into a grimace.

'You'll have to do better than that,' Friedrik said, his face reddening with every strained word. 'Much fucking better.'

Kaira knew she'd never be able to do better. The man was helpless – insane but helpless – and it was not in her to make a man suffer if he could not fight back. Even a man such as this, a man who would see hundreds sent into slavery just to line his own pocket.

She turned for the door, hearing him laugh as she opened it. Once she had slammed it closed behind her, she breathed a deep sigh of relief. Just being near Friedrik seemed to infect her; he was poison, a canker on her and this city. She raised a hand to her brow and felt a sheen of cooling sweat there.

'You all right?' asked Leofric, who was standing guard nearby.

Kaira nodded, then spotted Rag crouched down in the passageway. Kaira suddenly felt the bite of shame. This girl, this child, had been at Friedrik's side for weeks, months maybe. How had she managed to live with such a man? For a moment Kaira began to appreciate the girl's bravery.

But maybe she's not just brave. She must be cunning too, to have survived so long. Maybe she knows more than she's letting on.

'Rag, stand up,' said Kaira.

The girl obeyed. 'Won't talk, will he?' she said.

Kaira shook her head. 'No, he won't. He won't tell me anything. Can *you* tell me anything, Rag?'

The girl shrugged her shoulders. 'Don't know nothing,' she replied. 'I'm just Friedrik's pet. He don't tell me none of what he gets up to and I only know one of his hideouts and that won't be much use now he's not in it. Only thing I ever get to see is people being hurt. Only people I meet in the Guild come and go as they please. Now you've got Friedrik I might never see none of them again.'

'Then I need to get him to talk,' Kaira said, as much to herself as to the girl. 'But it can't be the Greencoats or the Inquisition. It can't be anyone who might have any links with the Guild.'

Rag looked doubtful, then brightened as though she'd had an idea, but the expression was gone as soon as it arrived.

'What is it?' Kaira asked.

'Well… there might be someone we can trust, but I don't know how good he'll be at making Friedrik talk. He might just as likely strangle him as soon as he sets eyes on him.' A mischievous smile crept onto her face. 'Friedrik'll shit himself when he sees him, though.'

THIRTY SIX

Nobul ached like someone had been using him as a doormat for a month. He had always healed fast, always been able to shake off the hurt, but he was feeling his years now. Nevertheless, he could walk and, at a push, he could fight. That was all that mattered. If the Guild were still after him – and he guessed after his party back at the tavern they most likely were – he'd need to fight soon enough.

As he walked the early morning streets he wasn't scared, though. Let them bloody come. Let them try to take him back and throw him in another dog pit. He was ready now. They wouldn't find it so easy to catch Nobul Jacks a second time.

A small part of him wanted them to come. Part of him looked forward to the fight. They'd tried to humiliate him, tried to kill him, but he'd paid them back for that. There were a dozen corpses as testament to it. He'd had his taste of vengeance, but his hunger was not satisfied. If he could remember the way back to that tavern in Northgate he'd most likely have gone there right now and killed anyone in there but he'd stumbled out of there delirious – wandering in a daze. He hadn't a chance of finding, let alone recognising, the place again.

Not that it mattered. As soon as he got his hands on Anton he'd go to work and no mistake. That little bastard would tell Nobul everything he knew – but most importantly, where he could find Friedrik. Then there'd be a reckoning. That little bastard had been responsible for the death of this son.

He'd been the one to order the hit that had seen his son bleeding to death on a rooftop. Without him and his fucking Guild, Markus would still be alive.

Nobul wasn't done by a long way. Right now though, he needed to get back to the Greencoats, back to Kilgar and let him know what had gone on. He trusted his serjeant; Kilgar was a man of honour, if a bit of a bastard. Better that Nobul had someone watching his back, especially if he was taking on the Guild – there was no reason to be foolish about it. Nobul Jacks might well have been able to handle himself in a brawl, but there was no point being reckless. With the rest of the lads behind him it'd be easier to find those scumbags and take them down.

When Nobul walked into the courtyard of the Greencoat barracks the lads were sat around like none of them had a care in the world. Old Hake was telling Bilgot, Dustin and Edric some tale about the old days. The three of them were listening intently; even fat Bilgot kept his mouth shut as the old fella went on. None of them noticed Nobul at first, and he scanned the courtyard for Anton. The little bastard was nowhere in sight, and as Nobul headed to the main building, Kilgar came out.

The serjeant stopped in front of Nobul, his mouth opening, most likely to ask where in the hells Nobul had been for the past few days, when he noticed the state of Nobul's face.

'What the fuck's happened to you?' Kilgar asked, though he didn't look that concerned.

'Had a run-in with some dogs,' Nobul replied, in no mood to go into details just yet. 'Where's Anton?'

Kilgar shrugged. 'I was going to ask you the same thing. I've not seen him for days.'

Hake had stopped his chatter now and the lads were looking over. 'What about you lot?' Nobul asked, turning to them. 'Anyone seen him?'

The lads just shook their heads. It was clear Nobul was in no mood to be pissed around.

'You all right?' Kilgar asked. 'Do you need some time off?'

Nobul shook his head. 'I've had enough time off.'

'Good,' said Kilgar, 'because you've had visitors, just this morning. They've brought you something.'

'Oh aye? Anything good?'

'Follow me and see for yourself.'

Kilgar turned and led Nobul towards the cells.

Down in the torchlit corridors beneath the barracks Nobul could see two figures waiting up ahead. One was a tall woman who looked familiar, though for the life of him he couldn't place her. She was broad at the shoulder, the features of her face strong and proud.

The second figure he did recognise, even stood as she was in the shadows. She looked at him, her eyes wide, fearful. That stung him a little bit. Out of everything he'd done back in that tavern, all the death he'd caused, frightening that little girl had been the one thing he'd regretted.

'You all right?' he asked Rag.

'Yeah, you?' she replied.

'I'll live,' he said.

He wanted to smile, wanted to thank her, wanted to take her in his arms and give her a grateful hug, but he didn't. Because as Kilgar opened the cell door, Nobul had a feeling he knew what was waiting for him. And this was not a time for thanks and hugs and gratitude.

This was his time for vengeance.

He was sitting on a chair, hands bound behind him, sack over his head. Nobul remembered how it felt to have a sack over his own head, remembered how it struck fear in your guts, how you didn't know where you were or who was watching or what they were going to do to you next.

'They brought him in earlier today,' said Kilgar. 'The woman's from the Sentinels. Says this here's—'

'Yeah, I've got a good idea who this is,' Nobul said, walking into the cell.

He was excited, almost gleeful. All he'd wanted for the past few days was to get his hands on this bastard, and now he had him. Might as well enjoy it.

Slowly he lifted the sack off Friedrik's head. When he looked up at Nobul, Friedrik seemed to go through a range of emotions – fear, confusion, recognition and back to fear again. Then he smiled.

'Wondered when I'd see you again,' he said.

Nobul just glowered at him.

'He's high up in the Guild, by all accounts,' Kilgar said. 'Is it who you were expecting?'

'Yeah, it is,' Nobul replied.

'How do you know him?'

'Let's say I've been lucky enough to have been his guest for the past few days.'

'Indeed,' said Friedrik, 'and what entertaining company you've been.'

Nobul took a step forward, his fist clenched, but before he could think where to begin, Kilgar took him by the arm.

'We need him talking, not dead,' Kilgar said. 'The woman, Kaira, said you were the only one she could trust with the job, though to be honest she didn't sound too sure about it.'

Nobul looked over his shoulder to where Kaira was watching from the corridor. Rag stood beside her, and he reckoned it was more likely the girl had been the one to say this was a job for Nobul.

Was she right? Could he get this bastard talking without killing him first? Only time would tell, he supposed.

'What do they expect me to do?' Nobul said. 'I'm no inquisitor.'

'That's what I've been saying,' said Friedrik. 'Surely it would be better for everyone if I was just turned over to the Inquisition. Then none of you have to worry about me anymore.'

Nobul shook his head. 'Do we look fucking stupid? We know you've got your grubby little paws into every nook and cranny of this city. Wouldn't surprise me if the Seneschal himself is in your pocket.'

Friedrik just shrugged. 'Then we appear to be at something of an impasse.'

'Yeah, we do.' Nobul turned to Kilgar. 'Leave me alone with him.'

The serjeant stared back uncertainly. 'Remember, we need him alive. I'd be as happy as you to see him dead, but we won't get any answers that way.'

Nobul didn't answer, and with no other choice Kilgar eventually conceded and left Nobul to it, walking out of the room and slamming the door shut behind him.

'Alone at last,' said Friedrik. 'Need me alive, yes? So what are we going to try? Strangulation? Beating me to a pulp?'

'You killed my son,' Nobul said.

Friedrik seemed to think on that. 'Mmm, don't remember that one. I'm not really into that kind of thing.'

'It was one of your murders went wrong. He was caught in the crossfire.'

'Ah, an unfortunate accident then? If it makes you feel any better, I'm sorry. We both know I'm not shy about killing, but even I don't relish the death of a child.'

'No, it don't make me feel any better. And I don't think you're sorry.'

Friedrik's expression darkened. 'Then you'd better get on with it, hadn't you?'

Nobul clenched his fists. He would have liked nothing more, and there was no one here to stop him. But if he didn't try to get Friedrik to talk Nobul knew he'd regret it. If he could bring down the Guild, or at least the men at the top of it, surely that would be vengeance enough. Surely that would mean Markus hadn't died for nothing.

'Where are the other bastards you work with?' Nobul asked. 'How do I find them?'

Friedrik shook his head, looking almost disappointed that Nobul wasn't going to kill him. 'Not this again. You know I'm not going to tell you. And big and tough as you are, there's nothing you can do that will make me.'

Looking at this sadist, sitting there all helpless, Nobul suddenly realised he would get nothing from him. You didn't rise to the head of the Guild without being stubborn to the point of insane. You didn't control every brigand and thug and thief in the city without being able to control yourself, without being able to resist blabbing even when your skin was flayed and your teeth pulled right out of your head. As much as Nobul would have loved to test that theory, he was sure he'd be wasting his time.

'May as well finish it right now then?' he said, taking a step forward.'

'Or,' Friedrik said, 'you could think about your future.'

Nobul stopped, looking down at the little man, wondering whether he should just strangle him. 'Go on.'

'I can make you rich,' said Friedrik. 'I can give you anything you want. The Khurtas are coming to destroy this place. You want a mansion far from here, filled with all the ale you can drink and all the whores you can fuck? I can make that happen. All you have to do is get word to my people and tell them where I am. I know we've had our disagreements in the past, but I'm willing to put them behind us. Think about it, Nobul, anything you want in the world and I can give it to you.'

'Anything?'

'Absolutely,' Friedrik beamed. 'You just name it.'

Nobul leaned in close, glaring at Friedrik, his words spat through gritted teeth. 'Give me back my son.'

Friedrik looked disappointed. 'I can see there's no reasoning with you, is there?'

Nobul didn't answer, taking the sack and putting it back over Friedrik's head before he was overwhelmed with the urge to pummel that face to mush.

Back out in the corridor, Nobul could only shake his head. 'There's nothing I can say, no threat I can give that will make him talk. I doubt anyone could.'

'So what do we do with him now?' asked the tall woman.

'We'll hold onto him,' Kilgar replied. 'Maybe something can be done with him later.'

'No,' said Kaira. 'I cannot risk losing him. I have pursued that man for a long time. There's too much of a chance he'll escape, even from here.'

'Trust me,' Kilgar replied. 'No one knows he's here but us four. And I'll have him watched by someone I trust.'

Nobul agreed. 'The more you keep dragging him across the city, the more chance someone will end up spotting him. He's safe enough here for now.' He didn't know whether he wanted Friedrik close to keep him safe or close to kill him. Either way it was best if he was within reach.

Kaira turned to Rag, who only shrugged in reply.

'Very well,' said Kaira, though the reluctance was clear in her voice. 'If he talks, send word to the Sentinels and I will come immediately.' With that, she and Rag left.

Out in the courtyard Nobul thought about Rag again. Perhaps he should have told her he was sorry and he didn't mean to scare her back in that cellar. That sometimes, when his mad was up, it wasn't too clever to be around him. But, truth be told, he was too tired. Dead tired – like he'd walked a hundred leagues – and he was in no mood for apologies.

'All right, lads,' said Kilgar, walking into the courtyard with a note in his hand. 'We've had a summons. Got some kind of special guard duty we're needed for. Get kitted up and let's go. Hake, you'll stay here. There's a special duty for you. Someone who needs looking after in the cells.'

As the lads went to get their gear together, Kilgar looked at Nobul. 'You coming?' he asked.

What else are you going to do, Nobul Jacks? Sit around on your arse waiting for someone to give you a back rub?

'Aye,' said Nobul. 'I reckon I am.'

THIRTY SEVEN

'**I**t's time,' she said.

Waylian had been standing for an age, waiting for his mistress to finish with her quill and parchment, scratching out some missive or other in the candlelight.

She stood up from her desk, straightened out her robe and ran a gloved hand over her grey hair. If Waylian didn't know better he'd have thought she was nervous.

He followed her through the Tower of Magisters, up towards the Crucible Chamber. This was the third time now, and it didn't make him any less apprehensive. The vast antechamber still rendered him awestruck; the imposing Raven Knights were just as intimidating as the first time he'd ever come to the place.

Once the bracelets were placed over Gelredida's wrists she stood close to him.

'This might be the last time we get to speak, Waylian,' she said in a low voice. 'So remember, it's imperative the vote goes in our favour. I will be vulnerable in there, but you may use any and all means necessary to protect me.'

'Protect you?' he replied. 'From what?'

She smiled at that. 'We'll see. Keep your wits about you. And don't hold back.'

Don't hold back? What did that bloody mean?

But before Waylian had a chance to ask, the vast doors were pulled aside, and the way in to the Crucible Chamber opened.

Gelredida raised her chin and walked forward. Waylian shuffled along beside her, smiling meekly at the Raven Knights as he passed them. Inside the huge chamber was an all too familiar sight: stone pulpits, stern faces. The air was tense, and as the doors were slammed shut behind him Waylian's heart almost jumped from his chest.

They were all here, stern Hoylen Crabbe, ancient Crannock Marghil, imposing Drennan Folds, young Lucen Kalvor and the amiable Nero Laius, though Waylian now knew that the latter was not quite as affable as he made out. But the presence of Nero bothered him less than that of a sixth figure in the Crucible Chamber.

Marshal Ferenz stood to the far right of the Archmasters' pulpits, and as Waylian and Gelredida entered he took his beaked helm from under the crook of his arm and placed it on his head. What that symbolised, Waylian had no idea, but he was sure he didn't like it one bit.

'I see we have a guest,' said Gelredida, before any of the Archmasters could acknowledge her. She gestured to Ferenz who stood like a statue at the end of the row. 'This is an unexpected breach in protocol. Is he here for my protection… or yours?'

'We were merely discussing some matters of security with Marshal Ferenz before you arrived,' said Nero with a smile. 'The matters we are about to discuss will be important to him and everyone who resides in the Tower of Magisters. It's only proper that he should be here. Do you object?'

Gelredida shrugged. 'Of course not. The more the merrier.'

Drennan Folds noisily cleared his throat. He looked uncomfortable, as if someone had put ground glass on his chair. 'Shall we proceed?' he said.

'We all know why we're here,' said Gelredida. 'I asked you to reconsider intervening in the coming invasion. Amon Tugha is almost at our gate. Without support from the Archmasters, and those that serve them, I believe this city will fall. You have had time to deliberate on this – what say you?'

Despite how uncomfortable she had seemed before coming here, Waylian could detect a note of expectation in her voice, as though she knew the outcome of today would favour her. The subsequent silence from the raised pulpits only served to confirm the notion, as the Archmasters held their peace, none of them wanting be the first to speak his mind on the matter.

'Come now,' said Gelredida. 'You were all very vocal a few days ago when I came to ask your aid. You've had time enough to think, what say you?' She glanced at each of them in turn, seeming to relish their discomfort. 'Lucen? Shall we begin with you?'

Lucen Kalvor looked up suddenly and regarded Gelredida with disdain, but as he realised his fellow Archmasters had all turned to him expectantly he slowly nodded.

'I have thought on this deep and long,' he said. 'It is clear Magistra Gelredida is right. We should support the armies of the Free States. The Elharim cannot be trusted. Steelhaven must not fall.'

'What?' said Nero suddenly, his amiable expression now gone. 'Preposterous, Kalvor. We were all agreed. For the good of this city we must remain neutral.' He glanced along the row of his fellows. 'Surely none of you can agree? Kalvor's just lost his nerve. The rest of us are still of one mind on this, surely?'

At first, silence. Then Drennan Folds looked up, and took a long and measured inhalation of breath before speaking. 'I too have reconsidered my position,' he said. Waylian could see that though he was talking to his fellow Archmasters, Folds was staring intently at Gelredida. 'And have decided to place my full support behind the Crown.'

'No!' said Nero. 'No, that's not what we agreed.'

'What say the rest of you?' asked Gelredida, ignoring Nero's cries of protest.

Hoylen Crabbe and Crannock Marghil glanced at one another, conveying some silent accord.

Crannock peered over his eyeglasses and said, 'I always doubted the wisdom of just standing by and doing nothing. An old man and his selfishness have no right to condemn this city. If the Archmasters must sacrifice themselves for the good of Steelhaven, then so be it.'

'Agreed,' said Hoylen Crabbe, his brow furrowed into a severe v-shape. 'The time for deliberation is over. Amon Tugha is at our door and has even been so bold as to threaten us. That cannot be tolerated. The Tower of

Magisters will stand shoulder to shoulder with the defenders of the Free States. You have your victory, Gelredida. Be grateful for it.'

'No!' screamed Nero, almost leaping from his pulpit. 'This is not what you all said!'

'Calm yourself, Nero,' Crannock said, raising a withered hand.

'I will not fucking calm myself, you old goat.' Nero replied, stepping down from his stone seat and moving beside Ferenz. 'You're all blind. You've been blinded by that woman.' He thrust an accusing finger towards Gelredida. 'I don't know what she's got on you, but it can't be enough that you would see this tower reduced to rubble beneath our feet. Amon Tugha has offered us clemency. It is madness not to take it.'

'The decision has been made,' said Drennan Folds. 'A majority decision has been reached. That is our way, Nero. You know that.'

Nero glared at them, then at Gelredida. 'Betrayers!' he said. 'Fools and cowards! You have condemned us all. I will not stand by and watch as this tower's guardians and magisters and apprentices are slaughtered because you are all too weak. It is time for a new order.'

'Stop being so dramatic,' said Hoylen Crabbe, climbing down from his pulpit and smoothing out his dark robe, the sigils embroidered there shifting into ordered rows. 'The decision has been made. Live with it. Now, if that's all, I have preparations to make.'

With an imperious gait he strode from his pulpit as though to leave.

'That's not all,' said Nero. 'Marshal Ferenz. Show them how serious we are.'

The huge Raven Knight took a step forward. From behind him he pulled a black-bladed dagger which he thrust into Hoylen's belly. The Archmaster gasped, his piercing eyes staring up at the beaked helm in accusation and disbelief before he collapsed to the floor.

Waylian almost fell over as he took an involuntary step back.

The Crucible Chamber was in uproar as Drennan, Crannock and Lucen all began bellowing in panic. With the manacles that bound their wrists there was nothing any of them could do against the colossal Raven Knight.

Ferenz took a threatening step towards the pulpits, but Nero held up a hand.

'No! Her next.' He gestured towards Gelredida. 'I've wanted to see that bitch dead for decades.'

Ferenz turned his helmed head. Waylian almost grabbed his mistress, almost screamed at her to run, but something in her defiant stance made him stop. Even as the Raven Knight strode towards her she didn't take a backward step.

Marshal Ferenz loomed towards them. Waylian stood there agog, fear striking into his gut like a hot iron. The dagger in Ferenz's hand dripped blood onto the granite floor and his footfalls echoed ominously.

'Waylian,' said Gelredida conversationally. He turned his head to look at her as she watched Ferenz bearing down. 'Now might be an excellent opportunity for you to demonstrate what you've learned these past weeks.'

What I've learned? Like what? How to summon lightning from the sky? Because I'm pretty sure I must have been elsewhere for that lesson.

Ferenz was less than half a dozen strides from Gelredida now.

'Any time now would be good,' she said, the slightest note of tension creeping into her voice.

So what are you going to do? There was a time you'd have loved the Red Witch to be gutted in front of you, but you're warming to the old dear, aren't you. Better bloody do something then!

Ferenz lifted his arm, raising the dagger high. Gelredida just stood there, waiting without a word of protest.

It's now or never.

The past few weeks ran through Waylian's head like a flood. The pages of books fluttered like sparrows' wings, inky words dripped from a thousand parchments. Things he'd heard, things he'd seen, things he'd barely understood, all coming and going in a flash of nebulous memory until only one word was left in his head.

'*Avaggdu!*' he screamed.

The vast beaked helm that encased Ferenz's head crumpled inwards as though crushed in the hands of an invisible giant. Blood spurted from the helm's twisted eyeholes and sprayed down on the gorget of the knight's armour.

Ferenz's arm slumped to his side, the dagger falling from his grip as he toppled to one side, crashing to the granite floor in an armoured heap.

Waylian stood there in the silence, eyes wide and staring. Then he clamped a hand to his mouth, too late to stop the fountain of vomit that spewed from his roiling guts.

Whether it was a consequence of using the magick or seeing Ferenz dispatched in such a gruesome manner he had no idea, but neither did he care as the contents of his stomach sprayed out between his fingers.

There was a gentle pat on his back as he crouched forward, sobbing the snot and puke from his nose and mouth. 'Well done, Waylian,' said Gelredida, as though he'd just solved some tricky equation rather than crushed a man's head with a word.

Nero let out an animal shriek.

Before any of the remaining Archmasters could restrain him he rushed to the marshal's armoured body. Too late, Waylian realised he was going for the dagger that Ferenz had wielded. Nero's eyes were wide with fury, his deadly intent obvious, but Gelredida was unable to act against him with the iron bracelets binding her power.

Ignoring the rancid puke running down his chin, Waylian dashed forward. He had no time to think, just bowled into Nero and they both went down. The Archmaster fought like an animal, snarling his fury. Waylian desperately grabbed Nero's wrist and focused on not being sliced by the dagger. If help was coming, it was slow in arriving; the other Archmasters just stood and watched. Even Gelredida did nothing, not even uttering a word of encouragement as Waylian fought for his life.

What did you expect, Grimmy? That she'd jump in to help you? That she'd risk having her throat opened when she's got dumb, obedient Waylian Grimm to do her dirty work for her?

He gritted his teeth as he rolled on the hard floor, wrestling with Nero. The Archmaster was a man grown but seemed no stronger than Waylian. As they struggled, Waylian could not take his eyes from the blade of that dagger, shining bright and moist in the torchlight.

Why is no one helping me? Why are they all just watching?

The unfairness of all this began to build in him like a pot of boiling broth. For every squeal and grunt Nero made, Waylian felt fury increase within him. As they grappled Waylian could not only smell the sweat and breath of the man trying to kill him, but sense his anger and frustration that he couldn't finish this meddling apprentice.

With a bark of fury, Nero managed to roll on top of Waylian. The dagger was between them now, the blade pointing downwards. Nero stared, his eyes wide with triumph as he pushed down with all his weight and Waylian got a familiar feeling he'd been here before. But as he stared into Nero's eyes he saw something in them, something dark, something forbidden.

It was as though he could read the secrets in those eyes, as though they showed him Nero's soul, and what Waylian saw there was black. This man was a traitor. This man had plotted against the Crown, plotted with its enemies, plotted to see this city fall that he might reap the rewards from its ashes.

But his plots were not over yet.

Nero was party to further dire schemes – a conspiracy that would see the death of... the queen.

Before the dagger could touch Waylian, something hit Nero hard across his head. He toppled to one side without a sound, leaving Waylian holding the black and bloody dagger in his hand. He stared at it, at the razor sharp blade, then at Nero, lying prone beside him.

'Do get up, Waylian. You're making the place look untidy.'

He looked up to see Gelredida standing beside him. In her hand she held a stone urn. It didn't even bear a crack after rendering the Archmaster unconscious.

Waylian stood, dropping the dagger to the floor. The other Archmasters had chosen to move forward now there was no danger of them being harmed.

'He's a traitor,' Waylian said, pointing a finger.

'That much is bloody clear,' said Drennan Folds.

'No. I mean, yes, but... he's plotting to kill the queen.

'How do you know?' Drennan stared accusingly.

'I... I saw it...'

The Archmasters looked at one another, almost more perturbed by Waylian showing talent with magick than by a member of their order being slain by one of their own.

'We don't have time for this,' Gelredida said. 'It's clear Nero has been playing us all for fools. He and Ferenz are in league with Amon Tugha. How deep that betrayal goes remains to be seen.'

'Indeed,' said Crannock. 'He should be handed over to the Inquisition immediately. They'll get to the bottom of this conspiracy.'

Gelredida shook her head. 'We have no time for that, but never fear. I am more than willing to put Nero to the question myself. I'm sure my methods will be most efficient.'

Waylian had little doubt she was right.

THIRTY EIGHT

Regulus had always known that coming north might be perilous, that he was most likely risking his life and that of his warriors. But back then the worst he could have imagined was an ignoble death, with no one to sing the tales of his passing – a quiet death in a far off land where he might never find his way to the stars.

He was forced to admit, his current fate was far worse.

They were locked in a dank and cavernous chamber, chained and humiliated. Rage burned inside him, fuelling the need to rend and tear his way out, to restore his honour in a swathe of blood and corpses. How he would make these Coldlanders pay for such an insult – how they would suffer.

He knew such thoughts were useless though; a waste of his waning energy. There was nothing he could do but wait while his fate was decided for him. No matter how much the fire inside demanded a blood reckoning there was little he could do to quench it.

His warriors shared his desire for vengeance, that much was clear. They wanted nothing more than to join him in the righteous destruction of their captors. Each one would gladly have given his life in pursuit of such retribution.

All but Janto Sho.

Regulus could see him staring from the shadows, what little light that encroached on the dungeon cell illuminating his eyes like baleful blue stars in the black night. Though he was silent, it was obvious he hated Regulus for bringing them so low, for leading them to this ignoble end. Janto had pledged himself to Regulus, fully expecting to die in the repayment of his life-debt, but now he was to die chained and dishonoured. Regulus could hardly blame Janto for his ire.

'How long have we been here?' asked Akkula, staring up at the barred window high above them.

'What does it matter?' Hagama replied. Regulus was sure the warrior would have displayed more annoyance had he the vigour to do so.

Akkula clearly did not sense the anger in his fellow warrior's voice.

'I'm starving,' he said.

'We're all starving,' growled Hagama. 'Now be silent.'

'Both of you be silent,' said Leandran. 'We have to save our strength. The opportunity for escape will arrive soon enough. If the Coldlanders wanted to kill us we'd be dead already.'

'Escape?' said Hagama, leaning towards Leandran, the chain that tethered him to the wall pulling tight. 'We are in chains. How will we escape? As for the intentions of the Coldlanders, none of us can guess what that scum has in mind. Perhaps they are gathering the people of the city that they might kill us in front of a baying crowd.'

'If you think like that, you're already beaten,' said Leandran. 'An opportunity will present itself in the fullness of time. Just wait and see.'

'You're an old fool!' Hagama snarled, baring his teeth.

'Leandran is right,' Regulus said, staring down the warrior. 'We must stay alert. Fighting amongst ourselves will only serve us ill. There will be time for fighting soon enough.'

Regulus hoped that was true. If his warriors did not find something to kill soon, they could end up turning on one another.

And why? Why would that be? Because you have brought them to this. You dragged them from their homeland to this place of weaklings and cowards, and now they are to be punished for it. You have brought them low – the punishment should be yours alone.

He felt his shame keenly. How Regulus missed the open plains of Equ'un. Things were much simpler there – fight or die. Had he been wrong to flee? Should he have stayed and died with the rest of the Gor'tana faithful to his father?

There was no use lamenting on what could have been. The decision had been made. Regulus took the blame, he hid from nothing. It was small consolation for his warriors though, forced as they were to share his fate.

Janto was still watching him from the dark and Regulus began to wonder what went on in that head. He must have loathed Regulus, and most likely wanted him dead. If they did manage to escape this place would Janto still be loyal? Would he still honour his debt?

He and Janto glared at one another for some time, ignoring the cold wind howling past the window and the damp rhythmic dripping of moisture from the ceiling, until finally Janto lowered his eyes and moved further into the shadow. A small victory at least.

A noise outside the cell roused the Zatani as they sat in chains. Bolts slid back, the sound of a key in a lock and the door was thrust open. Regulus squinted in the light of torches as several figures entered the cell.

'Don't give us no trouble,' said a voice.

Regulus stood up, his warriors doing the same. As his eyes adjusted to the glaring light he saw that the room was filled with a dozen northern soldiers in green jackets. They looked apprehensive, afraid, even though Regulus and his warriors were chained to the walls.

'What now?' asked Hagama. 'Is this our chance?'

Regulus assessed the men who had come for them. They were afraid – their weapons drawn, though none of them moved to attack. If there were to be any chance for Regulus and his warriors to make it out of this alive, they had to be careful. If they attacked now, chained as they were, they'd be slaughtered.

'Do not fight them,' Regulus said.

One of the soldiers held out a wooden pole, on the end was a shackle large enough for Regulus' neck.

'We don't want no trouble,' one of the soldiers repeated.

But what trouble could Regulus give? He and his warriors were at the mercy of these northern fools. Subject to their whims. The shame of it cut him deep, but still he did not resist as they secured the shackle around his throat. His chains were unfastened from the walls, and between three men he was guided from the cell.

They were not rough. These men did not drag him, but somehow that made it worse. That he was being coaxed like livestock, and allowing it to happen, only added to his humiliation.

Behind him he could hear the noise of his warriors receiving similar treatment. He could only hope they would heed his commands. Perhaps they would, perhaps not. Janto was unlikely to go without a fight; Regulus was unsure whether he wanted that or not. Perhaps one of them should at least show some defiance.

Regulus had to demonstrate wisdom, though. Had to show his leadership by example.

As he was conveyed down the darkened corridors, Regulus was taken back to his earliest memories, to a time when the Aeslanti ruled Equ'un with a clawed fist. To a time when they had conquered every tribe that stood against them. The Zatani had been a slave race then – in thrall to beasts.

Regulus had been only a child during that dark age, but he could still remember what it had been like before the Slave Uprisings. Before the Steel King had given gifts of Coldlander steel and sown rebellion in every tribe.

Now Regulus was slave once more. Now he was in thrall, not to beasts but to men. What would his father have said if he could see the shame Regulus had brought on the Gor'tana? A prince of the Zatani meekly leading his warriors into bondage?

Regulus decided not to think on it. Better he looked to finding a solution to their current predicament before one of his warriors did something they could not bargain or fight their way out of.

The corridor widened, and Regulus found himself flanked by yet more Coldlanders. As he approached the end, a door was flung open revealing a large chamber from which Regulus could hear the sounds of raised voices.

When he was dragged into the brightly lit chamber, he realised only doom awaited.

The room was huge and circular, tiered rows of seats rose up all around him, angry jeering faces staring down as though this were some arena and he about to fight. Yet the floor was not covered with blood-spattered sand, but hard stone, and there was little room for combat.

Steel rings were set into the stone slabs beneath his feet, and the chains that held Regulus' wrists were quickly tethered to them. Behind him, one of the soldiers who had conveyed him here still held the pole that secured the shackle around his neck.

As the rest of his warriors were brought in, the crowd's baying began to reach new heights of frenzy. Regulus could see that among them were mercenaries, their livery identifying them as the Hallowed Shields, the Midnight Falcons, the Scarlet Company – all leering down with hate. Every one of them had lost men in the fight with the Zatani. Regulus could not blame them for their anger. But neither could he forgive his captors for this ordeal. If there was a dispute then it should be settled by combat in the warrior tradition, not like this.

A robed man stood waiting for them. He held his hands up to the gathered mob and reluctantly its baying grew silent. Slowly, the robed figure drew back his hood. He was bald and bore a tattoo above his right eye, a sigil Regulus did not recognise.

The silence became uneasy as he fixed Regulus with a stare, bereft of any emotion.

'You are charged with heinous crimes,' he said in a voice flat and impartial. 'You have invaded our lands. Raided our villages, butchered our livestock.' Regulus bristled at the false allegations. He and his men had done no such thing, even though it had been well within their capabilities to do so. 'Then, after entering Steelhaven under the false guise of peace, you murdered men who would have otherwise defended this city.' At his words the mob surrounding them began to shout in agreement, some demanding justice, others demanding only execution.

'What are they saying?' asked Hagama.

Regulus could not answer him. How was he to say they were being accused of crimes they had not committed? He was the one who had brought them to this place. It was Regulus who had subjected them to this.

'It is the assertion of the Inquisition that you were sent here as agents of the Elharim invader Amon Tugha. That your mission was to sabotage the city from within, to do as much damage as possible in order to disrupt Steelhaven's defences.'

Regulus wanted to roar his defiance, but chained as he was he could do nothing. Perhaps they would have a chance to prove their innocence. Regulus had been taught little of the customs of the Clawless Tribes by his father but he knew something of their laws. They sometimes observed the traditions of trial by combat, but otherwise a lord or other elected nobleman would represent an accused party. Surely there would be some way to dispute these allegations. Surely someone would be their arbiter.

'The evidence against you is clear. Six men lie dead, twice that number wounded. No ally of the Free States would do so much harm to its people. Only an enemy, under pretence of friendship.'

'What are they saying?' Hagama demanded, this time his voice was raised high above that of the hooded man. Caught up in his rage, Akkula and Kazul roared along with him, cries of anger and defiance. Though Regulus was proud of their boldness, it only served to incense the crowd, who shouted back, howling like dogs, some spitting and throwing insults Regulus recognised only too well.

The robed man held his arms up again. Hagama, Kazul and Akkula fell silent as their cries of defiance grew hoarse.

'Confessions,' he said. The single word echoed around the circular chamber. 'Perhaps, savage, you will demonstrate some shred of honour and confess your crimes?'

'*Ordeal by fire*,' shouted a voice.

'*Put 'em to the fuckin' question*,' bellowed another.

Again the robed man's arms were raised for silence. Then he stared straight at Regulus.

'What say you, beast? Do you confess your crimes?'

Regulus knew that all his denials would be mocked and ignored. That a 'confession' was not what they wanted or cared for. They just wanted his blood.

'I came here to fight,' Regulus said, the strength in his voice silencing the onlookers. 'To defend this city alongside its people. To bring glory and victory to your queen. I have nothing to confess.'

'Nothing to confess?' said the robed man. 'Then we would ask none from you. We need no confession from animals.'

The crowd began to shout again, stamping their feet, the noise almost deafening. This was madness. Regulus strained to control his rage as his warriors each roared in defiance.

'All we need now is the sentence,' shouted the man over the din.

On a raised gallery, Regulus saw a door open. A second robed figure appeared from within, his face hidden beneath a dark hood. He stood for what seemed endless moments, waiting for the noise to abate, waiting for the sound of the Zatani to die down.

When all was silent once more, the tattooed man looked up and asked, 'What sentence shall be passed?'

The hooded figure at first said nothing, milking the silence. Regulus already knew the answer and simply offered a defiant glare.

'Death,' came the single word from the hooded man.

This time it was the crowd's turn to roar.

THIRTY NINE

The chamber was in upheaval. Men screaming in anger. Equ'un warriors bellowing their lungs out. It reminded Nobul of days long past. Days on the battlefield, sweating and bleeding and biting back the fear.

He held a chain that bound one of the Zatani. Nobul used all his strength, but still struggled to hold just that one arm. Any other day he'd have put it down to how tired he was, what he'd been through over the past few days, but he knew that wasn't the case. These were savages from the plains of Equ'un, former slaves of the Aeslanti, tempered in the fighting pits of the beast-men. Nobul was just glad they were in chains.

The Greencoats dragged them from the chamber. Now the sentence was passed it looked like the place might erupt at any minute. Kilgar led the way, shouting for them to move as fast as they could and to hold steady. It would only take one of these killers to escape its shackles and there'd be the hells to pay.

Nobul had seen first hand the ferocity of the Zatani and their prowess in battle at Bakhaus Gate. The Aeslanti had sent some of their Zatani slaves into the fray first – shock troops to soften up the Teutonian vanguard. They were formidable opponents and Nobul had no desire to fight them again. He'd been young and fit then – hungry for blood and glory. Now he felt every year weighing down on him as he dragged the raging warrior to his cell, and all Nobul's experience did nothing to curb the fear.

Back on the old days, when he was in his prime, he'd been scared almost shitless as he faced the enemy in the valley at Bakhaus. Now that feeling came rushing back to him. As the noise echoed down the corridor it wasn't victory Nobul remembered. It was standing beside a hundred other lads, some of them shaking, some of them weeping. It was gripping his hammer so tight he thought he'd never be able to let it go. It was looking all about him, trying to find somewhere to run but knowing there was nowhere.

No amount of victories would ever scratch out those memories. Not a thousand blokes patting you on the back, shouting their thanks, buying you drinks. The years had served to dull the memories well enough, but now here he was, reminding himself all over again what he'd faced.

They eventually managed to get the Zatani back to his cell and with difficulty chained him up once more. Bilgot gingerly unfastened the shackle from the warrior's neck and they stood back as the rest were brought in. There were six in all, most of them powerful looking. One appeared young and another very old, his head shaved, his dark flesh patchy, though he still looked as though he could do some damage. Even the weakest of these bastards was more than a match for your average man.

The noise in the room was deafening as they secured the warriors. Nobul gripped his short blade, looking for any sign of them escaping but there was none – though they made a lot of noise, the Greencoats managed to chain them up without incident.

'Right, everyone out,' said Kilgar.

None of the lads complained at that, practically falling over one another to get out of the door.

Nobul backed away as the Zatani thrashed against their bonds. It was taking all his nerve not to turn tail and run – though they were chained, these warriors still looked ferocious. He knew they were a fearsome enemy, but also a proud race. Something inside began to pity them, despite their ferocity. Something inside made him feel this just wasn't right.

Nobul was the last one out of the cell, and as he was leaving, he caught the gaze of one of the Zatani. This one wasn't roaring his anger, but was watching him intently. His black hair hung long over his shoulders and he was the biggest and most impressive of the group. It had been this one that spoke Teutonian and protested their innocence back in the inquisition hall. This one that stood proudly and defiantly while his fellows bellowed in rage.

As Nobul looked back at the warrior, he saw the keen intelligence in his green eyes. Nobul glanced at Kilgar, who beckoned him to leave, but he couldn't bring himself to move. Over a decade ago he'd faced warriors like this, had killed them, but he could sense this one was no threat to him. The Zatani had only been his enemy because they were slaves to the Aeslanti. After gaining their freedom it was said they had turned on their former masters, defeating them in a savage war. Perhaps they were not the enemy after all. Perhaps they didn't deserve such summary judgement. Surely what the Inquisition had done to these men was wrong.

'I'm sorry,' Nobul said, before he'd even realised it.

After a moment, the warrior responded. 'Keep your pity, Coldlander. We have no need for it.'

As their leader spoke, the rest of the Zatani fell silent.

'Come on,' demanded Kilgar, beckoning again, more impatiently.

Nobul stood his ground, though he realised how irrational it was. 'Close the door,' he replied, still staring at the dark-skinned warrior.

'Are you fucking insane?'

'Close the door,' repeated Nobul.

Without a word, Kilgar slammed the door to the cell shut and locked it.

The warrior watched him, his green eyes revealing no emotion.

'I'm Nobul Jacks.'

'Regulus of the Gor'tana. Prince of Equ'un,' the Zatani replied.

'It's good to meet you, Regulus of the Gor'tana. And I don't pity you, but I am still sorry.'

'I understand, Nobul Jacks. But your sorrow will not see us freed from this place.'

'No, I reckon it won't. Not much I can do about that.'

Regulus looked forlorn, beaten, and it made Nobul pity him all the more.

'To think, we came to fight for your queen,' said the warrior. 'To bring her glory. To bring death to her enemies. Now we will be slaughtered like livestock.'

'Why would you do that? Why come all the way north for someone to do your killing? There must be plenty of killing to be done back south.'

'There is indeed death aplenty back in my homeland. But the glory is here, in the north. Fighting to save the city of our liberator.'

'You mean King Cael? He's dead and gone.' *And some of us didn't shed too many tears over it neither.*

'So we have learned. Surely all the more reason to defend his kith and kin?'

Nobul could see the sense of it. And he'd be doing that very thing soon enough.

'It would have been good to stand beside you on the battlements,' said Nobul. He wasn't lying either – he'd have taken six Zatani at his shoulder when facing an army of Khurtas any day. 'But I guess that'll never happen now.'

'You are a warrior then, Nobul Jacks? But of course, I can see it in your bearing. Have you fought many battles?'

'I've fought enough. A long time ago now.'

'You have fought my people?'

That caught him off his guard. For a moment he considered denying it, but chained as these Zatani were there was little need to lie.

'Aye, I was at the Gate. Your people are great fighters. I hope never to face their like again.'

Regulus seemed to appreciate that.

'Would that I could have fought to win our freedom back then, but I was a child. The years were against me.'

'The years are against all of us, one way or the other,' Nobul said with a smile, as though he was passing the time with any old veteran. 'It's what you do with them that counts.'

'I fear I may not have used mine with the greatest of wisdom.'

'You don't know that yet.'

'You are right. It is best not to live with regret.'

'True enough,' Nobul said, though Arlor knew he'd gathered enough regrets of his own over the years.

The warrior crouched down, resting his back against the wall. Nobul glanced around at the other Zatani, watching in silence. One of them watched from the dark, his blue stare unmistakeably hateful.

Nobul turned back to Regulus and knelt down beside him.

'You don't deserve this. None of you do.'

The Zatani's face twisted into a smile. 'Perhaps none of us get what we deserve, Nobul Jacks. We are all condemned by fate.'

'Aye, that's true enough. You've just got to make the best of what gets thrown at you.'

'Indeed. And for what it's worth, I bear you no ill will.'

'That makes me feel a bit better, I suppose,' Nobul said, though he wasn't too sure it did. 'Good luck to you, Regulus of the Gor'tana.'

'And to you, Coldlander.'

Nobul pounded on the cell door twice. When Kilgar opened it he couldn't bring himself to look back at the warriors, chained and caged behind him.

Once more, Kilgar locked the door. When he turned Nobul expected him to give out a roasting, but the serjeant said nothing. The group of Greencoats made their way from the building in silence.

Back at the barracks all was unnaturally quiet. There was fear on Dustin and Edric's faces. Even Bilgot had lost his usual bluster. It was understandable. Nobul knew too well how the Zatani could unman you with just a glance of those eyes, let alone a flash of the claws and teeth. These lads should have counted themselves lucky they never went up against the Aeslanti, never mind Zatani warriors.

Nobul watched them as they all slipped away from the barracks one by one, without saying a word to him. He appreciated that; he wanted some time to himself.

With all the worry about rioters and invaders, discipline had slipped in the past few weeks. The Greencoats were even more slack about keeping guard than they had been when Nobul had first arrived, so it was nothing for him to make his way to the little room where they kept all the ledgers. Where the man who paid the wages kept his little desk.

It didn't take Nobul long to find what he was looking for. It was easy to search for a name and see where the man lived.

As Nobul made his way up to Northgate, all he could think about were those Zatani and how, after everything they'd been through, that leader of theirs appeared to hold no grudges.

Could Nobul Jacks have been that forgiving? Could he be slighted so badly and just put it down to fate?

The house was on a little street just west of the market. There was a single door at the front but Nobul wasn't interested in that. He made his way down a back alley, ankle deep in piss and shit. The night was drawing in fast and he could barely see where he was walking but he managed to find another door to the rear. Locked. Nobul nudged the single window beside it and it gave a little. A bit more muscle and it slid open. The sound of it was a bit too loud but Nobul didn't care, there was nothing to fear. Not for him at least.

Inside was dark. As his eyes adjusted to the light of a single candle he saw the one he'd come for. The lad was slumped over a table, empty bottle of spirits next to him, cup overturned. There was a knife too, just a few inches from his hand.

Nobul crept closer. Well, he wouldn't want to wake the lad up while he was sleeping so peaceful, would he. He picked the knife up off the table and rammed its blade into the doorjamb.

The sound woke Anton up with a start.

'Who's there?' he asked, his eyes looking all bleary as his hand felt around in the dark for a weapon.

'Thought you'd have been miles away by now,' said Nobul.

'Oh fuck,' Anton breathed in the dark. 'Oh fuck, fuck, fuck.'

'What's the matter? The Guild abandon you? They hang you out to dry when things went tits up?'

'They're looking for you,' said Anton, staring wide-eyed. 'They're probably watching the house right now. They'll be turning the city upside down after what you did. You shouldn't be here.'

Nobul shrugged. 'I'm willing to take the risk.'

Anton was shaking, and Nobul had to admit he liked that.

'What now?' Anton asked. 'You gonna kill me?'

Nobul stared at him awhile.

Well, are you? Isn't that why you came here? He's wronged you worse than most. After what you've been through, it's only right.

'I don't know,' Nobul replied. 'What do you think?'

'I think I'm a dead man.'

'Maybe that's what you deserve.'

'Then get on with it,' Anton screamed, rising to his feet.

Even in the gloom, Nobul could see tears in his eyes. He'd probably been waiting here to die for days. Had no idea what to do about it. He was only a lad too, didn't have a clue how to get himself out of this mess other than with a bottle of booze.

'Forgiveness is a difficult thing,' Nobul said. 'If I let you walk away from here, make sure you never fucking come back.'

Anton clearly suspected a trick. 'Honestly?'

Nobul nodded. 'Never come back.'

'I won't. I won't ever. You won't ever see me again.'

'Then you'd better make tracks, boy.'

Anton turned hurriedly. His bag was on the floor and he bent to pick it up.

And just like that, you'll let him go? Just like that, Nobul Jacks will take being treated like a cunt. That what you gonna do when the Khurtas get here — offer them forgiveness? And expect to survive the first day?

As Anton stuffed something into his bag, Nobul found himself taking a step towards him.

That's it. You're a cold bastard, Nobul Jacks. This city's gonna need cold bastards just like you. There's got to be a reckoning for what he did. Got to be some payback.

Anton was just there, his back turned, ready to start life anew, away from this city and its poison. Away from the Guild and the Khurtas and Nobul fucking Jacks.

And all because of your forgiveness.

Nobul's hands closed around Anton's throat. The lad gave a choked gasp, his last sound before the air was cut off. He struggled, but there was no escaping it.

Give him his due, he tried to fight, fingers scraping at Nobul's fists. The pain was good, and Nobul gritted his teeth, squeezing all the harder, tensing those arms for gods knew how long until Anton wasn't moving no more.

The lad finally fell dead to the floor.

Nobul looked briefly at that body lying there in the dark. It had been a quick death all in all.

That was about as much forgiveness as Nobul Jacks had left in him.

FORTY

Waylian could still taste the bile in his throat. All he wanted was a cup of water to wash the smell away, and perhaps a lie down to let his nausea pass, but Magistra Gelredida was in no mood to be stopped.

They were back in the bowels of the Tower of Magisters, back in the warren of passageways and chambers beneath the city, secreted away where no one could hear them. It was obvious why – Gelredida wouldn't have wanted anyone to hear the screams.

Nero Laius was stretched out on a block of wood, his arms and legs manacled tight. He was naked, his skin slick with blood and sweat, shivering in pain and fear. The block was set at forty-five degrees so Magistra Gelredida didn't have to stoop too low to administer to him. Nero had protested at first, had demanded to be released, had shouted that he was an Archmaster of the Crucible and he had the right to a trial. His protestations had soon turned to screams.

Waylian watched in horror, hand clamped firmly over his mouth as his mistress carefully selected her instruments and went to work.

She used the blades and hooks with precision, swift clinical strokes. At first she didn't even ask him any questions, just let Nero's screams ring out, echoing around the chamber. Waylian had clamped his hands firmly over his ears then, but after watching for several painful minutes he'd decided it was more prudent to cover his mouth. It wouldn't do to puke all over the floor again – he was making a habit of that, and it was just getting embarrassing.

'So, Nero,' said the Magistra, taking a step back. 'Archmaster. Keeper of the Ravens. And Master Diviner? It's a little remiss of you, isn't it? Not seeing this coming. Hardly a master of your Art.'

Nero whimpered his reply. As much as Waylian had feared and loathed the man, he still felt a little pity for him now. Blood ran in rivulets down his legs and into a little gutter that sat beneath the block. There were myriad cuts on his body and section of skin had even been peeled back and pinned in place with steel clips.

'You were clearly aided in all this by Marshal Ferenz. Are there any other Raven Knights involved in your little scheme?'

Nero mumbled something and Gelredida cocked her head, wincing in annoyance when she couldn't understand him. She grasped one of the steel clips in a gloved hand – now stained with blood – and twisted it.

Waylian looked away as Nero screamed.

'Yes!' he bellowed, blood and phlegm spurting from his mouth. 'I'm the Keeper of fucking Ravens! Of course some of the knights are on my side. I'll tell you who they are. I'll give you all their names. I'll tell you everything.'

Gelredida leaned back away from Nero's spit. 'I know you will,' she replied.

There was silence then, and in some ways that was worse than Nero's screams. Waylian could just about handle that, but the long quiet made him wonder what was to come next. Which new instrument would his mistress pull from her bag of tricks?

Instead she leaned in closer as Nero gasped for air. 'Your conspirators in the tower can wait, Nero. I want to know who you're working for.'

'You know who I'm working for.' Nero's voice was high and desperate.

'So say it.'

'Amon Tugha. I'm in league with Amon Tugha.'

'Yes, Nero,' she said with relish. 'That much is obvious. Why else would you be so keen for the Archmasters to do nothing in as the enemy besieges our city? But that's not the name I'm after.'

Nero stared at her, his eyes wide, tears running down his filthy blood-encrusted cheeks. When he said nothing Gelredida glanced across at her instruments laid out on the table.

'Waylian. Be so good as to pass me the saw.'

He usually obeyed without question, but Waylian couldn't bring himself to do it. As much as he loathed Nero, he didn't want to aid in his suffering.

Luckily he didn't have to.

'All right!' Nero screamed. 'There's a man in the city. He's an agent of Amon Tugha.'

'A name,' Gelredida demanded.

'He calls himself the Father of Killers.'

'Not good enough. Waylian, the saw.'

'That's all I know, I swear it.' Nero began to sob and whine. It was pathetic, Waylian knew, but he felt sorry for the man. 'If I knew anything else I'd tell you.'

'Then you'd better start thinking.'

Suddenly the sobbing stopped and Nero opened his eyes wide. 'He's known in the city's underworld. He runs assassins. The deadliest in the Free States.'

'And...'

Nero gritted his teeth, as though desperate to keep the truth in his mouth. 'They were the ones that attempted to murder the queen.'

She just stared at him, then held out her hand to Waylian.

Saw, Grimmy, I think she wants the saw.

'There's going to be another attempt,' Nero cried. 'The Father of Killers won't stop until she's dead.'

'What have you done to aid him in this, Nero?'

He shook his head vigorously, sweat and snot and blood flying from his damp curls. 'Nothing. I haven't done a thing, I swear it.'

She stared at him for the briefest of moments, then held out her hand again.

'All right! All right! He asked for help with some magicks, Elharim magicks. I didn't really understand. I gave him nails from a witch's coffin and mantikore venom, but that was all!'

Gelredida nodded, and backed away slowly. 'You know, I think I might actually believe you, Nero.' She turned and regarded her table full of instruments. 'But you realise I have to be sure.' She picked up the saw.

As she approached him, Nero began to scream anew. This time it was high pitched, like a cawing bird.

Waylian's hand tightened over his mouth, but it would do no good. The room felt as if it was spinning, his ears filled with sound as if a flock of angry ravens were pecking at his brain. He turned, his hand fumbling with the handle until he finally managed to open the door. It slammed behind him as he stumbled into the corridor. The noise stopped and Waylian felt relief wash over him, just before he threw up again.

He wasn't sure how long he waited in that dark corridor. Occasionally the moans and screams would escape through the door and he would wince as though he were in pain himself.

Count your lucky stars and say your prayers to Arlor you're not next on her list.

Eventually the door opened. Waylian tried to avert his gaze from what lay in the room, but he couldn't help seeing. There was little left of the Nero he'd known. Just a mass of mutilated flesh, now still and silent in the shadows.

Gelredida closed the door mercifully quickly, stopping to dab at her bloodstained robe with a filthy rag. Good job she was wearing her usual red – it disguised the amount of blood she was drenched in.

'Come along,' she said, as though she'd just finished pruning roses rather than a man's limbs. 'We must away to the palace, immediately.'

As they made their way up through the maze of passageways he realised his hands were shaking. The nausea was gone, so that was something. All he had to do now was cope with the memories of seeing a man brutally tortured.

Oh, and the fact that you crushed a man's head with the power of your will alone. There was that too. But one thing at a time, eh, Grimmy?

He took a deep breath when they got outside, which was a feat in itself considering how fast Gelredida was walking and how little breath he had to spare just trying to keep up. It was a relief to be outside, to clear his head, though it was racing with questions now he had a chance to think.

'Mistress, I don't understand.'

'Understand what?' she replied.

'The last time we asked the Archmasters to join with the city against the Khurtas they refused. Why did they change their minds so quickly?'

Gelredida glanced at him, and had he not known better he would have sworn there was a half smile on her face.

'That, young Waylian, was mostly down to you.'

'Pardon me?'

'Don't make me repeat myself. You know how tiresome I find it.'

'Of course, Magistra.' Waylian did his best to keep up as Gelredida squeezed herself through the thickening crowd. 'But I still don't understand.'

'Did you think those errands I sent you on were just for your health?' she said.

'Well... no. But I...'

'Milius the apothecary – what did you think of him?'

'He kind of gave me the willies.'

Gelredida chuckled. 'Yes, I'm sure he did. But then he is the foremost poisoner in the city. And I had to ensure he knew the ingredients for a very specific poison. One used not too long ago in the Tower of Magisters.'

'Someone was poisoned in the tower?'

'Come, Waylian. Surely you must have heard the rumours of old Archmaster Gillen's death? Who do you think it was I dissected in the lower chambers all those days ago?'

Waylian thought back to when he had first come to the city and the rumours he'd heard flying around the apprentice chambers. Archmaster Gillen had been Lucen Kalvor's tutor. Kalvor had succeeded him when the old man died quite suddenly.

'Are you suggesting Archmaster Kalvor actually killed Gillen?'

Gelredida shook her head. 'No, I'm not suggesting it, Waylian, I'm saying it outright. Those other fools in the Crucible Chamber are too blinded by Kalvor's charm and power to see it, but the signs were all there. The poison he used leaves almost no trace... almost. The evidence is there for those who know what to look for. There are only two people in the city who could have crafted such a potion. I'm one of them, Milius is the other. I knew if you went to him with a list of just the right ingredients it would spook Milius enough to try to kill you.'

'It would what?' Waylian stopped in his tracks, staring at his mistress. She'd put him in danger before, he knew that, but to stand there and admit it.

Gelredida stopped and looked at him. 'Come, Waylian. Don't be such a fusspot. You were never in any real danger. Had Milius succeeded in poisoning you I'm confident I could have found a remedy before you expired.'

You're 'confident'?

Waylian shook his head. 'What about the other business? Was my life in peril there too?'

'Of course not... not really.'

That's reassuring.

'So who is Josiah Klumm?'

Gelredida eyes shifted to left and right as though someone might be listening in. She had been happy to talk in public about Lucen Kalvor poisoning his former mentor but this, it seemed, was something she wished to keep private.

Satisfied no one was eavesdropping on their conversation, Gelredida moved closer to Waylian. 'Josiah Klumm is the illegitimate offspring of one Drennan Folds. If news of this was to become public knowledge it would be very embarrassing for the Archmaster.'

'So you blackmailed him? You threatened to tell his secret?'

The Magistra looked at him as though it was the stupidest thing she'd ever heard him say – and there was plenty to choose from.

'Of course not. I threatened to kill the boy. Now,' she said matter-of-factly, 'shall we be off? We have pressing matters to attend to.'

With that she set off through the crowd.

Waylian followed his mistress with thoughts of what he'd done coursing through his head. He was the one who'd brought Josiah Klumm to the Magistra in the first place. Did that make him complicit? Would Drennan Folds eventually want revenge? The prospect of that did not sit well at all.

'What about the other Archmasters?' Waylian asked, pushing his way forward to trot alongside his mistress. 'How did you persuade them to change their minds?'

'I didn't. I gambled on the fact that once Kalvor and Folds were on side the others would follow. Marghil and the unfortunately deceased Crabbe didn't disappoint. The only one I was unsure of was Nero, and once he'd shown his true colours I knew we'd won.'

'But we were nearly killed.'

Gelredida raised an eyebrow. 'Which is hardly the same as *actually* killed, is it, Waylian.'

He supposed it wasn't.

The rest of the way they walked in silence. Even as Gelredida passed through the gates of the Crown District she said nothing. The Greencoats on the gate stepped aside as though they had expected her arrival. When they reached the gate to the palace of Skyhelm, however, things weren't quite so simple.

Four Sentinels stood guarding the way, their spears shining in the winter sun.

'I must speak with the queen,' said Gelredida.

One of the knights looked down at her then shook his head.

'I need a hundred crowns and a good night's sleep,' he replied. 'But neither of us is going to get what we want today, old woman.'

Gelredida fixed her gaze on him.

Waylian could see the knight staring back from within his great helm. His three fellows shuffled uncomfortably. For some reason none of them could find the courage to speak and tell this old lady to be on her way.

After what seemed an age, the first knight suddenly moved from their path.

'All right then,' he said, his voice quaking slightly. 'Come in.'

FORTY ONE

I t seemed with every report from the front the news became ever more dire. The numbers of men lost, the increasing need for reinforcements, requests for supplies they simply didn't have, the villages burned, the townsfolk raped and murdered. The trail from Dreldun to the gates of Steelhaven would be thick with graves, yet the sacrifices made by the soldiers of the Free States might still all be in vain.

Janessa felt wretched. Felt that every man that was killed, every person that starved or died of cold or perished from infection was a result of her failure to make a deal with the Bankers League. And every passing day she knew the chances of her being able to ensure her city's survival were slipping through her fingers.

Of course preparations had been made. Garret and Odaka had done much, their military experience invaluable to the city's defence. They had tried to recruit fighting men from the teeming mass of refugees, but seemed to find only frail old men or keen but inexperienced boys. Odaka himself had told her that these would be the first to die once the Khurtas laid siege to the city walls. Janessa wanted to tell these inadequate recruits that they should return to their families, but how could she? The city needed all the defenders it could get. It would be lost without sacrifice.

Fodder, Marshal Farren had called them. Janessa could not bring herself to think of them like that. She could only think of them as old men and boys who were marked to die. Die because she had failed to make a deal with Azai Dravos to save her city.

Lamenting on it would do her little good, though, Janessa knew that. She had to move on. It was what her father would have done. In fact, King Cael would have proudly mounted Dravos' head on a pike for all to see – a warning to any others who might try to betray the Mastragalls. Janessa would never have gone so far, but after what Dravos had done she was sorely tempted.

But Dravos was gone and the business of state demanded her full energy.

Despite the vital importance of most of her business in court, the throne room was largely vacant. Chancellor Durket and her Sentinels stood close by, but most of her court had taken their leave. Marshal Farren and General Hawke had made their way back to the front, and Hawke had only gone reluctantly. Baroness Isabelle Magrida and her son still lurked within the palace but rarely deigned to come to the throne room. The lack of attendance was something of a relief.

It was with some regret then, that after all her business was done, she saw Seneschal Rogan make his way to the throne. The man moved like a snake, seeming to slide across the floor, his feet hidden beneath the hem of his drab robe.

'Majesty,' he said, dropping to his knees. 'I have come with matters that require your attention. It concerns an execution.'

Janessa felt the weight on her shoulders increase. With all she had to deal with and the threat to the lives of her people, were they now killing their own?

'Traitors to the Crown, Seneschal?' she replied. 'Has your Inquisition uncovered some plot?'

'In a manner of speaking, Majesty. And I thought the guilty parties in this case would interest you.'

'Why is that?'

Rogan smiled. 'Because they are foreign spies, Majesty. They are enemies of the Free States. Zatani from the southern continent of Equ'un.'

Janessa thought back to the awkward dinner in which Rogan and Odaka had quarrelled. The last she had heard the Zatani were being held in cells.

'These men have been condemned to death?'

'Regrettably so, Majesty. It became obvious these savages had only mayhem in mind. They are most likely agents of the Elharim warlord.'

'*Most likely*, Seneschal? You mean you're not sure? You mean these Zatani have been condemned on a guess?'

'Absolutely not, Majesty.' Rogan held up his hands, and Janessa was surprised at just how sincere he looked. 'Their guilt is beyond doubt. Three mercenary companies have had to bury their brothers as testament to the fact.'

'So they are condemned, Seneschal. How does this concern me?'

'The Zatani were in thrall to the Aeslanti, back when your father fought those beasts at Bakhaus Gate. Many say these savage tribesmen bear the blood of the Aeslanti in their veins. Bakhaus Gate was King Cael's last great victory. Surely this could be seen as a sign – that the execution of the Zatani is an omen of your victory to come.'

This was tenuous at best. Janessa could hardly see the relevance.

'Omens are no use to me, Seneschal. It's men and resources I need.'

'Of course. But morale on the streets is low. A public display, a reminder of old victories, might be just what the citizenry needs before it faces the Khurtas.'

Janessa had not even thought of such a thing. That her people might need to have their morale bolstered in such a way. But then who would think an execution might raise the spirits? That people could watch gleefully as someone was killed before their eyes – even if it were an enemy of the city?

What was it Odaka once said? That as the queen of this realm you must weigh every outcome, consider every option.

If this was what it would take to give her people the strength to defeat their enemy then she would sanction it. If these foreigners had come here to do harm to her city and its people, they had to die.

If only Odaka were with her now, he would know what to do. He had been a warrior of Equ'un after all, though obviously not a Zatani. They were of a rival tribe, savages, barely human if rumours were true. But was it not time for Janessa to make her own choices. She could not rely on Odaka to provide solutions to every difficult decision.

'Very well, Seneschal,' said Janessa, though the words almost stuck in her throat. 'You may have your execution.'

'Thank you, Majesty. You will of course be attending?'

Attend a public execution? The thought turned Janessa's stomach.

'I will not, Seneschal. I have more pressing matters.'

'But there are considerations of protocol. And it would do the city good to see you there… for morale, of course.'

In the absence of Odaka, only Chancellor Durket was by her side. As much as she was loath to do so, Janessa now turned to him.

'Considerations of protocol?'

Durket looked at her, blankly at first. Ever since she had been attacked by Azai Dravos, Durket had wandered the corridors of Skyhelm in a daze.

'Er… yes, Majesty. Monarchs are obliged to attend the executions of traitors and rival heads of state.'

'Then it seems I have little choice,' she said, taking no relish no the prospect. 'I trust you can make the arrangements, Seneschal?'

Rogan bowed and gave her a look that suggested the arrangements were more than likely already made.

Before he could make his fawning pleasantries and leave, marching figures entered the throne room. They were surrounded by four Sentinels, but this wasn't a close guard keeping a vigilant watch lest they try to harm the queen. This was a loose honour guard – one reserved for visiting dignitaries.

The Sentinels stopped, allowing the two figures to approach the throne. Kaira took a protective step forward, but Janessa held up a hand to stop her drawing her weapon.

An old woman halted in front of the throne. Though it was obvious she was indeed old, her age was impossible to guess. While her topknot of hair was silver, her eyes were sharply piercing. Her robe hung from her thin frame like a cloak from a hook and Janessa could see it was badly stained.

Next to her was a youth, who shuffled up beside the woman as though she might protect him from the gathered knights.

The old woman carefully took to her knee, the boy quickly doing the same.

'Majesty,' she said. 'I am Magistra Gelredida. I bring warning of a plot against your life.'

Seneschal Rogan took a step forward. 'Come now, Magistra. We all know the queen's life is in constant danger. I can assure you she is quite safe under our care.'

Janessa was about to tell Rogan to be silent – who was he to make such a presumption? – but it seemed the Magistra had even less time for his interruptions.She stood up, regarding Rogan with a withering look. To Janessa's surprise, the Seneschal of the Inquisition took a step back and held his peace.

'This is no ordinary plot,' the woman continued. 'It is one that goes to the very bowels of the Tower of Magisters. One that your personal guard may not be able to protect you from.'

Kaira moved in close to Janessa. 'If this is true, then attending a public execution would be madness, Majesty.'

Janessa nodded, a little relieved that she had a legitimate excuse to not attend.

'Public or not,' said Gelredida. 'Something dark is coming and there's every chance sorcery will be involved. Something only I will be able to protect you from.'

'If I may,' ventured Rogan. 'If something is coming, perhaps we should try to draw it out – rather than just delay the threat. A public execution it is known you will attend would be the perfect trap. We could make it a smaller affair than normal, set it within an environment we could control. The Magistra here could be in attendance to protect you.'

This was madness. Her life had already been threatened more than once in the palace. To now expose herself and her unborn child to catch some secret killer was the height of folly.

'Seneschal Rogan,' she said. 'I think it's clear—'

'No, he might be right,' said the Magistra. Even though Janessa had become unaccustomed to being interrupted these last weeks, she still thought little of the breach in manners. It was clear this woman was not to be silenced by anyone. 'A small public venue would provide the perfect opportunity for us to catch the assassin in the act.'

There was silence. Kaira was shaking her head, and it was clear she thought this madness, but something about the Magistra elicited Janessa's absolute trust.

'Very well,' Janessa agreed. 'We should endeavour to capture this assassin. With members of the Caste attending, I assume there can be little danger?'

She asked that question not just for her. In recent days she had endangered the life of her child, and there was no way she wanted to repeat that. If, as was rumoured, assassins were even now plotting her death she had to face them on her own terms, it was the only way.

Magistra Gelredida cocked her head. 'There is always danger, Majesty. But your safety will be paramount. Trust me on that.'

Without asking permission, the old woman turned and made her way from the throne room.

As she watched the old woman leave, Janessa wondered just how much trust she had left.

FORTY TWO

From the shadows of an alleyway, Rag stared at the entrance to the little tavern. It seemed to be taunting her, like it knew she was scared.

Come on then. What you waiting for?

Rag just sat in the dark, watching. She was good at that; had made a skill of it over the years. On the streets where she'd learned her trade it was almost as important as being a fast picker. Sometimes she'd sit for hours just watching – sizing up the best punters for the pinch. There was no point just rushing into it like a bulldog, risking getting caught for a few measly coppers. Having a keen eye for a fat purse could save you a lot of time and effort. Hells, it could save your life too. In such a tricky business as hers, brains beat speed and brawn every day of the week.

But is it gonna help you now Rag? Is it gonna save your neck this time or have you just been a bit too bloody clever for your own good?

Kaira had given her the chance to avoid all this. Right at the start she had said she'd take care of Rag, and she was true to her word. It wasn't enough for Rag, though, was it? Nothing was ever enough.

What would she do anyway, living in a barracks with a bunch of knights? Weren't no kind of life she wanted. Rag had always wanted to make something of herself. That was never gonna happen being lackey to some warrior woman.

Now though, as she sat staring at that door, it didn't seem like a half bad option.

At least you'd be alive, Rag. You'd get to survive. If that's enough?

Survival had never been enough for Rag. That was why she'd joined the Guild in the first place. That was why she'd risked her neck to come this far. Weren't no point turning back now.

You never did make things easy for yourself, did you, Rag?

She moved quick across the empty street and tried the door, half expecting it to be locked. It wasn't, and the handle turned easy as ever. The door gave a little creak as she opened it, but there was nothing she could do about that now. The raised voices from inside told her it didn't matter, anyhow. No one would hear.

Rag crept inside and shut the door behind her. She recognised the voices arguing in the bar and before she got round the corner she stopped to listen.

'We shouldn't fucking be here.' That was Shirl, all shrill and scared like a little girl.

'Where the fuck we gonna go?' said Yarrick, annoyed, like he'd heard Shirl's moaning one too many times.

'He's right,' said Essen, his voice sounding strange after having his nose flattened in that dark alleyway the night before. 'We stay here we're fugging dead for sure. Bastian's gonna come in and he's gonna have some questions we just can't fugging answer.'

'There ain't nowhere we can run to they won't find us,' said Yarrick. 'Runnin's only gonna make us look guilty.'

'We *are* fucking guilty,' said Shirl. 'We let them take him like we was nothing.'

'They were trained,' Essen replied. 'Weren't nothing we could do. You saw what that woman did to Harkas.'

Rag peered round the corner and saw the lads were crouched around the embers of the fire, Harkas standing back a ways staring into the flames.

'So what the fuck are we gonna do?' asked Shirl like he was almost in tears.

None of them seemed to have any answer. None of them had a clue what to do now Friedrik was gone and they were the ones that had lost him.

'We do nothing,' said Rag, walking into the room as confident as she could.

The lads all stood up at her arrival. Harkas just looked around all slow like he'd known she was there all along.

'Where the fuck have you been?' asked Shirl.

'Never mind where the fuck I've been,' Rag said. 'Start thinking about our story and how we're gonna stick to it.' The fat man looked at her like she'd slapped him but said nothing. 'If Bastian finds out we've lost Friedrik every one of us is gonna end up in the Storway with a rock round his neck. So we just don't tell him. Friedrik's fucked off before without telling anyone. No one knows where he goes or who he's with, so that's what's happened this time. He left last night; no one's seen him since. All right?'

Yarrick, Shirl and Essen all looked at her from beneath creased brows. Harkas watched her, his expression blank. It was clear they'd need a moment or two to think on it, and Rag just glared back, looking like she knew what she was on about. Like she'd tried to dupe the leader of the Guild before, and come out on top.

'This'll get us all killed,' said Shirl.

'No it won't.' Yarrick replied. 'She's right – no one knows we were with him when he got nabbed. We should just sit tight and wait for someone to come looking for him.'

Yarrick glanced over at Essen who said, 'Yeah. You're right.'

'Are you fucking barmy?' wailed Shirl. 'We're just gonna sit here and wait for them to come for us because she fucking says so?' He pointed an accusing finger at Rag.

Yarrick looked at Shirl like he'd just done a shit on his chair. 'She's the reason you're still breathing, lad. Wasn't for her we'd have had to leave you in a ditch to die somewhere.'

That was enough to shut Shirl's mouth for a while.

Essen went and got some more logs for the fire, and the five of them sat there waiting for morning. Rag's heart was thumping all the while, wondering what was gonna happen. Wondering if she'd done the right thing. This crew weren't the cleverest, or even the friendliest, but she didn't want to see them hurt on her account. Well, not all of them. Every now and again, as the night drew on, she'd see Harkas watching her from the corner of the room. She had no idea what was going on in that head of his, but then she wasn't too sure she wanted to know neither.

It was close to morning when the door burst open.

Palien wasn't the first one to walk in. He had men of his own – men who looked a damn sight more frightening than Shirl, Essen and Yarrick. Every one of them looked more like Harkas, though maybe not quite as brutal. They came in, taking their places around the edge of the bar like they already knew where to stand; where the best place was to look all intimidating. Rag counted six of them before Palien walked in, a wolf smile on his face, his hawk eyes glaring straight at her. He pulled a chair across the floor, like he was relishing the scraping noise it made. When he'd slid it as close to Rag as it would go he plonked down on it, his elbows resting on the chair's backrest.

'Where is he?' said Palien, staring straight at her.

'Who?' she replied.

Who? Don't be an idiot, Rag. It's obvious who he means.

'Don't play me for a fool, little girl,' Palien said. As she looked at him she noticed he never seemed to blink. That wasn't right, surely. 'We both know you're his little pet. He doesn't go anywhere without you knowing.'

'I don't know where he is. He left last night, went off on his own like he does sometimes. We ain't seen him since, have we?'

She glanced around, relieved when the lads all backed her up with their nodding heads, but it was obvious Palien weren't interested in their opinion.

'You expect me to believe that, do you, girl? You think he'd go somewhere without taking his little dolly with him?'

'He goes off on his own all the ti—'

'Don't fucking lie to me!' Palien stood up, flinging his chair out from under him. 'Where the fuck is he?'

'I don't know,' said Rag, pressing herself back in her chair but Palien reached forward, grabbed her shirt and pulled her up onto her feet.

'Tell me where he is or I'll gut you right here, I swear.'

Rag saw Palien's eyes glaring down from that face, saw his stupid moustache twitching with anger. Her hands were up as she tried to push him away and he shook her. It was then her hand slipped down to his belt and she could feel the coinpurse at his waist. It was full, secured with a single buckle, and it would be nothing to just open it and take his coin.

'She don't know where he is,' wailed Shirl taking a step forward. 'None of us do.'

Palien didn't have to say nothing; one of his men just walked forward and kneed Shirl right in his thigh. The fat man went down with a squeal.

'Friedrik won't be happy if you gut me, will he?' said Rag. 'You'll be in for it then.'

'Not if he's dead and gone,' Palien snarled. 'And I think he is. I think you might be the one that made it happen. I've been watching you, girl. Slinking around like the fucking tavern cat. You know something.'

'I don't, I don't—'

'Yes, you do.' His shake rattled the teeth in her head. 'And if you don't tell me, you won't leave here alive. None of you will.'

'All right, I'll tell,' she said, desperate. As she looked up, Palien seemed to calm, satisfied he'd done his job.

'I thought you might,' he said, with that wolf's smile.

'But I'll only tell Bastian,' she said.

Palien shook his head. 'No, girl, you'll tell me.'

Rag managed to tear her shirt free of Palien's grip. She stumbled back and steadied herself against a chair.

'No, I won't.' She stared Palien back in his hawk's eyes, trying to act more the hunter than the prey. She wasn't too sure it worked. 'I'll tell Bastian or I'll tell no one.'

'You'll tell me or—'

'Or what? What's Bastian gonna do when he finds out I've got news of Friedrik and you wouldn't let me tell him? What then?'

'How's he going to find out?'

Rag glanced around at the gathered crowd of thugs. 'You trust everyone here to keep their mouths shut, do you?'

Palien glanced around. At first he fixed every man with a determined stare, but it soon withered and died, only to be replaced with an arrogant raised eyebrow.

'Let's go see Bastian, then. I'm sure he'll want to watch while I cut little pieces off you.'

Palien signalled to his men, who bundled Essen and Yarrick towards the door. Shirl limped after. Two of Palien's thugs looked at Harkas but neither of them dared lay a finger on him. Rag could see them both breathe out a sigh as the big man followed along obediently.

There was nothing else that Rag could do but go along with them. Once again she was stuck in a spot she couldn't get out of. Out on the street she kept looking for a way out, seeing darkened alleys she could have scuttled into, yet half of her was determined to see this through to the end.

Palien led the way through Northgate, keener than anyone to see this over with. Rag followed, realising she had no idea where Bastian's hideout was, and the further they went the more uneasy she became. As they got to the middle of the district she saw something up ahead that made her stomach turn.

Brass railings surrounded a wide-open space that rose up to a dark hill. On top of the hill stood a creepy old tomb. Rag knew instantly what it was – everybody in Steelhaven knew about the Chapel of Ghouls. Word of its horrors had been used to frighten little children for years. Rumour had it that recently there'd been stirrings inside. Whether that was true or not it was still a bloody scary place.

They moved to an alley. Two men stood at the end, guarding some steps that descended to what must have been a sewer judging by the stink. With growing dismay, Rag realised that was where they were going.

The passageway descended deep under the street and a couple of Palien's boys had to lead the way with torches. Rag could tell they were headed right beneath the Chapel of Ghouls. The deeper they went, the worse the smell. How anyone could stay down here, let alone a rich man like Bastian, she had no idea.

Eventually they came to a big round chamber, damp walls, roots growing down through the roof. There was no fire and the air was chill, blowing in cold from somewhere.

Palien stopped in the middle of the room. He didn't announce himself, just stood there like he'd rung a bell or something, and was waiting for a servant to come scurrying.

It weren't no servant that turned up, though.

Bastian's men were all lean, not the big burly types Palien and Friedrik favoured. Their faces were gaunt, hungry, and they all dressed in the same dark gear and carried blades and axes and shivs of all sorts.

They came out of the shadows like they belonged there, the dark clinging to them like it didn't want to let go. Rag felt her hands start to shake and she clenched her fists in case she made herself look a twat.

When they were completely surrounded, Bastian walked out of the dark. In the scant light he looked more like a corpse than usual, like he'd just clawed his way out of the dirt. Rag was just glad that his eyes were on Palien, as those two dark sunken pools looked like they could kill all on their own.

'Well?' he said.

Rag could see all Palien's confidence was gone now; his eyes more rabbit than hawk. He drew a finger and thumb over his moustache before he spoke.

'Friedrik's gone missing. I was supposed to have a meet with him earlier but he never turned up. No one's seen him, and this little bitch won't tell me anything.' He gestured at Rag. 'She knows something, but she'll only tell you.'

Bastian glanced down briefly, casting his cold eyes over Rag like she was shit on his shoe.

'Yes, she will,' he said.

Silence then. Bastian weren't looking at her no more, but Rag knew it was her turn to speak. It was now or never. Time to roll those dice. Time to gamble with her life one more time. Maybe one *last* time.

'Friedrik's been caught,' she said. 'He's been taken by the palace guard.'

Palien looked round at her then. 'What? Where is he?'

Time to turn it on, Rag. Now or fucking never.

She took a step back, putting that face on and squeezing out those tears like her life depended on it. Which it most likely did.

'Please, Mister Bastian,' she said, just like she'd heard a dozen blokes say to Friedrik, just before they lost a finger or an eye. She pointed an accusatory finger at Palien. 'It was him what did it. It was him what betrayed Mister Friedrik to the guard.'

'You lying little bitch,' Palien barked. He took a step forward, and Rag stumbled back, squealing like she was a little girl, like she was terrified – it wasn't too much of a stretch.

Before Palien could reach her, there was a knife at his throat. One of Bastian's lean bastards was behind him. Palien stopped cold, like he'd been frozen in time.

'Go on,' said Bastian, looking on like none of this mattered a shit.

Rag knew it did matter. She knew either her or Palien was going to die down here in this stinky pit.

'I followed him. I saw him and Friedrik. I saw him lure Friedrik into the trap and I saw him take payment from them.' She pointed at Palien's purse, her eyes wide in fear like it was some bloated spider rather than a fat bag of leather clinging to his hip.

Without a word Bastian glanced at one of his other men, who moved forward and unbuckled the coinpurse from Palien's belt.

'She's fucking lying,' Palien said. 'Can't you see? She's a fucking liar.'

As he spoke, Bastian's man poured out the contents of the purse into his hand. He let some of the coins fall through his fingers until he finally found what he was looking for.

'What's that?' said Palien, voice rising in panic as the man handed it to Bastian. 'What is it?'

Bastian held something up. It glinted in the torchlight, shining like a beacon on a cliff.

'It's a little medallion,' said Bastian. 'Made of steel, crown and crossed swords on it. Only ever given out by the Skyhelm Sentinels. Very rare and worth a pretty penny on the black market. But then you already knew that, didn't you, Palien.'

'No,' Palien said. 'It's not mine.'

'Is this all they paid you to betray the Guild, or did you get gold too?'

'No, I swear. It's not mine.' His voice was rising with fear now.

'Then what's it doing in your purse?'

'It... It...' Palien stared at Bastian in panic. There was a tear running down his cheek now. Then his eyes turned to Rag. For a moment they had the hawk in them once more.

Just for a moment.

As he opened his mouth to speak again, most likely to put Rag in the frame, Bastian's man drew his knife across Palien's throat. Whatever he was about to say was lost as blood gushed from the wound. He fell to his knees, trying to claw his neck back together.

It seemed to take ages for him to die and Bastian didn't even stay to see the show.

Rag stayed, though. She watched Palien's every last breath.

FORTY THREE

T here was no way of telling the age of the amphitheatre. Kaira guessed it was older than the Temple of Autumn, perhaps even as old as Skyhelm itself. It sat in the centre of the Crown District, a crumbling stone edifice. The walls that surrounded it would once have risen a hundred feet, its tiered sides seating maybe five thousand souls, all come to watch whatever spectacle was on show. That spectacle no doubt involved blood and death to satisfy the crowd. Much like it would today.

Kaira had walked the amphitheatre from top to bottom. Most of its walls had crumbled. The place was still sealed off from the outside, though the tunnels beneath the floor of its arena were now open and laid bare to the winter sun. There was no sign of a trap. No sign of an assassin – or assassins – lying in wait to ambush the queen on her arrival. The place looked altogether peaceful and quiet. It wouldn't stay that way for long. Soon, on the scaffold built just for today, the execution would take place.

Kaira had heard about the Zatani, of course, and of their ferocity in battle. She had also been told of the crimes these particular tribesmen had committed. It didn't make sense to her. From all she'd learned of these men, they were noble warriors. Why would they come to the city under the guise of friendship and sacrifice themselves just to murder a few mercenaries? It was foolish to simply execute them. But it was not Kaira's place to question the decision. She had one purpose and one alone – to protect the queen.

A last circuit of the amphitheatre, just to ensure the rest of the Sentinels and assembled Greencoats were in place, brought her to the tree that had grown in the centre of the arena. Where once gladiators had fought for their lives, now stood a single leafless ash. Kaira found it symbolic that such a thing should grow where so many had died. She laid a hand on the bark, feeling its weathered surface. Before she turned away, her fingers traced something in the bark. Two nails had been hammered into the trunk and below them someone had carved a symbol. By the looks of it, this had been done quite recently. Kaira could make no sense of the marking. Perhaps it was some foreign language, or perhaps a message from one young lover to another significant only to them.

Well, there were no lovers here today.

Durket hurried into the amphitheatre, breathing heavily, his face red and moist.

'She's here,' he managed to say through his wheezing.

Moving past him, Kaira made her way to the entrance of the amphitheatre. Several dignitaries were already making their way inside: district commissioners, courtiers, stewards. Seneschal Rogan was there, of course, along with the High Constable and Baroness Magrida, though it appeared her son was not. Three mercenary captains were amongst the spectators, their coloured livery stark against the formal attire of the courtiers. Even Lord Marshal Ryder had chosen to attend with a contingent of his Wyvern Guard.

Kaira moved past them as she made her way towards the queen. Janessa stood surrounded by Sentinels, Merrick at her side, waiting for the crowd to enter.

Each one of her subjects who filed past gave a cursory bow or curtsy, but none of them tarried. They all seemed eager to enter the amphitheatre, to watch the coming show.

'Whose idea was it to hold the executions in this place?' said Janessa, whilst still acknowledging the fawning sycophancy of her court.

'Seneschal Rogan,' Odaka said. He was beside the Sentinels in full armour, his massive curved blade at his side. 'Had I the chance I would have advised against this whole—'

'You have already said. I am aware of your feelings on this, Odaka, but the decision has been made.'

'I must agree with Odaka,' said Kaira. 'This execution compromises your security, and I believe it serves little purpose.'

'Enemies of the Free States must be punished,' Janessa replied. 'No matter how distasteful we find the deed.'

'But here? In this place? And before a mob hungry for blood?'

'I like it no more than you,' said Janessa, as the Red Witch and her apprentice followed the last of the spectators in. The boy acknowledged the queen with a nervous bow as they entered. 'Here is as good a place as any. And we have presented a perfect opportunity for any would-be assassin.'

'Offering yourself up as a sacrificial lamb is madness,' said Odaka.

'I am well protected,' Janessa replied. 'Isn't that right, Kaira?'

No you're not. You're baring your neck in the hope of luring out the wolf and I don't know if I, or anyone else, will be able to stop it before your throat is ripped out.

'Yes, Majesty,' Kaira said.

Janessa gestured to the entrance of the amphitheatre. 'Shall we?'

Kaira led the way to where a special section of the arena had been cordoned off for the queen.

No sooner had they taken up their position than the first of the Zatani was brought in. He did not struggle, but walked proudly. His hands were chained, his mouth covered by some kind of steel mask, his neck manacled to a long pole. Kaira's heart sank to see the man brought so low. It sank further still at the crowd's response.

They began to boo and hiss like a bunch of children at a puppet show – this proud warrior reduced to the rank of villain in some mummer's farce.

Five more of the Zatani were brought out, four of them as tall and proud as the first, facing their fate with homor. The last one, huge and powerful with piercing blue eyes, writhed and bucked against his bonds, snarling behind the metal mask that bound his jaws.

All six were walked to the wooden scaffold at the far end of the amphitheatre and forced to kneel. Kaira could see the axeman standing to one side, checking the keenness of his weapon.

Once the Zatani were in place, Seneschal Rogan climbed up to the scaffold and silenced the onlookers with a gesture.

'Majesty,' he said, bowing across the arena to Janessa. 'Lords and ladies. We have come to observe an ancient rite – the execution of Steelhaven's enemies. Here are six men of the direst kind. Enemies of the Free States who would see our beloved city brought low. Traitors to the Crown and servants of the dread enemy Amon Tugha—'

'Gods, but that man makes me sick,' whispered Odaka, turning to one side rather than watching Rogan's performance.

'—the Elharim warlord who even now is only a few day's ride from the city.'

Some of the crowd had obviously not heard that news and began chattering in panic. Some even made for the exit from the amphitheatre, clearly eager to leave the city before the Khurtas arrived.

'It is with regret,' continued the Seneschal, 'that we have to carry out this necessary duty. Bring the first of the condemned.'

With difficulty, a trio of Greencoats forced one of the Zatani to rise to his feet. The warrior, on seeing the block and the executioner, began to struggle, but with his neck held fast there was little even one so powerful could do.

Before they could bundle him to the block, Kaira's attention was drawn by something curious – a movement in her peripheral vision. She looked towards the ash tree, its empty branches reaching up towards the pale sky. As she watched they shuddered, even though there was no wind. No one else had seemed to notice, so enrapt were they in the proceedings, but Kaira was unnerved by it. She took a step forward – the tree seemed to be swaying, although its trunk looked sturdy. As she came closer she saw the sigil cut into the bark beneath two hammered nails, that she had thought was some lover's carving, was now alive with writhing maggots.

Kaira stepped back. A wave of nausea hit her as she witnessed the corruption.

Again the tree shook.

She could hear Rogan in the background ordering the first execution.

The trunk of the tree creaked and groaned as it moved, bark snapped, branches shuddered into life.

With an ear-splitting crack, the ash tree split in two along its trunk.

The amphitheatre fell silent.

As though rearing its head, half the tree rose up. The branches, which before had reached up toward the sky, were now draped down its back like some ghastly mane.

'To arms,' Kaira cried. She recoiled, dragging her sword from its scabbard as screams rose up from the crowd.

With a violent wrench, the tree pulled itself from the ground. Loose soil and stone was dragged up as its roots formed a dozen rudimentary limbs, pulling it from the earth. Its branches writhed – like the tentacles of some colossal squid – and it raised its eyeless head, opening a toothless maw in a silent newborn wail.

The arena broke into uproar as the sight of the creature struck terror in the spectators.

Someone rushed past Kaira, a Sentinel knight, his spear held out to attack. With a growl of fury he pierced what seemed to be a leg of the monster, and Kaira stared horror as white cruor spewed from the wound. The hellish monster spun round, its mouth wide in a silent cry of pain. With a swipe of one thick branch it smashed the knight across the arena and into the fleeing mass of spectators where he landed with a sickening thud.

Kaira saw the ash tree turn ominously to face the queen. It seemed to lock her in an eyeless stare until, with the grinding of massive limbs, it moved towards her, dragging itself across the arena as those thick roots dug into the earth.

Kaira could hear Lord Marshal Ryder screaming at his Wyvern Guard, who duly rushed in disciplined ranks to stand in the creature's path. Sentinels ran to join them, raising shield and spear as the crowd fled.

Kaira felt unusually sluggish. Her injuries still troubled her, but she had to act.

The creature dragged its huge bulk ever closer to the queen, batting some unfortunate courtier from its path and sending him smashing into a pile of loose masonry.

Tannick bellowed to his men who rushed forward, chopping at the trunk of the ash tree and hacking at its flailing branches. White gore seeped from the creature, but still it battled on, tearing a path through the bronze-armoured knights that stood against it.

They would never stop it before it reached Janessa.

'Get the queen to safety!' Kaira yelled desperately.

Merrick tore his eyes away from the creature, grabbing the queen and pulling her from the dais. There was no way he could reach the exit from the amphitheatre, which was blocked by the monster's approach, so he guided Janessa into the crumbling tunnels of the arena, followed by several other Sentinels.

Kaira turned back to the foul monster, and saw its onslaught had been checked by the knights, but they looked unable to destroy it. They could never defeat such a creature; surely a thing born of such dark magicks would kill them all. She briefly wondered where in the hells that magistra had got to, but then all thought but battle was gone from her mind.

Gripping her sword tight, Kaira rushed to join the defenders.

FORTY FOUR

I t had dragged itself out of the ground with the sound of a thousand breaking bones. Merrick had watched as it turned its giant creaking head, pulling itself along on rotten twisted limbs. It wasn't until the killing started, and Kaira screamed at him, that anyone had moved.

And that was when Merrick grabbed Janessa's arm. Regardless of protocol, it seemed the right thing to do. He all but dragged her down from the wooden podium, slipping on the bottom step, almost sending them both sprawling.

The exit from the amphitheatre was across the arena floor. There were around a dozen knights in the way, their weapons flailing.

Merrick pulled the queen after him towards a gap in the broken wall. Odaka and two more Sentinels were right behind them, and that made him feel a little better. The break in the wall led to a crumbling stone passage. Merrick could see through the rotted mortar of the stone wall to the other side, to freedom, but there was no way through.

'Keep moving,' growled Odaka.

Merrick didn't have any quarrel with that, and he hauled the queen along the corridor. For her part, she made no complaint, following as best she could as the passageway reached a set of stairs. Merrick paused at the bottom.

'Up,' Odaka ordered. 'We will guard the way here.'

As Odaka and the two Sentinels took up positions, Merrick dragged the queen after him. Outside he could hear the sounds of battle; someone was screaming, there was a clash of steel on wood and something roared like a beast.

The staircase led to a rickety platform with passageways that led off to either side. Merrick picked a path, the one he thought might lead away from the carnage and pulled Janessa after him.

You've got no idea what you're doing or where you're going, have you. Get a fucking grip.

The passage darkened before they came out into another room, one with no exits. Merrick stopped dead. On the ground was the body of an armoured knight, a Sentinel. There was a single puncture wound in his breastplate, right above the heart.

Whoever had killed this Sentinel might still be around and Merrick was none too keen to meet him. He turned, ready to flee back down the stairs, but stopped as someone walked out of the dark passage behind them. For a moment he hoped would Odaka, come to find him and tell him everything was going to be all right.

Inside, he knew it wouldn't be.

The man was old, too old to have such a confident gait. His shoulders were wide, his hair and beard greying, but his eyes… those eyes were like two deep pools of winter staring out coldly as if they hated the world and would turn it to ice.

Merrick backed away, Janessa behind him, but there was nowhere else to go. They were trapped.

The old man held a sword at his side, the blade straight, the handle worked in a fashion Merrick had never seen before. He got the impression that, despite his age, this fella knew how to use it.

'No closer,' Merrick said, brandishing his own sword. 'I don't want to hurt you.'

The old man took two steps forward and stopped. 'You won't hurt me, boy. I am the Father of Killers. There is nothing you can do that would hurt me. But I have not come for you, I have come for—'

'Yeah, yeah, I get the picture.' Merrick dropped into a defensive stance. 'You've come to kill the queen, blah blah. I'm going to stop you, blah blah. Let's just get on with the fucking fighting, shall we.'

This seemed to amuse the old man, who walked forward, his guard down.

Never squander an opportunity, Ryder.

Merrick leapt to attack, feeling not a little guilty for taking the old man by surprise. It didn't matter anyway, as the old man batted the thrust aside, his sword coming up in a counter that Merrick struggled to avoid. He stumbled back as the blade almost took his eye out.

This was looking all too familiar. He'd had his fill of being humiliated by better swordsmen, he couldn't let this old man join the list.

Merrick struck again, this time totally focused. This time he'd make no mistake. Everything he'd learned from House Tarnath—

The old man parried again, and this time Merrick's blade almost flew from his grip. He was forced to dance back to stay out of the old man's range, Janessa moving along behind, staying at Merrick's back.

'There is nothing you can do,' said the old man. 'The end is inevitable. I will allow you to walk free. Leave your queen and I will let—'

Merrick struck in again. This time he managed to put a slice in the old man's robe, but the consequent counter was more ferocious than before. Merrick staggered back into the wall. He pushed Janessa out of the way as his opponent's sword cut in, taking a chunk out of the ancient stone behind him.

The Father of Killers moved like a phantom, in one place one moment, somewhere else the next. Merrick struck in again and again, but every blow was parried with ease. He thrust one last time and the old man's blade knocked the sword out of Merrick's grip. It clanged off the wall and came to rest some feet away and the Father of Killers bore down on him, each footstep carefully placed, his eyes never wavering from their immediate target.

'You have shown surprising courage in the face of certain death,' said the old man.

'Trust me – no one's more surprised than I am,' Merrick replied.

The Father of Killer's raised his blade.

Odaka Du'ur burst in through the archway with a savage cry. He was like an animal, his curved blade scything in and giving the Father of Killers little time to parry.

'Run!' Odaka screamed. Merrick needed no further encouragement.

He grabbed Janessa's hand and pulled her from the room. The sound of clashing swords rang out behind him as they fled.

FORTY FIVE

He had failed his warriors and led them to an ignominious death. The knowledge that they would die by the executioner's blade filled him with a shame greater than he had ever known. So when the fell monster dragged itself from the ground, Regulus Gor's heart had leapt. No longer would they be slaughtered for the delight of a baying mob. At least now they would die at the hands of a worthy opponent.

It had to reach them first, though, had to destroy those who stood against it. Regulus admired the warriors in bronze as they fought. They were organised, disciplined and died with honour.

He strained against his bonds as he watched, yearning to join them, but he could do nothing. Beside them the axeman, who moments earlier had been ready to lop Janto's head from his shoulders, stood dumbstruck, his axe held limp in his hand. What Regulus would have done for that weapon, for the chance to leap from the scaffold and take the fight to his enemy – to die a warrior's death.

As the Zatani watched helplessly, one of the soldiers in green ran towards them. Regulus realised it was Nobul Jacks, the one he had spoken to back in his cell. He looked angered. Someone was arguing with him, trying to pull him back, but could only do so in vain.

Nobul came to stand before Regulus, staring with apprehension but little fear. Then he unclasped the mask that held Regulus' jaws fast.

'Will you still fight for us?' he said. Regulus stared at him, aware of the carnage being reaped in the arena beyond. 'Will you fight for us now?'

Regulus smiled grimly. He had put his trust in these Coldlanders once and it had led him here, to be killed for the entertainment of a crowd. Could he really trust them now?

What does it matter? Say yes and take your freedom, to die here with a weapon in hand and blood on your lips.

'Yes, Nobul Jacks. I will fight for you.'

Nobul grabbed the keys and unlocked the manacles that held Regulus. Once released, Regulus stood to full height, looking down at Nobul. He could tell the Coldlander was ready to defend himself if he had to.

'My warriors and I will fight for you,' he said. 'But I will have the honour of entering battle first.'

With that he turned to the executioner. The man took a step back, holding his axe up as though it could shield him. Regulus wrested the axe from the hooded man's hands and leapt from the wooden scaffold.

He landed deftly and sprinted towards the fray. The great beast swung a writhing branch, sending gore and shattered armour flying.

With a roar, Regulus leapt past the armoured warriors in their desperate fight. He raised the axe high, bringing it down with a solid hacking sound against the thick wooden limb and the monstrosity raised its head high in a silent cry of pain. It struck out before Regulus could dodge away, and he was sent spinning through the air, somehow managing to hold onto the axe as it was wrenched free of the creature's flesh.

He landed heavily and the great monster bore down on him. Regulus leapt to his feet and braced himself, awaiting the onslaught. Before the creature could raise another massive branch to smite him, more figures rushed to join the fray.

Leandran leapt at the monster. He had found a fallen blade, and now raised it high. Akkula held a spear and rushed in low, impaling the creature's trunk while Leandran hacked at its thickest flailing arm.

Regulus flushed with pride, then joined them, rushing forward, his axe cutting in with swift staccato blows as he hacked at the monster, trying to fell it like the tree it had once been.

The trunk of the creature cracked as it twisted in an attempt to shake off the Zatani. Hagama rushed in then, adding another spear to the attack, screaming all the while as though the breath of his lungs had been put there by the Lord of the Wilds himself.

One of the bronze-armoured knights was quick to rejoin the fray, his sword flashing as he sliced great gouges out of the monster before moving out of range each time it had a chance to counter.

Regulus ducked, narrowly avoiding a great branch which swept down to smash him into the earth. Leandran was not so lucky. The monster grasped the warrior in a wooden limb and raised him high. Still Leandran battled, roaring in defiance right up until the creature smashed him into the ground head first. He lay there silent and unmoving. Regulus screamed in fury, his yell joined by Janto's as he raced past, leaping upon the creature's head and rending with tooth and claw.

Enraged at seeing one of their number so cruelly vanquished, the Zatani resumed their onslaught, more ferociously than ever. So furious was their assault that any bronze-armoured Coldlanders between them and the monster were forced to retreat from their path. Try as it might the monster could not land a blow on the Zatani. They attacked furiously then darted aside, moving with practised ease, each of them instinctively knowing what the others would do, where they would be, how they would fight.

Regulus came at the creature from the rear, his axe hacking the roots that supported it. The beast buckled, losing balance as it was tipped over by the spears of Hagama, Kazul and Akkula. Still Janto clung to the creature's face, bark and white gore flying every which way as he tore at it.

'Janto!' Regulus shouted.

As Janto looked up Regulus flung him the headsman's axe. The Zatani caught it deftly, raising it high with a roar before bringing it down to hack the head from the creature.

Still the monster writhed on the ground, spewing white gore. Regulus and his warriors stood back as the armoured Coldlanders rushed in, to hack the downed beast to kindling.

Regulus looked at the crumpled figure of Leandran, and saw Akkula already knelt at his side. The young Zatani looked up as Regulus approached.

'He has already gone on his way to the stars.'

The thrill of victory ebbed as Regulus looked down at the old warrior. Leandran had been a teacher to Regulus for many years, and his heart ached at the loss. There was no sorrow, though, no tears. Leandran had fought well and met his death as any Gor'tana should – in battle. It was a worthy end.

Once the sound of hacking had subsided and the beast was destroyed, a voice rose up over the calm.

'What are you doing? To arms! These criminals must be subdued!'

Regulus looked up to see a hooded figure he recognised. Rogan, he had called himself. The man was pointing an accusing finger at the Zatani.

'To your feet,' Regulus ordered, and his warriors moved to stand beside him. Janto's eyes were ablaze, his lust for battle far from sated.

One of the warriors in bronze, his helm bearing two mighty wings, took a step forward. 'These men have just helped us defeat a foe that would have murdered us all, Seneschal. You cannot seriously want them clapped in irons?'

'They are dangerous. Murderers,' said Rogan. 'I demand that—'

'Demand?' said the warrior. 'You demand?'

Regulus could see the other men in bronze moving to their leader's side, as ready for another fight as Janto was.

'I think they've proved their loyalty,' said a voice behind him.

Regulus saw it was Nobul Jacks who had spoken. He could not help but like this man. Could not help but think he was as honourable as his name suggested.

'This proves nothing. These creatures are dangerous enemies of the Free States,' said Rogan. 'They have been condemned.'

'They've shown where their allegiance lies,' said Nobul. 'Look.' He gestured at the fallen monster.

It was then the top of the amphitheatre exploded in a shower of stone.

FORTY SIX

Merrick pulled her up the worn stone stairs and Janessa clung to his hand as if her life depended on it. They came out onto another platform. Half the wall had collapsed and she could see out onto her city. It may as well have been a thousand miles away for all the good it would do her – there was no way down but for a hundred foot drop.

'We have to go back,' Janessa said.

Merrick looked around him, breathing heavily, his eyes wide. He knew they were trapped. 'You're right,' he said

He made his way back down the stairs but stopped suddenly as a figure made its way up. Janessa could barely look, could barely regard those stone-cold eyes without feeling their ice in her heart. There was no warmth about this man, just the chill of death.

'You have led me a merry dance,' said the Father of Killers in a voice like silk on steel. 'But it is now over.'

'Not another step,' Merrick said, standing before Janessa.

The Father of Killers smiled, but there was no humour there.

'You have no weapon. There is nothing you can do but die.'

Merrick backed away from the old man and the sword he carried that was dripping blood onto the stone. Janessa's heart gave a sickening lurch as she thought of Odaka fighting the Father of Killers so that they might flee – that the blood on that blade could well be his.

'I don't suppose you'd be willing to fight me unarmed?' Merrick said hopefully.

The old man's smile was gone as quick as it had come. He raised his sword, and Janessa held her breath.

Something clattered up the stairs. The Father of Killers turned to face the young man who had appeared, his face flushed, his robes dishevelled. Janessa recognised him as the Magistra's apprentice. The young boy rushed between Merrick and the Father of Killers.

'What are you doing, lad?' Merrick said.

'Trust me,' replied the apprentice, taking a deep breath.

Then he screamed at the old man as if it might blow him off the platform.

Nothing happened.

The Father of Killer's face twisted in frustration. He stepped forward, his blade poised to strike.

'Get out of the fucking way,' Merrick barked, pushing the boy aside. The point of the assassin's blade took him in the centre of his breastplate, the keen edge slicing through the steel plate as if it were parchment.

Janessa watched in horror as Merrick staggered to one side, clutching at his chest, his face twisted in pain. He was clearly trying to remain standing, but there was no strength left in his legs.

The young lad's face was twisted in fear and disbelief.

The Father of Killers ignored them both, his attention now fully fixed on Janessa.

'Shall we continue?' he said, like he was asking her to dance.

It was obvious no one else was coming to help Janessa. There was the sound of roaring from the arena below. The sound of weapons and battle. The rest of her Sentinels were all too preoccupied to save her now. The daemonic creature raised in the amphitheatre had been a diversion, the real threat hidden all along. Janessa had to admire how clever a move that had been.

'This will not seal Amon Tugha's victory,' she said, trying to stand up straight and proud.

'No,' said the old man. 'But it will help.' He took a step forward then stopped, looking at her askance. He regarded her with curiosity, as though he was weighing her up, judging her worthiness. 'Just one final question. What did you do to my son, River, to turn him against me?'

Janessa looked deep into those cold blue eyes – eyes without mercy, the last eyes she would ever see. Then she smiled. 'I offered him love,' she said. 'Do you even understand what that is?'

The Father of Killers narrowed his eyes. 'Do I understand what that is? I raised that boy. I taught him to be a man far greater than he would ever have been without me. I gave him abilities no southron has ever learned. I honoured him, and *you* ruined it all.'

'And I would do it again,' she breathed. And at that moment, she realised she would. That despite everything, despite the shame being with child might bring, she would do it all again, go through a hundred such trials, risk death a thousand times just for one more night in River's arms.

'By now he is dead,' said the old man. 'You can join him.'

Janessa closed her eyes.

'Just a moment,' said an old and tired voice from the stairwell. Janessa looked to see The Father of Killers glance around. If he was frustrated at the constant interruptions, he didn't show it.

Magistra Gelredida pulled herself up onto the last stair and breathed a sigh. Her apprentice moved from where he was cowering, but she raised a weary hand and waved him off.

'Come to die with your queen, crone?' said the Father of Killers.

'Hardly,' she replied, leaning heavily against the wall.

The old man's laugh was like the hiss of a serpent.

Without warning Gelredida threw something towards him. Janessa couldn't see what it was, couldn't make it out as it soared through the air. Without even having to look, the Father of Killers brought his sword up to slice whatever she had flung at him in two.

Then the rooftop exploded.

Janessa was flung backwards, blinded, deafened. When eventually she could open her eyes she saw the top of the amphitheatre had been blown off. Debris lay all around and a thick pall of dust rose up all around her. The dress she wore was torn and filthy and her ears were ringing.

The young apprentice was beside her, his face covered in dust. He was speaking to her, but at first she couldn't hear him.

'Are you all right, Majesty?' she finally heard.

'Yes,' she replied, staggering to her feet. 'Find your mistress.'

The boy nodded, wandering off into the dust to find Gelredida.

Janessa suddenly thought of Merrick, lying somewhere in the carnage, bleeding to death and she rushed into the dissipating cloud.

There was movement, and she stumbled forward, thinking it was Merrick. When she saw the drab and torn robes she stopped dead. The Father of Killers dragged himself along but one of his arms, his swordarm she assumed, was missing. He was pulling himself towards what remained of his sword; a broken hilt with a shattered blade. Before he could reach it Janessa stooped and picked it up.

The old man rolled over to look at her. She recoiled at the state of his face – half of it was a bloody mess but the other half filled her with as much horror. His eyes were no longer blue, instead shining with a gold light. His skin had grown less wrinkled and his beard had vanished to reveal smooth skin and a strong jaw. Though still unmistakeably the Father of Killers, he who had once been an old man was now youthful and, were it not for the injuries, might once have been handsome.

More magicks she supposed – the old man merely a guise, merely another Elharim trick.

'It appears I have failed,' he said, his voice weak.

'It appears you have,' said Janessa, looking down at him without pity. This was the man who had tortured her lover throughout his life, the man who would have seen her dead. He deserved no pity.

'When my master Amon Tugha comes to take your head tell him…' He took a pained breath. 'Tell him…'

Janessa thrust the broken sword into the Father of Killer's throat.

'I will tell him nothing,' she said through gritted teeth. 'He will know only that you failed. Your body will be burned and no one will care you ever existed.'

The light in those eyes slowly died, turning from gold to the colour of ash, as the Father of Killers' life ebbed from the wound in his throat. Janessa watched him and something in her fed on it. Something in her enjoyed watching him die.

She stood back then. The air had nearly cleared, the noise from down in the arena gone silent. Janessa looked around, desperate to find Merrick. She searched frantically until she found him beneath a pile of rubble.

Falling to her knees, she moved the detritus from his body. He was still alive, if barely. The wound in his chest was still pulsing blood, and a puddle had formed and begun to congeal beneath him.

At her touch his eyes flickered open. 'I wasn't expecting that,' he managed to say, a trickle of blood dripping from the side of his lips as he spoke.

'Don't try to talk,' Janessa replied, before calling out for help. The apprentice was helping Magistra Gelredida to her feet and Janessa looked at her pleadingly.

The old woman looked down and shook her head. 'There's little can be done,' she said and turned to leave.

Janessa looked down to see Merrick's eyes had glazed, his lids seemed heavy and he was struggling to keep them open.

'You have done a great thing, Ryder. Your sacrifice will not be forgotten.'

At that, Gelredida turned and looked with curiosity at the dying man. 'Did you say "Ryder"?' she asked.

'Yes,' Janessa replied. 'Merrick Ryder.'

'Step back,' said the old woman, kneeling beside Merrick's body.

Janessa rose to her feet and watched as the old woman carefully removed the scarlet gloves from her hands. The flesh beneath was black, the veins raised in a hideous spider-web pattern.

'Waylian, help,' said Gelredida as she began to unbuckle Merrick's breastplate.

The boy obeyed, and as soon as Merrick's armour was taken off the magistra laid her hideous hands on his wound. Quietly she began to chant, invoking whatever powers magickers channelled to carry out their deeds.

As Janessa watched, armoured figures came up the stairs desperate to find her. They tried to usher her away but, confident the danger had passed, she chose to watch in fascination as the old witch did her work.

In moments Merrick's eyes fluttered open and Gelredida reclined, stretching a crick from her back.

'He will live,' she said. 'Waylian, if you please.' With that the apprentice helped her to her feet.

'Thank you,' Janessa said as the old woman walked past.

'Don't thank me yet,' said Gelredida, her expression grim. 'This is just the beginning.'

FORTY SEVEN

N obul watched them as they feasted. It was just him and the five Zatani in the empty courtyard. They were beasts, giants, ferocious and untamed. Nobul had seen them up close before, had fought them, killed them, but that had been a long time ago. Back then he'd been scared half out of his wits, but you forgot all about the fear when the fighting started. There was nothing to fight now though – these men had given him their loyalty. Now all he had to do was watch them, and Nobul wasn't sure whether to be scared or not.

Their leader, Regulus, had offered him a life debt. Of course he'd refused. Nobul had no more right over the warrior's life than he did anyone's. These men owed him nothing. Nevertheless, they'd wanted to stay close to him, probably as he was the only one who'd shown them any kind of compassion. If you could call setting them free to fight off some magick-spawned monster 'compassion'.

The rest of the Greencoats were still at the amphitheatre, cleaning up the mess. Nobul was grateful for that, glad he hadn't had to hang around; he'd seen enough of what those magickers could do to last him a lifetime. The less he had to do with all that shit the better.

Not that dealing with this was any more appealing: what in the hells was he supposed to do with five Zatani warriors?

Regulus rose from the feasting, wiping his mouth on his arm. He turned and fixed Nobul with a determined look. But then these Zatani always looked determined. They always looked fierce.

Regulus crossed the courtyard to where Nobul stood. The warrior moved with an assured grace that Nobul marvelled at. He had never realised how impressive looking these creatures were, especially not when he'd fought them at Bakhaus Gate. You didn't have the time to appreciate those kinds of things when you were trying not to get killed.

'We must speak, Nobul Jacks,' said the Zatani.

'Now's as good a time as any,' he replied.

'I like you, Nobul Jacks. You speak plain. Just like a Gor'tana.'

'Thanks.' *I think.*

'My warriors and I have had much to discuss since you freed us. And we have decided to leave this place, unless we have certain guarantees.'

'Leave? After all you've been through to come here and fight for this city?'

'It is what we've been through that has made us come to this decision. We have been treated worse than animals – as enemies – when we only came to this place to offer our fealty. If we are to stay and fight for this city, concessions will have to be made.'

'I don't have the authority to—'

'If you cannot grant what we ask, then we will go. If we are forced to stay we will fight you.'

Nobul swallowed hard. 'What do you want?'

'First, we have travelled far. A journey that required we leave our armour behind. If we are to stand atop your walls and defend your people, we will need armour – Zatani armour, built by a craftsman.'

A smile crept across Nobul's face. He had abandoned his forge months ago, yet his hand still itched for a hammer. It was unlikely there was another man in the city who knew what Zatani armour looked like and could have forged it with his skill.

'That I can do,' he said with confidence.

Regulus nodded his thanks. 'The second demand is more important. We have lost a brother. A warrior of our tribe. We must have recompense for that.'

'All right. I'm not sure there's much left in the Crown coffers but—'

'No, you misunderstand. We do not require your worthless coins. We need a life for his life. A sacrifice as you might call it.'

Nobul felt the hairs stand up on the back of his neck. He asked the question but already knew the answer. 'You mean like a goat or a sheep?'

'No.'

Of course 'no'. Like it was ever going to be that bloody easy.

'There's no way that could happen. We don't just offer people up for sacrifice. That's not how things are done around here.'

'I understand, Nobul Jacks. You do not respect your gods or your dead as we do. It is no matter. We shall leave, then.' Regulus laid a huge dark hand on Nobul's shoulder. 'But I wonder if you might do us one last kindness. We would send our brother off to the stars.' He gestured to the body of the Zatani they had wrapped in linen. 'We would require a pyre.'

'I'll see what I can do,' Nobul replied.

With that, Regulus returned to his fellow warriors.

Nobul continued to watch them as the sun went down. The air grew colder, but Nobul chose to ignore the chill. There'd be plenty of cold nights to come, may as well get used to them.

Kilgar and the rest of the lads came back just before dark and the serjeant came to stand beside Nobul.

'How've they been?' he asked.

Nobul just shrugged. 'Pretty much as they are now.'

'The Seneschal's creating a right old shit storm. He'll tell anyone who'll listen this lot need to be killed.'

'Is anyone listening?'

Kilgar gave him a sly smile. 'Thankfully not. Lord Marshal and the High Constable both agree we'll need this bunch in the days to come. When the Khurtas get here they'll have a proper bloody surprise when we unleash this lot on them.'

'Yeah,' said Nobul with a frown. 'Not quite sure how to put this; but they're not sticking around for that.'

'What do you mean?'

'They've had enough. To be honest, the way they've been treated the past few days, I don't blame them.'

Kilgar cursed under his breath. 'Don't suppose there's anything we can do to change their minds?'

'Aye, there is. They want a human sacrifice to compensate for the death of their man there.' He gestured to the linen-wrapped corpse.

'They want a fucking what?'

'That's what they said.' Nobul shrugged.

'We just bloody can't.'

'That's what I thought you'd say. They'll be leaving just as soon as they've burned the dead one. I suppose setting up a pyre is fine?'

Kilgar nodded, though he obviously wasn't sure. 'It's the least we can do. See to it.'

The least they could do.

Was it the least they could do? Could they do more?

It didn't look like it. A sacrifice was a demand too far. Not that Nobul would have minded. There was one candidate in particular he loved to have offered up, but he'd never get away with it.

Would he?

The lads built a pyre by torchlight; there was plenty of wood in the store. Then they all stood back and watched the Zatani perform their ritual, growling in their alien tongue. Roaring and raking at their flesh with those claws. When that was all done, Regulus took a torch and lit the pyre. They were silent for that, just watching the sky.

Nobul had no idea what they thought was up there but it seemed pretty important to them. He found himself admiring the Zatani – their nobility, their loyalty. They'd fight for each other till death, and that was a rare thing.

In another few days he'd be atop the wall, facing the savages that were coming to destroy the city. How many lads would give their lives to watch his back? These Zatani knew a thing or two about courage, about brotherhood. It was madness to let them walk away when they could be fighting by his side.

As the fire burned in the courtyard, Nobul made his way down to the cells. The prisoner had been all but forgotten, and when Nobul turned the key and opened the door he half expected him to have escaped.

'Ah, Nobul,' said Friedrik with a smile. 'It's been too long. I've missed you.'

Nobul unlocked the manacles that secured the prisoner to the wall.

'Where are we going?' Friedrik asked. He sounded jolly, like they were going for a jaunt around the marketplace. 'I don't think I look my best. I hope it's nowhere important.'

Friedrik winced as Nobul grabbed him and dragged him out of the cell.

'You know my offer's still open,' said Friedrik. 'Let me go and you can have anything you want.' When Nobul didn't respond, Friedrik affected a solemn look even Nobul could see through. 'Look, I'm sorry about your boy, I truly am. If I could give him back to you, I would. But there must be something else you want.'

Nobul stopped in the corridor.

Friedrik wasn't sorry one bit. He didn't regret a thing.

Nobul looked Friedrik in the eye. 'Tell me where the Guild are, where your partners are, and you'll live.'

Friedrik looked back at him. He was clearly attempting to remain grave, but his frown turned to a smile and then to a laugh.

'That'll never happen,' said Friedrik. 'But I'll tell you what will – if you don't get me the fuck out of here, you're going to end up with a sack over your head again. You're going to end up worse than last time. We gave you a fighting chance then. Next time you'll be fed to the animals piece by fucking piece.'

'You first,' Nobul said, before dragging Friedrik up the stairs and out into the courtyard.

The funeral pyre was burning high now, almost level with the roof of the barracks. The Zatani still looked on in silence, and Kilgar and the lads kept a distance away from them.

Nobul paused for a moment, staring into those flames. He could feel Friedrik clawing at him, asking what the fuck was going on, but he ignored him. This was it. This was where everything would change. This was where he'd leave the last of his humanity behind.

For what you're going to have to do, that's the best place for it. Humanity is only there to burden lesser men.

Friedrik struggled as Nobul dragged him across the courtyard. Probably fear of the flames or maybe he'd guessed what was in store.

'Wait,' he shouted. 'Just fucking wait.'

Nobul dumped him on the ground before the Zatani.

'There's your fucking sacrifice. You'll get the rest of what you need as soon as I'm able.'

Regulus nodded his thanks and Nobul stepped back, away from the fierce looking warriors who now surrounding Friedrik.

'What's going on?' shouted Kilgar.

Nobul held out his arm, pushing the serjeant back. 'I've made a choice,' he said. 'They can have their sacrifice. Feel free to try to stop them.'

Kilgar looked on, but made no attempt to intervene.

Friedrik was on his knees, staring out from between the huge killers. All his arrogance, all his confidence, was gone now.

'Nobul,' he shouted, his voice breaking as the fear gripped him. 'I've changed my mind. I'll talk. All right? You fucking win, call them off.'

Too late. Far too late.

Regulus lifted his head and roared to the gathered stars. It was joined by a chorus as the other Zatani let rip. Friedrik began to scream.

He screamed for as long as he was able.

FORTY EIGHT

Merrick stared up at the ceiling, his finger tracing the two-inch scar just below his left nipple. When the witch had laid her hands on him and he'd felt life flooding back into his body it had been the worst thing he'd ever experienced. It was as if his soul was being twisted and torn, dragged back from somewhere dark and cold. Now, as he lay there thinking about it, his mind was plagued by the memory.

He should have died in that arena. Then he'd have been a hero, lauded as the queen's saviour, celebrated across the land. They might even have built a statue in his honour.

Not now, though. Now he was just another casualty. Just another nameless servant of the Crown, wounded in the line of duty.

Still, it beat the shit out of being dead, so he reckoned he shouldn't complain.

The door to the chamber opened. Merrick assumed it would be someone come to check on him, perhaps bring him food or water. So far he'd been treated like an invalid, even though the wound barely troubled him. It wouldn't do to let on though; he could easily get used to this treatment; being waited on hand and foot. Someone even came to clear his bedpan for him which was a privilege he was in no hurry to forego.

As he glanced across the room though, he realised the last thing his visitor would be doing was getting rid of his shit and piss.

Tannick Ryder closed the door behind him. He regarded Merrick, judging him, finding him wanting, as always. This time though there was something else in that glare. Was it compassion? Was it concern?

Don't be fucking stupid. Tannick Ryder doesn't know what compassion means. And he's likely more concerned about his horse than about you.

Despite his loathing for this man, Merrick still struggled to sit up, still slid his legs over the side of the bed. It wasn't just that he didn't want his father to see him lying there weak and vulnerable, he still felt the need to stand and show the man some respect. Merrick hated himself for that.

'Don't get up,' Tannick said. 'You need to let yourself recover.'

'I'm fine,' Merrick replied, rising to his feet. He was surprised at how easy it was. His wound merely felt tight, as if it had only recently knitted back together.

They stood there for a moment, and for the first time Merrick thought his father looked awkward, lost for words even. The old man just sighed, looking his son up and down.

For his part, Merrick didn't know what to say. The last time they spoke Merrick was made to feel a fool. Then his father had set one of his attack dogs on him. This relationship was anything but healthy.

'They say you showed great bravery,' said Tannick finally. 'They say you saved the queen's life. Some even say you should be granted lands and title for your courage.'

'They say a lot, don't they?' Merrick replied, though he had to admit, he quite liked the idea of lands and title.

'Look…' Tannick looked at the floor, at the walls, anywhere but at his son. 'I suppose what I'm trying to say is… you did well. I'm… I'm proud of you.'

Proud of him? Tannick Ryder was proud of him? It took all Merrick's strength of will to not glance out of the window to see if there was a pig flying past.

'I'm glad the fact I almost died finally made you proud. If I'd known it was that easy, I'd have looked for a fucking bridge to jump off years ago.'

Tannick bunched his fists, his jaw setting as he ground his teeth. He took a deep breath before speaking again. 'This isn't easy for me, Merrick. I know I may have misjudged you—'

'No,' Merrick replied. 'You've been right about me all along – useless, feckless, lazy – a selfish little bastard. That's what I am. That's what I've always been, and who have I got to thank for it?'

'I had duties to perform. There were more important things to consider. More important than me, than you—'

'Than mother?'

Merrick saw a flash of emotion cross Tannick's eyes at the mention of his wife. For a moment Merrick felt guilty about mentioning her, about using her as a weapon to stab at his father, but the old bastard deserved it.

It was clear her memory caused Tannick pain. He had lost her after all. Had been hundreds of miles away when she died. Merrick had always thought him a cold callous bastard, but looking at him now anyone might think that wasn't true.

'I'm sorry,' said Merrick. 'I shouldn't have brought her up.'

'No, you're right.' Tannick's voice had softened. It was almost gentle. Merrick had never heard his father speak in such a manner. It made him seem almost human. 'I wronged her, and I wronged you. I know that now. But I've come to make amends.'

Merrick shook his head. 'Make amends? You're going to give me back my childhood are you?'

'No,' said Tannick. All the strength and authority had returned to his voice. His moment of sorrow was past. 'I'm giving you the chance to join me. There's a place in the Wyvern Guard for you. A place by my side, if you'll have it.'

'A place by your side? What in all of Arlor's godsforsaken country makes you think I want to stand by your side?'

Tannick shook his head. 'I understand how you feel about me. I understand there's a lot of bridges need rebuilding. I am trying.'

Merrick looked at his father. He was trying, that was for sure. The fact he'd even come here to see Merrick must have been a real struggle for him. Was this his way of apologising for all he'd done? Should Merrick throw away this chance for conciliation, just like that?

'I'll think on it,' Merrick said.

'Good. That's all I ask. I'd be... proud to have you.'

With that the Lord Marshal turned and left Merrick alone.

He stared after his father for a long while, just standing there in that room, thinking about what had just happened. Back when he had thought his father was dead, Merrick would have given anything to see him again, to be offered a place by his side, to be told Tannick was proud of him

Now he had it, he wondered if it was worth a shit.

In the past few days Merrick had been through the hells and had almost died. Now his father deigned to come see him, to offer him a place in his Wyvern Guard, to call him a comrade. It was a poor second to being called a son. But then what had he expected? Tannick Ryder had never indulged in emotion, even before he'd abandoned his family. They were never going to hold each other in a warm embrace, never going to talk long into the night and share a jug of wine.

Merrick donned his shirt and put his boots on. When he opened the door of the chamber he felt the evening chill. He breathed it in, glad to still be alive. The dark shadow of death still played on his mind but he shut it out as best he could. No point moping. The Lord of Crows got everyone in the end, whether you worried about him or not.

Kaira was exactly where he thought she'd be, polishing her armour; her sword and whetstone sitting beside her waiting for her attention. Merrick waited rather than announce himself. The last time they'd spoken she had beat the crap out of him. Surely she'd be better disposed towards him now, after he'd saved the queen?

'Are you going to stand there all day?' she said, without looking up from buffing her breastplate.

'Wasn't planning on it,' Merrick replied taking a seat opposite her.

He watched her for a little longer, wondering if she'd say any more, wondering if she'd commend him on his bravery. The silence just wore on.

'How is the queen?' he asked finally.

'She's fine,' Kaira replied, still polishing. 'A little shaken, understandably, but unhurt.' Another pause as she rubbed vigorously at a troublesome spot on the armour. 'You did well.'

Will wonders never cease? A compliment from the ice maiden. Praise be to Arlor and all his beardy priests.

'I only did my du—'

'Don't,' said Kaira, looking up. 'Don't start talking about duty now. We both know it was nothing to do with that.'

Merrick felt himself getting annoyed. He'd saved the queen's bloody life, surely he deserved a bit of respect for that. Didn't he?

'No?' he replied, feeling his healing wound itch uncomfortably as his ire grew. 'So what was it to do with? I don't go around throwing myself on the end of swords just for the bloody laughs.'

'You tell me. Was it a chance to prove you're not a coward, or was there just no alternative – were you cornered?'

'Fuck you!' Merrick said, standing up and turning to leave. He stopped when he heard her chuckling.

'Whatever happened to that famous Ryder sense of humour?' she said with a smile. 'Started taking yourself seriously all of a sudden?'

'Being stabbed in the chest will do that,' he said, sitting back in the chair. 'When did you become a bloody jester?'

'Maybe I've learned from an expert.' She eyed him wryly.

'Anyway,' he said. 'I only came to tell you my father's been for a visit.'

'Really? Have you put the past behind you?'

Merrick shook his head. 'Not yet. He asked me to join him. In the Wyvern Guard, I mean.'

'And you're not sure whether that's the right thing to do?'

For a humourless, stone-cold maiden of the sword, Kaira had certainly become insightful.

'What do you think I should do?'

Kaira laughed and went back to polishing her armour. 'I think you should follow your heart, Merrick. What else can you do?'

'I could stay here with you and Garret. I could be one of the Sentinels. I think I've more than proved my worth.'

'Yes, you have. But is that what you really want? There's nothing for you to prove here, but to your father perhaps there is…'

'I don't need to prove shit to him,' Merrick replied.

Really? Don't you need to prove you're a fighter, a warrior deserving of the Ryder name?

'We all have to prove ourselves worthy, every day of our lives,' Kaira said. 'The hard part is picking what or whom you want to be worthy of.'

This was starting to get a bit deep, but perhaps she was right. Was Tannick Ryder worth all the bother? Would he even be able to make the old man proud? Did he really care?

He stood up. 'Thanks,' he said. 'I've got to go… polish something.'

Kaira gave him a nod and went back to her work.

As Merrick moved through the barracks his hand strayed to the wound at his chest. Was it all the proof he needed of his bravery? Or was it just a reminder that he wasn't quite as good with a blade as he'd have liked?

Who really gave a fuck? He was Merrick Ryder – he didn't owe anything to anyone. He'd done his part, saved the bloody queen, for Arlor's sake. What more could anyone want of him? What more could he give?

He guessed in the days to come he'd be likely to find out.

FORTY NINE

They sat around the fire, all five of them just watching the flames, listening to the wood crackling in the hearth. None of them knew what to do. There was no one to order them around now that Friedrik had gone, so they just sat and waited.

You should be running, not waiting. You should be on your way and not bothering to look back. You've ridden your luck enough for a hundred lifetimes and you're not yet thirteen winters.

Rag didn't run, though.

'Do you think they're gonna kill us?' Shirl asked in a little voice, saying what they were all thinking.

Rag shook her head. 'Don't be soft,' she replied. 'If Bastian wanted us dead we'd be corpses already.

That seemed to calm Shirl a bit, and she saw Yarrick glance at Essen looking a bit relieved. Of course she had no idea whether it was true or not. It would be just like Bastian to let them stew in their own fear for a bit, heating up their terror until it reached boiling, and then kill them anyway. She had no idea if they were going to die tonight or not. No point sharing that though, was there. The lads were already in a hole – no point digging them deeper into it.

Rag glanced over at Harkas, sitting instead of standing like he usually did, hardly visible, in the shadows. She could feel him watching though, staring from the dark, his eyes always on her.

He knows. He's worked out who it was that betrayed Friedrik, and when Bastian comes to kill us all, that's what he'll use to bargain for his life.

But *did* he know? If he knew, why hadn't he said anything when Palien was having his throat slit? Why didn't he speak up and tell Bastian then?

Rag sat back in her chair, trying to stay out of his eye line. She guessed she might never know; Harkas wasn't much for sharing. Whatever his intentions, she kept her eye on the door that led out of the place, just in case. First sign of trouble she'd be through it and away.

But you won't, will you? Even if you had the chance you ain't got nowhere to go.

After Palien had bled out through his neck and his body'd been left to drop to the floor she'd still thought they were all done for. Rag wouldn't have put it past Bastian to rid himself of all five of them without giving it a second thought, but he hadn't. He'd just told them all to be on their way.

So here they were, with nowhere else to go. They sat in the tavern, waiting for gods knew what, while the wood pile slowly went down.

Rag had no idea how long they'd been sitting there. Shirl's head kept nodding as he fought off sleep. Essen had wrapped himself in a blanket as the chill of the night crept into the bar and filled the shadows with cold.

None of them heard Bastian's lads enter.

They were the same lean bastards as had killed Palien and they filled the little bar in silence, standing in the shadows, lurking like ghouls waiting to reach out from the dark and take a victim. When Rag saw them her eyes went wide with the fear. None of the other lads noticed until the door swung wide, banging against the wall, and Bastian himself walked in.

Rag stared at his face. At those gaunt, skeletal features. The Lord of Crows himself, come to take them to the hells.

Bastian just stood there and all five of them stared back, not sure what to do. It would have been a fucking stupid thing to speak – no one was going to risk interrupting Bastian.

'I've been thinking,' he said finally, like he was carrying on a conversation from a moment before. 'It did cross my mind to have you all offed. You're not the best bunch the Guild has got, after all. But then Friedrik must have kept you around for something: perhaps your loyalty. Loyalty's worth a lot in these trying times. You did let him get captured, but then that was down to Palien, so I can't really blame any of you.'

He looked straight at Rag then, those eyes boring into her like a weevil in her flesh. Then he smiled slightly. It looked odd on his cruel face and it made Rag's skin go all tingly with the creeps.

'About Friedrik, by the way,' he said, the fire dancing off his sharp features giving him a daemonic look. 'Apparently he's been executed. So we won't be seeing him again. Consequently, all responsibilities for running this outfit pass to me. I've asked around and no one has a problem with that. I assume none of you do?' Rag didn't move, but she could see Shirl, Yarrick and Essen shaking their heads in the dark. 'Good. Then we can move on.'

One of those lean shadowy bastards brought a chair forward and Bastian sat in it, crossing his legs and straightening his black undertaker's jacket.

'War is coming.'

Bastian let his words hang in the air.

'We... we know, Mister Bastian,' said Shirl.

Typical Shirl – never could keep his bloody mouth shut.

'You've probably been wondering what your contribution will be to the war effort.' said Bastian.

Shirl glanced at the other lads. 'Actually... erm... no.'

'No,' said Bastian mirthlessly. 'Of course you fucking haven't. You were more than likely wondering how you're going to avoid the fighting and survive when the Khurtas come knocking.' The lads nodded. 'Well, I'm here to tell you. The Guild has been made an offer. One that will see us survive this whole shitty mess. Obviously there will be things to do in the coming days, but I won't entrust the important work to a bunch of useless fuckers like you. However, I'll need all the men I can get, so be ready. I'll have word sent to you when the time is right, so don't go far.'

His last three words were spoken like they were all a bunch of halfwits.

'No, Mister Bastian,' said Shirl, Essen and Yarrick in unison.

'Good.' Bastian stood up, his men already moving towards the door. 'You.' He pointed at Rag. 'Show me out.'

Show him out? Did he not know where the bloody door was?

She stood and walked beside him. Perhaps this was it. Perhaps she was the one would be getting it. The one with her throat slit as an example to the other lads not to fuck about. But as they went into the little backroom that led out on the street, Bastian stopped beside her.

He looked down and laid a hand on her shoulder. 'I know the rest of your crew hasn't got the brains of a dray horse between them. That's why I'll be relying on you to hold them together.'

'Yes, Mister Bastian,' she said without thinking, just grateful he wasn't going to kill her.

'There'll be a chance for you to prove yourself in the coming days. Friedrik always surrounded himself with fucking idiots – that was his way. He was arrogant you see, thought he was untouchable, that his reputation would protect him, but it's clear he was wrong about that. Still, he seemed to think you were different.' He gestured to the men around him. 'Now, as you can see – I don't surround myself with idiots. And after this whole Palien business I'm beginning to see what it was he saw in you. You're clever. There's potential in you, girl. You could go far.'

'Yes, Mister Bastian,' she repeated. 'Thank you.'

She resisted the temptation to add a 'sir' to the end of that. She didn't want to seem too much of an arse licker, after all.

Bastian nodded and followed his men out onto the street. The last of them closed the door behind him, shutting out the chill of night. Rag just stood there, thinking a while.

She could go far?

What the fuck did that mean? Was he grooming her for big things?

Inside she should have been jumping for joy, but all she felt was sick. It seemed that no sooner had she got past one trial she was jumping straight into another. He'd just put her in charge of this crew. Just promoted her. And all she'd had to do was tell a few lies and get a couple of people killed.

Rag wasn't even sure how she felt about it. There certainly weren't no guilt. The emptiness inside at learning she'd done for a couple of fellas gave her a bit of a fright.

Can't do anything about it now though, can you? May as well just get on with things – play the hand you're dealt.

She turned to head back into the bar and stopped. Harkas was just standing there. It was just the two of them, alone in that backroom. She looked up, trying to give him that same smile she'd given him a few days ago. This time she couldn't muster it.

'I've been watching you,' he said.

She'd never heard him speak before. His voice was pretty normal for someone so big.

'What do you mean?' she asked, playing all innocent, though it was clear there was no point in that now.

'No one else sees it,' he replied. 'But I do. They're all too busy talking, too busy with their own thoughts and words to look. But I stand there all quiet and I listen. And I watch.'

'Good for you,' said Rag, as panic welled up inside. The door was right behind her. Should she try to run? But she'd never make it before he grabbed her.

'I could tell you were trouble right from that first day. I don't know what Friedrik was thinking, but it's too late now.'

'Look,' she said feigning annoyance in the hope it would put him off. 'I don't know what you're on about and I don't really care. Bastian just told me to make sure you lot stayed in line and that's what I'm gonna do. If you've got a problem with it, see him.'

She hoped that would put him off; that the mention of Bastian's name might bring him to heel a bit. It didn't.

'Yeah, I bet he did,' said Harkas, bending low so he was at eye level. 'People like you, don't they?'

'Yeah,' said Rag, not too sure where this was going. 'I suppose they do.'

'I like you,' said Harkas, and Rag almost sighed with relief. 'You look out for your mates. What you did for Shirl... well... I won't forget that. And you're clever –more clever than Friedrik was. But then I suppose that's why you're alive and he's dead.'

'Yeah,' Rag said, feeling more uncomfortable now than when she thought he was going to kill her. 'I suppose it could be.'

With that Harkas turned and walked back into the bar.

He left the door open, and Rag could see in to the rest of the lads sitting by the fire. Would they accept her as leader? Would they do as she said?

Only one way to find out, she supposed, and walked back into the warmth of the tavern.

FIFTY

W aylian made his way up the tight winding staircase to Gelredida's chamber. He was still aching from the explosion in the amphitheatre, his eyes still gritty from the dust that had got in them.

The door to the Magistra's chamber was slightly ajar and as Waylian reached out to push it wide he paused. There was noise from within, as though someone were in pain.

Waylian's memory flashed back to that chamber deep beneath the tower of Magisters, to Nero Laius screaming in pain, crying for mercy, and he wondered if Gelredida had yet another victim in her clutches. As he peered through the crack in the door he saw it was only her, alone, her sleeves rolled up, her hands submerged in a bowl.

Though he knew he shouldn't, Waylian just waited and watched. He was taking a risk – chances were she already knew he was there – but he needed to know. Wanted to see.

Up on the highest point of the amphitheatre he had seen her remove those gloves and lay her hands on the Sentinel Knight's chest, bringing him back from the brink of death. Just as seeing such a feat of magick had struck him with awe, seeing the hands of his mistress, all blackened and cankerous, had filled him with horror.

He watched as she gently washed those hands, allowing the soothing waters to run over her tarnished flesh. With every gesture she breathed a sigh of discomfort until finally she finished.

'You can come in now,' she said without turning around.

I knew it! What an idiot to try to hide from the Red Witch.

Waylian slowly pushed the door open and stepped inside. He thought about speaking, to make an excuse, to tell her he hadn't seen anything, but why make things worse? Best just stand and take whatever rebuke she threw his way. But it never came.

Gelredida merely dried her hands gently and then carefully drew on her red gloves. She winced in pain as she did so, the livid flesh clearly tender to the touch.

'What is it, Magistra?' Waylian asked.

She glanced up at him, silently admonishing him for his question. Then, with a sigh, she answered.

'That night in the Chapel of Ghouls, I drew out a dark power from that dead girl. If I hadn't done so, the rite enacted by Rembram Thule would have been completed. Regrettably, that power is still within me, held in check, though eventually it will be my demise.'

'It's killing you?' Waylian asked, feeling a knot tighten in his stomach. The thought of losing Gelredida filled him with dread. He hadn't realised before how much his teacher meant to him. 'There must be some way to stop it?'

Gelredida shook her head. 'Unfortunately not. But we all die in the end, Waylian. And I have lived more than my share of years. With luck I'll be around long enough to see the Khurtas off.'

He stared at her as she busied herself tidying parchments on her desk. She spoke about her impending demise like she was planning a summer jaunt, like she was looking forward to the journey. Waylian wouldn't be so matter of fact about his own death. No wonder she had been so nonchalant about putting him in peril when her own life meant so little to her.

'Now, if that's all,' she said, stuffing scrolls onto a shelf, 'we have a meeting to attend.'

'There is one more thing, Magistra.'

She glanced at him expectantly. 'Make it quick.'

'In the amphitheatre? Up on the roof, the injured knight? Why did you change your mind and help him?'

Gelredida smiled. 'Many things hold power in this land, Waylian. Swords, crowns, banners. Even stones dug deep in the earth. Such objects can decide futures and mould fates. More powerful than any of them is *blood*. The man I saved carries the blood of an ancient line – the blood of a king. We can't just have a line of kings expire, now can we?'

'I suppose not, Magistra. Though it doesn't seem very fair that some are sacrificed while others are saved.' He looked down at his feet, wondering if that had been the right thing to say. It bothered him, though: why one man got to live because of luck of birth, where so many others died. No doubt he'd have been one of the ones left to die, if it had come to it.

'You will learn soon enough about sacrifices, Waylian, and why they must be made,' Gelredida said. 'One person cannot put themselves above the greater good. Above nation or religion. We are all part of the earth, some of us destined to be great tributaries, guiding the waters through the land, feeding it, making it grow. Some of us mountains, guarding the borders of nations, protecting its innocents from the machinations of invaders. And some of us are just flowers, given a short time to bloom under the light of the sun before we die.' She gave him an almost sympathetic look. 'Do you understand?'

'Yes, Magistra,' he replied.

'No, you probably don't. But one day you will, Waylian. Shall we be off?'

Waylian nodded. He had no idea where they were going or why, but he'd long ago learned not to argue over such matters.

They made their way down through the tower to the Great Library, where the door was opened for them by two Raven Knights. Waylian had never known those doors to be closed, day or night, but as he entered he understood why. The three remaining Archmasters were waiting within. Other than the Archmasters, the library was empty of students or scholars. It seemed a much larger and more imposing place when it was empty.

Drennan Folds and old Crannock Marghil sat at separate, but adjacent desks. Drennan was clearly none too pleased to be kept waiting. Lucen Kalvor leaned against a bookshelf, his face impassive, though he watched Waylian and Gelredida as they entered and never took his eyes from them. Waylian suddenly thought back to his part in Lucen's recent blackmail, and wondered whether the young Archmaster might hold a grudge. Only time would tell, but he'd be sure to refuse any food or drink Lucen ever offered him.

Magistra Gelredida stopped before the desks, standing and regarding them all as though she were about to start one of her lessons. For his part, Waylian hung back and listened.

'Well?' asked Drennan, his mismatched eyes glaring in annoyance. 'Why have you called us? And to here of all places?'

'Oh, I like it here,' answered Gelredida, and she glanced around the huge library as though she had built it with her own withered hands. 'The Crucible Chamber can be so… stuffy, don't you find? I also thought it was fitting since Archmaster Crabbe was Keeper of the Books, and his tragic death means he can't be with us.'

Waylian doubted any of that was true. It was more likely Gelredida wanted to meet somewhere she would have all her powers of magick available to hand. Meeting in the Crucible Chamber where her power was nulled had almost cost all their lives.

'It is a pleasant change,' said Crannock, his weak voice cracking as he spoke. 'But why the insistence on summoning us here?'

'Why?' There was scorn in Gelredida's voice. 'The Khurtas are almost at our door. There is no time to waste and much needs to be done.'

'Agreed. We had best seek out candidates to stand as Archmasters,' said Drennan. 'Two places need to be filled.'

'There is no time,' she replied. 'Preparations for the siege must begin immediately. We cannot squander what days remain on needless protocols.' Drennan made to argue but she held up a gloved finger. It was enough to silence him, and Waylian wondered if his illegitimate son was still squirrelled away in that cellar, the threat of murder still hanging over him like a dangling blade.

'What, might we ask, needs to be done?' said Crannock, his ancient jowls quivering in annoyance.

Gelredida looked up to Lucen who stood silently in the shadow of the bookcase. 'Archmaster Kalvor, you shall be the new Keeper of Ravens. When the war begins the magisters of this tower will be key to us winning it. In turn they must be protected by our Raven Knights. You will take command of them, make sure they understand the importance of their charges' survival. There may still be elements unsympathetic to our aims; Ferenz and Nero's betrayal could run deep. I trust you can root out any disloyalty?'

Lucen Kalvor raised an eyebrow. 'I'm sure I can manage that,' he said.

'Excellent,' smiled Gelredida. 'Then we must begin to muster the Caste. Crannock, you will take charge of all current magisters – tutors, scholars, retired veterans. They respect you. They will follow you.'

'Er... I...' said Crannock, but before he could argue she'd moved on.

'Drennan, you will take charge of all apprentices and neophytes. As of now they have full Caste privileges and will be allowed to practice magicks within the walls of the tower.'

Surprisingly, Drennan nodded his assent. 'Very well. Although many of them have already left the city. Most of our current intake are from wealthy families; on hearing the city was under threat those families did all they could to convey their young back home.'

'Then you will have to make do, Drennan,' chided the Red Witch. 'You're a resourceful man, I'm sure you'll manage.'

'I'm sure I will, as long as I have every apprentice available.' He glanced at Waylian, who had been unable to drag his gaze away from Drennan's scarred and milky eye. 'Will I be taking charge of yours?'

Gelredida smiled faintly, as though Drennan had made a poor joke. 'I'm afraid I will require Master Grimm at my side at all times. But he's not the most gifted of students, so it's doubtful you'll miss him.'

'Not the most gifted?' said Drennan, looking at Waylian once more. 'We all saw what he did to Marshal Ferenz. They're still scrubbing the floor clean in the Crucible Chamber.'

'An accident,' said Gelredida, as though they were talking about a minor mishap. 'Grimm tapped into the Veil by mistake. It happens.' Drennan opened his mouth to speak, but Gelredida raised that finger once more. The Archmaster was cowed like a browbeaten husband. 'If that's everything, I'm sure we all have much work to do.'

None of the Archmasters spoke, and Waylian began to wonder just how much power his mistress had over them. It took all his will to stifle a smile as the three men made their way from the library as though dismissed from one of Gelredida's classes.

'What would you like me to do, Magistra?' Waylian asked when they were finally alone.

She looked at him and offered a smile. The expression was almost motherly. Waylian wasn't sure whether to be comforted or horrified by that.

'Get some rest for now. There will be much to do in the coming days and sleep may be something you'll grow to miss.' With that, she walked away.

Waylian took a moment to glance around the huge library. He wondered if there might be some hidden tome somewhere that could be of use; that hid the secret to their victory over Amon Tugha. For a fleeting moment he thought he might look for it, as though he could make a hero of himself, as though he might single-handedly turn back the tide.

What on earth are you thinking, Grimm? Don't you remember what she said about mountains and rivers? And flowers? You're definitely one of the flowers. Maybe even a bloody weed. Best do as you're bid and get some rest.

He turned to leave through the huge doors and stopped. Something in the corner of his eye had caught his attention. Waylian made his way to the massive window, its panes covered in myriad coloured patterns.

Through a frame of clear glass he could see far to the north.

All along the horizon rose a black pall of smoke.

It was as if the world burned.

FIFTY ONE

The palace gardens of Skyhelm were empty but for Janessa, Kaira and the priest. No one else had wanted to attend, but Janessa didn't mind. No one else needed to be here, and it was doubtful he would have cared anyway.

Odaka Du'ur lay in the ground, his body wrapped in a sheet of silk. The Father of Killers had managed to do her harm after all, though not in the manner he had intended. Odaka had died trying to give Janessa a chance to escape.

There had been little time to study the proper burial rituals of Equ'un. So, this had seemed the only suitable way. Odaka had served her father for many years and it was only fitting that the funerary rites of the Free States were observed at his burial.

She had picked the gardens for his interment to always have him close, at least in spirit. Now Odaka was gone who would advise her? Chancellor Durket? It was unlikely he could muster an opinion on anything other than what to have for dinner. Seneschal Rogan? The more Janessa learned about that man, the less she trusted him.

As the Priest of Arlor recited his litanies Janessa looked down at Odaka's body. He had given his life for her, like so many others in the arena. How many more would lose their lives in the days to come? How many of them would do it in her name? She had to be worthy of such sacrifice, had to be strong.

Surely she had proven that strength already when she took a broken sword and ended the Father of Killers. Was it enough? Would she need to dig deeper?

She had certainly begun in the right way – two of her foes were dead by her own hand. Only days ago she could never have dreamed of such a thing, but now it was as though she yearned to face her enemies, her hand itching to hold the Helsbayn and wield it in a real battle. In the next few days she might well have her chance.

As she listened to the priest's words, she laid a hand on her stomach. How much longer would she be able to hide the fact she was with child? Should she even try? And how could she justify fighting, leading her people to battle, putting herself in harm's way, with a life growing inside her?

No use thinking on it now. Should Amon Tugha smash the walls of Steelhaven it wouldn't matter anyway. She would be dead.

The priest had finished now. He stood with his head bowed, waiting for Janessa. Should she say any words? But what use were words now? Odaka would not hear them. He must have known how much he meant to her. Her only sorrow was that she could not thank him for his sacrifice.

'Majesty,' someone called from behind her.

She turned to see a young man, his livery denoting him a palace servant, trotting towards her across the gardens.

Kaira moved to block his path. Since the arena, she had been more vigilant, more protective, than ever.

The young man dropped to his knee several steps away from Janessa.

'Speak,' she said, annoyed that Odaka's burial had been interrupted.

'Apologies, Majesty,' he said, rising to his feet, 'but you have been summoned to the War Chamber. The armies have retreated from the front. Duke Bannon Logar is here.'

'Very well,' Janessa replied. 'Tell them I am on my way.'

She looked back at Odaka in his grave. She had wanted to stay while it was filled, to see him properly interred, but it seemed there was no time. But he of all people would have understood.

'Goodbye, my friend,' she whispered, as she and Kaira made their way inside.

She did not change for her meeting. She wore a plain gown, a fur cloak about her shoulders. Perhaps something more regal might have been appropriate, but she was not about to keep her generals waiting.

Kaira led the way, opening the door to the War Chamber then moving aside to allow Janessa to enter. As she did so, the four men inside stood. They had been sat about the table of oak and iron in silence, none of them speaking until she was there to hear their words and advice, and decide what action to take.

The cloak about Janessa's shoulder suddenly felt too heavy. Nausea gripped her, but she bit it back. She was stronger than this.

'My lords,' she said, gripping the back of her seat. Each of the four men bowed.

On one side of the table stood General Hawke and Marshal Farren of the Knights of the Blood. Each looked wearier and more haggard than the last time she had seen them. They must have seen much battle in the intervening days. Hawke in particular looked like an old man in his heavy armour, his beard filthy and unkempt.

To the other side stood Lord Marshal Ryder in his bronze armour. Next to him was a tall man, broad at the shoulder and fierce in the eye who must have been Duke Bannon Logar of Valdor. He was about as old as Hawke, and his white armour was battered and rent, but he looked ready to do battle right here and now. As Janessa looked at him she thought at first he looked nothing like his son, the late Lord Raelan Logar, but then the old man smiled, and the family resemblance was obvious.

'Duke Logar, Majesty,' said Lord Marshal Ryder, gesturing at the old man. Janessa proffered him a nod and he returned it.

'It is good to finally meet you, my lord,' she said. 'I have heard much of your bravery. A trait you clearly shared with your son.'

A flicker of sadness crossed Bannon's face. 'Thank you, Majesty. I know he thought highly of you.'

Janessa wasn't exactly sure how much of that was true but she acknowledged his comment with a smile. 'Shall we?' she asked, gesturing to the chairs. When she had sat, the four men took their places at the table.

There was a moment's silence before Janessa realised that she was leading the meeting. She was entirely in charge of proceedings. These men were her war council and they would only speak at her command.

But what would she ask? She had not been trained in the ways of war. What little she had learned of men and supplies over the last few weeks would scarcely be adequate here.

'Tell me where we stand,' said Janessa.

Seems as good a way to start as any.

None of them appeared eager to speak. General Hawke seemed interested in the polished sheen of the table. Marshal Farren glanced to Duke Logar who took a deep breath before beginning.

'Not in an advantageous position, Majesty, all truth be told,' said Bannon. 'No mercenaries are left within the city. Since we have no money to pay them, they have abandoned Steelhaven to its fate.'

'Bloody cowards,' muttered Marshal Farren, but Bannon ignored him.

'We estimate the Khurtas are no more than a day's ride to the north. They will be here soon. Within the city our troops are fatigued, but ready to fight. Lord Marshal Ryder has three hundred Wyvern Guard, Marshal Farren another two hundred Knights of the Blood. General Hawke and I have only five thousand foot and one thousand horse remaining between us, with which to defend the city walls. Our position is grave, Majesty. There are most likely more than forty thousand Khurtas making their way here. I wish I could give you some news to cheer you, tell you we had allies, but there's no one coming to assist us.'

'Thank you, Duke Logar,' replied Janessa. 'That is most… enlightening.'

More silence, until Tannick Ryder cleared his throat. 'The walls of Steelhaven are high, Majesty. Impregnable, some say. Amon Tugha's Khurtas are savages from the steppes of the north; they have no skill at besieging fortress cities.'

General Hawke shook his head. 'Don't underestimate them,' said the old man. 'They razed Touran and they've taken us by surprise at every turn. They have magicks, they have engines of war and they have the Elharim warlord.'

'What's the matter with you?' said Lord Marshal Ryder. 'You sound as if you're scared of him. He's one man leading a bunch of barbarians.'

Duke Logar laid a hand on Tannick's forearm. 'General Hawke speaks true. I wish it wasn't so, but we've seen it. On their own, the Khurtas would be easy pickings, but under Amon Tugha they are a force to be reckoned with. They have dogged our every step from Dreldun. He's outwitted us in every battle.'

'He won't outwit us here,' said Tannick

'How can you be sure?' replied Marshal Farren, staring from beneath a creased brow, left eye twitching, his red gauntleted fist clenching as he banged on the table. 'You weren't there. You haven't seen him.'

Tannick Ryder glared across the oak table. 'I'll see him soon enough.'

Janessa had witnessed about as much of their posturing as she could bear. If this was what it meant to convene a meeting of her council, she could well do without it.

'My lords,' she said, and was relieved when they stopped their bickering and looked at her. 'I understand you and the armies you lead have been through a great deal these past weeks, and much has been sacrificed for us. For that we are grateful. But Lord Marshal Ryder is correct. We need to look ahead. We must find a way to defeat Amon Tugha and his horde, not dwell on past defeats.'

'Indeed, Majesty,' said Duke Logar. 'We *will* find a way.'

Janessa nodded her thanks to him, but as she did so she felt a sudden spasm in her gut. Marshal Farren began to speak, but Janessa could barely hear his words. She glanced towards Kaira, who stood motionless a few feet away. Janessa was suddenly desperate to catch Kaira's eye, but her bodyguard seemed to be listening intently to what Farren was saying and failed to notice.

The room began to swim as the pain in her belly grew. Something stabbed at her from the inside and it took all her will to quell a cry of pain. She could not show weakness in front of these men. She was their queen and despite their experience in war it was expected she would lead them.

Lord Marshal Ryder had joined in now, speaking over Farren. It appeared the two men were at loggerheads but all Janessa could hear was a torrent in her ears. She clenched her fists, her nails digging into her palms. It was no good; she could stand it no longer.

'My lords,' she said, rising to her feet. The four men halted their bickering and instantly stood up. 'I am feeling…' *Another stab at her loins.* 'We will continue this later.'

As she turned, Kaira was at her shoulder, but Janessa shook her head as her bodyguard tried to aid her. Fighting the pain with every step, Janessa walked from the war room as best she could and Kaira closed the door behind her. As soon as it was shut Janessa collapsed against the wall, gritting her teeth in agony.

How she made it back to her chamber she had no idea – she moved through the corridors in a daze. The pain was almost unbearable and it took all her will not to scream.

Once in her chamber Janessa slumped on to her bed. Something ran down her leg as another white-hot stab of pain coursed within her.

'What is it, Majesty? Shall I summon the surgeon?'

'Yes,' Janessa screamed, any thoughts of keeping her unborn child a secret outweighed by her fear and pain.

She pulled up her skirts, feeling blood running in a steady flow between her legs. Kaira had already rushed for assistance, but as the agony inside Janessa reached a peak she knew it was already too late.

FIFTY TWO

K aira had dragged the surgeon from his bed. In the end, however, nothing could be done to save the child. Janessa had wailed and thrashed as the surgeon made sure she did not bleed to death. As Governess Nordaine and the surgeon did their best to calm the queen, Kaira gathered the tiny body in a discarded blanket and held it in her hands. It weighed almost nothing and was small enough to fit in her palm.

Once Janessa had calmed and succumbed to the mercy of sleep, Kaira asked Nordaine to take away the small body, sure that the governess would treat it with the care it deserved. Before the surgeon left, Kaira reminded him of the need for discretion. He gave no word of argument to that.

Once he was gone, Kaira watched over Janessa as she slept. The girl would have to cope with her loss, and it was another battle she would have to fight alone. It only served to make Kaira feel helpless, knowing how little she could do for the girl she was charged to protect.

After what seemed like hours, Janessa finally stirred, and Kaira moved to her bedside, laying a hand on the queen's brow. The girl opened her eyes and looked at Kaira, at first hardly comprehending what she saw.

'It's me, my queen. It's Kaira.'

Janessa gave no response, but glanced away towards the window. Tears were beginning to well up in her eyes and Kaira could see her anguish.

What was she supposed to say? What was she supposed to do?

Kaira sat on the bed beside Janessa and stroked her red curls, now matted and unkempt.

'There is nothing to fear, Majesty. Your child is safe with Vorena now.'

Janessa said nothing.

Kaira was filled with pity for her. The young queen had lost so much, and so recently. Not just her child, but also her father and her most trusted advisor.

She was just a girl, lost and alone, charged with facing a battle-hardened warlord with a sorely depleted army. It was a responsibility Kaira would not have wished on anyone.

'Is it a clear day?' asked Janessa.

Kaira looked down at this girl who seemed so small and vulnerable. This girl with the weight of a kingdom on her shoulders.

'I... I do not know, Majesty,' she replied, rising and moving to the window.

Kaira looked out onto the Crown District and the city beyond. There was bustle and noise drifting in from the north. The city knew what was coming and it did not lament. It moved with urgency, preparing itself. Over it was a grey sky, the winter chill giving the air a strange calm.

The calm before the storm.

'No, Majesty. The sky is dark, but—'

'It is no matter,' said Janessa, and Kaira turned to see she had risen from her bed. She stood unsteadily, using the bedpost for support, but there was a determined look to her eyes. 'It is still a good day. A day for a new beginning.'

Kaira moved towards her. 'Majesty, you must rest.'

'I've rested enough, Kaira. I've hidden from this for far too long. I've filled my head with worthless thoughts. That will all change.'

Kaira wanted to argue. To tell her that she didn't need to do this now, that there would be time aplenty later. That she had time to mourn her loss.

But she didn't. The Khurtas were almost here. The time for rest had passed. If the people of Steelhaven were hoping for some miracle to come and save them, they would be disappointed. The only thing that would save them was grit and fight and sacrifice.

'What would you have me do, Majesty?'

Janessa fixed Kaira with a determined stare. 'I will need armour. Armour fit for a queen. And my sword.'

Kaira smiled. 'Yes, Majesty,' she said.

Janessa smiled back, and in that moment Kaira felt proud. Felt ready to follow this young girl anywhere she would lead.

FIFTY THREE

C aptain Garret had told Merrick how sorry he was to lose him, how he'd have been proud to have Merrick among the Sentinels when the Khurtas arrived. Merrick didn't believe him. This was what Garret had wanted all along – for Merrick to be reconciled with his father, for them to be together, side-by-side, fighting for queen and kingdom.

It wasn't quite so simple though – this was no reconciliation, after all. There was no hugging one another and lamenting the lost years. This was just a chance for Merrick to prove his worth. To show his father what he was made of. He had a long way to go, but it was a start.

And it was a bloody painful start and no mistake.

Merrick knelt in the middle of the courtyard, surrounded by armoured Wyvern Guard. It might not have been so bad if he hadn't been stripped to the waist. He'd seen these bastards stripped down themselves, and there wasn't a one of them didn't have a better shape to him than Merrick. In itself, that might not have been so bad – if it wasn't for one of them tapping holes in his arm with a needle.

Tattoos were for whores and sailors, or so Merrick had always thought. Clearly he'd been mistaken, because they were for the Wyvern Guard too. The bloke beside him had been going at his shoulder for an age, and Merrick had long since started sweating from the pain. It hadn't been so bad at first, and he thought he'd be able to handle it no problem, but as time went on it started to hurt like the hells and Merrick had taken to clenching everything he had that would bloody clench.

Keep it together, he'd told himself, *this won't last forever*. It was weird how slow time seemed to go when you were in constant fucking agony.

'Done,' said the tattooist, wiping the blood from Merrick's arm with a rag.

'Thanks,' Merrick replied, suppressing what he actually wanted to say, his shoulder burning like it was on fire.

Tannick walked forward, carrying his massive sword, his helmet covering most of his face.

'Stand,' he said, his voice stern and commanding.

Merrick rose to his feet, doing his best not to show any discomfort. He was being inducted into an order that showed no pain or fear. Now wasn't the time for whining.

'You bear the mark,' said Tannick. 'But do you bear the will to serve?'

Merrick had already been drilled in the ceremony and knew the words. Whether he believed them or not was another matter.

'I bear the will,' he replied. 'And the courage.'

'Show me,' said Tannick holding out the sword.

Merrick didn't hesitate. He'd never been surer of anything in his life. There had been a time, and not too long ago, when he would have balked at this, taken the piss, laughed at the solemnity of it all. Not now.

With his right hand he grasped the blade, feeling its keen edge break the skin of his palm. It stung, but only for a second, as he removed his hand and made a fist. Without waiting for instruction, he walked to the barrel that sat in the centre of the courtyard and held his hand over it. He could smell the wine inside. How he wanted to just stick his head in and take a long gulp of it. But he didn't; he held his hand over the barrel and let the blood run from his fist until he could squeeze out no more.

About a dozen Wyvern Guard walked forwards then, each one holding a goblet. Merrick saw that one of them was Cormach, the man who had bested him so easily in the palace gardens. Each man dipped in his cup and then held it up.

'Wyvern Guard,' said Tannick. 'We have a new brother. Let his blood mix with yours, now as it will in battle.'

With that the dozen knights drank deep of their cups, swilled the wine around their mouths and then one after the other spat it back into the barrel. Merrick noted that Cormach swallowed his mouthful and just spat in a gob of phlegm, but then what had he expected?

When they'd finished, one of the knights offered him a goblet. Again Merrick didn't hesitate, dipping it into the wine barrel. As he raised the full goblet to his lips all he could hope was that he hadn't fished out Cormach's gobbet. Thankfully, as it went down it just tasted of wine, and he drank deep, gulping in the wine as if it was the last drink he'd ever have.

He was surrounded then. Someone took the goblet from his hands and the dozen knights began to deck him in armour. Gauntlets, vambraces, greaves, breastplate and the rest, all strapped on. The lad who buckled the rerebrace to his upper arm was none too gentle either and Merrick fought back a grimace against the pain from his new tattoo.

When they'd finished they stood back, revealing Tannick standing there with that bloody great sword again. *Bludsdottr* they called it, an ancient name for an ancient blade.

'You've shared our blood, Merrick Ryder. Are you with us until death?'

There was silence. This was it, devoting his life to this crowd of nutcases.

It was all he'd ever wanted

'I am with you. Beyond death and to the hells,' Merrick replied, kneeling and kissing the blade Tannick held in his hands.

With that a cheer went up from the gathered Wyvern Guard. Each man came forward to pat Merrick on the back or hug him in brotherhood. It reminded him a little of his days in the Collegium of House Tarnath where he'd learned to fight. Back then, he'd never appreciated any of the camaraderie, considering himself above it – but this was different. This felt like he belonged, not least because his father was in charge here. And because he'd been given the choice of joining with these men, not forced into it at an early age, whether he liked it or not.

As he was welcomed by his fellow knights Merrick could see his father standing and watching.

Was that a smile on the old bastard's face?

No, you must have just imagined it.

As the knights laughed and helped themselves to wine, clearly none too concerned about what exactly they were sharing, Tannick walked over.

'You're one of us now, lad,' he said. 'Make me proud.'

'I will,' Merrick replied. 'Don't worry about that.'

They looked at each other, and for a moment Merrick wondered if his father was searching for any sign of doubt. It was too late now, though; he'd taken the mark and said the words. Merrick wasn't about to show any regrets. When his father eventually gave a nod, Merrick knew he'd passed the test.

'There'll be chance to prove yourself soon enough,' said Tannick. 'I for one can't wait.'

With that he turned and, as he did, Merrick spotted something of a mad glint in his eye. Whether he should be worried about that, only time would tell.

As he stood there, Merrick sensed someone at his shoulder. He turned to see Cormach Whoreson glaring at him with dark eyes, his face looking anything but welcoming.

'One of us now, are you?' he asked.

Merrick glanced down at his bronze armour. 'It certainly looks that way,' he replied.

'Takes more than a suit of armour and a few words to be a man of the Wyvern Guard. Takes steel and blood and heart.' He tapped the centre of his breastplate. 'Think you've got that in you?'

Merrick fixed Cormach with as icy a glare as he could muster. He reckoned it came somewhere between frightened kitten and surprised washerwoman. 'I know I have,' he replied.

For a moment he thought Cormach might try to stare him down, might call him out and they'd have to draw steel. Before any of that could happen, Cormach smiled.

'Yeah, course you have,' he said.

Merrick smiled back. Had he won this bastard over after all?

He turned back to the rest of the men, about to ask for a goblet of his own, when Cormach punched him hard on the arm, striking his armour with a dull thud right where his tattoo was. Merrick almost screamed, gritting his teeth and letting out a low moan.

'Welcome to the Wyvern Guard, cunt,' said Cormach, before he walked off and pushed his way towards the barrel of wine.

Welcome indeed, thought Merrick. *What the fuck have I let myself in for?*

FIFTY FOUR

T he song of steel was not a pretty tune. But Nobul Jacks played it regardless, played it like he never had before.

It had fast become obvious he would never be able to achieve what he wanted alone, so two forges and their smiths had been requisitioned by the Greencoats to help him craft armour for the Zatani. It felt strange to be back in the Trades Quarter, back at his old job, but it was also somehow liberating. No longer did he feel constrained by lack of coin or pressure from the Guild. For the first time in what seemed like an age he was able to take pleasure in his work, revelling in the sound of hammer on steel, the smell of white hot metal, the bright flash of spark on anvil.

This was what he was born to do: to craft mighty armour with nothing but the keenness of his eye and the strength in his arm. To create and fashion and hone, rather than destroy.

But Nobul knew there would be destruction enough to come. There would be carnage and, gods willing, he would be in the middle of it. Not that the will of the gods mattered a shit. They wouldn't help him, or this city. The only thing that would save Steelhaven was a dirty bloody fight to the death. And Nobul Jacks knew how to do that all right.

Sweat poured off him as he went at it in the little forge. The fire burned white and he was stripped to the waist, enjoying the feeling of strength returning to muscles that had for too long been allowed to go soft. As he paused, reaching for a jug of tepid water to slake his thirst, he heard a commotion outside.

Laying his hammer down on the anvil, Nobul opened the door, letting the chill from outside cool his moist flesh. The noise was like an urgent hum, and Nobul watched as a gathering crowd hurried northwards up the street.

He stepped out, not bothering to put on a shirt, feeling the welcome winter cold on his skin. An old man, stick rattling on the cobbles, shuffled past him as fast as he could.

'What's happening, old fella?' asked Nobul, grabbing him by the sleeve of his jacket. It was a stupid question. Nobul already knew what was going on. It could only be one thing.

'The Khurtas,' said the old man. 'They're bloody here!'

With surprising strength he pulled his sleeve free of Nobul's grip and hobbled off up the street.

Nobul Jacks smiled, his mouth widening into a grin. They had arrived, at last.

He grabbed his shirt and pulled it on, feeling the moist cotton stick to his flesh. Swinging the door to the forge shut behind him he moved off northwards with the thronging mass of city folk.

It was an odd feeling, moving along with the mass of bodies, seeing the concern and fear on their faces where he was just expectant... excited even. This was what he'd waited for. This was his time.

Nobul reached Fernella's house and paused for a moment outside. He had butterflies, like a child waiting to receive their solstice gifts. As he banged on the door he could hardly contain himself.

When Fernella opened it she had what he'd come for already waiting for him by the door.

'Knew you'd be coming,' she said. 'Knew what you'd be coming for as well.' Nobul didn't answer, just looked at that box. 'Take it then, lad. I'm not standing here with it all day.'

He reached out and picked it up, feeling the weight of it in his arms.

'I appreciate it,' he said.

'No need for that. You just look after yourself,' she replied.

This might be the last time they ever saw each other, and maybe he should have thought of something nice to say. Nothing came to mind.

As he turned, he heard her shut the door behind him.

The walk back to the forge was quick, but would have been quicker if he hadn't been moving against the crowds. People shoved past in their eagerness and fear, but Nobul barely noticed. Once he'd reached the forge he laid the wooden box down on a table that stood against one wall. Then he took a step back.

This was it. Open up the box and there's no going back. Once he had its contents in his grip he knew the old days would be back again – and the old Nobul Jacks.

Was that what he wanted? Those days of blood and slaughter he'd tried for so many years to leave behind him?

But they weren't behind you, were they, Nobul Jacks. They were never behind you. The old Nobul Jacks has always been here, sleeping maybe, but he's woken a few times in recent weeks and plenty of people are dead because of it.

As he reached out to open the clasp of the box, he noticed his hand was trembling. He gritted his teeth, flicked the clasp and opened the lid. It was stiff on its hinges, but then it would be after all these years. The contents were still there though, wrapped in a black rag.

Nobul reached inside, grasping the haft and pulling it out, then he unwrapped the rag and let it drop to the ground.

He stared at the hammer. Hefted its weight. Was reassured by the feel of his palm on the leather grip. Admired the carven head, the relief pattern resembling interlocking chains. And he remembered.

Remembered Bakhaus Gate. Remembered the Aeslanti running at him, roaring for all they were worth. He remembered the feel of solid impact, the blood, the dead. He remembered that roar of his own, that victory cry. The emotions it stirred had been left unfelt for more than a decade.

No, the old Nobul Jacks had not returned.

He had never been away.

Nobul walked to a shelf beside the door. On it lay the completed pieces of Zatani armour, but that was not all he had crafted since coming to the forge. He reached out, grasped the black iron helm in his hand and looked down at it. It might not be the same as the one he'd worn at Bakhaus, but it was close enough. Anyone who'd been there would be sure to recognise him. Anyone who hadn't would know him from the legends.

With helm and hammer in hands, Nobul ventured back out onto the streets. They were all but deserted now, everyone having rushed north to the wall. As he neared it, he could hear the people of Steelhaven, some wailing in lament, some shouting angrily, spitting their rage and defiance out onto the plains.

Nobul pushed his way through the city folk. Some turned angrily as he did so, but on seeing his grim visage not one of them said a word. Eventually he stood on the northernmost battlement, surrounded by the people of Steelhaven. They all looked out at the sight. All stared in awe at what had come.

To the north was an army. A host of thousands. The savage Khurtas had finally arrived with their warlord – the immortal Elharim, who had ventured far from his homeland to claim Steelhaven for his own.

Nobul Jacks donned his black iron helm, lifted the hammer to his shoulder, and waited.

EPILOGUE

T hey called it Aluk Vadir. It was a bustling port, not like Steelhaven, not huge and imposing, but it had still been busy in recent days. River guessed busier than it had been in many years.

A score of battleships, each carrying a huge trebuchet, had already set sail from the dock, making their way across the Midral Sea. River watched that dock from the balcony of a chamber set high up on the side of a smooth-sided tower. But his mind was not troubled by the ships that even now were making their way towards his home.

All River could think of were the men he had killed.

Forest had told him there were only five men. Just five, and evil men at that. River had considered that an acceptable number. Only it hadn't been just five, it had been those five men and their guards, their sentries and, when necessary, their servants. River had found the old ways, the killing ways, had come back to him all too easily.

As he stood there on that high balcony in the stifling night heat, he was filled with regret. Regret for all the lives he had taken. If Jay knew what he had done she would hate him for it. She was gentle, an innocent soul, and she would never understand, even though he had only done it for her. To protect her from the Father of Killers.

And what else could he have done? He had made a vow, and to the Father of Killers no less.

River turned as he heard the old man fumble his key in the lock of the door. As he entered River caught his scent, unwashed and musky, wine on his breath and the aroma of pipe smoke on his clothes.

Abda Jadi shuffled inside, closing the door behind him. He had been the one to give River his targets at Keidro Bay. He had been the one to draw up the contract River had presented to his marks, written in strange foreign script and eventually signed in blood.

'A quiet night out,' said the old man. 'Streets are all but deserted now the last of the ships is making ready to leave.'

The last of the ships that would bring carnage to Steelhaven. River clenched his fists, feeling remorse for his part in it.

'Our business is done then?' asked River.

'Yes, I suppose it is,' replied the old man. He was staring, his fingers toying with the soiled white robe that covered his body. River saw a bead of sweat run from beneath Abda's headwrap.

Something was wrong. It was hot, but this old man was used to it. Surely he would not be sweating unless…

River ducked on instinct, dropping to the floor as something tore through the air. The arrow whipped in, cutting through where he had been standing a moment before. Abda Jadi was not so quick, taking the arrow in his throat.

As the old man staggered back, gripping his neck, River pulled out his blades. The assassin burst through the window, his weapons already drawn.

'Forest,' River had time to whisper, before he was on the back foot, his blades quick to parry the rapier and poniard that cut in at his face.

This could not be. He had made a vow. The Father of Killers had promised him.

But had he? He had only promised Jay would live – he had never promised to spare River.

Forest said nothing, attacking with all the speed and venom River had come to expect from his brother. At first River was hard pressed to parry the blows, and Forest's rapier cut a line through his jerkin, slashing the flesh. He ignored the pain, twisting aside, grabbing Abda Jadi, who still stumbled in his death throes, and thrusting him towards Forest.

His brother just pushed the old man out of the way and took a step back, breathing hard from his exertions. It was clear his skills were rusty and he had not fought for a while, but then it was a long journey from Steelhaven. River on the other hand, still had the killer in him.

The two went at each other again, the only sound their weapons ringing off one another. As Forest's rapier came down in another thrust, River caught the guard in one of his blades, twisting it and pulling it from his grip. He ducked Forest's short blade and hooked his own weapon behind his brother's leg. It sliced Forest's calf and he grunted in pain, staggering as River stabbed in again, taking Forest in the forearm and causing him to drop his poniard.

With the advantage of his momentum, River bore down, knocking his brother back. They both fell to the ground and River held one blade to his brother's throat, the other raised for the killing blow. Abda Jadi had breathed his last and with the old man's dying gasps finished, there was silence in the room.

Forest smiled. It was obvious he was in pain, but he fought it, just as River would have done.

'What are you waiting for, brother?' he asked. 'Do it.'

River stared into Forest's eyes. There was no fear there. It was as though he wanted to die. As though he had been waiting for it, expecting it, yearning for it.

'Why have you come here? Why not just let me go?'

'The Father will never let you go, River. Just like he will never let *her* go.'

'He made a vow.'

'He does not honour vows with traitors,' Forest replied, seeming to take some small delight in River's unease. 'He owes you nothing. By now she is most likely dead. Her city will fall soon after.'

River growled, raising his blade to strike.

But this was his *brother*. He had already killed one, could he really kill another?

River stood, looking down at Forest bleeding on the floor of the chamber. His brother was helpless and gravely wounded. He would be lucky to survive. Perhaps he was best left to the fates.

'Do not follow me, brother,' River said. 'If you ever come back to Steelhaven, I *will* kill you.'

Forest did not answer. If he lived, perhaps he would heed his brother's warning.

Perhaps not.

Without another word, River ran for the window and leapt out onto an adjacent rooftop. What little breeze there was sweeping in from the Midral was warm, almost inviting.

The dock was not far from the tower, and River ran the whole way. He could see the last ship was almost ready to cast off and he rushed to the end of the pier where men were busying themselves loading the last of the ship's supplies. Without a word River joined them, taking a wooden crate from one of the dock labourers and making his way up the gangplank. No one paid him any attention as he walked onto the ship's deck. No one said a word as he laid down the crate and made his way to the bow. No one saw as he crouched low in the shadows and waited for the captain to call for sail as they cast off.

As the ship cruised out of dock and made its way northward, River could not take his eyes off the far horizon. It might be days before he saw Steelhaven, and he knew each one of those days would be torment until he knew whether Jay was still alive.

River had to believe she was. If she were not, he vowed that there would be more deaths.

Many more deaths.

THE STORY CONTINUES IN BOOK THREE OF
THE STEELHAVEN TRILOGY…

LORD OF ASHES

A WORD FROM THE AUTHOR

If you reached the end of *The Shattered Crown* and enjoyed the second Steelhaven novel then I wonder if you could do me a small favour. Honest reviews of my books help bring them to the attention of other readers, so I would be very grateful if you could take five minutes and leave a review (it can be as short as you like) on the book's Amazon page, Goodreads, or any other social media you're into. Thanks in advance.

EXCLUSIVE FREE CONTENT

Building a relationship with readers is very important to me. I occasionally send newsletters with details on new releases, special offers and other bits of news related to my novels. If you sign up to my newsletter I'll send you the **WORDHOG OMNIBUS**, which includes an unpublished book and short stories, including one that leads up to the events in this novel.

You can get your content **for free**, by signing up to the mailing list on my website at **WWW.WORDHOG.CO.UK**.

ABOUT THE AUTHOR

R S FORD has worked as a roleplaying game developer and computer game writer, while also carving out a career as a novelist. As well as epic fantasy, he also writes historical fiction under the pen name RICHARD CULLEN (his debut, *Oath Bound* was longlisted for the Wilbur Smith Adventure Writing Prize 2022). He'd love to have a proper job, but isn't qualified to do anything other than make up stories about blood-soaked maniacs.

He now lives back in his hometown of Leeds. If you want to hear some more from him you can follow him on Twitter at **@rich4ord**, or Instagram as **thewordhog**.

Printed in Great Britain
by Amazon

32864910R00239